All the Stars

Book One in the Love Under the Arizona Sky Series

Hilary Dartt

Also by Hilary Dartt

Love Under the Arizona Sky Series

The Whole Sky

To the Moon

Arizona Heat

Pure Luck

Sweet Luck

Terrific Luck

Christmas Luck

The Mint Creek Ranch Series

My Favorite Story

My Favorite View

My Favorite Place

The Seedling Homestead Series

A Summer of Wonder

A Dream of Home

A Promise of Forever

The Intervention Series

The Dating Intervention

The Marriage Intervention

The Motherhood Intervention

The Garden Club Series

Jasmine's Pact

Studying Sequoia

Just Holly

All the Stars

Book One in the Love Under the Arizona Sky Series

Hilary Dartt

To my dearest friends.
You make life sweeter.

Chapter One

TAYLOR

Taylor Cole had an obsession with the mail. Over the course of the past month, she'd memorized the mail carrier's precise schedule. At exactly 2:52 p.m. every day except Sunday, Lynette (they were on a first-name basis) rounded the corner onto Pleasant Street, her mailbag slung over her left shoulder, resting on her right hip. Taylor couldn't help but picture the stacks of envelopes in the bag as Lynette finished the first block at 2:54 and started the second block — where Taylor lived — immediately thereafter. Taylor often wondered how a person could keep such an exact schedule, day after day. But Lynette did it. She was as punctual as the church clock that chimed every hour on the hour.

From inside her living room window one Friday, Taylor watched the intersection of Walnut and Pleasant Streets. Sure enough, just as the clock on her phone ticked over to 2:52, Lynette came around the corner, as purposeful and energized as ever. Taylor's heart beat faster.

Up until the week before, Taylor had rushed out her front door as Lynette began dropping mail in slots on that first block. Sometimes she paced the second block while she waited. Despite the anticipation that began anew each day, Taylor had the introspection to realize her waiting, like a cat preparing to attack an unsuspecting mouse, was just the other side of creepy. She decided to wait until Lynette stepped onto the second block before walking out to the sidewalk.

Her body feeling borderline jittery, Taylor made her way to her own mailbox. Lynette gave her a friendly wave, and when she (finally) made it to Taylor's mailbox, she said, "Hello, Taylor."

"Hi, Lynette!" Taylor said, hoping her voice sounded cheerful and not maniacal. Lynette's wide-eyed expression made Taylor realize it was the latter. "I'm sorry," she said, rushing to add, "It's just that I'm still waiting —"

"For the approval letter," Lynette said. "I know, and with your enthusiasm, I have confidence it's a sure thing."

She pulled a stack of mail out of her bag and handed it to Taylor. Within a fraction of a second, Taylor knew: today's mail did not contain an approval letter. All her Internet research said approval letters came in big manila envelopes, not regular little envelopes. Suddenly feeling very heavy, she sighed. "I don't think I got one today, though."

"Chin up," Lynette said, gently tapping a knuckle against Taylor's chin. Taylor saw compassion in the other woman's eyes, and it made her want to cry.

"Thanks, Lynette." Taylor walked back up the path toward her front door. As she pushed it open, she became aware of her posture, slumped and dejected, and almost certainly with a cartoon rain-cloud over her head.

Disappointment is okay, she reminded herself. Everything unfolds in its own time.

She sat at the kitchen counter to sort the mail, separating the junk from the important stuff. A hand-addressed envelope caught her eye. The return address read *Kristi Mendez, Prescott Bank.* Taylor's heart pounded so hard she could see its beat in her field of vision. The envelope shook as she tore it open. Kristi Mendez from Prescott Bank had handwritten the letter on a sheet of bank letterhead. It was dated the day before, printed in neat but loopy handwriting.

Dear Ms. Cole,

I received your application for a business loan. I'm sorry to say that at this time, Prescott Bank cannot offer you a loan. That being said, I, personally, am intrigued by your business idea. Sugar Pine Barn sounds like a viable business that could enhance the lives of people in this area. I could sense your enthusiasm and dedication. The one thing missing for me right now is proof of concept. As a lender, I'd like to see something of a track record. The numbers look good on paper, but I need to see that you can maintain the enrollment numbers you outline in your business plan. And that comes from experience. I encourage you not to give up. I'm confident that, when you find the right lender — and you will — you will get the approval letter I'm sure you are hoping for.

Kristi Mendez
Senior Loan Officer, Prescott Bank

Taylor felt a tear roll down her cheek. It was the fourth rejection letter she'd received out of the six applications she'd turned in over the summer. Each one sent a fresh wave of disappointment through her. She folded the letter and put it in the junk drawer, atop the others.

Taylor swallowed, hoping to get rid of the tightness in her throat. Then she closed her eyes, took a deep breath, and visualized what she wanted. This exercise — which she'd read about in a magazine article — usually helped her overcome her disappointment and keep her focus where it should be: on her goal.

One day, in the not-too-distant future, Taylor would own Sugar Pine Barn, an all-inclusive equestrian center. Surrounded by horses and horse people, she and her team would train local kids in horsemanship, dressage, roping, barrel racing, and more. One day.

In need of a pick-me-up, Taylor glanced at the clock. Rita's

Diner didn't close for its afternoon break for fifteen more minutes. If she walked fast, she could make it inside and order with ten minutes to spare — and hopefully chat with Sal and Rita. They always had good advice. Well, she amended, not always. But when it wasn't good advice, it was entertaining. Like the time Sal told her she should always boil chicken before barbecuing it.

Brushing tears from under her eyes, she headed out. Even in her state of disappointment, Taylor couldn't help but appreciate the walk between her house and Rita's. The hot August day had reached triple digits, but she was cool in the shade of the century-old trees lining Pleasant Street. The sunlight came through the leaves, sparkling as it hit the stained-glass windows on the Victorian houses in her neighborhood. Just being outside, in her hometown, lifted her spirits.

"Good morning, Miss Taylor. And how is our lovely lady librarian today?" The baritone voice caught her off guard at first, but she relaxed as soon as she realized it belonged to Umbrella Jack, who often lived on a bench near her house. He'd told Taylor before that he loved to hang out on Pleasant Street, "as aptly named as it is." At the moment, he lounged at the base of a tree, his tattered umbrella in one hand. He cackled, his mouth wide open, revealing gaping holes where a few molars should have been.

"Sorry to scare you, Miss Taylor! I could see you were deep in thought."

Hand on her chest, Taylor laughed. "I guess I was. How are you today, Jack?"

"I'm fine. Real fine. Thanks for asking. You have a nice day, now, you hear?"

"Things can only go up from here."

In a mere half-second, the man's expression morphed from relaxed to alarmed. "Everything okay, Miss Taylor? What's the matter? Is someone messing with you?"

"Oh no," she said. "It's nothing like that. You know I want to open my own barn one day."

"And you will, too."

Jack might not have all his marbles, but his confidence gave Taylor a boost.

"Not this week, I won't. I got another rejection letter and I'm feeling a bit down."

"Aw, now, honey," Jack said. "Don't go getting discouraged. Let me tell you something, girl. Never confuse a single defeat with a final defeat. You hear me?"

Again, Taylor felt the pressure of tears behind her eyes. "Okay, Jack. I won't." She squared her shoulders. "That's really good advice."

"It is." Jack shrugged, laid his head back against the trunk of the tree, and closed his eyes. "Wasn't me who said it. It was F. Scott Fitzgerald. That old-time author."

"But you shared it with me," Taylor said. "Thank you."

His voice was near a mumble when he answered, "You're welcome, darlin'. Any old time."

As she continued to make her way toward Rita's, Taylor thought back to how her love affair with horses started, all those years ago.

She was just a little girl, so small that every evening, when her dad got home from work, he'd scoop her up and swing her around, her feet above their heads. Her dad worked hard to support their little family of three, so hard that she felt like she rarely saw him. So hard that when he was home, he was often in a state of stress or exhaustion or both. But every evening, without fail, as soon as the dinner dishes were clean and put away, he'd hold out his hand and say, "Shall we?"

Taylor would slip her hand into his and they'd walk out the front door together. Their route was always the same: north on Bridle Path, west on Saddlehorn, and straight to the fence at the end of the road. The horse expected them, and when she noticed them coming, she trotted to meet them — and to accept the carrots they brought in their pockets.

If she wanted to spend time with her dad, all she had to do was suggest they go for a walk. The two of them, and sometimes her mom, would head out the door and toward their equine friend. At some point, they started calling her Freckles, and Taylor always felt like they had a special bond.

When her mom was there, her dad would exclaim, "See? What did I tell you, my love? Our daughter! A magician with animals!"

Within a year or two, her begging paid off: her parents leased her a horse — a retired barrel racing horse named Sugar — and enrolled her in riding lessons. Taylor was such a natural on horseback that her instructor suggested she try barrel racing.

Taylor spent hours of her life with Sugar. Those were the happiest memories from Taylor's childhood, and she just knew she wanted her whole life to be about horses when she grew up. She dreamed of running a place for kids like her — kids who loved horses.

Only, her dad was completely against it.

He'd dreamed of entrepreneurship, himself. His vision: a bakery. He yearned for it. Wished for it. Wanted nothing more than to offer his customers the delight of a perfectly made sweet treat. But his parents had told him that if he wanted to be an entrepreneur, he should choose more wisely. They'd give him a loan to get started, but only if he did something sensible, like accounting.

So, a young groom with a baby on the way, he made what he always referred to as the sensible choice. He went into accounting, and Taylor knew he regretted it for the rest of his life. He didn't quite say so, but he did say that if Taylor wanted to spend time with her future family, she should absolutely not go into business for herself. Instead, she'd do better to pursue a reasonable job, like teaching. Something that would change lives, but that wouldn't take over *her* life.

A dutiful daughter, she followed her dad's advice. Becoming a school librarian enabled her to spend time with young people. It also gave her stability and weekends, holidays, and summers off.

She liked it fine, but it wasn't her dream. Her dream was to be an entrepreneur, famed for a beautiful barn and the experiences she provided there. Maybe her horses and students would even appear on the cover of local magazines. Her dream was to also have a family: a husband, a handful of children, and an ugly shelter dog. She wanted it all.

This thought caused chills to rush over her skin, and a new wave of emotion to flush her system as she pulled open the door to Rita's Diner.

Chapter Two

JUDD

Judd O'Connor knew at eight years old that his destiny was to be a cop. He remembered the moment — and the events leading up to it — with the extreme clarity someone has when they've watched a movie dozens of times. As an adult, he had, in fact, relived that day hundreds of times. Every shift, practically.

One particular Friday afternoon was no exception. Judd was running patrol, watching the clock for the end of his shift. Twenty more minutes, and he'd be off, for three full days. Twenty more minutes and he could go home, feed his horses, take off his boots, and relax. It had been a long week, one of those weeks so packed with calls, he felt like he aged ten years. He replayed a few of them in his mind: the welfare check where he'd found an old man, unable to get up after falling and breaking his hip; a toddler left alone in a car in the grocery store parking lot, which at once angered Judd and made him pity the single mom who hadn't wanted to wake her sleeping baby while she ran in to get him formula; the call about Umbrella Jack, the infamous local who insisted on walking through the taco drive-thru, and wouldn't move from the pick-up window because he felt he had to convey an important message from the aliens. Judd shook his head at that one. He'd bought the grizzled old guy a couple of tacos and a soda and convinced him to sit in the shade and eat them before the aliens came.

Out of nowhere, the memory hit Judd as he drove down Gurley Street, downtown Prescott's equivalent of Main Street.

Moviemakers loved to give car accidents major foreshadowing. If they recreated that morning in Judd's life, they'd have the camera focus on mundane tasks like the making of breakfast, conversations around the table, getting ready for the day.

But there was nothing mundane about the day of the accident. It was a special day: his sister's birthday. If someone set up a movie camera in the O'Connors' kitchen, it would capture their traditional pancake breakfast. A sizzling pan, the smell of bacon frying. It would capture Judd's sister, Katy, wearing the special birthday hat, laughing as their mom sang an opera version of Happy Birthday over a stack of fluffy pancakes.

The camera would follow them all out to the car. Judd and his sister would good-naturedly argue over who got to ride in the front seat, and he would end up letting her have it because it was her birthday. Shotgun meant she got to play DJ. Judd remembered the way she looked back at him over her shoulder, her smile devilish as she put on her favorite teen boy band CD. Normally, that would make him grumpy, but because it was her birthday, he just smiled back at her. He surprised himself by singing along, and their mom surprised both of them by joining in. And then, mid-chorus, it happened.

Judd's memory showed him the event in snatches: the semi truck right in front of them, its horn blaring, a split second of silence when they all stopped singing, and then the impact. Metal on metal. Glass shattering. For what felt like a very long time, everything was silent. Judd thought maybe he was having an out-of-body experience. He'd already died, and his ghost was looking around at all the damage. From his spot in the center of the backseat, the scene looked dark. Maybe hours had passed and it was already nighttime. Then he realized: it was dark because their car was underneath that giant semi truck. It blocked the windshield — no, it had obliterated the windshield. A sound broke the silence. Judd recognized it right away: his sister's voice, moaning. It wasn't a whine, like when she tripped and fell and wanted attention to soothe her pride. No, this was the sound of real pain, like the time she stepped on an ant hill next to the barn, and an angry army of red ants retaliated on her poor bare foot.

"Katy," he tried. No sound came out, so he tried again. "Katy."

Her answer was a louder moan. He scooted up, thinking he could talk to her, but his stomach lurched when he saw the side of her face. Her skin was pale. There was blood. Her eyelid twitched like she was trying to blink, but her eyes barely opened. His mom looked much the same way, only her eyes were closed and still. He felt sick.

"Mom?" No response. "Mama?" No response.

"Katy," Judd said, trying to keep the rising panic out of his voice. "Katy, it's going to be okay."

He had to get help. He could see now that the whole front end of the car had buckled, and the dashboard pinned his mom and sister into their seats. What could he do? Hands shaking, he unbuckled his seatbelt. He started to scoot across the backseat behind his sister's seat and had to curl up his legs to get to the door.

But he couldn't open it. The door wouldn't budge. *Right.* All the doors locked automatically when the car was in drive. He would have to reach into the front seat to press the unlock button. But the unlock button was missing. It must be part of the mess that was now the entire front of the car.

Katy moaned again and panic gripped Judd like he'd never experienced before. His whole body felt tense, stiff. He could taste something coppery in the back of his throat. His heart beat hard, and he felt lightheaded, like he'd stood up too fast. He knew he should take a deep breath. It was what his mom always told him to do when he was upset. But he couldn't. He couldn't breathe at all. Hours passed. Maybe minutes. Maybe even seconds. Then, sirens. At first, Judd thought the sound might be more moaning from Katy, but then he realized someone must've called 9-1-1.

"We need an ambulance," Judd said, more to himself than to Katy or his mom.

A pounding noise made Judd jump. Someone was banging on the door across from him. Shouting. "Can you hear me? Get away from the window."

Judd did as he was told, curling himself into a tight ball in the center seat. Another loud crash, the sound of glass shattering, the voice, much clearer and louder. "Are you all right, son? Come on, let me get you out of here. Careful, now."

The man reached through the window and grabbed Judd under the arms. Judd gripped his shoulders and the man hauled him out.

"My mom," he said, as soon as his feet hit the ground. "My sister."

The man wrapped an arm around Judd's shoulders and pulled him close. "I know, son. Someone called 9-1-1. Hear the sirens? They should be here any minute."

Some invisible force pulled Judd toward the car, but the man held him firmly in place. "I know you want to go to them. But you don't have the right tools."

Thinking back on it from an adult perspective, Judd realized that man, that stranger, had done him a great kindness by not letting him get close enough to see the damage again, from outside the car. In that moment, though, his body pulled away from the man.

"They'll be here soon," he said again. "They have special tools they can use to get those doors open. Now, I'm not going to say something stupid like, 'Don't worry.' Because you *are* worried. But I'm going to be honest with you. There's nothing you can do right now. But these guys? When they show up, they can help. Look now, here they are."

Sure enough, a police cruiser pulled up next to Judd's mom's car. A policeman jumped out, and when Judd would have run to him, to start pleading with him to do something, to save his mom and sister, the man continued to hold him still.

Watching, Judd thought it seemed like the police officer already knew what he needed. He'd opened the trunk of his patrol ca and pulled out a giant metal tool. He didn't waste any time closing the trunk. A second later, another cop showed up. This one, a lady, didn't even stop her car all away before she opened the door. She jumped out and ran up to the first guy. Judd realized then that he was crying, his chest heaving, tears streaming down his face.

"They're doing everything they can. I promise you that. That tool there, that's called the Jaws of Life. They'll use it to cut open the doors."

Judd was vaguely aware of people gathering around, watching. His focus remained on the cops who were trying to free his mom and sister, but he registered an ambulance pulling up, and a fire truck. Again, it felt like lots of time passed, and then finally, *finally*, the police stepped away from the car and the paramedics rushed forward, pushing a stretcher.

Suddenly, the strong arm that had encircled his shoulder for the past several moments slipped away, and the man was crouching in front of him, his hands on Judd's shoulders. "Now, you're not going to like hearing this. But I don't want you to watch anymore. They got your mom out. And your sister is next. But sometimes, seeing the ones you love getting strapped into a stretcher, put in the back of an ambulance, and driven away is — well, let's face it. It's pretty awful. I know you don't know me, but I hope you can trust me."

Judd looked into the man's kind brown eyes and thought that he *could* trust him. He nodded. Swallowed. Turned around.

"Good. I think the next thing we need to do is decide where you're going to go. Come on over here."

The man led Judd to his own car, and Judd noticed red and blue lights flashing in the back window.

"You're an undercover cop?"

After popping the trunk, the man turned around. "Yes. I'm sorry, I should have introduced myself. I'm Mike Larson. I'm a detective. I just happened to be nearby when the accident happened, so I stopped to see if I could help. You thirsty?"

He handed Judd a bottle of water, and Judd opened it and took a drink.

"Is there someone we can call to come get you?"

"My dad," Judd said. "He's at home. He wasn't with us because it's my sister's birthday, and we got her a new swing set. Mom took Katy and me out of the house so he could set it up. And then we were going to surprise her."

The detective nodded. "You know his number?"

Judd gave him the number, which he dialed quickly. While he waited for Judd's dad to pick up, he said, "What's your last name, son?"

"O'Connor."

Detective Larson gave him a nod and then said, "Mr. O'Connor. This is Mike Larson with the Springfield Police Department. I have your son here. Your family has been in an accident. The boy is fine, but paramedics are taking your wife and daughter to the hospital. I can meet you there."

Modern-day Judd swore as he almost ran a red light and slammed on the brakes. He couldn't let that long-ago morning take him out of the present moment like that. A few months before, the police department had brought in some "mindfulness expert" to help the guys on the force with stress. Judd was convinced it was woo-woo hippie stuff, but he had found her relaxation technique helpful a couple of times. While he waited at the red light, he used it: he tensed and relaxed each of his muscles in turn, starting with his eyes, working his way down to his jaw, his neck, his shoulders, and his arms. The light turned green, and he took a deep breath.

Driving by the park, Judd saw some kids kicking around a soccer ball on the field. He checked the clock. It wouldn't hurt to join their game for the last fifteen minutes of his shift. He parked and let dispatch know where he was before he got out of his patrol car. The uniform was definitely too warm to play soccer in, but he didn't care. Especially when a few of the kids recognized him, lifting their hands in waves, smiling, calling out to him.

"You be forward," said Augie, the kid Judd had early on identified as the leader. Judd nodded, and Augie, long, curly black hair flowing behind him as he went, ran back to his spot.

The two teams spent a few minutes rallying, and Judd did his best to make sure everyone got a little play time. The kids liked to talk trash, and Judd usually laughed it off, engaging only once in a while when it seemed like a kid was getting too big for his britches. He was already wiping sweat off his forehead when Little Jerry (a perfectly imperfect nickname for the hulking twelve-year-old who probably wore size fourteen shoes) hollered, "That's all you got, Officer O'Connor?"

No matter how serious the game got, they always called him Officer O'Connor. Judd shook his head at Little Jerry, grinning.

"Come on, big guy," Jerry called. "You know you were bragging last weekend. Said you'd beat us all with one hand tied behind your back. Which doesn't mean anything, since you don't use hands in soccer."

"Not what I said," Judd hollered back. "I said —"

"Whatever, man. Let your soccer do the talking."

Laughing, Judd did just that. Using his fanciest footwork, he grabbed the ball from Little Jerry's teammate. He faked out a few of the kids as he dribbled up the side of the field. Some of them pretended to trip, rolling in the grass while Judd made his way to the goal. Most of them were laughing when Judd gave the ball a good, hard kick and it sailed right into the net.

Although Judd didn't showboat, the rest of his team did, running around, arms raised, whooping like a bunch of hyenas. That's when Judd realized one of his favorites, Zion, wasn't on the field. That kid had a killer hyena laugh ... and he was *always* there.

"No Zion today?" he said to Little Jerry.

"Nah, man, he hasn't come around," Little Jerry said. "You seen Z, Augie?"

"Nope," Augie said. "Haven't seen him. Anybody?"

A murmur rose among the rest of the kids, most of whom shook their heads.

"How long?" Judd asked. Sweat dripped down his back. He decided he'd stop and get an iced coffee on his way home.

A few boys shrugged. "A while," Augie said, and Little Jerry added, "A couple weeks?"

"Anybody try checking up on him?"

Another murmur, containing negative responses.

"Maybe we should, though," Augie said.

"Wouldn't hurt." Judd checked his watch. "All right, fellas. I've got to go." He turned on his best mega-watt grin, threw out his arms, palms up, and turned in a slow circle. "You're welcome for that amazing display of talent."

A mix of cheers, disappointed groans, and friendly goodbyes followed him as he jogged back to his car.

———

Judd was so deep in thought as he approached Rita's Diner that he almost smacked into the door as someone else opened it. The sounds of the bell ringing and a feminine, "Ooh!" jolted him back into the present moment, the latter sending a thrilling shiver down his spine.

When he saw the woman who opened the door — and got a look at the light sprinkle of freckles on the bridge of her nose — Judd's reflexes took over. He went to step around the woman so he could hold the door open for her, and as he did, he caught a scent of citrus. He didn't have time to enjoy it though, because the woman jumped forward to grab the door handle at the same time he reached for it. An awkward scramble took place. They both froze, and the woman giggled, again igniting a little flame of pleasure in Judd's body.

"Sorry," she said. When they made eye contact, he had another physical reaction. This one felt like a jolt of recognition even though he was certain he'd never seen her. *Interesting.*

Her eyes were the prettiest color, gray with undertones of green. He found himself standing there, trying to define that color.

Snap out of it, O'Connor. "Let me get the door."

She nodded, and then gave a funny little curtsy. "Thank you."

"My pleasure," he said, the word *pleasure* sounding way too suggestive.

He managed to keep his gaze from roaming down her backside as he followed her to the counter, but just barely. He did, however, notice and appreciate her slim frame and the gentle curve of what was surely a toned butt. At the counter, Rita, the diner's owner, greeted the woman with her usual friendliness. "Hey, Taylor. I just saw Lynette go by. Anything in the mail?"

Judd saw the woman's shoulders slump, just a little, and just for a fraction of a second, before they straightened again.

"Another rejection. Every note brings me one step closer to that 'yes,' right?"

Her voice was a little too cheerful, a smidgen too bright.

"I'm sorry, hon. You're going to get that 'yes.' I just know it."

"Thanks, Rita. Until then, I'll keep at it."

"That's all you can do. When Sal and I started this place, it took us a year to get the loan. At the time, that felt interminable. But it was worth it. Everything has worked out like a dream. Isn't that right, Sal?"

Rita's husband, Sal, answered from his customary spot at the counter. "That's right, Taylor. It all worked out like a dream. Your business will, too."

An impulse had Judd taking a step forward as the woman opened her purse to get her wallet.

"I'll get her coffee, Rita," he said.

Both Rita and the woman looked at him, obviously shocked. He smiled at Rita, and then at the woman.

"It only seems fitting, since I caused our near collision this morning."

She laughed again. "Oh, I don't know. I think we were equally at fault. I wasn't paying attention." A coy smile on her face, looked at his name tag. "O'Connor. I'd love to know the first name of the guy who's buying my coffee."

Out of nowhere, he was blushing. Like he had in the seventh grade when Mira Flores handed him a love letter from a secret admirer, and he made the mistake of reading it right there in the middle of math class. "Judd." He held out his hand. She took it. There wasn't a tingle or an electric shock or a warm sensation. But there was a moment. Their eyes locked, they both grinned, and something passed between them.

"Taylor," she said.

"It's nice to meet you."

"Likewise."

Judd could hear the amused smile in Rita's voice when she said,

"Taylor, coffee's ready," and he realized they were still standing there, hands clasped.

As if the same realization startled her, Taylor jumped and dropped his hand. The grin remained on her face as she turned away to get her coffee off the counter. "Thanks, Rita."

"You're welcome, hon. And remember, keep on keeping on. You're going to get that, 'yes.'"

"I hope you're right." She turned to Judd. "Thank you for the coffee."

And with that, she was gone. He imagined himself staring after her as she went out through the door but didn't want to give Rita any extra ammo. She was always trying to set him up, and he could already see her wheels turning.

But she didn't say anything about the encounter. She simply asked, "The usual, Judd?"

"Yep. You know me too well." She smiled and went to make his cold brew.

"How's your week been, son?" Sal wanted to know. "How's business?"

"Same old, same old," Judd said. "People getting crazier every day."

"Ain't that the truth. Just yesterday, we had a guy come in asking if we sold fish bait. I told him, we sell hot dogs. I hear the catfish in Willow Lake go for those. He looked at me like *I* was the crazy one."

"Must be something in the water," Judd said.

"Must be," Sal said.

Rita reached over the counter with Judd's drink. "Your usual."

He walked out while marveling that this visit to Rita's had been decidedly unusual ... in the best way possible.

Chapter Three

TAYLOR

Determined to make her dream reality, Taylor followed the advice in almost every personal development book she read. Each morning, she spent five full minutes visualizing her ideal life.

The Wednesday that launched the new school year was no exception. Still lying in bed with her eyes closed, she imagined her perfect morning, letting herself experience it with all five senses.

She woke, energized and fresh faced, and brewed coffee, enjoying the rich, nutty scent of it while going over her entrepreneurial to-do list. Birds sang outside her window, their cheerful song echoing her mood. She was a business owner, a proprietor. When her coffee was ready, she poured it into an expensive travel mug with *Boss* etched on it.

Sipping away at her coffee, she sat down at the computer to look over the barn's daily, weekly, and monthly schedules: riding classes, grooming classes, and barrel racing and roping practices.

Once she was confident the schedule was in order, she showered and got ready to go. She lathered herself up with expensive, creamy body wash, and dried off with the fluffiest towels money could buy.

Then she put on designer jeans and luxury leather riding boots, and a nice sweater that made her eyes stand out.

Taylor didn't actually care about name brands. But treating herself to the finer things would signify that she believed in herself.

Dressed and ready for the day, she'd head out to the barn. There, the scents of horses and leather and dirt greeted her like old friends. The dogs barking (because a barn wouldn't be complete without a dog or two) announced the arrival of a big brown delivery truck. She'd meet the (very sexy) delivery driver at the front gate, for once having enough confidence to give him an actual greeting, to look directly into his eyes.

In that day's visualization, the delivery driver bore an uncanny resemblance to that sexy police officer from Rita's. She offered him a hot coffee, and he followed her inside. She felt like such a vixen as she poured his cup, leaning forward to give him a peek at her cleavage. After she handed the mug to him, he came toward her, unable to resist her charm. Her skin tingled as he wrapped his arms around her waist and pulled her in for a kiss.

The imaginary record playing in the background screeched to a halt as Taylor's second alarm blared, signifying that her visualization session was over.

"*This* is my real life," she huffed, turning over to switch off her alarm. She wasn't an entrepreneur. She didn't own Sugar Pine Barn.

And she certainly didn't have the confidence to make eye contact with the delivery guy. Or *any* good-looking guy (although, she thought, she *had* shared a moment with that police officer at Rita's).

In real life, she was Ms. Cole, librarian at Prescott High School. Ms. Cole was almost the exact opposite of Taylor Cole, entrepreneur. Sure, she brewed her coffee in the morning, and went over her mental to-do list while she waited. A typical day's activities — shelving books, helping students research, entering new books into the library's system in the computer — were *fine*. Her constant companions were books, which were just about her favorite people on the planet, and the reason she'd taken the job (in addition to the fact that her two best friends worked at the high school, as well).

Taylor's phone rang. Her spirits lifted when she saw it was her best friend, Rose Coffey. She tapped to connect, and although she rushed to turn off her camera, she didn't do it quite fast enough: she caught a glimpse of her disheveled hair and the puffy skin around her eyes before the screen went blank.

"Turn your camera back on," Rose said by way of greeting. "Girl, you know I've seen you in a worse state than the first day back for teacher workdays."

Smiling, Taylor obeyed and flinched as her own image reappeared. "You're right. Nothing will ever compare to the morning after senior prom, but my daily bedhead gets worse with age."

Rose's laugh came through the phone like music, and Taylor couldn't help but smile.

"That may be true, but you do clean up nice. You ready for today?"

"I was ready for today before I realized I don't get to live my fantasy."

"You could, you know."

Taylor sighed. They'd had this conversation too many times to count. "I know. Are *you* ready for today?"

"I think I'm ready. Celeste was playing dress-up with my shoes, and at this point, I can find only one pair — and it doesn't match."

As if on cue, Taylor heard a squeal, and Rose's five-year-old daughter Celeste ran through the frame behind Rose.

"Celeste! Didn't you want to say good morning to Auntie Taylor?"

Less than a second later, the little girl was back, her chubby-cheeked face and wild mess of black curls taking up the screen. "Good morning, Auntie Taylor! I get to go to school today! Just like you and Mommy! Want to see what I'm wearing?"

"Absolutely," Taylor said.

"Mommy, hold this," Celeste said, handing her mom the phone so she could step back and offer Taylor a full-length view. "It's a princess dress, see? And here's my shoes."

She stuck out one foot, showing off a clear plastic high heel, which she wore over a sock with ice cream cones on it.

"Very nice," Taylor said. "The only thing I think you're missing is a crown, maybe. Do you have one?"

Celeste looked up at Taylor and grinned. "Course I do. You know that. Be right back."

Taylor said, "Sounds like she's ready for a great day."

Rose turned the camera toward herself again and smiled. "Yes, thank goodness."

The closer Taylor got to work the less she felt like the confident business owner of her daydreams. She parked in her assigned spot, which looked like exactly what it was: an afterthought. Someone had forgotten to assign her a staff spot, so one of the janitors, Mr. Jim, took pity on her and spray-painted one in a non-spot in the dirt at the far corner. She was grateful, but she'd almost rather park in the student lot, where at least it wouldn't be so obvious that she was forgettable.

Taylor glanced around the parking lot. Most of the teachers drove cars that suited their personalities. Elizabeth Tinsel's light yellow Volkswagen beetle sat near the entrance to the lot, its top down, a small bouquet of daisies in the bud vase. Johnny Mac drove a muscle car, naturally. He may be a science nerd, but with his military retirement, he could afford the sleek hot rod. And Taylor? As she started walking, she looked back over her shoulder at her own set of wheels. A gold sedan with four doors, it screamed — no, *whispered* — boring librarian.

There, at Prescott High School, Taylor Cole fit in among the staff just like her car did among the others in the parking lot: she was practically invisible. Except to Rose and the third member of their trio, Jessie Monroe.

As if she'd conjured them, they drove in, one after another. Sharing a workplace with Rose and Jessie, at least, brought a smile to Taylor's face. She reached Rose's car first, and Rose, a chaotic mix of curly blond hair, a loud greeting, a giant grin, and an outfit that checked all the boxes for color, texture, and pattern, embraced Taylor. "Good morning, Sunshine!"

"Good morning," Taylor said, squeezing her back.

Jessie joined them, and after another round of hugs, they headed for the library, where the whole staff would meet.

Since it was a teacher work day, the campus was much quieter than usual, and Taylor took a moment to notice the birds chirping, the trees' leaves shimmering, and the morning sunshine reflecting off the windows. Teachers stood in small groups outside the main building, talking and laughing. As Taylor and her friends went by, people greeted Rose and Jessie, who responded in kind, with friendly waves and wisecracks.

Inside the library, Rose and Jessie got pulled into separate conversations, leaving Taylor to find them a table. She chose her favorite spot, the little table by the window, with three cushy chairs.

Taylor was already settled when Jessie rushed up, pulled out a chair, and sank into it. "Sorry, Taylor," she said, taking her notebook and pen out of her bag and setting them on the table. "I didn't mean to make you find us a seat."

Taylor waved her off. "You're just so much more of a social butterfly than I am."

A minute later, Rose joined them. Taylor noticed the dark circles under her friend's eyes and reached out to squeeze her hand. "You okay? You look tired."

Rose nodded. "I'm fine. I was up half the night looking for a new place."

"What?" Jessie said. "You just moved into this place. Right? Or am I losing my mind?"

Rose blew out a breath. "No, you are not losing your mind. Celeste and I moved in two weeks ago. I should have known the listing was too good to be true. It's fine, it's just that I'm surrounded by college students. They're all so sweet. They dote on Celeste. But they're also really noisy. Let's just say they keep different hours than my five-year-old and I."

"Have you tried those apartments off McCormick Street?" Jessie wanted to know.

Rose shook her head. "No go. I did check, but they're out of my price range, being right downtown."

The sound of a cowbell interrupted their conversation. The trademark signal of the principal, Ernie Vasquez, the bell brought the one-hundred-person staff to silence in a matter of seconds.

"Good morning," Ernie said. Everyone chorused, "Good morning."

"I'd like to open today with a refresher on our mission. And then, I've brought in a guest speaker to inspire you."

While Ernie talked, she let her mind wander once again to her ideal day as a business owner. After waving goodbye to the sexy delivery driver, she'd walk the property, greeting the horses in the barn and checking the arena fences.

"Ms. Cole," Ernie was saying, while one of her friends kicked her under the table.

Taylor blinked.

"Would you be willing to do that?"

Do what? "Yes?"

"Thank you!" Ernie beamed.

The staff gave her a polite round of applause, and Taylor did her best to keep her lips still when she asked Rose and Jessie, "What did I just agree to?"

Smiling and applauding, Jessie said, "To meet the breakfast delivery guy at the front of the school and bring the food back here."

"Great," Taylor said. She stood up. The applause died down. Quite out of nowhere, Taylor felt the sting of tears. And then, hearing footsteps behind her, she dashed them away with the heels of her hands.

"I'll help you," Jessie said. "We can't have a repeat of that time Mr. Carnegie asked you to carry in all the new textbooks by yourself."

Taylor groaned. "Thanks." She tucked her arm into Jessie's. They stayed linked together as they walked to the front office, where they loaded a spare audio-visual cart with the boxes of pastries and cartons of coffee.

"One day, I'll be the one ordering breakfast for all my staff," Taylor said as they walked. "Not the gopher for the principal."

"I can't wait," Jessie said. "You could do it, you know. Resign at the end of this year. Open Sugar Pine Barn next fall."

Jessie was a great friend. The truth was, she believed in Taylor more than Taylor believed in herself.

Taylor sighed. "I know."

Back in the library, Taylor, Rose, and Jessie arranged the breakfast on a long table at the back of the room. Once everyone got their food, Ernie announced that the speaker was there.

Taylor had glanced at the day's itinerary when Ernie emailed it the week before. She knew the speaker was a former educator whose claim to fame was that she had started some kind of reading program, which quickly became a nationwide hit.

She thought she might wander off into dreamland again, but then the speaker walked through the door. One glance told Taylor exactly what she needed to know: this woman radiated happiness and contentment. Confidence. Undoubtedly, she wore a designer suit, and those heels probably cost as much as a month's worth of gas for Taylor's invisible car. But it wasn't just her outfit that caught Taylor's attention. No, it was the way this woman carried herself.

"Good morning," she said. "I'm Rebecca Easton, founder of Reading Circles."

The entire Prescott High School staff must have been as mesmerized as Taylor was. "Good morning," everyone said.

"You probably know that my program has become a household name across the country," Rebecca said. "I've sold hundreds of thousands of licenses. Yes, to the tune of hundreds of thousands of dollars. But, believe it or not, I'm not going to talk a about my reading program. The numbers tell the story, so I don't have to. I'm here today to tell you the story of a transformation. A story of passion."

Taylor leaned forward, her elbows on the table.

"In my first life, I was an eighth-grade English teacher. Room four, Sunnyside Prep. Kids would show up in my class, unable to read the textbooks."

Taylor's fellow staff members were nodding. They'd seen it. So had she.

Rebecca went on, "I wanted to help each and every one of them. But, I had one hundred and eighty students. Not all of them struggled. But you know how hard it is to give these kids personal attention. I should have mentioned earlier that I'm a huge nerd when it comes to reading. I spent most of my graduate career researching reading. After about a decade in that eighth-grade classroom, an idea started to form. I thought, what if I could help more than just one hundred and eighty kids a year? What if I could create something that would give thousands of kids, or, if I was really thinking big, *tens* of thousands of them, the fundamental reading skills they need?"

Taylor felt herself sitting up a little straighter. The speaker's words resonated with her. Taylor felt it, too: the desire to do more.

"I probably don't have to tell you, I was afraid to leave my job. Yes, teaching is hard. Exhausting. It's also beyond rewarding. Plus, it's secure. And you get weekends and summers off, right? You can't beat that. And my benefits were pretty good. But at a certain point, my excitement overtook my fear. I started small. During the day, I went to school, just like I always had. I taught my kids. I did the best I could. And in the evenings, I worked on my program. Once it was done, I convinced our local school board to use it at the elementary school. The results were incredible, if I do say so myself."

Rebecca flashed her audience a cocky grin, then laughed. "I was confident," she said, "but also, to see how much those kids improved their reading skills was truly life-changing for me. And for the kids, too, of course."

More chuckles.

"Now, I know your school is set to start using my program this year. And I just wanted you to know about the driving force, the motivation, behind it. It's not coming from some big corporation, some money-hungry non-educators. It's coming directly from me. From my heart. From my desire to help kids ... and make your job easier. And although my main reason for coming today was to introduce you to the program, and to myself, I hope I've also inspired you. You all are in education because you love kids."

"Most of the time," Johnny Mac muttered. People chuckled.

"True," Rebecca said, smiling. "I want you to know that if you have a dream to change their lives, you can. As Walt Disney said, if you can dream it, you can do it."

Chapter Four

*J*UDD

Judd almost didn't hear the call come through on his portable radio.

"Do you copy?" The dispatcher's voice sounded urgent, borderline irritated.

"I copy," he said. "Could you repeat?"

"We have a nine-six-two at Willow Lake and Willow Creek. Can you respond?"

An injury accident. Judd looked at his watch. Five minutes until his shift ended. He bit back a sigh. He was looking forward to getting home. But, this was what he signed up for. It was his calling.

"On my way."

He put the air conditioner on full blast and flicked on the lights and sirens as he pulled out of Rita's parking lot, then requested more information from dispatch. At least two cars were involved, and the ambulance was already on its way. Almost every time he got a hot call, Judd relived the day of his own accident.

The pancake breakfast. Katy in the birthday hat. The mild scent of maple syrup and bacon on his and Katy's clothes as they got in the car. His sister smiling at him from the front seat. The semi truck's horn honking. The impact. The silence. Katy moaning. He shook his head to clear it, took deep breaths to stop his hands from shaking. That was *years* ago.

When modern-day Judd arrived at the scene, he could tell immediately that it was the kind of accident where someone could have died. It wasn't as much about the position of the cars as it was about the energy of the people around them — rushing toward the epicenter, pulled by a need to help.

Bystanders wrung their hands or talked on their phones, worry lines etched into their expressions. One man tried to pry open the driver's side door of one car, while another stood off to the side, running his hand through his hair. Judd took in the scene within a fraction of a second before throwing his patrol car in park and rushing toward the cars, himself. Before he even traversed the several yards, he realized: one of the cars was dripping gasoline — which meant a fire, or worse, an explosion, could happen any second.

"Get back!" The man working on that door turned to give Judd a piece of his mind. Judd pointed at the puddle on the ground. "It's leaking gas! It could catch fire!"

Understanding crossed the man's face, and while he backed up, he shouted, "The driver's unconscious." He pointed at the other car, a pickup truck. "That guy came barreling through the intersection, hit her car pretty hard. It spun around. Her brain is probably scrambled eggs."

Judd nodded. "Thanks, man. The fire department is on the way."

He knew he had to work fast. The car, a small sedan marketing experts would call a "gas sipper," had crumpled. It reminded Judd of the way his dad used to crush his soda cans. He didn't have time to use the Jaws of Life, so he opted for breaking the woman's window. He was sure his mind was playing tricks on him — he kept thinking he heard the whooshing sound of fire igniting, and the hairs stood up on the back of his neck.

Even in the moment, he recognized his fight-or-flight response. His hands shook, his heart pumped hard, he could taste the copper of adrenaline in the back of his throat. His body wanted to flee. But he had to stay, to fight, for this woman who couldn't fight for herself. He used a tool to break the window, hoping the glass shards wouldn't cut the driver, but knowing the alternative would be worse. The glass shattered, and he used his bare hands to peel it away. The woman didn't have any obvious external injuries. Judd didn't see any blood, and by some miracle, none of her body parts were pinned or trapped. He wished there was some kind of clock counting down to the explosion, like there would be for a bomb in a movie. But, no. That didn't happen in real life. Finally, his flight response subsided, and calm certainty came over him. Behind him, someone was yelling, "Back up, everyone! Back up! The gas is leaking!"

Judd reached across the driver's body and unbuckled her seatbelt, then hooked his arms under hers and started lifting her out.

"Right behind you, O'Connor." Judd recognized the voice. It belonged to Nicky Frye. They'd gone to the police academy together, and Nicky was about as steady as anyone Judd could hope to have at the scene.

"Nicky." Judd gave him a quick nod in greeting. "I've got her upper half. If I pull her out, you could come in and get her hips."

Nicky nodded, and stepped close to the car as Judd lifted the woman out.

Even as Judd's body went through the motions as quickly as possible, carrying the woman to the backboard the paramedics brought, laying her down, standing by while they put on the neck brace, checking the woman's pockets for identification so he could try to find a family member, his mind took note of the other driver involved in the accident, who had gotten in his truck and was backing it up. He felt the anger stirring in his belly, a dragon armed with venom.

As soon as the paramedics loaded the woman into the ambulance, Judd made eye contact with Nicky. He could literally feel his blood boiling in his veins. He felt his molars grinding together as he hooked a thumb at the offending driver and said to Nicky, "Can you believe this guy?"

"Oh, no, man," Nicky said.

"What do you mean?"

"You're getting that look, my friend. I think it's best if you hit the office, write up this report, and go home."

If it were possible, his friend's comments made Judd even angrier. He was fairly certain steam was coming out of his ears.

He knew he should take a deep breath, maybe several. But instead, he flashed Nicky a grin and said, "I'm good, man. We're just going to have a little chat."

It was the equivalent of, "Hold my beer," and they both knew it. But Nicky didn't try to stop Judd as he marched toward the pickup truck.

Chapter Five

As inspired as she was after the guest speaker's talk, Taylor felt that old sense of wistfulness envelope her as she walked back to the parking lot with Rose and Jessie at the end of the day.

"What's the matter?" Jessie said. "You seemed so energized by that talk and now you seem ... well, sad."

"You're always so good at reading my mind," Taylor said.

"And your facial expressions," Rose said. "You look like you could cry."

They had reached Jessie's car, a Jeep Wrangler with huge tires. It screamed *fun*.

"I mean, look at your car."

Jessie's attention snapped to the Jeep. "What? Did some high schooler come in here and key it while we were in our meeting?"

Taylor laughed. The Jeep was Jessie's baby, her dream car since childhood. "No. At least not that I know of. Your car is so *you*. And look at Rose's car."

Taylor gestured to the bright blue SUV. "It's the perfect combination of practical and whimsical. And look at mine."

All three of them looked toward the corner of the parking lot, where Taylor's car blended in with the aging asphalt and the dirt surrounding it. After a long second of silence, Rose and Jessie looked back at Taylor. She could tell her point was starting to sink in.

"It gets you from point A to point B?" Rose tried, grimacing.

"Yeah," Jessie said. "It's reliable. Dependable. Like you."

"I'm grateful you think of me as reliable and dependable," Taylor said. "I don't know how to put it into words, exactly. Hearing that lady speak today, it made me realize, I want to be like her. Confident. Fulfilled. Passionate. Pretty, for goodness' sake. Going my own way. You know?"

"You *are* pretty," Rose insisted, sounding so much like Celeste, Taylor had to laugh.

"You know what I mean. I want to wear makeup and do my hair and —" she gestured at her beige skirt suit —"find clothes I feel amazing in. Like you two. Not like the boring, nerdy librarian."

Jessie was nodding, but Rose started to say, "Nothing wrong with —"

Taylor cut her off. "I know. There's nothing wrong with being a librarian. But let's face it. I applied here because you two were working here."

"And because you love books," Jessie added, like she was explaining the concept to a three-year-old.

Taylor laughed. "Thank you for trying to make me feel better. But the fact is, I don't feel like this is what I was made for."

Awareness dawning in her eyes, Rose said, "You feel like you were born to be the owner of Sugar Pine Barn."

"Yes," Taylor said. "But —"

This time, Jessie interrupted Taylor. "But more than anything, you want a family. And you're afraid that owning a business would mean you couldn't be there for a husband and kids."

"See? You guys get me. The two things I want most are at odds with each other."

Rose and Jessie looked at each other, something passing between them, unspoken.

"What are you guys thinking?"

"I'm just going to come out and say it," Jessie said.

Even though Taylor suddenly felt nervous, she nodded. Anything coming from Jessie came from a place of love. Even if it hurt to hear.

With one last glance at Rose, Jessie said, "What if that's just a story you're telling yourself? I mean, you say you wish you were more confident, and you wish you could start your business, but sometimes it feels like you're stuck. What if you just started taking the steps to become more confident? Wear makeup, if you want to! Style your hair! Go crazy and buy new clothes! Take the steps to launch your business and find love!"

"That's a lot," Taylor said.

Rose grabbed Taylor's hand. "It *is*! And she's right about all of it. You've said it before: you wish you were brave enough to change your wardrobe and do your hair and all that. And you wish you could run a business and have a family. Well, why not?" Her voice rose in volume and intensity. "Things are different now, Taylor. There's all this information out there about work-life balance. Your dad didn't have that. Not to say you won't have to work hard, but it's a *thing*. People do it. It's going to be hard work. But if anyone is capable, it's you. Have you heard that saying that starting a business is the best personal development journey of all time?"

Taylor shook her head, unable to speak. Could her friends be right? Could she make a change, just like that?

"Well, I have," Rose went on. "And you know we think you're fantastic. We believe in you. But, since we are being totally honest, I think we both agree that it's time for you to start believing in yourself. You've already admitted that you don't feel confident. I'm pretty sure you can change that. Even if it's one baby step at a time."

Rose looked at her watch. "I've got to go. I told Celeste's teacher I would be back any minute. But we're still doing dinner tonight, right?"

"Right," Taylor and Jessie said.

"Great," Rose said. "See you at Taylor's at five."

After saying good-bye, Taylor's mind started to work. She had an idea, and she was pretty sure her friends would be excited to play along.

———

When the doorbell rang at five o'clock on the dot, Taylor didn't quite make it to the door before Celeste flung it open. "Party time!" She ran up to Taylor and threw her arms around her knees.

"Party time, huh?" Taylor said, and Celeste replied, "Yep. Mom brought you a grown-up drink. That's how I know it's party time."

Coming through the door, Rose held up a bottle of peach-flavored vodka. "Party time!"

Jessie was right behind her, arms raised and hips swaying as if music already played.

"It's party time!" Celeste squealed. "Pick me up, Auntie Tay!"

Taylor hoisted Celeste onto her hip. "I think you're going to be too big for this by next week."

Celeste laughed, wrapped her arms around Taylor's neck, and nuzzled the side of her face.

"Pour us some drinks, Rosie," Taylor said, "because I've got a big favor to ask you."

A minute later, the women (and Celeste, with her cup of lemonade) toasted an evening of fun.

"Your favor?" Jessie said.

"Remember when we used to watch that show, the one where all the dancers compete?"

Taylor said.

Rose and Jessie nodded.

"I don't remember that one," Celeste said.

"That's because you weren't born yet," Jessie said. "But it's still on. Maybe we should have our weekly girls night again and we can all watch it together."

While Celeste bounced around the living room, excited about girls night, Taylor said, "Remember that guy, the hip-hop dancer? He was so good at hip-hop but on one episode, he had to do this slow number. Remember that?"

Her friends nodded. "Yeah, I do," Jessie said. "He was so good-looking."

"He was so *nervous*," Rose said.

"Why was he nervous, Mommy?"

"He was nervous because he had never done that kind of dance before," Taylor said. "But you know what the judge said to him?"

"What did she say?" Celeste said.

"She said, 'I know this style is new for you. The best thing you can do is to *act* confident. If you're not confident, *pretend* you are. Keep on pretending until you believe it.'"

"Ah," Rose said. "I think I see where you're going with this."

"Me, too," Jessie said.

"That's what I need. But I need help."

"I'll help you!" Celeste said, making them all laugh.

"Thank you," Taylor said. "You're the best, you know that?"

"What do we do?" Celeste wanted to know.

"For starters, I'm hoping your mom and Aunt Jessie will do my hair and makeup. And help me find something cute to wear."

For the next hour, Rose and Jessie primped and plucked and powdered Taylor. They sipped cocktails, too, and the honesty flowed right along with the drinks.

"I've always thought you had the most beautiful eyes," Rose said as she applied eyeliner and shadow. "But you didn't seem to notice that, yourself."

"I mean, I guess I've always thought they were a nice color," Taylor said, "but I didn't want to, you know, be full of myself, or something."

Behind her, Jessie clucked her tongue, pulling the straightener through Taylor's hair. "There is absolutely nothing wrong with playing up your best physical attribute. The eyes are the window to the soul and all that."

"Right," Taylor said. "I have heard that. But still." She shrugged.

Growing up, smarts and work ethic always took precedence over physical characteristics. Her parents rarely complimented her looks — physical traits, outfits, or otherwise. They raised her to believe hard work and providing for a family were the keys to fulfillment, and traits like responsibility were invaluable.

And, her entrepreneurial father told her that her dream of opening a barn was too pie-in-the-sky. He offered a service people needed: accounting. But something like horseback riding lessons? If she remembered correctly, his exact words were, "Horses are pretty, Taylor, but they're expensive and they take lots of work. If you saddle yourself with that" (he chortled at his own pun) "you'll never have a family."

Even all these years later, his words still stung.

But ... what if he was wrong? Just as he'd believed he had to work around the clock to run his business — which many people no longer did — perhaps his belief about how she could run a horse-related venture were outdated, as well. Nowadays, as Rose pointed out, entrepreneurs found ways to strike a balance between work and family.

"It's just hard to change a lifetime of thinking a certain way," she said.

"Right," Jessie said. "But you have to start somewhere. This is that place. Now go look in the mirror."

The results were astonishing. She still looked like herself, only ... more. Jessie had styled waves into her hair, and they framed her face, rather than hanging limp like they usually did. The makeup, as minimal as it was, brought out her eyes and cheekbones and lips. She actually looked *pretty*, which she would never admit out loud. But she didn't have to.

"Your face says it all!" Rose said, her voice a squeal as she came up behind Taylor. "You *like* it. You know you look hot." She pretended to lick her finger and made a sizzling noise when she touched Taylor's shoulder.

Celeste laughed. "You do look *hot*, Auntie Tay!"

"I'm glad we've taught your five-year-old a new and exciting phrase," Jessie said.

"And now for the outfit," Rose said. "Take us to your closet."

After a few minutes of sliding hangers along the rod, passing up tops and pants and dresses, Rose and Jessie looked at each other, and then at Taylor.

"I know, it's in pretty bad shape, isn't it?"

"I think we can do better," Jessie said. "This closet screams 'School Librarian.'"

"Is there anything in here that isn't a neutral?" Rose said. "We didn't plan on this, but we're going to have to make a quick stop at Fashionista."

The outfit her friends chose for Taylor was exactly what she would have chosen for herself, if she were living her dream entrepreneurial life rather than her actual librarian life. The dark jeans and high-neck tank top were casual, yet sophisticated. The sandals and jewelry dressed up the outfit, and Taylor couldn't remember the last time she felt so good in her skin and clothes.

"I love this," she told Rose and Jessie as she turned in a slow circle for them outside the dressing room. "I feel so good."

"Good," Rose said, no nonsense. "I want you to do what we talked about earlier. Pretend you're already the owner of Sugar Pine Barn. Act like the woman you want to be."

A big feeling rising up inside her body, Taylor nodded. "I will. I'm her. This will be fun."

At first, it was difficult. When the hostess at the Hideaway asked her how many were in their party, she had to consciously straighten her posture and infuse her voice with confidence, rather than stating her answer like a question like she normally would. "A table for four, please," she said, looking into the hostess's eyes and offering her a smile. "In the area with the kids' zone."

The hostess beamed at her. "Right this way."

Taylor found herself sitting up a little taller than usual, perusing the menu with a more adventurous attitude. "You know," she said, "I think I'm going to go big tonight. I've always wanted to order the pirate's booty platter, but I've never wanted to say, 'booty' to the server."

Her friends laughed. "Go for it!" Rose said. "I can't wait to hear this."

Celeste spent the next several minutes making herself laugh as she repeated, "Booty!"

When the server came to take their order, Taylor glanced nervously around the table and said, "I'd like the pirate's booty platter, please." Although she felt a tide of nervous giggles threatening, she held it in check.

The server didn't even bat an eye. After everyone else ordered, he walked away, and Taylor said, "I can't believe I avoided ordering that dish all this time. The guy was completely unfazed."

"Yeah!" Jessie said. "It's on the menu. I'm sure people order it all the time. It comes with a mini pot of melted butter, for goodness' sake."

The server delivered a basket of warm cheddar-garlic biscuits, and everyone dug in. While they ate, Jessie said, "I think we're already ready to take this to the next level."

Taylor froze, mid-chew.

"She looks terrified," Rose said to Jessie, and Jessie nodded. "Sure does. But this is going to be fun. I've been keeping my eye on the bar. There's a guy. He's here alone —"

"No way," Taylor said, her heart racing. "I am not asking anyone out tonight."

"Then you'll be relieved to know that's not what I had in mind," Jessie said. "I just want to see you strike up a conversation. Offer to buy him a drink. It's completely safe. We'll be right here, watching."

"The two of you here, watching, is even more nerve-racking," Taylor said. "I can embarrass myself just fine without an audience."

"Just remember the dancing show," Jessie said. "All you've got to do is *pretend* you are a flirtatious, sexy babe. Before you know it, you'll feel like you are."

Her mouth suddenly dry, Taylor nodded. Her friends looked at her from across the table, expectant and excited. She didn't want to let them down. She could do this. She stood up, and as she walked away from the table, Celeste called, "You got this, girl."

Taylor was laughing when she slid onto the barstool next to her target. He gave her a funny look, like he wasn't sure if she'd actually meant to sit down next to him.

In return, she flashed him a smile. "I couldn't help but notice you've been sitting alone for a while," she told him. Good. Her voice sounded normal.

"To be honest, I was waiting for someone. But I think she's a no-show."

"Someone, as in a date?"

"Yeah, but online dating is brutal. As many people flake as show up."

"I'm Taylor." She offered him her hand and he shook it, smiling at her for the first time. "BP," the guy said. "Stands for Brian Poland."

"Can I buy you a drink, BP?"

He shrugged. "I mean, I won't turn it down. But also, chivalry is not dead. So I've got next round."

Uh oh. Was Taylor into this for two drinks now? She decided that even if she was, she could always order a soda or an iced tea. She didn't have to throw them back with a stranger. "Deal."

Without any of the pressure she'd normally put on herself to be *more* (more chatty, more funny, more pretty), Taylor found the conversation flowed easily, from typical topics, like what they did for work and where they'd grown up (he was a traveling nurse and grew up in a small town in Kansas), to deeper ones, like what they envisioned for their futures.

Although Taylor found BP charming and friendly, she didn't find him attractive. Besides, he was based out of somewhere in the Midwest, and she didn't want to get involved with someone who lived three quarters of the way across the country. So, when he said he'd better get going after their second round, a Guinness for him and a Shirley Temple for her, she wished him well and went back to join her friends.

Once he was out of earshot, they let loose, offering her high-fives and congratulations.

"You looked so good, talking to that guy like that!" Rose said. Jessie added, "I've never seen you so confident with a guy!"

Basking in their compliments and excitement, Taylor felt herself grinning. If this is what it felt like to embrace the new Taylor Cole, she'd take it.

———

Riding high on the success of the evening — Taylor couldn't believe how much she enjoyed being the confident version of herself, even if she was just acting — she cranked up the music as she pulled out of the Hideaway parking lot to drive home. She danced along, grinning wildly, glad no one could see her. Her phone vibrated, and at the next stop light, she took it out of her purse just to make sure neither Rose nor Jessie needed help getting home.

But no, it was a couple of texts from each of them, in the group chat. First, the flames emoji from Rose. Then, a couple of photos Rose had taken while Taylor sat at the bar, chatting with the stranger. A car horn sounded behind her. She looked up. The light was green. She should probably look at the pictures later ... but another quick glance wouldn't hurt.

While driving, she swiped through the photos, watching herself become more relaxed. If she were a stranger, she would describe the Taylor in her friends' pictures as flirtatious, fun, maybe even coy in one or two. She might even say she looked sexy, and although the light makeup and hairdo helped, it was her bearing that made the real difference.

She looked like she felt strong. Feminine. Powerful. Like she was the kind of woman who could do anything she wanted to do.

Then, right in the middle of her reverie, the sound of sirens made her jump. Startled, she looked up from her phone and realized she'd crossed the centerline. Worse, she was heading straight for an oncoming car. Not just any car, but a police cruiser. On reflex, she yanked her steering wheel to the right. Her heart rate spiked as she passed by the cop, and raised even faster when she realized he was making a U-turn to get behind her. She pulled over immediately. She considered the consequences for driving into oncoming traffic. Certainly a ticket. Possibly jail time. *Jail time?* She wondered how long the stay was for that infraction.

Chapter Six

Judd

*K*aty *has probably already fed the horses,* Judd told himself. *You can go home, crack open a cold one, and relax. You can completely avoid humans for the next three days.*

And that's when he saw it. A tiny gold sedan coming toward him, in his lane. Another careless driver. Another person who didn't care about consequences. Judd sighed. That driver was a menace to society. Yes, he was more than an hour into overtime. But he couldn't in good conscience let that person stay on the road.

So, the anger still red-hot, he turned on his lights and sirens.

The driver's reaction was almost comical. Any other day, Judd would have laughed. The gold car swerved into its own lane, not even thirty feet from where he had stopped in his. It passed him, and Judd caught a glimpse of the driver before he turned around. He saw a flash of wavy brown hair and a toned, bare arm. That was it.

To her credit, she put on her turn signal and pulled over right away. Still, Judd felt the anger bouncing around inside his body like the ball in a pinball machine as he called in her license plate and got out of his car.

———

TAYLOR

All the excitement Taylor experienced just a moment before disappeared. Fear replaced it. Was the universe trying to tell her she wasn't meant to feel powerful? Immediately after her first taste of being unstoppable — and it had been just a taste — there she was, swerving into the wrong lane and getting pulled over and likely hauled off to jail.

Still, her fear gave way to interest (at least, partially) the moment she saw the cop in her sideview mirror. As he walked toward her car, she couldn't help but notice that he was built. His legs looked muscular in his uniform pants. He had a trim waist and wide shoulders and his shirt sleeves were tight around his biceps.

The Taylor Cole who'd sat at the Hideaway bar just a few moments before would say something like, "Yummy," but the Taylor Cole who had just gotten pulled over for swerving into oncoming traffic — or, more precisely, an oncoming police car — felt suddenly nervous.

She put her hands on the steering wheel like her dad taught her. That way, she remembered, the cop would know she wasn't hiding a weapon. And also, he couldn't see her hands shaking. She cursed the universe when he stopped next to her window, and his ... package ended up at eye level. Despite the lecture she was surely about to receive, she felt a jolt of electricity power straight down to her nether region.

The first thing she noticed when he bent down to make eye contact with her was that his face was just as perfectly sculpted as his gorgeous body. He had a nice, strong chin. A nose that looked like it had been broken once, maybe twice. And his eyes were the most striking hazel color, brown with a sunburst of golden green.

His eyebrows were to die for. Only, at the moment, they were drawn together in what looked like a very angry frown. Taylor tried for a smile, but it felt more like a grimace.

Then it hit her: it was *him*. The cop who'd bought her coffee a few days before. The sexy man-god who'd made more than one appearance in her visualizations since.

"Crap."

As distracted as she was, she didn't remember to roll down her window until he knocked on it — three fast, angry-sounding raps with his knuckles. She pushed the button and waited for what felt like forever.

The police officer spoke then, and she didn't even register the words he chose, because she was too busy enjoying the deep richness of it, and the way it made her entire body hum.

"Did you hear me?"

This isn't good.

———

*J*UDD

Judd did his best to look imposing as he approached the car. He made a point of stopping at the driver's window before leaning down to make eye contact, hoping the pause would give the driver time to understand just what a mistake she'd made.

Realizing she hadn't rolled down her window, he heaved out a frustrated sigh and knocked on it. She jumped a little and rolled it down. Again, something at which he'd probably chuckle if he wasn't on his second overtime call of the day.

When he bent down, and their eyes met, the anger dissolved. Like magic. A completely different feeling replaced it. Was it ... No, impossible.

It *was* the woman from the coffee shop. Taylor. But she was a stranger. He could never feel such unbridled lust for a stranger.

But look at her, a voice murmured in the back of his mind. He did. He noticed her eyes first. They were the most interesting shade of blue gray. Long, thick eyelashes framed them. She had a dusting of freckles across the bridge of her nose, which he found at once adorable and alluring. And although her mouth was twisted into a grimace he assumed was guilt-induced, he wouldn't hate kissing it.

Kissing it? What was he thinking? And how much time had passed while he stood there, staring at her like some crazy person? *Snap out of it, O'Connor.*

"Do you have your license and registration? Proof of insurance?"

She returned his stare, her lips parted just slightly. God, she was beautiful. He had to snap out of it. "License, registration and insurance?" he repeated.

"Oh! Yes!" She held up her pointer finger. "License, registration, and insurance coming right up."

As irrational as it was, his gaze flicked to her left hand when she leaned across the center console. No ring. He admired the length of her torso when she reached into the glove compartment. His hand would fit perfectly just there, in the curve between her rib cage and her hip. He deserved a good punch in the nose, and had to resist the urge to give one to himself.

She straightened up and handed him two slips of paper. He snatched them, afraid that if his skin touched hers, he might ignite.

"I just have to get my license out of my purse."

"Go ahead," he said, feigning boredom, even though he was interested. Very interested.

Judd had a near photographic memory and an uncanny ability to remember random pieces of information. He wouldn't soon forget the Pleasant Street address on Miss Taylor Cole's registration and license. And her birthdate: September 10. She was just a year younger than he was.

Typically, he would ask a driver whether she knew why he pulled her over. But he didn't feel comfortable remaining in close proximity to Taylor Cole, of Pleasant Street, born September 10.

So he said, "Sit tight. Be right back," did an about face, and returned to his car, butterflies in his stomach like he was back in junior high school.

While Judd waited for dispatch to get back to him with any information about Taylor's drivers license, he thought about his reaction to this complete stranger. This completely beautiful stranger who couldn't possibly be his type (if she drove that carelessly, how did she live the rest of her life?).

The dispatcher interrupted his thoughts. "All clear. No warrants or suspensions."

Well, *that* was a relief. He didn't have to arrest her. Although, he could think of some fun they could have with handcuffs.

What is happening, here?

Judd needed to get the traffic stop over with. He had to return her license and write her a ticket. The only way to quash the attraction he was feeling was to shut down his human side.

He was used to that — he did it every time he encountered a scene so terrible it made him question whether he was really cut out for his job. He'd never done it because of a beautiful woman, but the process should be the same. He could compartmentalize all day long. With a new resolve, he got out of his car and walked up to Taylor's. He handed back her license. "Thanks," she said. Her voice didn't affect him at all. Not one bit. It didn't send those butterflies into a frenzy or a shiver over his skin.

"Do you know why I pulled you over, ma'am?"

"Yes."

He thought he detected a hint of sarcasm, and he told himself it wasn't cute at all. "Care to enlighten me?"

Her lips twitched. He'd been right. They were kissable. Fortunately, he had no interest whatsoever in kissing her.

"I was in the wrong lane."

"Why were you in the wrong lane?"

Taylor put her forehead on the steering wheel for a moment. When she straightened back up, a strand of hair remained across her face. Brushing it away would be totally inappropriate, Judd reminded himself. He hooked his thumbs into his belt while he waited for her response.

"This is embarrassing to admit, but I was looking at some pictures."

At that, genuine aggravation returned. Not, he realized with a start, because she'd made a bad driving decision, but because he was worried. About her. "You know how long it takes to crash into someone? Less time than it takes to look at pictures."

At least she had the decency to look even more embarrassed and remorseful. "A split second. I know. I'm sorry."

He hadn't expected that it. Most people tried to explain away their actions, rationalize their dangerous behaviors. He had to know.

"What kind of pictures?"

Surprise registered. "Some pictures from an evening out with my friends."

"Huh." With her friends. *No boyfriend? Don't ask for specifics, O'Connor.* "I'm going to have to write you a ticket."

She simply nodded. "I understand."

At that point, he didn't even *want* to write her a ticket. He wanted to get away from her, from the way she made him feel. He filled out the form anyway, handed it to her, and without another word, walked back to his car.

"And now, if I could just get home."

———

*T*AYLOR

Driving home, Taylor chastised herself. Why had she been so stupid as to look at those pictures while she was behind the wheel? Talk about vanity. A grown woman, admiring photos of herself flirting with a stranger. She groaned.

"That vanity just cost you a couple hundred dollars," she told herself. "Minimum."

The sun had started its descent, transforming the sky into a soft, dusky rose that melted into peach. Taylor put on her turn signal — she'd be extra careful from now on — and turned onto Gurley Street, the main drag through downtown. Her train of thought returned to that sexy cop. O'Connor. If they'd run into each other anywhere else, she thought as she turned onto her street, laughing at her own pun, she probably would have asked for his number.

Who are you kidding? You never would've asked for his number. You would've sat there and hoped that he asked for yours.

Besides, she didn't need someone that uptight and prickly in her life. Still, she couldn't stop seeing images of his biceps, imagining his arms around her, his mouth on hers.

She parked in her driveway and said into the silence, "I think someone needs a cold shower."

Not for the first time, she noticed how quiet it was in the house. Living alone was lonely sometimes, she thought as she changed into pajamas. Taylor didn't consider herself a needy woman. She wasn't one of those girls who always had a boyfriend, or even dates lined up.

Still, she knew what she wanted: a long-term partner — eventually, a husband — someone with whom she could watch TV at night while sharing a bottle of wine, or a couple of beers. If only she could have that *and* her dream business. But she knew from experience that it wasn't possible.

Her friends claimed it was, but their lives proved otherwise. Rose, recently out of a bad relationship with Celeste's dad, had sworn off men for the foreseeable future. And for Jessie, romance wasn't a priority.

As she brushed her teeth, she watched the movie reel of possible situations in which she could have met the smokin' hot Officer O'Connor again and not pissed him off. They could have met on the Courthouse Plaza, where they were both out for a stroll ... and he could have offered to buy her ice cream. They could have met on a hiking trail and shared a magical moment when they spotted a bald eagle, or a family of deer.

"Get a grip, Taylor," she said. Her voice echoed into the silence.

She had to think about something else. Intending to text Jessie and Rose to tell them about the ticket — not about the guy who gave it to her — she picked up her phone after getting in bed.

Thank you for the great pictures. Unfortunately, I was so busy gawking at myself that I almost ran head-on into a police car. Yes, he wrote me a ticket. I would blame you, but I guess there's a price for vanity. She added a winking emoji, hoping to keep the tone light.

Jessie wrote back immediately. *Oh no! I feel like I should help you pay for it. I sent you half those pictures.*

Feeling slightly better, Taylor wrote back, *No, this is not on you. I shouldn't have even looked at my phone.*

Jessie responded, *But you looked so darned goooooood. Bummer, though. I'm sorry.*

No worries. Sleep well.

Same to you.

Taylor knew Rose would respond eventually. She was probably going through the official bedtime routine with Celeste: bath, pajamas, reading, singing, and finally, bed. That, too, Taylor wanted. She would wait until she had a partner. She saw how much work parenting was, especially for Rose as a single mom. But on the rare nights when she babysat and put Celeste to bed, she found the routine almost magical.

Feeling especially lonely, Taylor turned off her bedside lamp, and although she told herself not to, she thought about Officer Judd O'Connor until she drifted off to sleep.

Chapter Seven

When Judd pulled up at his family's property fifteen minutes after leaving Taylor, he saw his sister coming out of her house. Which meant she hadn't fed the horses yet. Good. He still felt off and could use the rhythm of their ritual to get grounded. She waved at him and changed direction to meet him at his parking spot. Her smile was infectious, and he found himself smiling, too.

She wrinkled her nose. "You're late. Rough afternoon?"

"You could say that," he said.

"Then why are you smiling?"

"Because you are." He punched her gently on the shoulder.

She winced and rubbed the spot where he'd made contact. "I shouldn't admit this to you, because I'm sure you are dog tired, as late as you are. But I sort of waited for you. I didn't feel like feeding by myself tonight."

"Everything okay?"

She laughed and stretched her arms. "Everything's fine, except my entire body is on fire from this new class I took at the gym. I was going to make you do the heavy lifting."

"Fair enough. The only workout I got today was a little bit of soccer. So I could use some heavy lifting."

"Perfect. Well, go change and I'll meet you in the barn."

Judd did what he was told. He'd learned long ago that while his mom trumped both of them, Katy trumped him. He made the walk to his own house, which sat fifty yards or so from where he parked. He took off his duty boots and vest, feeling thirty pounds lighter already. Then he changed into sweatpants and a T-shirt and put on his cowboy boots. Down at the barn, Katy was already at work, loading the wheelbarrow with flakes of alfalfa.

"Nice. I like the sweats-and-boots look," she told him. He rolled his eyes and asked, "How was your day?" while adding more flakes to the wheelbarrow.

"It was okay," she said. "But more importantly, why did you look so ... *weird* when you got home?"

"That's just my face, you little punk," he teased. "Are you saying I'm weird-looking?"

"The weirdest. Obviously."

Judd considered lying to his sister, telling her he was just extra tired after the long shift. But he had never lied to her, and he wouldn't start now.

"It's stupid," he said, grabbing the wheelbarrow handles and pulling it toward the first stall in the barn. "Just before my shift ended, I got a call about an injury accident."

"And let me guess. You lost it on some poor driver."

Judd wondered, for a split second, why Katy would say that. He dismissed the thought as quickly as he had it. "That wasn't the worst of it. After we cleared it, I was heading home, right? There I was, minding my own business, and this little car comes creeping down the road. In my lane."

"Creeping?"

"Yeah. Traveling really slowly. Don't make fun of my word choices. I don't make fun of your outfits."

"This is the guy who's wearing cowboy boots with sweatpants. And besides, you do make fun of my outfits. So?"

"So." Judd dropped a couple of flakes into the stall where he kept his horse, Tiny. "It's obvious when the driver sees me, right? She jerks her wheel and gets right back in her lane."

Katy stopped, mid-stride on her way to the stall across the walkway. She raised her eyebrows at him. "She?"

How in the world she had picked up on that, Judd didn't know. But women had their ways, he knew.

"Not important."

Katy gave him a look that said something like, *I know it* is *important*, and said, "So.

You read her the riot act."

"Why do you keep saying stuff like that?"

"I don't know," Katy said, coming back to the wheelbarrow as he pushed it to the next stall. "It just seems like you've been a little, I don't know, tightly wound lately. Most of your stories include you losing your mind on people."

He offered a grunt in response, and as they went about their chores, he couldn't help but picture Taylor Cole, of Pleasant Street, and some activities that would surely help him unwind.

———

"Judd met a pretty girl today," Katy announced an hour later, when the O'Connor family gathered around the table for their weekly dinner.

Judd's parents looked at each other and then at Judd, their eyebrows raised. Judd shot daggers across the table at his sister. "I admit, I did," he said. "But nothing's going to come of it. She was pretty, but she was driving into oncoming traffic. I *was* that oncoming traffic and although she was obviously embarrassed, I hate to think how she lives the rest of her life."

"And yet..." Judd's dad said. His mom's eyes twinkled.

Judd glared at Katy, who smiled back, her expression as sweet as almost-rotten fruit.

"And yet, nothing," Judd said. "I'll probably never see her again."

"Nonsense," his mom said, making a dismissive motion with her hand. "This is a small town. You'll see her again."

"But it's true," Katy said. "Our little Judd is a recluse. Work and go home. That's it."

Judd shook his head. The shortcomings of his social life drove many dinner table discussions.

"True," their dad said. "We need to get you off this property, son."

"I like it here. There're no crazy people."

He gave Katy the side-eye, and everyone laughed. The conversation flowed on to their mom's rose garden and the upcoming wine and cheese festival, which Judd would do everything in his power to avoid. He volunteered to do clean-up, and his parents sat on barstools at the counter while he washed dishes and wiped down the counter. Katy read in the living room, interjecting every so often. The evening was so pleasant, he didn't realize how long he'd gone without looking at his phone.

No technology at the dinner table was an O'Connor family rule. Judd sometimes found it difficult to resist the urge to do a quick Internet search or share something he'd seen earlier with his parents and sister. He also recognized that the break from screen time allowed him a respite from an almost-compulsive need to check his work email, respond to text messages, and stay on top of the police department's call log, twenty-four seven.

When he did get back to his phone that night, the text message he received from his sergeant, Michael Barnes, set his nerves and his teeth on edge (again): *My office. 0500 Thursday.*

Judd respected the heck out of Barnes, a long-time law enforcement officer he considered a mentor. He also feared him.

Being called into your supervisor's office at the start of your shift was akin to being summoned to the principal's office. It was rarely, if ever, a good thing. What could Barnes possibly want? Standing in the entry of his parents' house, Judd ran through a list of potential reasons Sarge would want to see him. He wasn't one to waste time. He'd handle a small matter, like a little overtime or a detail from one of his reports, or, come to think of it, an unfinished report, with a phone call.

A straight-A student, Judd never got sent to the principal's office. But he imagined he would have felt somewhat like he did reading that text. He cursed himself when he noticed butterflies in his stomach. Butterflies!

Worse, he went on to overthink his response. Should he send a thumbs up? A simple *Okay*? He decided on, *No problem*, and hoped he'd be able to sleep that night.

———

"Listen, O Connor. You're probably aware I've gotten some calls about you."

Panicking, Judd glanced from one side to the other, as if someone might be there to corroborate Barnes's claim. Judd knew he'd left some unhappy drivers in his wake over the past several months. But was it any more than usual?

"Receiving a couple of calls about a particular officer isn't too concerning," Barnes went on, and Judd felt himself start to relax. "But in your case, it's more than a couple. More than a few, even. You know, Judd, have you ever watched a cooking show?"

Judd shook his head.

"My wife loves to watch cooking shows. There's this one host, a chef, I can't remember her name. But instead of giving recipes with actual amounts, she says things like, 'add a generous palmful of Italian herbs.' This morning, when I got the most recent call about you, O'Connor, I thought, you know, it seems like I've gotten more than a generous palmful of calls about O'Connor."

"Really?"

Barnes leveled a gaze at him. People saying things like, "Really?" was one of Barnes's pet peeves.

"Right. Sorry."

"Has something been going on, O'Connor? Something at home, maybe?"

Judd's mouth felt extraordinarily dry. He was almost positive that if he opened it, sand would come out. "No, sir."

"Nothing? You can't think of anything? Your parents okay? Your sister?"

Judd shook his head. "They're fine, sir. Nothing out of the ordinary. Everything is the same as always."

He pictured his family's property: the rolling hills, the houses nestled among them. The trees shading the fields, the horses grazing. The nighttime sky sparkling with stars. It was a slice of Heaven, and increasingly, the only place he wanted to be. Maybe *that* was different.

Barnes leaned back in his chair. The leather creaked. He folded his hands behind his head. "Well, that's too bad. I admit, I was hoping you would tell me some circumstances exist, circumstances causing you to act out of character. Giving you what many people have called a short fuse, or a bad temper."

Judd took a deep breath and racked his brain. "A short fuse?"

Barnes inclined his head forward. Repeating what he said was another pet peeve. "That's what they said."

"I mean, maybe I lost it with the one guy, who was swerving in and out of lanes on the highway because he was trying to feed his dog perfectly-sized morsels of chicken nuggets, *while driving*."

The memory got his adrenaline going. Again.

Barnes didn't speak, so Judd filled the silence. "And I might have been a little gruff with the lady who almost caused a wreck after poking herself in the eye with her mascara wand."

Again, Barnes responded with silence and eye contact. "Right. Those were some of them."

Am I about to get fired?

"No, you're not about to get fired. I could see the question plain as day in your expression." Barnes leaned forward again, his elbows on the desk, his fingers interlaced. "Look. I'm going to be straight with you. I've seen guys like you. They come in as rookies, on fire, ready to change the world. I love to see that. But what happens is, you're so excited to change the world that when you encounter these people — idiots feeding their dogs perfectly-sized morsels of chicken nuggets while driving — over and over again, you get frustrated. You realize that, even if you're changing the world a little at a time, those idiots are still going to be out there, being idiots."

Judd felt his shoulders slump. It was as if Barnes could read his mind. That's exactly how he'd been feeling the past couple of months. Even if he hadn't quite put his finger on it until that very moment.

When Judd looked up at Barnes, he saw that he was nodding. "I nailed it, didn't I? You know how I know all of this, O'Connor? It's because I used to be you. You should have seen me as a rookie, man. I was *hot*. Those tones came over the scanner, I was the first one to turn up the volume, take the call. I was dressed and ready thirty minutes before every shift, listening to the police scanner so that if a call came in, I could take it. This was my *calling*, man. You feel me?"

Judd nodded. Swallowed.

"But then I started getting angry. So angry. I lost my mind on a drunk driver who darn near killed a little girl. An innocent little baby. That guy gets out of his car, and is walking over to me, barely able to stand up straight, but without a scratch on him."

At the memory, a vein bulged at Barnes's temple. The muscles clenched in his jaw.

"I was mad. I pictured wrapping my hand around that guy's neck and — who am I kidding? I *did* wrap my hand around his neck. I squeezed. He's spluttering, you know? Drunk as all get-out, spitting all over the place."

Judd had never heard that story. But it resonated. He knew the feeling of wanting to throttle someone. "So what happened?"

"Some guy off the street ran up and grabbed my arm. Snapped me out of it," Barnes said. "Someone called it in the next day. Guy deserved it, but some Good Samaritan wanted to protect him, I guess."

"Or they wanted to protect you from ruining your career."

Barnes's eyes lit up as if he hadn't even considered that. "Good point, O'Connor. I got admin leave for that. But anyway. Bottom line? I think you need a bit of a break," Barnes said.

Oh, no. Barnes wasn't going to bench him, was he? Judd was not cut out to be an administrative guy, a paper pusher. A desk job would be the absolute end of him. He would die of boredom. The only thing worse than a desk job was —

"School resource officer."

"What?"

Barnes's eyebrows, fuzzy black caterpillars, inched closer together and drew downward.

"I mean, excuse me?"

"I said, I found you a position as a school resource officer."

"A school resource officer?" The words tasted like acid. "Are you kidding me?"

Barnes smiled. "O'Connor. You know I don't kid."

"But —"

Barnes held up a hand, and even though that stopped Judd from speaking out loud, he ran through all the different ways he could complete that sentence:

I need to be out on the street, arresting bad guys.

A school resource officer isn't a real cop.

I don't deserve this.

This will be the end of my career.

"Who will cover my shift?"

There. Logistics would get Barnes's attention. He wouldn't leave a shift uncovered.

"I've already taken care of it. You have the next few days off. Your new assignment begins on Monday. First day of school."

Judd wanted to argue. He wanted to throw himself at Barnes's feet and beg him to change his mind. He wasn't above that — being demoted to school resource officer was cause enough. But it wouldn't change Barnes's mind. Nothing would.

Judd thought he might throw up. Or scream. But *that* might get him fired. So he did the only thing he could think of: he pressed his lips together, gave Barnes a curt nod, and walked out of his office.

Chapter Eight

T AYLOR

The first day of school. It wasn't her dream life, but Taylor had always loved the fresh start of a new year. She was up, caffeinated, and showered by six, which left her thirty minutes to play with her hair and makeup. That was kind of a treat. Her night out with the girls had left her inspired, and she was surprised to find that the act of caring for herself made her feel as pretty as the end result did.

She pulled into her non-spot at 6:40 and walked into the library for the annual First Day of School Staff Breakfast Meeting (Principal Vasquez capitalized every word in the title of every event). Jessie was already there, and she raised her eyebrows when Taylor walked in. "Looking good."

Taylor smiled at her. "You are, too, but that's nothing unusual."

A frazzled Rose rushed in a minute later, pinning her hair into a bun as she practically ran over to them.

"Everything okay?" Taylor and Jessie asked at the same time.

"It's fine," Rose said, finishing her bun and smoothing her hair. "Sort of. Not really. Celeste was up all night, thanks to our college apartment-mates. She finally fell asleep at four. I let her sleep as long as I could, tried to get her to stay asleep in the car on the way to daycare. But she woke up. She's a disaster."

"Maybe they can get her to nap at daycare?" Taylor said.

"I hope so. I don't think they really nap in the second-year preschool class, but I know that if she falls asleep, they'll leave her alone."

Principal Vasquez rang his cowbell. "Good morning, staff," he called, his voice singsongy.

"Good morning, Mr. Vasquez," they all responded, equally melodic.

"Welcome to the new school year," he beamed. "It's going to be a great one. Before we dive into the food and the business, there is one small staffing change of which I want to make you aware."

Ernie's gaze darted around the room. He raised up on his tip toes, obviously not finding whoever he was looking for. Footsteps sounded outside the library door, and the shiny toe of a black boot appeared. A well-built, very sexy man in uniform appeared next. Taylor gasped just as Rose and Jessie said quietly and perfectly in sync, "Oh, *hello*." She gripped one of their wrists in each of her hands and squeezed.

"Ah," Ernie said. "There he is. Staff, I'd like to introduce you to Officer Judd O'Connor, our new school resource officer. He's been assigned to Prescott High School, and I trust that you will all make him feel welcome. I was going to ask him to give a speech, but I think I will save that particular humiliation for Wednesday's after-school professional development meeting."

Judd. Taylor couldn't believe it. Rose and Jessie both looked at her, foreheads wrinkled in concern.

"It's him," Taylor hissed, thinking she would give absolutely anything to be able to slink back and disappear behind her friends so he wouldn't see her.

She couldn't though, and their eyes locked just as he raised his hand and said, "Hello."

She saw recognition in is, and felt a rush of energy shoot through her body, settling soundly between her legs.

This isn't good.

---

*J*UDD

Judd did his best to offer a friendly smile while the principal introduced him as if he were an important member of the staff. Meanwhile, he took stock of the people he'd be working with for the indefinite future. Several times, he had to consciously unclench his teeth.

His first thought was that the members of the high school staff were a much more motley crew than the members of a police department. At one of his typical squad meetings, most people were in uniform, creases ironed, collars buttoned, boots shined. Those who weren't in uniform were just as squared away. Slacks and button-up shirts were required, along with a badge and gun.

He hadn't expected a similar vibe at the high school but was still surprised when he looked around and saw some teachers wearing jeans, others wearing business suits, and still others wearing every variation of "professional" from hippie skirt and sandals to a tuxedo. He could swear one guy was dressed as a Viking.

Like a jointed wooden puppet, he lifted a hand in greeting. Just as he said, "Hello," he spotted her. Taylor Cole. The woman who had occupied the forefront of his mind since he'd pulled her over three days before. She looked ... mouthwatering. Her blouse at once showed off her curves and left something alluring and mysterious to Judd's overactive imagination. His eyes locked with hers, and he realized she was ... terrified? She was blushing, which he found adorable, and grasping the hand of a woman on either side of her.

He told himself he was relieved she looked upset. Yes, she was gorgeous, but the very last thing he needed was an office romance. He was already in trouble at work and couldn't afford for Barnes or anyone else to think he was in an inappropriate relationship with a co-worker.

And yet. Something inside him sparked when their eyes met. He realized with a start that everyone in the room stared at him expectantly. With no small amount of effort, he tore his gaze away from Taylor and looked at the principal, Ernie Vasquez, who'd greeted him at the campus gate at six a.m.

"Would you like to introduce yourself? Tell us a bit about why you're here?" Ernie — as the guy had instructed Judd to call him — grinned at him, charming and jovial. "No speech! Like I said, I'm saving that. Just an informal introduction."

Judd quashed the urge to blurt out, "I'm here because I'm being punished, given the lamest possible position on the planet."

"Sure," he said instead. "I'm Judd O'Connor. I've been with the Prescott Police Department for seven years." He nodded.

"And what brings you to our campus, Officer O'Connor?"

In his mind, Judd groaned.

"In our department, we rotate through these special assignments. It's my turn, lucky for you."

He flashed his best cocky grin. The quip earned him a couple of chuckles but did not make him wish any less that he could turn on his heel and march away from the library, and the spotlight, and the stupid School Resource Officer position. And Taylor Cole, whose very presence made him feel like he would burst into flames at any moment.

———

One perk of being the school resource officer: Judd got his own office. And it had a door. Which meant that when things got too people-y, he could hide out. He spent the first two periods of his first day getting to know the campus, walking the hallways and saying hello to students between classes. He quickly realized the school was a microcosm of the rest of the world: most of the kids responded in a friendly way, some of them seemed a little standoffish, and a few seemed to straight-up dislike him.

Judd realized right away that he walked the place in hyper-alert mode — and not for the usual reasons. His eyes were peeled and his ears were pricked for any sign of Taylor Cole. He hoped his peering into every single window he passed looked more like curiosity than investigation. He had no idea what position Taylor held at the school. She could be a teacher or an aide or the vice principal. What he *did* know was that their paths would cross eventually.

He couldn't wait.

By lunch, he still hadn't seen her. The sense of anticipation felt heavy.

He remembered waiting for things as a child: Christmas morning, the mailman on the day he was expecting a new *MAD* magazine, his Shrinky Dinks to shrink in the oven. He also remembered his mom saying, "Judd, honey. A watched pot never boils. Walk away, keep yourself busy for a while and it will happen before you know it."

The library door stood open, and Judd looked inside. Reading had always held a sort of magic for him. Although he probably couldn't spend much time there, he figured it wouldn't hurt to look around, see what the school had. He walked inside and inhaled. The scent of books greeted him, and he felt right at home. He heard footsteps coming from the other end of one of the rows. He slowed down, but the person who owned the footsteps didn't. Her head down as she looked at an open book in her hands, she ran right into him. He grabbed her arms to keep her from losing her balance. In that instant, he inhaled something other than the scent of books — she smelled glorious (a word he would never use in real life, but one that most accurately described the fresh, citrusy scent). They recognized each other at the same time.

"You," she said, taking a step back.

"You," he said, releasing her arms.

"What are you doing here?" she demanded, before immediately saying, "I'm sorry. I mean, is there something I can help you with?"

This is interesting, Judd thought. Taylor seemed as flustered by his presence as he was by hers.

"I'm —"

"Judd O'Connor, new School Resource Officer, I know."

She knew his name. And, if he wasn't mistaken, she was blushing again. Which was devastating. It highlighted those freckles on the bridge of her nose. He was a goner. Only, he reminded himself, he wasn't looking for romance. He was on a mission: get in, get out, get back on the road. Still. Judd couldn't resist trying to disarm her prickliness with a smile. "I've always loved a good library," he said, shrugging. "I just thought I would come in, see what books you have."

A spark of interest flashed in her eyes.

"Well, we've got a little bit of everything," she said. "But I don't imagine you'll have much time for reading while you're here. Since you'll be, um, patrolling and all."

Was that sarcasm? No, she couldn't know what this assignment meant to Judd — a demotion only slightly better than being fired — so he brushed off his own prickly reaction.

She straightened her posture and said, "You're welcome to look around."

The longer he could spend in her presence, the better, he thought. "I will, thanks."

He could feel her watching him as he headed toward the stacks. Patrolling, indeed.

A little voice in the back of his mind said *You could always patrol the library*. He'd imagined the halls of a high school would be mundane at best, but this assignment was already proving beyond interesting.

Chapter Nine

The idea for a rodeo club had brewed in Taylor's mind for the past few years, but she never had the courage to take it to Ernie. Until she'd received that letter from Kristi Mendez, Senior Loan Officer at Prescott Bank.

It was just the motivation Taylor needed. Something had to change. She refused to experience the denied-bank-loan disappointment over and over. It was time to take action. A rodeo club would give a lender the proof of concept Kristi mentioned. If Taylor could build the club into something kids were excited about, bankers like Kristi Mendez wouldn't be able to pass her up.

Taylor was now operating as the new, confident version of herself. So, Wednesday morning, she parked in her non-spot fifteen minutes earlier than usual and headed to the main entrance, where Ernie stood, greeting students, teachers, and staff as they came in.

"Ms. Cole!" he called as she approached him. Her hands started shaking, and she felt sweat prickling her skin. "Good morning!"

Taylor cleared her throat. Rather than facing him, she stood next to him, looking out over the parking lot.

"You going to be part of my greeting committee today?" he asked.

"Yes," she said, finally chancing eye contact. He looked calm and friendly, as usual. She took the plunge. "And, there's something I want to talk to you about."

She waited while he said good morning to a few students, calling each one by name. After they passed, he turned toward her. "So, what did you want to ask me?"

Taylor cleared her throat again. Silently, she recited her affirmations. *I am confident. I can create what I want in life. I can do hard things.*

"Well, the thing is, I don't know if this will fly or not, but I've been thinking about it for a couple of years —"

Ernie held up a finger, then turned away to greet a few more students. Taylor sighed. *I am confident.* She was just going to have to spit it out. When he turned to face her again, she hurried to say, "I'd like to start a rodeo club. At the school."

"A rodeo club, you say?"

"I know it's not strictly academic, but I thought it would be fun for some of the kids. And rodeo is a great skill. It teaches responsibility. A little math. And we could definitely tie in some academics. If it won't work out, that's okay, you can just tell me."

Again, Ernie held up a finger, eyes twinkling with amusement. "Are you trying to talk me out of it before I can give you an answer?"

Taylor exhaled, offered a weak smile. "No."

"Good. I think it's a fantastic idea."

Suddenly, she felt like she could float if she wanted to. "You do?"

"I do. I assume you do too, so why do you sound surprised?"

"I don't know," Taylor said, her voice breathy with relief and excitement. "I guess I just wasn't sure what you'd think."

"I love it," Ernie said. "In fact, I think it's a *fantastic* idea. We don't have anything like it. The thing is, we don't have horses or a barn. There's nothing saying you can't have a horse club without horses, but I assume you have a plan for hands-on rodeo, if you've been thinking about this for a while?"

A rush of adrenaline filled Taylor's veins, and her heart beat so fast she almost couldn't breathe. "I, uh, did some research. Contacted a couple of local ranchers. I found someone willing to work with us. If you're willing to work with me on transportation and the legal stuff — liability forms, whatever."

Ernie raised his eyebrows at her. "I have to say, I'm impressed. I love the idea. I love your enthusiasm. And I'd love to support you. As long as you can find another staff member to run it with you, you can start next week."

Another staff member?

Ernie must have seen the question in her expression. "School policy. Every club has to have at least two staff members."

As quickly as Ernie's "yes" had boosted her spirits, this bit of news deflated them. She couldn't think of another staff member who would want to take on the extra responsibility of helping run a club.

"Oh, okay," Taylor said. "I guess I'll ask around."

"We'll all be together this afternoon at the regular Wednesday staff meeting. Why don't we ask then?"

"Okay, sure." Taylor could scream. Not only was her dream of starting a club going down the drain, but that afternoon, she would face public rejection.

———

Taylor spent the entire day agonizing over whether anyone would volunteer to run the rodeo club with her.

Rose couldn't do it, Taylor thought as she shelved the books students turned in the day before. She didn't want to miss a minute with Celeste if she could help it. And Jessie had taken to caring for her elderly neighbor.

But, almost one hundred other people worked at Prescott High School. Surely *someone* would have an interest in horses. Or take pity on Taylor and agree to help her. During second and third periods, the science classes came in to research for their essays. Chatting with the kids, helping them find books, and asking questions about what they were studying provided a good distraction.

Fourth period ticked by so slowly, Taylor forced herself to dust the shelves.

Apparently, Taylor didn't feature in Officer O'Connor's thoughts like he did in hers. He hadn't returned to the library since their collision on Monday. Taylor couldn't quite put her finger on why that disappointed her so much.

At long last, the final bell rang, which meant the staff meeting would begin in ten minutes. Taylor was torn between waiting at the library door to give each person a warm welcome, or hiding behind her desk until Ernie forced her into the spotlight. In the end, she decided on something in between: she stood behind her desk and waited, planning to say "hello" as people came in.

When they did, it was in pairs or groups of three, some laughing as they talked, some deep in conversation. One commonality between them: none of them seemed to notice Taylor. Maybe things would change if she were more outgoing, she thought. Maybe if she'd stood at the door. This was, after all, her space. It seemed as though hours passed. Finally, Jessie and Rose entered, and unlike the rest of the staff, they came right up to Taylor.

"I did it," she said to them. "I asked Ernie if I could start a rodeo club."

"And?" Rose said.

"He said it was fine —"

Both of her friends squealed and held up their hands for high fives. Taylor shushed them while high-fiving them, not wanting to draw attention. The room had quieted, and Taylor hissed, "I just have to find someone to run the club with me."

The gravity of the statement hit Rose and Jessie immediately, and they began searching the crowd for candidates. Taylor could hear their whispered discussion over who would make a good partner ("No, he'd accidentally let the horses out of the corral and they'd wind up on the street." "Yes! Maybe. She stepped up and ran the chess club once."), but she had eyes only for Officer O'Connor.

He was the very last person to walk in, just as Ernie did his rhythmic clap to get everyone's attention. Taylor watched as his eyes scanned the crowd. When they locked on hers, she experienced a palpable jolt. Then he smiled, his eyes crinkling at the corners, and the nerves that had been zipping around her body settled.

That's interesting.

"Good afternoon, everyone," Ernie said.

"Good afternoon, Principal Vasquez," the staff answered.

Taylor managed to shift her focus to her boss.

"From what I've observed, we've had a great start to the school year. We've had a few glitches, but as always, you have handled these things with extraordinary aplomb. I believe this will be the best year yet at Prescott High School."

A few people clapped, and someone let out a whoop.

Principal Vasquez held up a hand. "We have a few matters to attend to."

Instantly, Taylor's nerves sprang back to life. Her eyes sought officer O'Connor, as involuntarily as her heart continued beating. He was looking at her, which made her smile. Again, involuntarily.

Taylor blinked, hoping to give herself a mental reset, so she could tune in to what Ernie was saying. When her fellow staff members reacted, nodding in agreement or acceptance, Taylor realized just how tuned out she was. Or tuned in — to the arguably sexy police officer who stood across the room.

Snap out of it.

The meeting droned on, Taylor's anxiety increasing in intensity as if it were a balloon expanding and expanding and ready to burst.

Finally, after months passed while Ernie talked about fall sports, homecoming themes, and a new math program, he gestured at Taylor, palm up.

"Our final item today is Ms. Cole's announcement ... er, request! Go ahead, Taylor."

"Oh." She hadn't been expecting this. She'd been expecting Ernie to make the announcement, to beg someone to step up and run the club with her.

The room went dark. Her co-workers became an audience, seated quietly in red velvet theater chairs. A giant spotlight anchored somewhere on the ceiling shone down on her, making her sweat. Suddenly, a microphone materialized in front of her. She swallowed, certain the microphone amplified the sound. Resisting the urge to shield her eyes from the imaginary spotlight, Taylor licked her lips. "Oh. Yes. Um. I'm starting a rodeo club?"

Crickets.

She could feel the eyes of her best friends boring into the side of her face and had no choice but to look at them. They gave her double thumbs-up, nodding encouragement.

She nodded back and took a deep breath. "For years, I've wanted to start a rodeo club," she said. "And it's finally happening. I'm so excited to share my love of horses with the kids. The only catch: I need someone — another adult — to run the club with me. School rules."

She gave Ernie a look, and someone chuckled. Then, more crickets.

Her fellow staff members looked everywhere but at Taylor. Her face began to burn. Would no one step up and help her out? After all the meetings she'd hosted in the library, all the fundraisers she'd supported, buying popcorn and baked potatoes, and all the research she'd done for her colleagues when they begged her for help making their lessons more interesting?

She could cry. She *would* cry, if she didn't get out of there.

Looking down at her feet, she tried to think of all the ways she could disappear. A trap door in the floor. A secret passageway through a bookshelf. Combustion.

"I'll do it."

Her heart leapt. Her eyes prickled with tears, brought on by relief. The voice belonged to a man, of that Taylor was sure. But who?

Judd O'Connor. He stood at the back of the group, his hand raised, his eyes on her, and a smile on his lips.

———

*J*UDD

Judd didn't know what he was thinking. Yes, he had horses, had grown up with them, and horsemanship and rodeo were as natural to him as breathing. But he didn't need another obligation. All he wanted was to get back on patrol. Except. There was something about Taylor that made him lose his senses.

And, okay, maybe he *did* know what he was thinking. A moment ago, Taylor stood in front of the entire Prescott High School staff, obviously terrified. Mortified.

The principal was putting her on the spot.

When Ernie asked for a volunteer to step up, a person could hear a pin drop. To Judd, it seemed like everyone in the library held their breath. Judd did, too. If he held it much longer, he'd probably pass out. Meanwhile, Taylor stood there, her eyes fixed on the floor. She looked miserable, and the only thing Judd could think to do was to take that misery away. So, he raised his hand and said, "I'll do it."

Suddenly, the tension eased, the pressure releasing like the air being let out of a balloon. Taylor's shoulders relaxed and the crease between her eyebrows disappeared. And Judd exhaled.

"Great!" Ernie said, then did the same rhythmic clap he'd used at the beginning of the meeting. Everyone else followed suit.

"Meeting dismissed!" Ernie said.

As the staff filtered out over the library, Taylor came over to Judd, a friend on either side of her.

"Thank you so much," she said.

If he wasn't mistaken, it looked like she wanted to hug him. Which he would have liked. Instead, she grabbed both of his hands, the contact sending warmth right up his arms. He had the insane urge to kiss her, but figured that was a huge no-no.

Maybe next time, when her friends weren't around.

What was this woman doing to him? They were co-workers — at a job he planned to leave as soon as possible. Starting a romantic relationship with her would do nothing but put his real job in jeopardy, and he couldn't afford that. But still. Her hands in his made his heart beat just a little faster.

"You're welcome," he said. "I could tell it was important to you."

Taylor nodded. "It is. So important."

"I'm Rose." Taylor's shorter friend, the one with wild, curly blonde hair, held out a hand. Judd had to let go of one of Taylor's hands to shake Rose's, and she gave him a knowing smile.

"Nice to meet you," he said. He turned to the other friend, who stuck out her hand as well. "Jessie. Thank you so much for doing this."

Just as he was wondering why the two of them didn't step up, Jessie said, "We'll help out however we can. Neither one of us can take on weekly meetings, though. Rose is a single mom, and I've become the unofficial caretaker for my neighbor. This has been a dream of Taylor's for a long time. I know she appreciates this."

For her part, Taylor looked adorably shellshocked, and Judd couldn't wait to see just how much she appreciated him stepping up.

Chapter Ten

*T*AYLOR

Wednesday after school, Taylor went to the store and filled her cart with poster board, markers, glitter, and everything and anything she hoped would make her posters so appealing, kids couldn't help but sign up for rodeo club. She may or may not have added googly eyes to the cart — she couldn't remember. Her eyes were bleary with shopping fatigue ... and her thoughts kept returning to Judd.

Not that she wasn't glad he had stepped forward and volunteered to help with the rodeo club. But, *why?*

The answer made her tingle in all the right places: because he was attracted to her. And, she thought, her face growing hot for the millionth time as her imagination took control, she was attracted to him. Holding his hands after the meeting had given her some wild ideas — ideas she couldn't act on with Rose and Jessie flanking her. Ideas she *wouldn't* act on. But still.

"I need wine."

After adding a bottle to her cart, she made her way to the front of the store to check out.

A glance at her watch revealed it was almost five o'clock. "I can't believe you killed two hours in here, woman," she said to herself. "You must've gotten carried away."

"I would say so."

She'd heard the voice only a couple of times, but she recognized it right away. Her body reacted before she even turned around to make eye contact with him. And again with the blushing. She'd always thought it was funny when, in old-fashioned romance novels, ladies swooned when they saw handsome men. But suddenly she understood. She was *this close* to swooning in that moment. Judd was wearing a plain gray v-neck and jeans that hugged his thighs. And she was drooling. She swallowed.

"You must be Judd's new co-worker."

Taylor hadn't even noticed the woman standing next to Judd. If it were possible, her face got even hotter. It was obvious right away that the two of them shared genes. The woman was drop-dead gorgeous, first of all, and she had Judd's calm green eyes and strong eyebrows.

"I'm Katy," she said, extending a hand.

"My sister," Judd rushed to interject.

"Yeah," she said. "Since my doofus of a brother apparently forgot his manners."

"Taylor."

Katy grasped Taylor's hand and gave it a firm shake. "It is so very nice to meet you."

Judd elbowed his sister, who grinned up at him impishly. She obviously adored him. And, even though he scowled at her, he looked amused.

Katy gestured at Taylor's cart. "Is this for the horse club Judd was telling me about?"

Taylor looked at Judd, who gave the tiniest of shrugs.

"It is," Taylor said. "Although, I didn't realize quite how much I had stacked up until I headed for the register."

Katy laughed. "I get it. You should've seen what I put the whole family through when I ran for Student Council President in sixth grade."

"Craft explosion," Judd said, using his arms to mime one. Taylor's eyes immediately went to Judd's biceps. Katy noticed. She gave Taylor a knowing grin, and Taylor blushed. Yet again.

"We could help you," Katy said.

Taylor froze. What should she say? What if Judd didn't *want* to help? Certainly he had plans for a Friday evening. After a couple of seconds, she realized they were waiting for her to answer. She gulped. "I mean, I couldn't ask you to —"

"You didn't," Katy said, matter of fact. "We offered."

"I'm sure you have something else to do."

"We don't," Katy said. "Besides, we want to help you. Don't we, Judd?"

Taylor saw him give Katy a look, but his smile was warm when he looked at her. "We do."

Taylor's heart melted, just a little. Here was a man who was obviously smitten with his sister. Making posters for the rodeo club was probably not how Judd wanted to spend his time, but he was going to do it anyway, because his sister wanted him to. That was pretty adorable. She could hear Rose and Jessie in her mind now: "Aww."

"Well, that *would* be really nice. I could use the help."

"Why don't we go to Rita's?" Katy said.

"That's perfect," Taylor said. She felt guilty stealing their evening, but Katy didn't seem to mind. She grabbed Taylor's cart and started wheeling it toward the checkout.

Judd and Katy were waiting next to the trunk of Taylor's car when she got out of her car.

"Go ahead, load this guy up," Katy said. "He has big muscles from hauling bales of hay his whole life."

"So does she." Judd jerked a thumb at his sister, who held out her hands.

Taylor, tempted to ogle Judd's muscles but preferring to do so in private, followed instructions, hooking several bags of craft supplies onto each of Judd's waiting hands. She then gave the package of poster boards to Katy and grabbed the remaining bags herself. Even with his hands full, Judd managed to open the door for her and Katy, a chivalrous gesture Taylor liked.

Because they had bags hanging from their hands, she had to turn sideways to go through the door. Deciding whether to face him or go in with her back to his front almost paralyzed her. She went for facing him, and didn't miss the chance to inhale his clean, woodsy smell as she did.

Being that close to Judd shorted the wires in Taylor's brain, and she was relieved when Katy took charge, leading them to the corner of the diner and pushing two tables together.

"I think it's late enough Rita won't mind us taking over a few tables," she said. "This will be perfect."

Katy's chattering alleviated some of the awkwardness, but not all of it. Every step of the way, she could feel Judd's presence, a certain energy vibrating between them.

She'd never thought of the diner as a romantic setting, but sudden, vibrant images of Judd laying her out on the tabletops came into her mind. At that moment, the heat that rushed to her face had nothing to do with embarrassment. She had never reacted this way to a man before.

Judd gestured for Taylor to set down her bags first, and the fact that this meant she was leaning over in front of him made her whole body heat up yet again. And so what if she found herself taking a little longer than necessary?

Once they'd unloaded their supplies, Katy continued to direct Judd and Taylor, telling them where to put the markers, glue, and glitter.

"I've heard more than once that I can be a bit overbearing," she said at one point. "But I love getting things done. Do you have any specific ideas? Any must-haves?"

Still in a bit of shock at the way the evening had unfolded, Taylor shook her head. To her surprise, Judd laughed out loud. "This is the effect my sister has on lots of people. There are no words, right?"

Katy shot Judd the death stare then, and Taylor smiled in response. "It's okay," she said. "I appreciate the help. I admit, I was starting to feel a bit like I had bitten off more than I could chew."

"See?" Katy said to Judd. She slid a clean poster board out of the package and set it on the table. "I've been brainstorming ever since we ran into you at the store. How about, 'Come ride with us?' Or, 'Saddle up!'"

"That's cute," Taylor said. "I like it. Saddle up! Come to rodeo club."

Katy handed the pack of markers to Taylor. "Okay, you get started."

She pulled out another piece of poster board and handed it to Judd. "Come up with something clever. I know you can do it. I just remembered an errand I have to run. I'll be back in two hours."

And just like that, she was gone. Taylor and Judd stood at the back of Rita's Diner, poster boards in hand, staring at each other.

———

*J*UDD

Judd couldn't decide whether to kill his sister (figuratively, obviously), or offer to buy her a beer. There he was, quite suddenly alone with Taylor, and he didn't know whether to laugh or cry. Surveying all the supplies laid out on the table, he wondered if Taylor was sane. Maybe she didn't plan to use everything, but it was a lot of work for one person.

"Your sister's nice," Taylor said, interrupting his thoughts.

Judd chuckled. "That's one word for it. I also like to call her conniving, interfering, and bossy."

Taylor set her poster on the table and picked up a marker. "I guess everyone feels that way about their siblings sometimes, but I still think yours is nice."

She bent over to start writing and smiled up at him. He thought then and there that he would never be the same. There was something special about this girl, something about her smile that completely disarmed him.

"Katy is pretty great. To tell you the truth, you looked like you had your hands full when we saw you at the store. I'm sure her plan involved helping you." *And quite possibly, giving us some alone time.*

Taylor had gone back to writing. She finished *Rodeo Club* in big bubble letters and sketched out *First meeting this Friday* below that.

All she said was, "Hmm," and Judd had to stop himself from dissecting all the possible meanings of that single sound. Her long hair kept falling over her shoulder and getting in her way, and he was far too tempted to pull it back and braid it. That vision, though, had his fingertips tingling and another not entirely unpleasant feeling swirling down to his lower half. In desperate need of a distraction, he finally pulled out his own piece of poster board and picked up a marker.

"So why a rodeo club?" Judd asked.

She told him how her love affair with horses started when she and her dad took their evening walks, how those moments with her parents were among her best memories. She told him how hard her dad worked, how tired he was at the end of each day, but how, whenever they stepped out the door after dinner — and especially when they stopped to talk to the horse — he lit up.

"As I got older, I got really into horses. I was a barrel racer in high school, but I learned all the events. Well, most of them. I never tried bull riding or bronc riding. But I did team roping and steer roping. I always dreamed of opening my own equestrian center, where kids could come and learn about horses. I'd have open practice times for adults, too, but kids were — *are* — my primary audience."

She went silent, lips pressed together. Judd guessed she didn't talk much about her dream, which he could tell was close to her heart. "I think it's a great idea," he said. "I grew up with horses — still have about a dozen on the property — and it did me so much good. I think it's great for kids."

"That's good to hear," she said. "My parents think I'm crazy. My dad was self-employed, and he always tells me working for yourself takes over your life. I wish it didn't have to be that way. I mean, I enjoy being a librarian, but when I imagine waking up every day and getting to go to the barn and hang out with kids and horses all day — that seems really great."

They both worked in silence for few minutes.

"I have to admit, I'm surprised at how good your posters are," Taylor told him. "Impressed, too. You're pretty crafty, for a guy."

Judd smiled, but didn't look up at her. He was hard at work putting stripes on the block letters he'd made. "Katy wasn't joking. She tortured us all when she ran for Student Council President in sixth grade. And all throughout high school. She was always spearheading something. Never a horse-related club, but homecoming activities, a math club, fundraisers, you name it. My parents made us help each other with stuff like that. Forced bonding, they called it. I made posters. She accompanied me on shopping trips to help me pick out my outfits. I drove her to track practice on weekends, and she helped me with my math homework. Never tell her this, but I actually enjoy making posters."

"Sounds like you had a lovely childhood."

"We did," he said. "Even if she's a pain in the butt sometimes. Like this evening."

He saw a shadow of doubt pass over Taylor's face. "Not that I'm not happy to be here," he rushed to explain. "But honestly, I feel a little like we intruded on your poster making. What if you had plans?"

"The only I plans I had were the bottle of wine and these poster-making supplies," Taylor said. "And, to be honest, we're probably better off without the wine."

Quite unexpectedly, Judd pictured the two of them sharing a bottle of wine. Not in Rita's diner, but outside, during a picnic, or under the stars. He bit his tongue. He'd never imagined picnicking with a woman before. But there he was, imagining laying Taylor out on a blanket, stretching his body alongside hers, running his fingertips over her skin.

His jeans suddenly felt tighter.

Think about football, he told himself. *Think about driving. Anything other than laying down with this beautiful woman.*

TAYLOR

"I'm pretty confident all your poster making is going to pay off," Taylor told Judd a while later. "If we don't get at least a few kids to sign up, I'll be surprised."

"Do we need a certain number of kids to start the club?"

"I think the minimum is five. But I'm not sure." Taylor felt her anxiety pick up, a buzzing in her veins. What if they didn't have enough people to form a club? It would be devastating for her, and it would mean all of their work that evening was for nothing. Even worse, it would mean another delay in getting her business up and running.

Again, it seemed as though Judd could sense her thoughts, or at least her feelings.

"I'm sure we'll get at least five," he said. "Maybe even twenty."

"I'll be really disappointed if we don't have enough," Taylor said, thinking "disappointed" didn't even come close to summing up her feelings.

"We'll cross that bridge when we get to it." Judd put the cap on his marker and grabbed Taylor's shoulders. His hands felt strong and certain. Looking into her eyes, he said, "Don't worry. Yet. Let's just enjoy the process, okay? Making posters is fun, right? And as an added bonus, you get to hang out with me."

How did he know precisely what to say to make her feel better?

"That's true," Taylor said. "Hanging out with you *has* been fun. More so than I expected." When Judd's eyes widened, Taylor clapped a hand over her mouth. "That didn't come out how I meant it! It's just that, when Katy said the two of you would help me, I was so nervous! I thought you'd hate it. I didn't know you secretly love poster making!"

"Fortunately, in my profession, one develops a thick skin," he said, his eyes twinkling. "And since you're being honest, I will, too. I was pretty nervous, myself. I couldn't decide whether to kill Katy or hug her when she crashed your evening. I wanted to spend time with you, but I wasn't sure you wanted to spend time with me."

Taylor's heart melted then and there. "It's been really nice," she said. "I almost wish I'd bought more supplies, so we could spend even more time together."

At this, he raised an eyebrow, and they both laughed. Taylor knew, in that instant: she was completely smitten.

Chapter Eleven

When Taylor pulled into her non-spot the next morning, she was surprised to see Judd standing there, a paper coffee cup in each hand. Her heart did a little flutter, a lively jump. When she got out of her car, Judd handed her a cup. "Sustenance."

"Thank you," she said. "I could get used to greetings like this."

He stood close enough that she could smell his cologne, and she found herself wanting, desperately, for him to kiss her. But that was off limits. Still, the moment lingered as they stood there, grinning at each other. She snapped out of it first. "I guess we'd better hang those posters before the first bell rings."

"Right." Judd took the posters from Taylor and tucked them under his arm. As they walked through the parking lot side by side, Taylor noticed everything looked bright and beautiful that morning. The sky was a bright, undiluted, blue, and a few puffy white clouds added cheer. Birds sang from the tops of the buildings.

"Beautiful morning," Judd said.

"It is," Taylor agreed, suddenly giddy.

They walked in silence for a few more minutes, and Taylor

couldn't help but notice how natural it all seemed. Almost as if they were already a couple. *This could become a daily routine.* She lost herself in another daydream: one morning, they'd wake up together and share a decadent breakfast of cinnamon muffins. They'd shower together, and their morning lovemaking would make them *almost* late. As they arrived at school, they'd be laughing about the near-miss.

As they passed through the high school's main entrance, Judd interrupted her thoughts. "I've been thinking. We've got to be strategic about this, right?"

Taylor felt her lips twitch and looked up to see his expression was perfectly serious.

She nodded. "Yes. What were you thinking?"

"I was thinking, where does *everyone* go? Is there a spot where, every day, almost every student will see one of our posters?"

Taylor nodded. "I see where you're going with this. Everyone has to go to the cafeteria. So maybe we hang one in there. And almost everyone goes to English or Language Arts. So we should definitely hang one more in that hallway."

"Great. Now, who are our most likely suspects? I mean, rodeo club members? Which students are most likely to come to the club?"

"The farm kids," Taylor said. "And maybe a few nerdy kids who wish they were farm kids. And I don't mean that in a bad way. That was pretty much my profile as a teenager."

He smirked at that. "Good thinking."

The two of them spent the next half-hour hanging the posters, and Taylor couldn't help but be hyperaware of Judd's body, and the way hers reacted to being in such close proximity. Every time he leaned across her to tape the corner of a poster onto the wall, or straighten a poster to make sure it was level, she felt pleasant little chills all over her skin. By the time they were done, she felt warm and tingly everywhere, especially below the belt. The anticipation was just delicious.

"I'll walk you back to the library," Judd said to her when they'd hung all the posters.

The tingling got even stronger.

"Tell me you're not trying to impress Officer Hotpants O'Connor," Rose said to Taylor the next evening.

Taylor had enlisted her friends' help baking treats to entice kids to join the rodeo club. The three of them measured and mixed and tasted while Celeste sat at the counter, working on homework, tracing triangles, rectangles, and circles. "Officer Hotpants," she murmured, making herself giggle. Taylor, arm sore from mixing batter, smiled. "Obviously. And also, I'm hoping to impress the students. If they experience for themselves the pleasure of a perfectly baked chocolate chip cookie, they're going to tell their friends there are cookies at rodeo club. And I can grow my empire." She cackled, doing her best impression of a villain's evil laugh.

"But," Jessie said, "your first priority is impressing Officer Hotpants."

Taylor made a couple more rounds with her mixer. "Who's to say he's even single? A guy as good-looking as that? Doesn't say on the market very long."

"So you've thought about it," Rose said, and Jessie said, "Of course she has."

"He wouldn't have spent all evening with you, making posters, if he had a girlfriend," Rose said, and Jessie added, "Or, he would, and he's a dastardly scoundrel."

Taylor paused, held up a finger, and said, "Unless it was out of pity."

Although, when she thought back to how the evening had ended — the look of longing in his eyes when they said goodnight and parted ways without so much as a handshake — she felt pretty certain he was single.

Celeste put down her pencil. "Well, how are we going to find out? I mean, if he has a girlfriend or not."

Taylor paused her mixing to take in Celeste's serious, thoughtful expression. "Good question."

"I suppose we could stalk him," Rose offered.

"What's that?" Celeste wanted to know.

Taylor shook her head. "I'm pretty sure stalking people is illegal. Stalking a police officer might get you an even worse charge."

"You could just ask him," Celeste said, and Jessie gave her a light tap on the shoulder. "I like your thinking, Celeste. Good strategy. Direct and to the point."

Celeste smiled and went back to tracing shapes.

Taylor considered. She *could* ask him. But wouldn't that be too ... forward? She put down her mixer and cleaned the batter out of the beaters.

"Now what are you doing?" Celeste asked.

"I'm rolling the dough into balls. Want to help?"

Celeste looked to Rose for permission. Rose leaned over to look at her worksheet. "You can help. You only have one more row to do."

"Yes!" Celeste hopped off her stool and went around the counter.

"First, we're going to split this cookie dough in half," Taylor said. "Then we'll split each half into half again."

"And then half again?"

"Right," Taylor said. "Until we have twenty-four pieces. And then we make each one into a ball."

They got to work, Jessie and Rose correcting papers at the counter across from them. Taylor let herself get lost in the rhythm of separating the dough. Her mind wandered once again to Judd. What would it be like to have him here, in her kitchen? The idea produced a strong wave of longing, and she decided she'd better keep herself cemented in the present moment before she got carried away.

"Once we get these in the oven," she said to Celeste, "we can start the snickerdoodle batter. Want to help me with that once you finish your worksheet?"

Celeste, intent on rolling her dough into a perfect ball, tongue sticking out between her lips, nodded. "Course I do."

Taylor set the completed balls on the baking sheet. "Okay. Finish your worksheet."

Celeste hopped off the stool and ran off to the bathroom.

"She's so cute," Taylor said to Rose, who gave her a wry smile.

"Yes. She is cute. Especially when she listens, which she does so much better for you than she does for me."

"That's because you're her mama," Jessie said, wrapping an arm around Rose's shoulders. "And a darn good one. It would be unnatural if your child listened to you one hundred percent of the time."

Rose leaned into Jessie's hug. "Thank you. It means a lot."

The doorbell rang. "That's dinner," Taylor said.

A few minutes later, the four of them sat around Taylor's dining room table, a feast of takeout Chinese food before them.

Jessie picked up the container of broccoli beef and spooned some onto Celeste's plate, and then her own. "So. Taylor."

"Jessie."

"What else are you going to bake to get into the heart of Officer Hotpants?"

She handed Taylor the broccoli beef and picked up the sesame chicken. As Taylor served herself, she said, "Who said I was trying to bake my way into his heart?"

"Okay, into his pants, then," Rose muttered under her breath. Taylor gave her a playful swat on the arm. "Rose Coffey! I have no such intentions!"

Rose blinked at her, all innocence. "Don't you?"

Taylor pressed her lips together as she thought about it. Did she? Judging by the way his pants fit, in them was probably a nice place to be.

———

Judd

Friday afternoon when Judd walked into the library, his jaw dropped. Baked goods of every shape, size, and color covered the surface of an entire table. In Judd's estimation, that was eighteen square feet of cupcakes, cookies, cinnamon rolls, and breads.

Taylor stood behind the table, pretty as a picture, making adjustments to the placements of individual goodies. Judd imagined saying, "I think I'm in love," but an incredulous, "Did you make all these?" came out.

Obviously, dummy, he thought. But Taylor just smiled at him, making him all warm and fuzzy inside.

"I did," she said. "Along with the help of Rose's daughter, Celeste. I thought we might entice more people to join. It might border on bribery, but whatever it takes."

"Can I have a taste?" He didn't even try to hide innuendo on that one, and he could tell from the way she paused, went absolutely still as the tip of her nose turned pink, that she picked up on it. *Good.*

"Not until everyone gets here," she said, her voice prim.

He felt a little chastised, and for some reason, that turned him on. He put his hands behind his back, as much to keep from picking up a cookie as to keep from walking around the table to kiss her.

"You seem nervous," he said, and again, she froze.

"Really? You can tell?"

He shrugged. "Yeah. I can tell."

"You got me. I *am* nervous. This club means a lot to me. It's one way I can do something with my passion. You know? Something official."

"I get that. Even though you won't let me have a taste" (he shot her what he hoped was an over-exaggerated dark look). "I'm confident that if you keep up this baking, word's going to get out. We'll have the biggest and most sugar-high club in Prescott High School history."

She laughed and the sound came out almost as a sob. "I can't keep baking like this. I was up most of the night. I think I got about an hour of sleep."

Judd had the strongest urge to take Taylor in his arms, to comfort her, to reassure her that everything would turn out fine. He also had the strongest urge to run out of the room and gather up as many potential rodeo club members as he could, by force if he had to.

"We should have written, 'Free baked goods' on the posters," he said. "That would bring them in here."

"Maybe we should have," she said. "I thought about it, actually. But ultimately, I want kids in here who love horses."

Judd thought that said something about her character. Taylor Cole was someone who wanted to enjoy the process — not just a quick win. He imagined she had tenacity and perseverance, both of which he would value in an eventual spouse.

Spouse? Was he actually thinking about spouses?

"You okay?" Taylor said.

Judd shook his head. "I'm fine. Just thinking about how we could entice people to come to the club." That sounded believable.

"Well, if your amazing poster-making skills don't do it, I don't know what will. Don't worry, I'm sure they'll come."

Now *she* was the one reassuring him. Judd could kick himself. Fortunately, at that moment, two students walked in.

"Olivia! Scarlett! I'm so happy to see you!"

Judd felt a smidgen of relief. One of them — Olivia — looked at Taylor and then back at Judd, a smirk playing on her lips. He could practically read her thoughts ... and her thoughts were that she could practically read *his* thoughts. He shouldn't be surprised. Women had almost magical powers for picking up on relationship dynamics — hadn't his sister done the same?

Besides, he could see how it might seem rather suspicious that he'd volunteered to help Taylor with the club. He returned Olivia's knowing smile, gave her hand a nice, firm, professional shake, and directed her attention to the trays overflowing with sweet treats.

The girls acted like they hadn't even noticed the stacks upon stacks of goodies, and Judd figured they were more interested in the potential for romance between their two adult rodeo club leaders.

Well, he thought as he watched them take éclairs from the trays, so was he. Was there anything wrong with that? Another minute passed and a young man came in. Judd thought he recognized him as one of the juniors who hung out in the quad.

"Henry!" Taylor called, obviously delighted he was there. The kid made a beeline for the table and helped himself to a brownie and a couple of cookies. The three students seemed to know each other. They started talking about an assignment they had in biology, and

Judd found himself watching the door, hoping at least two more students would show up.

Just as he was wondering if there was a deadline for gathering five club members, Taylor handed him a brownie. "Relax, O'Connor. They'll either come or they won't. We might as well enjoy the fruits of my labor while we wait."

The brownie felt dense in his palm, and he held it up to his nose for a sniff before tasting it. It smelled like Heaven, and tasted even better. His gaze held Taylor's while he reveled in the pleasure.

I am in trouble.

———

T AYLOR

Taylor was devastated. She knew she should be grateful that three students showed up for the club's first meeting, but three wasn't enough. Even though she'd told Olivia, Scarlett, and Henry they would wait a few minutes before starting, she already knew: no one else was coming. So at ten minutes after three, a heavy feeling in the pit of her stomach, she put on her best smile (albeit a forced one) and said, "Welcome to the first official meeting of the Prescott High School rodeo club!"

Olivia and Scarlett clapped, which lifted Taylor's spirits a little. "As you can see, I have made way too many baked goods."

"Is there such a thing?" Judd said. "That means more for the five of us, right?"

Henry pumped his fist and grabbed another piece of cake.

"True," Taylor said, her spirits lifting just a little more. "Be prepared to take some of this home."

As Judd and the kids helped themselves, Taylor said, "The first thing you should know is that we have to have five people in order to make this club official. We have until the first competition, which is three weeks from now, to get our numbers up."

"There are competitions?" Judd said.

Taylor laughed. "Yes, Officer O'Connor. There are competitions. With judges. And prizes."

The way she said his name, her tone just this side of bossy, invoked an image of her straddling him. His pants suddenly felt a little tighter.

"Ooh, prizes," Scarlett said.

Taylor held up a hand. "Yep. But don't get ahead of yourself. We can't go to competitions or win prizes if we don't have enough club members. I need you guys to recruit your friends."

"These *are* my friends," Olivia said, gesturing to the other two kids.

The kids left a few minutes later, hands full with boxes of baked goods they planned to bring home to their families.

"They seem like nice kids," Judd said to Taylor.

She looked at the door, wistful. "They're great kids. But we've got to get some more, or we won't have a club at all."

"I'm sure those three have more friends, right? If each of them invites one friend, we have six."

Taylor shook her head and began packing the last of her goodies into the brown boxes she'd brought. "I'm afraid these three are kind of loners. They're my library nerds — and before you worry that I'm being offensive, they call themselves that. They make up their own social circle. I highly doubt each one of them has another friend, certainly not a friend close enough to convince to join our club."

Judd nodded. "I like how you called it 'our' club."

Taylor smiled. "Well, it is."

"Okay," he said. "I'm sure we can think of other recruitment ideas."

Bolstered by his confidence, Taylor stacked the boxes at one end of the table and brushed the last of the stray sugar and flour into a tidy pile with her hands. Judd came over to help.

"You know, you could have made half of these, and been up only *half* the night," he said.

I'd like you to keep me up half the night. A parade of sexy images marched through Taylor's mind: her in an apron (and nothing else), waiting for him to come into the library; Taylor pushing all the baked goods off the table so they could get frisky right then and there; Judd naked while she fed him chocolate chip cookies, kissing leftover chocolate off the side of his mouth.

He interrupted her fantasizing. "What would you say to a brainstorming session?"

Again, hopelessness hit her. "You think there's anything we can do to salvage this?"

"Definitely." He sounded so certain, which strengthened her resolve.

Brushing her hands together over the trash can, she gave him a single nod. "Yes. Let's have a brainstorming session."

Chapter Twelve

JUDD

Taylor looked so forlorn during the meeting, Judd felt his own heart ache. He'd do everything in his power, he decided as they parted ways, to get this club going.

An interaction caught Judd's eye as he walked through the breezeway between the gym and the football field. The end-of-day bell had rung an hour before, and any students who didn't play sports should have cleared out by then. Two students, both boys, leaned against the brick wall of the gym. They looked casual enough, until they spotted Judd. If his life were an old Western movie, the sun would have glinted off his badge and startled them. The two boys jumped, obviously guilty. Judd had spent his time observing criminal behavior for long enough to recognize someone up to no good. As he continued walking toward them, they both made to leave, splitting in opposite directions.

"Hold on a minute, guys," Judd said. Then, recognition dawned. "Zion, my man!"

Zion — the superstar soccer player missing from the match the week before — had the decency to look chagrined.

"Hey, boss," he said, his eye contact fleeting like the flicker of a lightbulb going out.

"It's been a while," Judd said. "I haven't seen you over at the field. I missed having my main winger there the other day."

The kid shrugged and looked away, the way people do when they don't really want to have the conversation they're being forced to have. "I've got stuff going on."

"Everything okay? I was worried."

"You don't need to worry about me, man," Zion said, making a dismissive gesture, offering a too-bright smile. "I'm all right."

Zion's friend had frozen, watching the exchange as if it were a bomb about to go off.

"Who's your friend, here?"

"He ain't my friend."

"That true?" Judd asked the other boy, who shrank into himself. Judd had seen that before, too, and wanted to tell the kid that no matter how hard he tried, he couldn't become invisible.

The kid shrugged. "I mean, we're, like, acquaintances, I'd say."

"What's your name?"

"They call him Raven," Zion interjected. Although the name was laughable, and something he and his squad would make fun of after finishing up a conversation with potential criminals, Judd didn't laugh. No, his curiosity was piqued. Why was Zion trying to protect this other kid?

"What's your real name, son?"

"You're not my dad."

Judd rolled his eyes, ground his molars together.

"Do you want to tell me your name? Or do I need to arrest you?"

Raven lifted his chin in defiance. "You can't arrest me. You ain't nothing but a school cop." How that kid knew exactly which buttons to push, Judd didn't know. But he wasn't going to let some delinquent teenager, especially one who went by the name Raven, cause him to lose his temper.

"I'm sorry to tell you that you have your facts messed up. I most certainly *can* arrest you. So you can tell me your name, so we can both get out of here, or I can arrest you. I'll find out your name either way."

The kid's shoulders slumped, just a little. "Leviticus. Snipe."

Well. If Judd thought he was exercising his ability to keep from laughing at the name Raven, it was even harder to do so at Leviticus. No wonder the kid went by Raven. It was a huge improvement. Judd glanced at Zion and thought he detected a flicker of amusement in his expression. He quickly looked away. "All right, Leviticus. Why don't you get on home? Just don't let me catch the two of you doing whatever this is again."

Leviticus took off, head down, not wasting a moment. Zion looked as if he would do the same, but Judd held up a hand and he stopped.

"Look. I know a drug deal when I see one."

Zion inhaled, probably about to deny it, but Judd stopped him with a small shake of his head. "I could haul you both in, gather evidence, come up with charges. But you're a good kid. You said you have stuff going on. Anything I can help you with?"

For a beat, maybe half a second, Zion looked like he might cry. But then he shuttered his expression and said, "No, man. I'm good."

A lightbulb illuminated, then. "Listen, man. I know we don't know each other very well. But I've seen you on the soccer field and I know you're coordinated as hell, and even smarter. I need a favor."

Surprise, then doubt registered on Zion's face. "From me?"

It was a risk, but one Judd thought just might pay off. "There's this club."

Zion took a few steps back, hands up in a dramatic show of objection. "Oh, no. Clubs are not my thing."

"Will you just hear me out? It means a lot to me."

Dropping his hands, Zion shook his head. "Those puppy dog eyes, man. What is it?"

"A rodeo club."

The standoffishness disappeared and Zion laughed out loud, covering his mouth with one hand. "A horse club? You're serious?"

Maybe it hadn't been a good idea. Judd thought about backing down, telling Zion to forget it. But then he pictured Taylor's face, and how disappointed she'd looked when only a handful of kids showed up at the meeting. Maybe he needed to try a different approach. Guy to guy. "It's not for me. It's for a friend. Taylor Cole? The librarian?"

The kid's eyes lit up. He *was* smart. "Oh, I see what's happening here. There's a *lady* involved."

He was positively enjoying himself. Judd smiled. "It's not like that."

"You lie. I've seen the lady in question."

Judd ignored that. "The thing is, we need a minimum of five kids for the competitions."

"Back it up. Competitions? *We?* Don't tell me *you're* in charge of the horse club with the lady librarian."

Judd shrugged. "They needed another staff member, and nobody else came forward."

"Ah, I see. So you're hoping to be the hero, here. Come into the horse club meeting with another kid, and win the heart of Taylor Cole, the *fire* librarian."

"Wait, wait, wait," Judd said. "You're crossing the line. You can't call her *fire*, you're a student."

"But you were thinking it."

Judd shook his head, decided on a change of subject. "Look. If you can come to the next meeting, along with ... Raven, I'll keep quiet about the interaction I saw today. But that's a one-time pass. I can't look the other way again. You've got to keep things on the up and up. You're a smart kid, athletic. You have potential. I won't stand by and watch you screw up."

For the second time, Zion looked emotional.

"Fine, I'll come to the horse club. No guarantees I can get Raven. He's a real tough guy, you know?"

Judd felt his lips twitching. He hadn't looked like such a tough guy when he scuttled away a few minutes before. Or when he had admitted his real name. "Right. But you'll try. Because he won't feel like a tough guy when I'm hauling his butt into juvie."

Zion nodded. "I'll try."

———

Judd got home before Katy did, and he went ahead and started the chores. He felt almost like he was dancing as he moved between the stalls, carrying hay and alfalfa. He greeted the horses by name, and took the time to give each one a neck rub or a friendly pat.

"I take it the first rodeo club meeting went well."

Judd jumped at the sound of his sister's voice. He chastised himself. He was typically a lot more aware of his surroundings, and he hadn't heard her car pull up.

Turning to face her, he shrugged. "It was okay. I mean, the baked goods she made to make the first meeting special? *Great*. I brought some home for you. But the turnout? Not so great. Only three kids showed up. We need five for the club to be official."

Falling into step beside him, Katy started loading hay into the wheelbarrow. "That's a bummer. What can we do to get more kids in there?"

Katy might be a pain in the ass sometimes, but he loved her. He didn't want to get too mushy, though, so he said, "That's exactly what Taylor and I are going to discuss at our brainstorming session. Over dinner."

Katy whistled, nice and long ... long enough that his cheeks and ears started to burn. He held up a hand. "Don't go getting all excited. It's just dinner. To brainstorm."

Katy looked at him over her shoulder. "That's what you're *saying*. But we both know you were just looking for an excuse to ask her out. No wonder you sounded so happy when I got here."

Judd heaved a flake of alfalfa over a stall door. "You got me. Where should I take her?"

The truth was, even though Katy liked to tease him, she gave solid dating advice.

"You want somewhere nice, but not too fancy. Comfortable, but classy."

Considering his options as he started checking the horses' water dispensers, Judd suddenly began to imagine Taylor in the space with them. Even though he'd only seen her in librarian clothes, he thought she'd be pretty easy on the eyes in jeans and boots.

"I could bring her here," he said to Katy, who said, "Judd O'Connor. I've never heard you even consider bringing a girl home on the first date."

Again with the blushing. "You're right. Maybe on the next date."

"Ooh. Already planning a second date?"

Chapter Thirteen

*T*AYLOR

J udd knocked on Taylor's door two minutes before seven o'clock. Grabbing her purse, she rushed to answer it, then took a settling breath before she opened it. The sight of Judd in a button-up shirt and dark jeans, set her heart all aflutter. He was, without a doubt, the handsomest guy who'd ever stood on Taylor's front step. Her mouth went dry. She swallowed.

"Right on time," she said to him.

He blinked, and she realized that he looked just as stunned as she felt.

He put a hand on her shoulder and gave it a gentle squeeze. "You look really nice."

The way he said it, holding eye contact, opened up a connection between them.

"Thank you. You look really nice, too."

They stood there, staring at each other, Judd's hand on her shoulder, sending a pleasant current through her body. Finally, he said, "Shall we?"

"Yes!" Taylor said. "Let's."

After Taylor locked her door, Judd offered her his arm, and she slipped her hand into the crook of his elbow. Again, her body felt energized at the contact. If they didn't stop touching each other, she didn't know if she could make it through dinner without combusting. He opened the passenger door for her and she climbed up into his truck.

When he got in, she said, "This is a big truck," and immediately felt silly. Wasn't there some joke about men with big trucks?

Judd laughed. "It gets the job done. I use it to haul hay and pull the horse trailer, so it definitely serves a purpose. And, to be honest, I think it looks pretty cool."

"It does look cool," Taylor agreed. "And that's so awesome that you have horses. I'm jealous."

"It *is* awesome. They're so much fun. Each one has its own personality. Maybe you can come out to the ranch one day and spend time with them."

Was he already asking her for a second date? "That would be nice," she said. She saw Judd let out a breath. Trying not to smile, she said, "So where are we going for dinner?"

"I thought we could go to Curly's. The menu has a little bit of everything, and it's a fun atmosphere."

———

*J*UDD

Judd couldn't get enough. He had the startling thought that there would never be enough dinner dates to satisfy the need building inside him. "Pretty great place, right?"

"I love it," she said, her focus on the ceiling, where at least a hundred different colored glass globes hung.

Judd found himself smiling, as she faced him again. When their eyes met, he could almost feel the sensation of his heart unlocking. That scared him so much he rushed to pick up his menu.

After they ordered, he couldn't believe how easily the conversation flowed. They talked about her work, his work, their families, their childhoods.

"So, you grew up with horses?" Although only a couple of days had passed since they worked on posters at the library, Judd was impressed that Taylor remembered the piece of trivia Katy had mentioned.

"Yeah," he said. "My family owns property, and we've always kept several horses. Katy and I were both on horseback before we could even walk."

"I would've loved that," Taylor said, and hearing the wistfulness in her voice, Judd was tempted to reach across the table and take her hand.

"Owning horses was a huge childhood fantasy of mine," she told him. "I read all the horse books, checked out all the novels and nonfiction books I could get my hands on. Like I said, we leased a horse and kept her at a barn, but I would have loved to have her in my own backyard."

Before he realized the words were out of his mouth, Judd was inviting Taylor to the house for a ride. Her eyes lit up. He felt like he'd just been awarded lifetime tickets to Disneyland.

"Really? You'd let me come over and ride your horses?" Judd didn't know if it was the wine they shared going to his head, or his constant state of arousal since he'd been sitting across from her, letting his eyes roam over every square inch of her, from her fingertips to her jawline to her very kissable neck. But the innuendo had him looking down at his plate, clenching his teeth to keep from laughing, or worse, blurting out that she could come over to ride any time.

He choked out, "I would really like that."

When he made eye contact again, the look of pure joy on her face actually warmed his heart. "Then it's a date."

"Speaking of dates," Taylor said, "we haven't talked all about the club. And we have a deadline coming up."

That wasn't like him. Typically, Judd was the most task-oriented guy around. If he was supposed to meet someone to talk about something specific, then that topic was first order of business. He'd probably even show up with an outline.

"You're right. The conversation was just so good, I forgot what we were here for."

"Honestly? I did, too."

They spent a few minutes discussing options, and decided that they'd pass out flyers the following Monday.

"Meanwhile," he said, "should we exchange numbers? That way we can, you know, text each other if we come up with any good ideas. For rodeo club."

She was already reaching for her phone. Her eyes met his, twinkling with mischief. "For rodeo club."

They must have sat there grinning at each other for a full minute before she finally said, "Okay. Ready."

She sent him a text that contained only a horse emoji, and then offered to split the check with him. He insisted on treating — he was old-fashioned that way, and plus, Katy might have his head if she found out he didn't pay for dinner.

When he parked in front of her house a while later, he was surprised to feel a sudden sense of sadness.

"I don't want the evening to end," Taylor said, her words mirroring his thoughts.

He reached across the console and took her hand, interlacing his fingers with hers, noticing how well their hands fit together. "Me, neither."

Even though Judd could stay in close proximity with Taylor indefinitely, something else tugged at his attention: he wanted to see the daily log for the police department. Still, as they walked up the path to her door, he found himself pulling her into his arms. She smelled so good, and the desire was strong to press his lips against hers and pull her hips against his. The way she melted into him, it seemed like she wouldn't mind. He leaned back just enough to look into her eyes, and she tilted her head in response, granting permission.

He reacted, pressing his mouth to hers. Gently, at first, and with more urgency when the fireworks started. Taylor's body relaxed, as if this were the kiss she'd been waiting for. She ran her hands up his arms and into his hair, and he suddenly ached for *more* of her.

If he didn't walk away now, there was no guarantee he wouldn't tear off her clothes and have his way with her right there on the doorstep.

With reluctance in every fiber of his being, he ended the kiss, and noticed with satisfaction — and another wave of desire — that the contact had messed up Taylor's hair and made her lips slightly more plump. He brought his forehead to hers and tried to slow down his galloping heartbeat, while noticing she seemed just as breathless as he was.

"I'd better go," he said.

She nodded in agreement, and then took his face in her hands and gave him one more kiss that left him reeling as she said good-night and let herself into the house.

———

*T*AYLOR

Taylor smiled when her phone chimed a couple of hours after Judd left. More accurately, she thought, after they shared a mind-blowing kiss and *then* he left.

When are you free to come ride horses?

Right that minute probably wouldn't work, although her body had been pulsing with need since he'd kissed her that way. Instead, she typed, *This weekend?* and then immediately wondered if that answer would make her come across as too needy. Was there some kind of waiting period before a second date? Maybe she should have asked about the following weekend.

But his response came through right away: *Sure. I'm free. One of the perks of working Monday through Friday.*

Before she could respond, another message came through: *Tomorrow?*

She shrugged, feeling herself smiling and her heart thudding in her rib cage. *Sure.*

How about six?

Waiting until six p.m. felt like waiting an eternity. But she could keep herself busy, she supposed. *Sounds good. What do I wear?*

To her surprise, he responded with a smiling devil emoji and then, *Glad you asked.*

She typed, *I didn't mean it that way,* and then quickly erased it. Maybe she hadn't, but she liked the thought of him thinking she had.

She could be flirtatious, too. *You're the expert,* she typed instead. *I'll wear whatever you tell me to.* That time, he didn't respond right away. She would have loved to see him in that moment, to get a sense or whether the conversation was affecting him the same way it was her. After a few more seconds, his message showed up on her screen. *I like where this is going. For horseback riding, I'd suggest jeans and sturdy shoes. Boots, if you have them. What you wear underneath is up to you.*

"Underneath?" Taylor groaned, even as slow-burning fire made its way from her stomach to her lady parts. Underneath, indeed. She had never even considered what to wear underneath her clothes on the second date. And there she was, thinking about getting completely naked on her second date. Heck, she would get completely naked right that second if Judd showed up at her door.

Chapter Fourteen

TAYLOR

When Taylor pulled up at Judd's property Sunday evening, he was leaning against the fence, waiting for her. Her breath caught. He looked like he belonged in one of those Western calendars where each month featured a shirtless cowboy. Quite suddenly, she was picturing Judd shirtless, imagining sculpted abs and arms, rippling muscles in his back. And then she was picturing herself running her hands all over him, feeling his warm skin under her palms. And then she felt all hot and bothered, and reluctant to get out of the car in case he could tell.

She took her time putting her car in park and gathering her things.

It was absolutely unfair for a man to be as sexy as that, she thought, finally opening her door and putting one foot on the ground. It was enough to make a woman lose her self-control. Taylor gulped, stood, and closed the car door. Judd finally moved from his post. He walked toward her, and the way he smiled and said, "Hey, beautiful," did something to quiet the nervous energy.

His jeans hugged his body in all the right places, and Taylor's gaze made an involuntary trip down to his button fly (and what was very obviously behind it) and back up to his face. Naturally, he noticed. The man was a trained observer, after all. The old Taylor would attempt to hide the fact that she was ogling this sexier-than-sexy cowboy, but the new, confident, Taylor said, "I like you in this uniform almost as much as I like you in the other one."

Surprise registered on his expression, and then he laughed, the kind of head-thrown-back belly laugh that was totally contagious. She was laughing, too, when he finally got control of himself.

"Thank you very much," he said. "That's one of the best compliments I've ever received."

———

Judd

Judd couldn't remember a time he'd ever been so aroused by a simple greeting. But watching Taylor get out of her car, rake her eyes over his body, the hunger plain as day on her face, he considered canceling the horseback riding plans, throwing her over his shoulder, and taking her to his bed.

Fortunately, reason prevailed. It was only their second date. He wasn't the kind of guy who took a woman to bed on the second date. *But maybe I should be.*

"Let me show you the barn," he said, his voice sounding strangled to his own ears.

She fell into step beside him. "This place is gorgeous. You said your family had property, but you didn't say it was a pristine ranch, straight out of the movies."

"Well, when you put it that way, I guess it is. I grew up here, so I don't really think of it as anything other than home."

"You're very lucky."

"That's true," he said.

And, taking in the place with Taylor's perspective in mind, he thought, he *was* lucky. To enter the property, Taylor drove up a tree-lined drive, which seemed downright luxurious in the desert. She emerged from under its shady canopy to a view of the barn, freshly painted, dark red against the backdrop of green pasture dotted with granite boulders and more lush trees. The main house, a classic farmhouse, sat off to one side, pretty as a picture. And, to the other side, one smaller house for each O'Connor sibling sat within walking distance from the barn. He didn't realize he was sighing until Taylor said, "I bet this is the only place you can really relax, right?"

How any woman could gain such an understanding of him, so quickly, took his breath away. "It is."

They'd reached the barn, and he pulled open the sliding door. "Welcome."

———

*T*AYLOR

An immediate sense of calm settled over Taylor when they walked into the barn. Horses on either side of a wide walkway poked their heads out of their stalls, ears pricked and eyes bright with curiosity. One of them, reddish with a white patch on its forehead, looked from Judd to Taylor and back to Judd again, then made a *pffft* sound.

Taylor couldn't help but laugh. "I'm not sure what that means, but I hope it's not a complaint."

"He's probably just in shock. I never bring women in here."

Taylor hoped Judd couldn't see her smile in the shade of the barn. She changed the subject. "It's so cute, how they're all coming out to greet you."

"They're probably just expecting food."

"Oh, I think it's more than that," Taylor said. "They seem happy to see you."

Judd walked up to the horse that made the funny noise. It leaned into his touch when he rubbed its neck. "I'm always happy to see them, too. This is Knickerbocker. He's Katy's horse."

"It's been years since I've been this close to horses. He's giant."

"He is." Judd moved on to the next stall, where another huge horse waited. It bobbed its head in greeting. "Hey, guy. This is Tiny."

"He is *not* tiny."

"He's not. At all. This is my horse. And," he said, moving to the next stall, "this is my mom's horse, Rosie."

"She's a much more reasonable size. Can I pet her?"

"Yes!"

He gestured for Taylor to walk in front of him. He didn't leave much space for her, and when she approached the half-door where Rosie stood, Judd put a hand on her waist and used his free hand to guide hers up toward Rosie's smooth cheek.

Instead of paying attention to the sensation of the horse's hair against her palm, Taylor couldn't help but focus on the feel of Judd's calloused hand on hers, his body warm and strong against her back. Her breath caught.

"She's pretty sweet, right?" he said, and she nodded, thinking *he* was pretty sweet.

"And it just feels so peaceful in here."

"It's definitely my happy place. Nothing else like it."

Judd walked to the wall at the far end of the barn, where Taylor saw saddles and tack hanging.

"I'll saddle up Tiny and Rosie, and then we can head out."

"Can I help?" she asked.

He smiled at her, and she practically melted right there on the spot. "You could, but I wanted this to be relaxing for you. Why don't you watch this time, and you can help next time?"

If she hadn't felt like melting a second before, she really felt like it then. *Next time.* She followed him into Tiny's stall.

"Hey, bud," he said. He set the saddle on the floor and ran a hand down the horse's neck. "How are you doing today? Good? It's a really nice day. Want to go for a ride?" Again, the horse seemed to lean into Judd's touch, and Taylor found herself thinking she would do the same.

"I always like to have a little chat with them before I saddle up," he told Taylor as he lifted up the saddle. "Seems more polite than just tossing this old thing on, you know?"

"That's very thoughtful."

He laughed. "It's the same way with people. At least, I think so. I find it's more pleasant for everyone if you pave the way with a little friendliness."

He fastened the saddle strap and straightened up. Then he saw the look on her face. "What?" he said.

"I don't think you paved the way with much friendliness when you pulled me over that day."

He gave her a stern look, but she could see the humor in his almost-smile. "That was different. You were driving on the wrong side of the road and almost killed me. Just kidding. You were going really slow. The truth is, I was coming off a rough shift."

"I'm really sorry."

He grabbed her hand as if he were in a hurry to make contact. "I didn't mean for you to apologize. I reacted more strongly than I should have. It's been a rough couple of months. But that's a whole different story. Let me grab another saddle."

He dropped her hand, effectively ending the conversation, and leaving Taylor curious. What had made the last few weeks rough? And did it have anything to do with the reason he was working at the high school? She spent the next few minutes watching him put the saddle on Rosie, and then the bridles on both horses. She found herself noticing — and enjoying — the way his body moved, strong, graceful, and certain. She wondered if he moved that way in bed, and felt her body heat up at the thought. This was only their second date. She shouldn't think about Judd in bed. At least, not yet. But, she thought as he finished up and led the horses toward her, smiling, it was hard not to.

———

*J*UDD

Judd felt almost giddy at the thought of going for a ride with Taylor. That was unusual. Typically, his enthusiasm level fell somewhere between mild and just a touch more than mild when it came to spending time with any woman. *That's because usually, work is the most interesting thing in your life, and everything, even women, pales in comparison.*

Judd wondered whether his feelings for Taylor would change when he went back to his regular job. But then he offered her a boost into the saddle, giving himself a close-up view of her butt in her jeans, and decided they wouldn't. The woman had an effect on him. One that made him question, for the first time ever, whether it might be possible to give work the backseat.

He let his hand rest on Taylor's thigh while she picked up the reins. "Do you feel ready?"

"I'm ready."

She looked so comfortable on the back of the horse. Like she belonged there. Not just on the horse, but at his house. In his life. In that moment, the air between them felt charged. Judd found that he liked it. He gave her a smile he hoped didn't convey all the strange feelings he was having. Then he mounted his horse and they walked out of the barn side-by-side.

"So I poured out my heart to you the other night while we were making posters," Taylor said after they had ridden for a few minutes. "Tell me about you. How did you come to be the school resource officer? Isn't that a special assignment?"

Judd scoffed before he could stop himself. "I guess you could call it that."

She looked over at him without speaking, giving him time and space to answer. He liked that. He probably shouldn't admit how he felt about being a school resource officer, but something about Taylor inspired honesty. He could feel her eyes on him, and the way she studied him. A gentle chill ran over his skin, as if she were actually running her hands up his arms and down his back.

"I can't believe I'm about to admit this to one of my new coworkers," he said, "but the high school is the last place I would choose to be."

He sensed no judgment when she asked, "How come?"

"It's hard to explain without sounding like a jerk. I know some officers who love the role. They enjoy being around kids, developing relationships. And that's great. But what I want is different. I belong out on the road, on patrol. Responding to calls, saving lives, catching bad guys."

Taylor smiled at him. "So you're an adrenaline junkie."

Returning her smile, he said, "Well, yes. That, too. But there's more to it."

As the horses walked along the shady creek bed, Judd shared the story of the childhood car accident that set him on his path. He started at the beginning, with the traditional pancake birthday breakfast, and finished in the present day, with the way that memory seemed to crop up more and more frequently, igniting his temper every time.

"So, effectively, after one too many outbursts, I got myself demoted." Her lips were twitching in that adorable way they did, and she said, "Well, it's no wonder you looked like you wanted to hurt me that night you pulled me over."

Judd felt the tension leave his shoulders. If a woman could find humor in that moment, she was a keeper. "Partially. I had just come off a really bad accident where a guy was texting and almost killed someone. So yeah, I was pretty hot under the collar when you tried to head-on me."

She faux-glared at him, and he smiled. "Well. I'm sure you believe a librarian is a pretty glamorous job," Taylor said. "But like I said the other day, it's not what I want to be doing, either. I mean, I love the kids. But I feel like I'm meant for something more, too. So for now, I remind myself that at least I have the chance to interact with the students. Maybe influence one or two. Save the day with a certain book recommendation when they're researching for projects."

She shrugged, looking at once forlorn and resigned. If they weren't on horseback, he would give her a hug. Instead, he reached over and squeezed her elbow. "I get it. And I have a feeling you're going to open that barn one day."

"Thanks," she said. "And I have a feeling you'll get back on the road one day."

He almost said, "That day can't come soon enough," but instead offered a quiet, "I hope so."

"And thanks again for your help with the rodeo club," Taylor said. "I know it might sound silly, but I feel like this is a step in making my business a reality."

It didn't seem as though Taylor thought any less of him after his confession. Judd didn't know why that meant so much to him, but it did. He felt a little lighter having shared with her his real feelings.

"So," she said, "will you be the school resource officer for the whole school year?"

"My sergeant didn't give me an end date. Before meeting you, I would have said I hope to get out of there as soon as possible, but I have to tell you, my feelings have changed."

"At least a little?" Taylor asked. She winked at him, and as he laughed, he realized that for the first time in as long as he could remember, he felt content.

———

TAYLOR

Taylor could get used to this. The rhythm of Rosie's gait rocked her into a meditative state as they followed the creek, under the shade of the trees. Next to an incredibly handsome man, who, like her, had bigger dreams, wanted more for his life.

"Can I show you something?" Judd asked.

"Yes, please. This place is so beautiful."

"We'll have to dismount."

When Judd led Tiny off the trail, Rosie followed. Taylor watched Judd dismount in an easy, graceful motion. He tied Tiny's reins onto a fence post, and then came over and stood next to her. "Want help?"

She did want help, but only because she could almost feel his hands on her waist, easing her down. Saying so felt shamelessly forward, so she declined. "I think I've got it."

"All right," he said. He took a step back, and she pressed her left foot down into the stirrup, swinging her right leg up and over the horse's back. She started to let herself down, expecting to feel her foot make contact with the ground. But it didn't. Before she knew it, she was descending a lot faster than she expected, her foot still stuck in the stirrup. Just as she braced for impact, she felt Judd's hands on either side of her rib cage, hoisting her back up, pulling her away from the horse to disengage her foot from the stirrup. She should be thinking about how grateful she was that he had saved her from that fall, but her mind wouldn't focus on anything other than the feel of his hands on her body.

Taylor felt breathless — and not because she had almost fallen on her butt in front of this incredibly handsome man. Catching her was probably a reflex for him, but she found it unbearably romantic. Not to mention the way her body seemed to fit against his. His arms around her waist, his face next to hers, felt like the most natural things in the world. Even after she regained her balance, she leaned against him, okay with the fact that he might think she was doing it to recover. She could feel his biceps, his thighs, and his day-old whiskers on her cheek. No man anywhere should have the right to smell that good. The pine scent of his soap mixed with just the faintest bit of sweat.

That's pheromones, said a vixen-like voice in the back of her mind. *It science. It's not your fault you find him irresistible.*

"You okay?" he asked. His voice sounded huskier than it had before. So he was affected by the contact as well.

As he should be. The smug little voice piped up, sending a thrill of confidence through Taylor.

"I'm fine. Thank you so much for catching me. Losing my balance was embarrassing enough. But falling right on my butt would have been even more so."

A low, rumbly chuckle escaped, and Taylor felt the vibration in his chest, against her back, and the warmth of his breath next to her ear.

The old, average Taylor would freeze at a moment like that. Fight or flight would kick in, and she would extricate herself from the situation as quickly as possible. Flight 101. But the new, confident Taylor wanted to sink into his embrace, and didn't bother disentangling herself just yet.

"You smell good," Judd said, and at that, Taylor was grateful he was propping her up. Otherwise, she would have swooned. For sure.

"So do you," she said.

"As much as I would love to stand here like this all afternoon, there *is* something I'd like to show you. I mean, if you'd like to see it."

Taylor gave her sigh a dramatic flair. "If there's no way you can show it to me while we are standing here, like this, then I guess we'd better separate."

There was that chuckle again, and that feeling like she might swoon. Judd released her, and she knew she'd spend the rest of the afternoon concocting scenarios in which she could get him to put his arms around her again. She turned around to face him, and he was smiling at her with what looked like genuine affection. *I'm falling for this guy.*

"Come on." He took her hand and led her farther off the trail, through a copse of thick trees.

"This is where Katy and I used to come when we were kids. As soon as we finished our morning chores, our parents would kick us out of the house 'til lunchtime. We always came here first."

Taylor was unreasonably touched by the fact that Judd wanted to show her his childhood hangout. While simultaneously reminding herself he probably took women there all the time and doing silent, feminine squeals in her mind, she let him lead her into the trees. A sudden, serious thought interrupted her internal dialogue to point out that he could very well be leading her to a remote location that would soon be the scene of her death. They came to a giant boulder. It rose like a wall in front of them. Was this a dead end? Maybe it really was the spot where he planned to murder her and bury her body.

"There's no way out," she said.

Judd laughed. "There is. It's just up."

He took a step to the left and pushed back a couple of low-hanging branches to reveal a smaller rock, one they could easily climb onto.

"You first." He offered a hand to help her up. She took it, marveled at the way little shivers traveled all over her skin, and stepped up. She would have kept hold of his hand, but she realized right away this little trip was more of a climb and would require her to go on all fours. He was suddenly right behind her, so close, their bodies were pressed together. What was this man doing to her? Hands on her waist, he chuckled again, and the low rumbling sent a bolt of heat straight to her lady parts.

"Wasn't quite this cozy when we were little. Go on and step up to the next rock." She did, way too conscious of the fact that this brought her waist level with his eyes. She scrambled up to the next one. She could hear more rumbly laughter behind her, and found herself as amused as she was aroused.

"Now which way?"

"Start heading to your right."

Taylor did, scrambling higher, the feel of the granite cool and rough on her palms.

"How will I know when I get there?"

His voice came back, much closer behind her then she realized. "You'll know."

A few minutes later, she did. She'd reached the end of a peninsula, which seemed to jut into the sky. The view was unbelievable. Before she had a chance to take it all in, Judd was there, beside her. He linked his fingers with hers but didn't say anything right away. Taylor's heart beat wildly against her rib cage. She couldn't tell whether it was from exertion, or from pure joy at the way he had taken her hand.

Then there was the view.

The earth spread out beneath them, a wide valley punctuated with smaller, sparkling granite rocks, prickly pear cactus with their bright pink flowers, and a rainbow of wildflowers Taylor couldn't name. And the sky. It blazed a bright blue, and white clouds hung in it, glowing, illuminated from behind.

"Wow," Taylor said, a feeling of deep gratitude clogging her throat with emotion.

"Yeah. That's what I was thinking. Taylor looked over at Judd, and realized he'd been watching her as she took it all in.

"I've always liked the spot, but I've never seen it quite like this." While he was speaking, Judd released Taylor's hand and put both of his on her waist, turning her to face him. A breeze came up, blowing a few strands of hair across her face. Judd brushed them back and pulled her hair into a ponytail.

With one hand he held onto that, and with the other, he cupped the side of her face. Just before she closed her eyes, she noticed again the startling color of his eyes: every shade of green with a sunburst of gold in the middle. A girl could get lost in those eyes. A girl could get lost in that kiss.

His mouth was on hers, his lips firm and warm. She wanted him closer, and she slid her arms around his waist, pulling him in. She'd heard of kisses described as explosive, like fireworks. But this was lava. A slow, hot burn. And she was fireproof. She could submerge herself in the kiss and emerge like a phoenix, a whole different version of herself. Judd must be able to feel the sense of power he instilled in her, and he took the kiss deeper, parting her lips with his and slipping his tongue between them. His free hand made its way down to her rib cage, the edge of his hand barely grazing the side of her breast. More heat. More fire. The movement stoked fire within him, too. He let go of her ponytail and brought that hand down to her hip and around her lower back. He hooked his thumb into a belt loop, letting his fingers brush the top of her back pockets. Taylor groaned, the sound escaping her before she realized she'd gotten completely lost, tied up in the kiss, the contact, the man. Judd reacted, bringing one hand up to cup her breast. That nearly undid her, and literally made her weak in the knees. She wanted this, with him. She wanted more than this. The view, the kiss. Sex. He had roused something in Taylor she hadn't even known was there. And she liked it.

Chapter Fifteen

Looking forward to the next rodeo club meeting, Judd felt like a kid anticipating Christmas morning. If anyone had told him he would ever feel this way about a meeting for a school club, he would have said they were crazy. But there he was Friday, counting down the hours until the end of the school day.

As had become routine, he walked the halls during breaks, saying hi to kids, many of whom he knew by name, and many who had started greeting him first. Judd considered that progress.

During the longer break between second and third periods, he went in search of Zion, who hung out under the stairs behind the science building. Notably, that seemed to be the popular hangout for the rougher kids — the pot smokers and troublemakers. He made eye contact with Zion before calling his name, and didn't miss the little eye roll the kid gave him before separating himself from the group. He met Judd far enough outside the circle that people wouldn't overhear them talking.

"Hey, man. How's that left kick coming? You been practicing? Are you still painfully right footed?"

Zion's posture softened a bit at the talk of soccer, which had been Judd's intention. "Nah, man. *You* ain't been at the field. Nobody else can stack up against my right foot. So why bother?"

Feeling a little flattered, Judd shrugged. "Yeah. This new gig has got me working Monday through Friday. Five days a week instead of four. Which means I need to be home on my days off. Take care of the horses, stuff around the property."

"*You* have horses?" Genuine interest sparked in Zion's eyes.

"Yeah. And they're a lot of work. But as soon as I ditch this position, I'll be back on the field. So you should probably practice with that left foot if you want to stand a chance when I get back."

The kid gave him a conspiratorial side eye. "This isn't the best place to hang out, is it?"

As tempting as it was to open up to Zion about how much he disliked being at the school — maybe as much as Zion, himself, did — Judd went for professional. "Not if you want to play soccer, it's not. But. If you want to go to horse club ..."

At that point, Zion's head dropped forward, making Judd laugh out loud. "Can't say I want to do that. But I guess you're going to make me. Right?"

Judd put his hands on his hips. "I can't actually *make* you. But I'm here to strongly encourage you. We need the bodies. And remember, I need you to bring your friend. What was his name, Leviticus?"

Zion smirked. Judd felt like maybe they were forming an actual connection. "Something like that. But you can call him Raven."

"Bring Raven with you, all right?"

"Nobody makes Raven do nothing. But I'll try. I know you've got to win the heart of the sexy librarian."

Judd shook his head as he walked away.

During fourth period, Judd was in his office when the principal, Ernie, knocked on the door. "Come on in," Judd said. "Have a seat."

"How's it going?" Ernie asked as he sat down across from Judd.

"It's going," Judd said. "The kids are starting to recognize me. I'm learning my way around. Now, if someone would just bring me donuts, I'd be set."

Ernie smiled. "I'm sure we could arrange that. I heard Ms. Cole has a penchant for baking."

Judd couldn't tell whether Ernie was teasing him, and the last thing he needed was for this boss to think he was unprofessional, so he changed the subject. "What brings you to my office, Mr. Vasquez?"

"Listen, I heard there's some kind of *drug ring*," Ernie said, using air quotes. "This is high schoolers talking, so I don't know how it compares to what you guys deal with over at the police department. But whatever it is, it sounds like it warrants some investigating. Supposedly, the leader, the main man, if you will — is a kid named Leviticus."

Suddenly, the conversation seemed a lot more interesting.

"Personally," Ernie said, "I can't imagine a kid with a name like that playing lord over a crime ring." He waved a hand, dismissive. "To each his own, I guess. Anyway, I was hoping this might be something you could check out, nip in the bud before it gets any bigger."

Judd's wheels were already turning. If Zion could get Raven to come to the rodeo club meetings, Judd could find a way to squeeze the information out of the little punk. He thought with some regret that the investigation might be a bit of a distraction from Taylor, but at the same time, he could already feel his adrenaline pumping at the idea of keeping his skills somewhat sharp.

"This is right up my alley," he told Ernie. "I'll start working on it today."

"Great. Your boss, Sergeant Barnes, wasn't it? Said you're great at investigations. I'm confident you'll be able to take care of this for me. I appreciate it."

On his way out, Ernie paused in the doorway and turned around. "By the way, how is the rodeo club going, anyway?"

Judd hoped his expression didn't convey the attraction he felt for Taylor — the real reason he'd volunteered to help her — and did his best to mask his features before he spoke. "We're going to have to recruit some more members. Taylor — Ms. Cole — says we need at least five to make it official."

"I'm sure it will all work out. Taylor is a very charming woman." Ernie actually winked at him before walking out the door.

———

TAYLOR

At lunch, Taylor met Rose and Jessie at their usual picnic table under the flowering apricot tree outside the library.

"So, how was your date with Officer Hotpants?" Rose asked, and Jessie added, "Yeah. Don't think your one-sentence text message gives us enough detail."

"You want me to tell you everything?" The confidence was back, and Taylor felt like quite the vixen.

"Everything," they said.

She dished. She told them how she felt when she saw Judd at his house. How sweet he was with the horses. How he promised to let her help saddle them up *next time* (at that, both girls said, "Aww"). She told them about the ride, climbing the boulders he used to climb as a kid, and, naturally, the kiss. *The kiss.* Reliving it made Taylor hot all over. Rose and Jessie fired questions at her.

Rose: "Is he a gentle kisser? Or a firm kisser?" Before Taylor could answer, Jessie asked, "Did he use tongue right away or was there a delay?"

"What did he do with his hands while you were kissing?" Rose asked, and Jessie asked, "What did he say after?"

"Wow," Taylor said. "That's a lot of questions. Suffice it to say, it was toe curling and spectacular. And he used his hands in exactly the right way. The kiss left us both speechless. There will *definitely* be another date. Hopefully, one with more kissing."

Lunch ended and fifth and sixth period dragged by. Finally, *finally,* the end-of-day bell rang.

And there was Judd, pretty as a picture, looking downright edible himself, walking into the library with ... was that student a potential rodeo club member? He couldn't be. Taylor didn't know the kid's name, but she recognized him as part of the group that hung out under the stairs behind the science building. He'd come into the library with his classes a few times, and usually declined her help. He seemed to know his way around, and also was the role model for efficiency, finding what he needed quickly and then waiting at the table nearest the door for the teacher to dismiss the class. Her mind completed that thought process in a fraction of a second, and that's how long it took her to realize Judd was watching her carefully, gauging her reaction.

"This is Zion," he said. "He's going to try the rodeo club."

Taylor nodded. "I'm Ms. Cole. But you probably know that."

Zion looked at his shoes. "Yes, ma'am."

Taylor looked at Judd, thinking, *Where did you find this kid? And how did you pull off getting him here?*

Judd smiled back, as if they were sharing some kind of inside joke. Which made Taylor feel all warm and fuzzy inside.

"Zion has invited a friend. Leviticus. Also known as Raven."

At that point, Taylor could hear the barely contained laughter in Judd's voice and it was all she could do to keep a straight face.

"That's great! I'm sure Officer O'Connor told you we need two more people to make our club official."

At that point, Zion made eye contact. "He did. But I don't want you getting your hopes up, Ms. Cole. I'm not sure how excited Raven is about horse club."

Judd gave Zion a light, friendly punch on the shoulder. "But we're going to *make* him excited, right?"

Zion shrugged. He looked doubtful. "I guess so."

Olivia, Scarlett, and Henry walked in, and Taylor watched as all of them noticed Zion, standing there next to Judd. Surprise registered on each of their faces.

"Hi, guys!" Taylor was sure they could hear the forced cheer in her voice. "This is Zion. He'll be joining us today."

Downright chatty when it was just the three of them, Taylor's library nerds mumbled greetings.

"What's on the agenda for today, Ms. Cole?" Judd asked.

Taylor beamed at him. "So glad you asked. First, I should tell you that once we have five consistent club members, we'll be taking a bus over to the Mint Creek Ranch for our meetings. For today, though, we're going to talk about what the competitions entail, and then I'm going to have each of you do a little report on an event."

"This sounds an awful lot like school work," Zion mumbled.

"It'll be fun," Taylor said. "I just want to make sure we all know what we're getting into. I wrote each event on a slip of paper. Draw one, and I'll give you an hour to work on your report. We'll present at the end."

Taylor held out the bowl containing the slips. If she wasn't mistaken, she saw Zion's eyes light up as he read his selection.

"What did you all get?" Judd asked.

"I got horse grooming and care," Henry said. "Pretty standard."

"Olivia?" Judd said.

She held up her slip. "Barrel racing."

"Scarlett?"

She wrinkled her nose. "Steer roping. Which seems hard."

"I'll help you," Taylor said.

"Which leaves you, Z," Judd said to Zion, and Taylor wondered how they'd gotten on first-initial basis. Zion held his slip of paper in both hands. Although he didn't look up when he said, "Bull riding," Taylor thought she could see his lips sliding upward in an almost-smile.

Someone cleared his throat from the doorway, and the whole group turned. Another young man — must be Raven, Taylor thought — stood there, his whole body drawn into itself, clearly indicating he'd rather be anywhere else.

The smile that came to Taylor's face then was natural; the kid's posture and bearing were comical. "You must be Raven," Taylor said. She glanced at Judd, who looked smug. Which she found adorable. He confirmed he was proud of himself when he said, "Our fifth member."

"Come on in," Taylor said to Raven, and he obeyed, eyes on the floor.

"We just picked the reports we're going to do today," Taylor said. "There's one left."

Raven held up his hands. "I don't report, man. I'm only here because this guy said I had to come." On the words, *this guy*, Raven jutted his chin at Judd. Again, Taylor had to keep herself from laughing.

"All right. Maybe you'll change your mind."

"I won't."

Taylor raised an eyebrow at Judd, who shrugged. The library nerds shuffled their feet, uncomfortable.

Taylor took a deep breath to fortify herself. "I've set up a laptop for each of you to research, so you should have everything you need. Go ahead and get started, and let us know if you have any questions."

Olivia, Scarlett, Henry, and Zion walked over to the computers. Raven made a show of sitting at one of the desks without a computer, leaning on the desktop in a way that conveyed his boredom. Judd winked at Taylor, and walked over to sit down next to Raven. "Tell you what. If you grab that slip of paper and do the report, I'll bring pizza to the next meeting."

"Pizza?"

"Yeah. It's like a giant round piece of bread with tomato sauce and cheese on it, and stuff on top. Like meat. Pepperoni, sausage, bacon. Sometimes vegetables."

Not amused, Raven said, "I know what pizza is, bro. I'm saying, you're willing to bring pizza, and all I gotta do is a little report?"

"Well, yeah."

Raven looked skeptical. "Maybe next time, man."

Judd shrugged and stood up. The kids worked in near silence for the next hour, their fingers clacking away on the keyboards. Taylor expected her library nerds to do thorough reports. What she didn't expect was for Zion's report to be a verifiable masterpiece. He had slides with photos, graphics, videos, and full paragraphs. At one point while he was talking, Taylor looked over at Judd, who looked back at her with raised eyebrows and a thumbs up. By the time he was finished presenting it, Taylor thought she knew enough to get on the back of a bull and stay there for eight seconds if she had to.

As he promised, Raven stayed away from the laptops, but Taylor saw him watching his fellow club members with interest.

It was a start, Taylor thought. There was some promise. If they could just keep Zion and Raven coming back, maybe the club could be a success.

———

Judd

Judd couldn't say who was more surprised by the skill with which Zion made his presentation: himself or the library nerds. Taylor seemed downright delighted, so much so that was the only emotion she conveyed. She bounced on the balls of her feet, her hands clasped together at her waist, her smile as wide as he'd ever seen it. It was pretty darned adorable.

"You guys! You *all* are rock stars! I can't believe how well your reports turned out."

"Zion's was the best," Olivia said, and Judd watched Zion's gaze drop to the tops of his shoes as a blush crawled up his neck.

"It was really good," Scarlett said. Zion scratched the back of his neck, eyes still firmly downcast, refusing to smile.

It was a new side of the confident, grinning soccer star with whom Judd was familiar.

"This obviously isn't your first rodeo," Taylor said. "Pun intended."

Judd saw Zion start to roll his eyes, and then stop.

"Yeah. I grew up around rodeo. I've gotten on the back of a bull or two."

"How long have you been at it?"

Zion shrugged and looked down again. The tips of his ears were still a little pink. "Since I could walk, I guess. My uncle taught me."

Taylor looked at Judd over Zion's head. Her eyebrows were raised, excitement palpable.

"You think he'll ever come in as a guest speaker?"

Judd didn't miss the shadow that passed over Zion's face.

Again, he shrugged. "I don't know."

Taylor seemed to sense his unease, and changed the subject.

"You guys all did great today. I can't wait until our first competition. This club has some real promise. See you next week. Same time, same place."

When all the students were gone, Judd turned to Taylor. "So? What did you think?"

Taylor laughed, the sound like music. She came toward him and wrapped her arms around his waist. "What I think, Officer O'Connor, is that you are some kind of miracle worker. Not only did you fill out our rodeo club roster, but you brought me some kind of rodeo prodigy. And I think that I am very, *very* appreciative. She nuzzled his neck, and then kissed him just under the chin.

"Well, *I* think I'm going to have to keep earning your appreciation."

He couldn't believe how much fun he was having. She kissed him again, this time on the throat, which turned him on far more than was appropriate in a high school library.

"What do I get if I bring two more members next week?"

Taylor tilted her head back and kissed him on the mouth. "I guess we'll just have to see."

A voice from the open doorway startled them. "Isn't there a rule about PDA on campus?"

Judd released his grip on Taylor, but she held onto him.

"Rose," she said, drawing the name out into two syllables. "You interrupted our moment."

Looking about as embarrassed as Judd felt, Rose leaned up against the door frame, and said, "I'm sorry. I didn't mean to spoil anything. But I thought we were meeting here at four forty-five."

"Oh!" At that point, Taylor practically jumped away from Judd, then looked up at him with the guiltiest, cutest expression on her face. "Yes. I remember. I just got distracted."

"I'll give you a minute." Smiling, Rose turned around and walked away. Judd could hear her footsteps receding.

"Well, I guess I'd better leave you to it." Taylor reached for him again and this time put her forehead against his. "I'm sorry about that. We made plans to go look at an apartment. Rose and her daughter are living underneath a bunch of college students and their schedules don't exactly line up."

"That's nice of you to go with her."

"What are friends for? It's always nice to have a second opinion making big decisions."

"That's sweet. Listen." Judd didn't know exactly how to say what he wanted to say. But he knew he had to tell her. She took a step back, holding onto his hands, looking into his eyes.

He took a deep breath. "I don't know exactly how to say this."

Her concern was palpable. "You don't want to do the club anymore."

Judd felt himself smiling. "That's not it. I do want to do the club. I just wanted to say, I really like you. I like spending time with you. When we're together, I can finally relax. Just be. I've never had that with anyone else."

Taylor was silent. Judd wondered if he'd said too much. He waited. Then suddenly, she smiled, as bright and beautiful as the first warm spring day after a long, frigid winter. Relief swept through him.

"Well, it seems we're making confessions every time we're in the same space, doesn't it? In that case, you should know that I really like you, too. When I'm with you, I feel more confident. Like I can do anything. I like that. I want to feel like that all the time."

"Then maybe we should spend more time together."

She nodded. "We definitely should. But right now, I've got an apartment viewing to go to. Want to do dinner tomorrow?"

"I would love to do dinner tomorrow."

"Then I guess it's goodbye for now."

Taylor leaned toward him again, pressing her lips to his. She gave him a light, friendly peck, but the conversation they'd had made Judd want more. He took her head in his hands and kissed her again, doing his absolute best to convey all the different feelings he had for her. Affection, tenderness, attraction. Taylor responded, kissing him back with matching intensity. He could get lost in that kiss. He never wanted it to end. He wondered if it was what Heaven was like. Then he realized he'd never felt that way about anyone, ever. Taylor Cole was special. And he wouldn't let anything get in the way of him proving that to her.

Chapter Sixteen

TAYLOR

"Well," Rose said when Taylor climbed into the passenger seat of her car a few minutes later, "I think I got a fever from all the heat coming out of that room."

Taylor blushed fiercely. "It *was* pretty hot in there."

"I'll say. I thought it was rodeo club, not making-out club."

Taylor gave her friend a gentle slap on the arm. "Oh, stop it. I just hope I haven't made you late to pick up Celeste."

"We have plenty of time. But even if you had, it would be totally worth it. I got a good, healthy dose of romance just from watching the two of you."

Taylor shook her head. "So where is this apartment?"

"It's over off Willow Creek." Rose backed out of the parking spot and Taylor glared at her own car as they drove past it. A new car, one with more personality, was priority number two, right after getting that business loan.

"Is it in that new complex, near the grocery store?" Taylor asked.

"Yep," Rose said. "That's the one." She tapped her thumbs on the steering wheel, which made Taylor think she was nervous.

"It seems nice."

"I should hope so, for what they're charging. Honestly, I'm not sure if I can afford it. It's going to be a real stretch. But I've heard they let you choose whether you're on the bottom or top floor. And maybe even where you are in the complex. So hopefully I can find something that will allow Celeste — and me — to get some sleep."

Taylor offered what she hoped was a reassuring smile. "If anyone can make it work, you can."

They pulled up at Celeste's daycare, and Taylor put a hand on Rose's arm to stop her from getting out. "You know, you just have to make this work for one more school year. And then Celeste will be in kindergarten and you won't have to pay for full-time childcare. You can do it."

Rose let her head fall back against her headrest. "Thanks. That's the only thing that keeps me going."

"You've got this. Come on, let's go in."

Rose may feel like she was struggling, Taylor thought, but she'd managed to get Celeste a spot in the best daycare in town. A retired kindergarten teacher ran the business out of her home, which was completely set up for preschoolers. At the moment, most of the preschoolers were in the shady backyard, drawing with sidewalk chalk or painting with water.

When Rose and Taylor reached the spot where Celeste was playing, Taylor noticed right away she was the only one who had mixed the two activities. She painted on the patio with a paste she'd made of chalk and water. Her hands were coated in the chalk paint, and she was creating some kind of flower garden with it.

"I think your kid is a genius," Taylor whispered to Rose, who dropped her forehead into her hand. To Celeste, Taylor said, "Is that a flower garden?"

Celeste froze, looked up, and yelled, "Auntie Tay!" She jumped to her feet and leapt toward Taylor, ready to throw her arms around her. Rose, with the reflexes of an experienced mother, stuck out an arm to stop her. "Hold up. I don't want you to get your chalk paint on Auntie Tay's nice work pants. But that is a lovely piece of art you've made."

As if she'd only just noticed the mess she'd created, Celeste looked at her palms and then the backs of her hands. "Thanks," she mumbled, distracted. "I guess I gotta go wash my hands."

While Rose gathered Celeste's things and Celeste washed her hands, Taylor let her mind wander. What would her life be like when she had kids? They could come to the barn with her after school and on breaks. She imagined a little version of herself, or Judd, tagging along, helping with barn chores. At the end of the day, they'd go home to Judd, who would be so happy to see them.

By the time they got back to the car, Celeste was chattering away, and Taylor was so immersed in her full-fledged fantasy that she hadn't heard much of what she had said.

Rose reached across the center console and put her hand on Taylor's forearm. "Where'd you go?"

Taylor laughed, and decided to go for full honesty. "Oh, I was just having a little daydream about my future life, with my own charming five-year-old and my husband waiting at home."

Rose glanced at her, eyes narrowed, an eyebrow raised. "Interesting. Very interesting."

———

*J*UDD

The evening after the first rodeo club meeting, Katy met Judd at the barn and called him out as soon as she saw his face. "Oh my gosh! I can't believe this! You are totally smitten."

"What?" He changed direction so she couldn't see his face.

"I know what you're doing." She relented, starting the chores while he thought about how to respond. They worked in silence for a few minutes, until Katy couldn't help herself any longer. "Just tell me! What happened today?"

Judd grinned at his sister while he threw some alfalfa into Knickerbocker's stall. "Let's just say I was the hero of the rodeo club meeting. And Taylor was not shy about expressing her appreciation."

"Judd Michael O'Connor! Please tell me you didn't do anything that's going to get you fired!"

"Geez. I thought you'd be happy for me."

Katy paused, a scoop of grain in her hand. "I *am* happy for you. But from where I'm sitting, you're *this close* to losing your job. And even though it's been stressing you out for a while, I don't think you're ready to give it up. Are you?"

Judd turned toward her, his hands on his hips. "What makes you think I'm 'this close' to losing it?"

Exasperated, Katy dumped the grain into the bucket. "Oh, I don't know. Maybe the fact that Barnes stuck you on SRO."

She was right. Judd turned around again. "I'm not going to get myself fired, Katy. All we did was kiss in the library."

"'All you did'? Geez. If a simple kiss has got you all hot and bothered, I don't want to be around when you finally take her to bed."

"Hold up. First of all, how do you know it was a 'simple kiss'? Second of all, this has gone too far. I can't have my sister talking about me taking my girlfriend to bed."

"Girlfriend?" Her eyebrows wiggled.

"Lay off, will you?" He made sure to infuse his voice with just enough seriousness that Katy would stop nagging him, and just enough humor that he wouldn't hurt her feelings.

"What about you?" Judd said a minute later as they grabbed their rakes and started shoveling soiled hay out of the stalls. "Got any romantic prospects on the horizon?"

"Not a single one. All I do is work, anyway. Not like I have time for romance."

"Work and go to the gym."

"True. But gym rats aren't really my type."

After they had checked all the waterers and finished mucking the stalls, Judd told Katy, "I think I might need your advice."

She clicked her tongue. "I *knew* it! You can't help but talk about this! It was just a matter of waiting you out. Although, big brother, I'm not sure why you're asking for my wisdom. I'm obviously not striking it rich in the dating world."

"But you *are* a girl."

"I am. So hit me with it."

Finished with the chores, the two of them headed toward the barn door. Judd slid it closed and said, "I'll walk you home." They set off toward her house. "We agreed on dinner tomorrow night. I wanted to bring her flowers. Is it too soon? What kind should I buy? I want to send the right message."

"And what message is that?" She leaned toward him, bumping his upper arm with her shoulder.

"A message you'll probably make fun of."

"Probably," she said, her tone agreeable. "But as you know, I'm always looking for a reason to make fun of you."

"Isn't that the truth."

"So?"

"Right. The message. The message is something like, 'I really like you. I can't stop thinking about you. I'm not ready to say I'm in love with you, but I really really *really* like you.'"

"Awww," his sister said, before falling silent to consider. "Okay. I like this message. I think I can get behind it. Based on what I've seen, I think Taylor is a soft, pink flower type of person. Probably not roses, but not carnations, either. I'm thinking peonies. Or stock. Those are both really nice. And I think they convey your message."

By that time, the two of them had reached Katy's front door.

"Thank you," Judd said.

"Anytime. And Judd? Be careful, okay? I don't want you to risk losing your job if this office romance gets out of hand."

"I will," he promised. Walking away, he had the unusual and surprising thought that he was more concerned with keeping Taylor than he was with keeping his job.

———

TAYLOR

Rose and Celeste loved the apartment complex, so much so that they spent a few hours touring all the various floor plans. By the time Taylor got home, it was too late to cook. She decided to order takeout from the diner, and as she riffled through her kitchen drawer to find the printed menu, she came across the rejection letter she received the week before.

She unfolded it and read it again. Kristi Mendez, the loan officer from Prescott Bank, thought she had a solid business idea. She said she was confident Taylor would find the right bank. Fueled by renewed confidence from the successful club meeting and the powerful energy she'd recently discovered, Taylor made a decision.

She wasn't going to wait around for the right bank or the right loan officer. She was going to make her business so attractive, the next banker she encountered wouldn't be able to pass it up. The idea swirled around inside her body, a lightning bolt of energy building.

But how?

That was the question she had to answer.

What if the club became so popular it went Prescott-High-School viral? Wouldn't that be something like proof of concept?

Taylor poured herself a glass of wine and sat down at her kitchen counter, where she always kept a pad of paper and a pen. When she applied for business loans, she'd included the money-making components of her potential business. She wrote them down on her pad: lessons, open arena time, and special events.

Special events. She underlined that, twice and took a sip of wine.

Pulling in five club members might be difficult, but with the number of farm and ranch kids at the school, she had no doubt she could attract more than enough competitors to raise a decent amount of money — and attention.

Nodding, she wrote down *Competition*, and underneath it, potential events: *Barrel racing, steer roping, team roping, mutton busting* (that last one was for smaller kids, but she thought high schoolers might get a kick out of it).

The club could charge entry fees for each contestant, and maybe even sell merchandise during the event. She'd have to find a place to host the event, but the owners of the Mint Creek Ranch had already agreed she could use their property for club meetings ...

For the first time in a long time, maybe ever, Taylor felt like she was taking control of her future. Instead of waiting on someone else, she was taking action. And it felt good.

She wished she could call one of her friends, but Rose was probably rushing through a condensed dinner and bedtime routine after apartment hunting. And Jessie was over at her neighbor's house for the evening, helping pack up her belongings for a major yard sale. Taylor sighed.

You could call Judd.

She could, she thought, acknowledging the helpful little voice in her head. But what if he was busy? What if he thought the idea was silly? No, she wouldn't bother him now. She could run this idea past him the next day. For the moment, she would let herself imagine people showing up to watch the competition, cash dropping into the cash box for the rodeo club.

She couldn't *wait*. She could keep track of her expenses and her profits, and prove to any lender that she could do it. She could run a successful business. But. She had to get Principal Vasquez's permission, first.

Her phone chirped, alerting her to a text message. She almost ignored it, as much fun as she was having brainstorming about the rodeos she could put on, but then wondered if it was Rose with news about the new apartment, and went to check it. The message was from Judd, and seeing his name on the screen gave Taylor a pleasant little jolt of surprise.

What are you doing?

Smiling, she typed, *I just had an idea. I wonder if we could turn horse club into a mini business, to prove to potential lenders that it could be profitable. My imagination got a bit carried away. I was over here planning events — smaller versions of rodeos — the club could put on to raise money. Kids who compete could get involved without a commitment. And we could rake in the cash! And, you know, it would be proof of concept and I could get that business loan.*

His response came back right away. *Let's do it.*

Taylor felt a huge grin spreading across her face. *Let's do it*, he'd written. He was all in.

I love that that's how you responded. I don't know where to start. And we have to get permission from Ernie. He could put the kibosh on this whole thing.

Judd responded, *We'll make the idea un-turn-down-able. Should we discuss this over dinner tomorrow night?*

Could he be any more wonderful? *I'd love to.*

———

JUDD

Judd woke up the next day thinking about Taylor. He loved that she'd shared her idea with him, and he was starting to develop an idea of his own. Out of habit, he turned on his police scanner, just like he did every morning. Radio traffic was relatively quiet. A little disappointed not to catch any action, Judd turned it off and went about his morning routine.

By the time he pulled into his front-row parking spot at Prescott High School (another nice perk), he had a solid plan for getting into the drug ring Ernie mentioned. Thinking about Raven's birth name, Judd chuckled as he got out of the car, his mind focused on his mission. A little investigation would spice things up while he was here.

Not that things need much spicing, he thought, remembering the kiss he shared with Taylor the day before.

Reliving that moment while at school, in uniform, was probably not prudent, so he adjusted his pants, dropped off his lunchbox and briefcase in his office, and went in search of Raven.

He walked past bleary-eyed teenagers, most of whom looked like they hadn't gotten enough sleep. During the first days at his new job,

Judd had observed that for the most part, teenagers were pretty quiet in the morning, clutching coffee mugs and energy drinks, and speaking in mumbles. As the day wore on, the volume in the halls increased. As Judd expected, Raven was under the stairs behind the science buildings, leaning against one of the pilings.

Originally, Judd had planned his morning patrol as just that: a patrol. He figured he'd walk right past Raven, scope things out, get a feel for the kid's vibe when he wasn't in the middle of a drug deal. But coming up on him, alone, seemed like an opportunity Judd couldn't pass up. Greeting him would be natural, since they'd met twice (albeit, under awkward circumstances).

"Good morning," Judd said. Raven offered a quick lift of his chin. Judd chose his next words carefully. "How's it going?"

Raven shrugged.

"You don't know? Or you don't want to talk?"

"Both, I guess."

"All right," Judd said. He left it at that and walked away.

Chapter Seventeen

TAYLOR

Taylor heard Judd pull up in her driveway and opened the door before he knocked. His gaze raked over her body as he said hello, which had been her intention. Taylor's pulse quickened at his reaction — his voice went husky when he told her how nice she looked (she had bought a new dress, bra, and panties for the occasion), and he stepped closer to her and wrapped his arms around her waist. She considered telling him they should stay home for their date. She wouldn't mind at all if he explored the miraculous bra and matching panties.

"You smell good, too," he said. "If I didn't have such fun things planned for us this evening, I'd ask if we could just stay in."

"I was thinking the same." Her own voice came out so sultry, so sexy, she could almost envision herself as a woman in a romance novel. Judd put enough space between them to kiss her. It was a greeting and a promise wrapped into one. The promise traveled right down the center of her body.

"Where are we going?" Taylor asked once they were in his truck.

"It's a surprise. One of my favorite places."

Taylor felt a rush of pleasure at the fact that Judd was showing her another one of his favorite places. She told him so, and he grinned at her across the cab. "I have to tell you, I'm just as excited to share all these spots with you."

It seemed like he wanted to say more, but his attention returned to the road.

"Should we put on some music?" Judd pushed the power button on the truck's stereo, and heavy metal blasted from the speakers. Taylor winced and covered her ears, and Judd rushed to turn down the volume.

"Is that your idea of music?" she teased.

Judd laughed, but Taylor noticed a shadow pass over his features. "Yes. When I'm in a certain mood, it is."

"And what mood is that?" She kept her tone light, but wondered what could possibly put him in a mood that would call for that harsh, angry music? She felt Judd's energy shift. His grip tightened on the steering wheel, the muscles in his forearms flexing.

"I was feeling a bit frustrated about my employment situation."

Taylor nodded. "Still anxious to get back to the road?" Judd glanced at her again, as if to gauge her reaction. "It's fine. You can admit it." She put a hand on his shoulder and felt some of his tension ease.

"Yes. The school resource officer position is *fine*. And you being there is the absolute highlight of the job."

Taylor's heart warmed at that.

Judd went on, "It's hard not to be out there, catching criminals. I heard a call on the radio this morning. A guy running from the cops. If I were on shift, I would have raced over there to help out the guys. But my hands were tied. I suited up and went to *school*." He shrugged and offered her a sad smile. She wanted to hug him, to somehow infuse him with happiness, but she settled for giving his shoulder another squeeze.

"I'm sorry. If it's any consolation, you being at school is the absolute highlight of my job, too."

The smile he offered then was genuine. Judd reached down and changed the radio station. When a few twangy cords of a country song came through the speakers, he arched an eyebrow at her. "Better?"

"Much. What does *this* station say about your mood?"

"I'm not sure if it says romance, or cold beer," he said.

"A cold beer does sound pretty good."

"Then you're in luck, because my special plans for us happen to include ice-cold beer." They had reached the base of Granite Mountain, and Judd pulled into a spot in the trailhead parking lot. "I hope you're willing to work up an appetite."

Taylor's insides went molten when they made eye contact, the innuendo hanging between them.

"I'm already hungry," Taylor said.

Judd opened the center console and handed her a package of trail mix. "To tide you over. But you've got to make it to the top of the mountain for your actual surprise." Judd removed a backpack-style cooler from the truck's backseat and put it on.

"You're carrying that to the top of the mountain?"

"Yes. Something I will do only for the most beautiful woman in Prescott. It's heavy."

They spent the next hour hiking, trekking up the steep trail, between boulders and wildflowers, through pine trees and oak shrubs. Although Taylor munched on trail mix most of the way up, she really had worked up an appetite by the time they reached the summit.

"Hope you're hungry," Judd said.

"So hungry," Taylor said. "But also thirsty." Judd removed the backpack and knelt next to it. He pulled out a blanket and spread it on the ground.

"Then I think it's definitely time to crack open a couple of these." He pulled out two cans of beer, the condensation so thick on them, Taylor's mouth watered. Judd open the first one and handed it to her, and then opened the second one and held it up so she could tap hers against it.

"Cheers to a cold beer on a hot day," he said. "And, more importantly, cheers to spending this beautiful evening with an even more beautiful woman." They both drank then, long and deep. The bubbles fizzed in Taylor's mouth, and she thought it just might be the most refreshing drink she'd ever had.

They sat down on the blanket and Judd took out two sandwiches wrapped in waxed paper, two bags of chips, and a small white bakery box.

"This is really nice." He shrugged, as if he hadn't made the most thoughtful picnic and made Taylor practically swoon on the spot. "I wanted it to be special."

"Did you make all this?"

"Most of it. Katy made the cookies. I'm supposed to tell you I made them, but I feel like I should be honest about their origins. Mostly in case they're not good."

"I'm sure they'll be wonderful."

"Katy has spent a lot of time in the kitchen. She says she only spends as much time in the gym as she does because she likes eating baked goods."

Judd's mention of baked goods reminded Taylor of the first rodeo club meeting, and brought Taylor's nerves about the possible rodeo event back to the forefront. She sighed, and again, Judd seemed to understand.

"Thinking about your great idea for a rodeo event?"

"How'd you guess?"

"You looked all wistful." He handed her a sandwich. "It's going to be a hit. If anyone can pull this off, you can."

"Thanks," she said, feeling bolstered "I just keep picturing Ernie saying a rodeo event is too much. Too dangerous. Too *something*."

"I doubt he will. But imagine how you'd feel if you didn't even try. You'd be kicking yourself for sure. And you're not on your own. I'll be right there with you."

"You have no idea how much that means to me."

"You're welcome." He winked at her. "I'll admit, I originally volunteered to help you with the rodeo club because I thought you were hot." Taylor raised an eyebrow at him. A devilish light in his eyes, he said, "I'm just being honest. But now that I've gotten to know you better, I'm hooked. And not just on the club."

If he was trying to turn her into a pot of melted butter, he was well on his way. While Jessie and Rose had always supported her, Judd's support felt different. The girls were her best friends. They had to cheer her on. Coming from someone she'd only just met met, hearing the words felt different somehow.

As they finished their picnic dinner, the sun set, turning the sky into a rainbow of soft colors.

"Are you ready for your surprise?" Judd said.

"Ready," Taylor said.

He sat behind her, and she leaned into his embrace as the stars came out, twinkling. The scene was breathtaking.

"Wow," she breathed. "I've never seen the sky quite like this."

"Just keep watching," he said. "It gets better."

The sky darkened even more, accentuating the bright light from the hundreds of thousands of tiny pinpricks that were the stars.

"Look at all the stars," she said.

"Pretty amazing, right?"

"So amazing."

As they sat together, watching the stars, their bodies touching, Taylor's nerves from moments before felt a lifetime away.

———

The next day, Taylor and Judd met at the high school entrance — Ernie Vasquez's morning post — and asked for a lunchtime meeting. Ernie raised a curious eyebrow and agreed, and Taylor spent the entire morning outlining and re-outlining the argument she planned to share with him. When the end-of-fourth-period bell rang, Taylor went flying out the library door, only to stop abruptly when she heard a voice behind her. "A beautiful woman such as yourself should be far more aware of her surroundings."

"Judd!"

He caught up to her, and they started walking together. "Sorry! I didn't see you! I was in such a hurry to get to our meeting."

"I could tell. Nervous?"

Taylor slowed down, and made a show of taking a few deep

breaths. "I guess I need to calm myself down, or I'm going to botch this meeting."

Judd, the picture of calm, said, "Well, I seriously doubt you would botch it. But a few more deep breaths might not hurt."

Taylor counted out her inhales and exhales as they walked.

"Besides, think about it this way: I can think of almost no way the benefits don't outweigh the risks of us putting on a rodeo event. The whole process is educational for our club members, right? Real life, hands-on stuff. And Ernie seems like a reasonable guy."

Still doing her deep breathing, Taylor considered. It was true. Ernie *was* a reasonable guy. And putting on an event was educational. The rodeo club members would have to plan and budget and execute. Plus, as she had outlined that morning, the money they raised could go toward competition fees. Other clubs did car washes or spaghetti dinners. Chances were good Ernie would approve of rodeo events.

"You're right," Taylor said. "I should stop stressing myself out."

They'd reached the school office and Judd held open the door. Ernie spotted them from behind his desk and called them in. Judd pulled out a chair for Taylor and waited to sit down until she was seated, which she found ridiculously chivalrous.

"How can I help you two?" Ernie leaned back in his chair.

Judd inclined his head toward Taylor, giving her the floor.

She nodded. "We'd like to start holding small rodeo events to raise money and awareness of the club." She cursed herself for not coming up with a stronger opening.

"Tell me more."

This was her chance. "First and foremost, all high school rodeo events require teams to pay fees. So it would be natural for us to charge entry fees, which we could then use to to pay for our team members to enter local and regional competitions. Adding this event-planning component to our current curriculum — which involves horsemanship and the actual rodeo events — would give our team members the opportunity to learn about marketing, sales, and budgeting. We know these events come with a certain level of liability, but the way Judd — I mean, Officer O'Connor — and I look at it, these are all important skills. We were hoping to host events one evening per month."

Realizing she'd barreled on, much like a runaway train, she stopped talking and inhaled. And waited for Ernie's response. He pursed his lips, considering.

Finally, he said, "You got it. When do we start?"

Almost as if she were having an out-of-body experience, Taylor felt her mouth drop open and her head swivel to the right. She made eye contact with Judd, who smiled back at her, smug. She could practically hear him thinking, "I told you so."

Her head swiveled back toward Ernie. "Great. Thank you. How about two Fridays from now?"

Normally, she would have thanked him profusely, expressing her long-winded appreciation. But she figured she had better make the plan and get out of Ernie's office before he changed his mind.

"Sounds great. Why don't you announce this at the assembly on Friday? Get some interest going."

Taylor's mind raced. If they announced a rodeo event, it became *real*. They had to do it. They had no choice but to move forward. Her throat constricted. She couldn't speak. It was what she wanted, but this was big. Was it possible? Would students sign up? Would they show up?

Judd must have read the panic on her face because he cleared his throat and said, "Yes. We'd love to announce it at the assembly Friday."

Ernie nodded. After a short pause he said, "Well, if that's all you guys needed ..."

"That's it, sir," Judd said. "Thank you for your time."

As she was still frozen to her spot, Judd took Taylor's elbow and practically hauled her to standing. He gestured for her to walk out ahead of him. As she did, she started to regain her senses. The meeting had lasted all of forty seconds, and they'd gotten exactly what they wanted. Taylor couldn't believe it.

———

JUDD

Completely enamored with the excitement shining in Taylor's eyes, Judd felt his own excitement rising as they walked out of Ernie's office. "I'll walk you back to the library," he told her.

Taylor gave him a conspiratorial smile, then looked behind them to make sure no one was within earshot. "Good. That'll give us a chance to talk about how well that went. That was amazing!"

He grinned at her. "I told you he wouldn't turn down the idea."

"And I trusted you! I just expected it to be a lot harder to convince him."

"Why? It's a great idea."

Seeing her smile in response, knowing how much his words meant to her, made his heart melt. "It is. Now we just have to put it into action."

Taylor interlaced her fingers with his and gave his hand a quick squeeze, then broke the contact. By that point they'd reached the library.

"I wish I could stick around," he told her. "But I promised Ernie I'd do some investigations this week. So I've got to go do some patrolling."

"Aw," she said. "I wish you could stay longer too. But the youth of our world need you, Officer O'Connor. Go get 'em."

Judd winked at her, hoping his expression didn't betray him. The last part of what she said hit him right in the gut. It was something a wife might say to her husband every morning when she sent him off to work. Akin to the whole, "Have a great day, see you tonight," thing. Or, "Be safe."

Why couldn't Judd stop himself from picturing Taylor as Mrs. O'Connor? It was crazy. He did not plan on there being a Mrs. O'Connor (other than his mother).

He'd better get his head on straight, or he would never be the same when he got back to being a real cop. So, like he often did, Judd put Taylor — and all the strong feelings he had tangled up in her — into a neat and tidy little box, which he closed, locked, and put on a shelf in the back corner of his brain.

Then he went in search of Raven.

The short meeting with Ernie took up just enough time that Raven had already gotten through the cafeteria line. In fact, when Judd spotted him, he was almost done eating. *Perfect timing.*

Judd walked the perimeter of the room, letting his eyes roam over the different groups of students. He could tell when Raven spotted him. The kid stiffened and then immediately looked down at his tray. Even though Judd wasn't looking directly at him, Raven's actions showed guilt, plain and simple. Judd wondered what he'd been up to, with whom, and when. The possibility existed that he hadn't done anything yet, and looked guilty for whatever he was planning.

Judd would just have to keep an eye on him. He walked out the side door of the cafeteria, and then positioned himself near a window that gave him a view of Raven and the whole room. Raven couldn't see him, but Judd could watch his every move. He finished eating, and Judd saw him look around the cafeteria. Judd wondered if Raven was looking for *him.* He didn't seem to see Judd, and his shoulders sagged in relief. Which meant the likelihood was high that he was about to cause mischief. He got up, tossed his trash into the trashcan, set his tray on top, and walked out the door. Judd took a few quick steps to his left so he could see which way Raven went, and almost ran smack into him at the corner of the building.

It was all Judd could do to keep from laughing. "Hey, man." Raven mumbled a response, but looked downright terrified. Another indicator of guilt. "Everything okay?"

"Yeah."

"Where are you headed?"

Raven shrugged, broke eye contact. "I don't know. Nowhere."

"I didn't know Nowhere was a place."

That earned a half-smile, the lift of one corner of Raven's mouth. "Yeah, well, it's where I'm headed."

"All right. Have a good time."

At that point, Judd couldn't very well follow him — he'd notice. So, he carried on in his original direction, letting Raven go in his. If Judd hurried, he could make it to the hangout where he'd seen

Raven that morning. Making it look like he'd ended up there by accident would be difficult, but it didn't end up mattering because when he got there, Raven was nowhere to be found. Judd wondered if he really had been going to Nowhere.

As Judd walked back toward the quad where most of the kids hung out after eating, he thought about the other kids he'd seen around Raven. It was kind of a motley crew. Some of whom he'd expect to ingest nothing more risky than coffee; others who'd smoke pot, and still others who might go for the harder stuff. Mushrooms, cocaine. Despite his bad attitude, Judd still had a hard time seeing Raven as the mastermind of any larger-scale operation.

The quad was quiet that day. Judd spotted the library nerds, standing together at the edge of the Student Council group. They called out to him, he walked over to say hello.

"Where's Ms. Cole?" Olivia asked, that mischief he was starting to recognize shining in her eyes.

Was he smiling? He was. It had happened without him even noticing. "I don't know, actually." He didn't want to tell them he knew she was finishing up her lunch in the library.

"Look at that," Henry said. "He knows where she is."

"Yes," Scarlett said. "He just doesn't want us to know that he knows."

Judd raised his arms in an exaggerated shrug. "Would I lie to you guys?"

Olivia smiled. "No. But you would omit the truth, to keep up your professional façade."

This girl can read me like a book. "I can neither confirm nor deny."

There. That should do the trick.

The three kids exchanged knowing looks, and Judd decided to change the subject immediately.

"Have you seen the other two guys? Zion and Raven?"

Another look passed between the members of the trio.

"We don't exactly travel in the same circle," Scarlett said. "I mean, except for rodeo club, now. But if I had to guess, I would say they're either under the stairs by the science building, or in that weird area by the art room."

"Thank you. I'm going to go track them down."

————

Taylor

The night before the assembly, Taylor lay awake, watching the shadow of the tree outside her window, cast by the moon, dancing in the slight breeze.

The rodeo club meant so much to her. She wanted its success more than anything, because it would open the door for her future business.

Her speech had to be outstanding. Then, the rodeo events had to be great. Her motley crew of club members had to be organized and work well together as a team. And she had to make it all happen.

At four-thirty a.m., she finally gave up on sleep. Before leaving the house at six forty-five, she stood in front of her full-length mirror. She looked more confident than she felt. And, if she did say so herself, she looked pretty. As she drove to school, still caffeinating herself even though she'd had more than enough coffee, she checked off all the important talking points of her speech.

She'd introduce the club and its members. Then she'd talk about the events. They would be a fundraiser for the club, and they would also be fun. They would give students the chance to showcase their skills and compete against one another. There would be prizes. (Taylor had no idea what they'd be, but they would exist.) She would have a sign-up sheet available. She nodded and tapped her thumbs on the steering wheel.

"You can do this," she told herself as she parked.

All Taylor had to do was get through the first five periods of the day without running to the gym like a maniac. Once she got to school, she rushed across campus and into the library, head down, determined to keep herself busy.

She'd arranged for her club members to come to the library before the assembly so she could give them a rundown of what she'd cover. The library nerds met her at two o'clock sharp, which Taylor expected. What she didn't expect was for Zion and Raven to show up a full minute early.

As always during assemblies, sounds of chattering and laughter filled the gym. Ernie Vasquez stood behind the podium, and Taylor and Judd, the rodeo members flanking them, stood off to one side behind him. He did his renowned rhythmic clap, and a few students quieted down, copying him. He repeated the clap a few times until a hush fell over the gym. Raising both arms, he said, "Good afternoon, Prescott High School!"

The students chorused, "Good afternoon, Mr. Vasquez!"

Ernie talked about the first weeks of school: successes, learning opportunities, updates. Nerves kept Taylor from listening carefully, and Ernie's voice and all the other sights and sounds felt like a blur.

Ernie stepping away from the podium seemed quite sudden to Taylor, who felt Judd grab her elbow and steer her toward it. Olivia, Scarlett, and Henry stepped forward with her. Zion and Raven hung back. Taylor blinked, trying to clear her hearing. It was a few seconds before she realized the buzzing sound was polite applause. She cleared her throat into the microphone and the sound echoed. "Hi," she said. Through the speakers, her voice sounded uncertain and tinny. *You can do better than this.* "As you know, I am Ms. Cole, the librarian."

In the bleachers, a student gave a loud whoop, which gave Taylor a boost of confidence. She went on, "You may not know that I've started a rodeo club here at the high school." Another shout. She smiled, lifted her chin, squared her shoulders. "First of all, we're always welcoming new members. So if you're interested, see me after this assembly. Just as importantly, we're going to be holding some fundraising events."

Silence.

Raven was beside her. She hadn't even noticed him moving.

"Would you allow me to speak, Ms. Cole?" he asked.

His formal manners caught Taylor off guard, but she nodded,

her head bobbing quickly. She took a step to her right, shifting the others over as well.

Raven's voice came through the speakers, friendly and confident. "These aren't your grandmother's fundraisers. We ain't holding bake sales or car washes. You are invited to participate in the Prescott High School Rodeo Club's inaugural rodeo competition."

To Taylor's surprise, the students in the bleachers sat up a little straighter and leaned forward in reaction to Raven's words.

"Help me out, Henry," Raven said. "What events will we have?"

Henry was at the podium in a flash. "Glad you asked, my man."

Taylor chuckled on the inside, but maintained her composure on the outside.

Henry said, "We'll have barrel racing, steer and team roping, and maybe bronc riding if we can get it through our insurance people."

A few kids laughed, and Taylor started to relax. If nothing else, students were listening. They might get a few sign-ups after all.

"Any other details, Ms. Cole?" Henry said.

Olivia arrived at the podium next. "May I?"

Taylor nodded.

"The entry fee is fifteen dollars for each event. You can enter as many events as you like. There will be prizes. And remember, it's all for a good cause."

Judd inched closer to Taylor. "You look like you're in complete shock," he said through clenched teeth. Almost giddy at that point, Taylor thought he'd make a good ventriloquist.

"I am." Following his lead, she kept her lips still.

"I am, too," he said. "This is great. You've barely had to speak."

"Truer words were never spoken," Taylor said. A fit of giggles threatened to take over. Her shoulders threatened to shake with hilarity. But then, another surprise quelled the giggles. Zion stood at the microphone. Taylor felt her body freeze. His first word, "Yo," made Taylor think she would faint on the spot. "What's up Prescott High School," he said, and much to Taylor's surprise, the students cheered.

"Listen, y'all," Zion went on. "These events are going to be off the hook. I know my teammate, Olivia, mentioned prizes. There's also going to be *sur*prises. You guys have got to come check it out. You won't be disappointed. We got sign-up sheets down here."

He held up the clipboard Taylor had set up, and she wondered how he'd gotten it. Before she had too much time to think about it, though, Ernie was back, and she, Judd, and the rodeo club members were shuffling off to the side.

"Sounds like a great time!" Ernie said. "I know we have lots of talented horsemen and horsewomen in the audience, so I hope to see some of you signing up to support your fellow students. And Ms. Cole and Officer O'Connor. Assembly dismissed. Come on down and sign up."

The chattering resumed as students stood and stretched. Watching the door, Taylor saw hordes of students flowing out of it. Disappointment settled on her shoulders. But then Judd nudged her, and when she looked at him, he pointed his chin toward a small group forming, clustering around Zion, who held the clipboard so people could write on the sign-up sheet. Taylor felt her mouth drop open. "No way. They're signing up."

She could hear emotion clogging her voice, and her throat felt tight when Judd said, "They sure are."

"Any idea what surprises he was referring to?"

"None whatsoever."

Chapter Eighteen

JUDD

Still riding high from the success of the assembly and Taylor's reaction, Judd didn't even notice the volume was turned up on the police scanner in his patrol car until he heard the hot tones come through. The assured voice of a dispatcher followed: "All units, we have a two seventy-three in progress. Requesting an available unit to nine forty-five West Creek Drive. RP states her parents are fighting and throwing things. That's a two seventy-three at nine forty-five West Creek Drive."

Two seventy-three. That was a domestic violence call.

Judd should ignore it and head straight home. He wasn't on shift, so no one was counting on him to show up. But domestic violence calls were the most dangerous for cops. And he *knew* it wasn't a coincidence that he got into the car just as the call came out. It was a sign. He flipped the switch for the lights and sirens, made a quick U-turn, and heard the sound of his tires peeling out as he floored it and headed toward the address.

Surprised he was the first one there, Judd thought again that his presence was meant to be. After throwing the car into park, he jumped out and ran the short distance to the door. Instead of hearing the sounds of a fight in progress (yelling, crying, furniture and dishes hitting the walls), he heard nothing at all. That scared him even more than all those other sounds would have.

He knocked on the door. "This is the police. Anybody home?" More silence. He knocked again, harder. "Anybody home?"

Still nothing. Judd raised his arm to knock again, and nearly jumped when the door opened. At first he thought it had opened on its own, but then he looked down and realized a little girl, maybe six or seven, stood there. She looked up at him, her eyes wide in her pale face.

"Hi," he said. "Are your parents home?"

The little girl nodded. "They're home."

"Do you think I could talk to them?"

The little girl shook her head. If it were possible, her eyes got even bigger. "No, I don't think so. They're havin' a fight. My mama says she can't have a conversation when she's fightin' with daddy. I'm supposed to watch some cartoons."

She gestured at the living room behind her. The TV was on, volume low, the bright colors and singsong voices in stark contrast to the eerie silence he'd heard from outside.

"What's your name?"

"Lily." She held out her hand to shake.

"Judd."

"Nice to meet you."

"Likewise." He considered asking her to go and get her parents, but he couldn't be certain what she would find. "Do you think it would be all right if I came in, took a look around, maybe tried to talk to your parents, myself?"

Her mouth formed a little *O*, and she shook her head, fast. "No. I don't think it would be all right."

Judd heard sirens approaching, and a second later, the sound of another car pulling into the driveway. A car door slammed, and footsteps approached. It was Judd's friend Nicky — Judd could hear him speaking into his portable radio, telling dispatch where he was.

Surprise registered in his expression when he saw Judd, but he got right to business. "Whatcha got?"

Judd gave him a quick synopsis. "So, I haven't looked around yet." He turned to Lily. "This is my good friend Nicky. Why don't I wait with you while Nicky takes a look around?"

Lily nodded, and her expression became grim. "Nicky, you might want to get out your taser."

Judd and Nicky exchanged a look before Nicky disappeared into the house. More sirens, more footsteps, more cops. Within a matter of minutes, they'd sorted out that the little girl's parents had gotten into an argument about who had used the frying pan last. Each of them blamed the other, and neither of them wanted to wash it so they could start cooking dinner. The wife had picked up the frying pan and hit her husband on the side of the head with it.

Naturally, that enraged him, and he grabbed the closest weapon he could find: a two-pronged serving fork. He tried to hit his wife with it, and ended up slicing her arm with one of the tines. Naturally, that enraged the wife, who began swinging madly with the dirty frying pan. Eventually, she knocked him out. Then she went into the bathroom to clean herself up.

As wrapped up as she was in the first-aid process, she claimed, she didn't hear Judd banging on the front door. The husband came to about halfway through the wife's telling of the story. He blamed her for the entire mess, starting with the dirty pan. Because the husband had lost consciousness, Nicky called an ambulance to take him to the hospital. Just as the paramedics were closing the doors on the back of the ambulance, the wife murmured, "Oh. Maybe I *did* use the pan last. I just remembered I cooked a cheese crisp for lunch."

A few minutes later, Judd was in his car about to leave when Nicky knocked on his window. As Judd rolled it down, he noticed Nicky's eyebrows were drawn together.

"What's up, man? Everything okay?"

Hands on his hips, Nicky said, "I don't know. Is it?"

"I thought you guys had it under control. I was going to head home."

"What are you doing here, O'Connor?"

Oh. "I was on my way home, and I heard the call come out on the scanner. I was close."

His friend was nodding, now, like Judd's explanation was exactly what he expected. "Right. But you're not on patrol. At least, you're not supposed to be. You're supposed to be taking it easy. Chilling out."

Judd felt his hackles rising, and even though he knew his quick anger response was the reason he was off patrol, he felt powerless to stop it. "So you're telling me that if you were driving home, in uniform, in your patrol car, and you heard that call come out, you would've gone straight home?"

Nicky held up his hands, surrendering. "Look. I'm not saying that. All I'm saying is, we're worried about you."

Judd literally saw red — it colored the edges of his vision. "'We,' huh? You guys have been talking about me?"

Nicky, obviously exasperated, shook his head and pinched the bridge of his nose. "I'm glad you came. I am. We both know any domestic violence call could get ugly, quick. But also, you need to give yourself that mental break, so you can come back to work. Like, full-time."

"I just realized I have somewhere to be." Judd knew it was childish, but he rolled up his window and started backing up without a proper goodbye.

And he *had* just remembered he had somewhere to be: He had completely forgotten about the celebratory dinner date he and Taylor planned. He checked the time. If he hit all green lights, he'd be able to change and pick her up on time. Just barely. Feeling sick to his stomach, he drove away. In the rearview mirror, he saw Nicky watching him.

TAYLOR

As far as Taylor was concerned, dinner wasn't nearly enough to properly celebrate the day's successes. After school, she bought the sexiest set of lingerie she'd ever dared to put on, and went home to prepare for dinner ... and whatever came after. Everything would be perfect.

She'd figured out the lacy, strappy contraption, and felt ultra feminine and powerful.

On the dining room table, she set a bottle of expensive bourbon, a thank-you card, champagne in a bucket of ice, and two glasses.

After arranging and rearranging the items, she finally forced herself to sit. She tried to read a magazine while she waited for Judd, but she found she couldn't settle. Even though her eyes skimmed the words in an article, her brain didn't register them.

Where *was* he? It was unusual for him to be any later than five minutes early. She picked up her phone and went back through their text conversation to make sure she wasn't misremembering the time. She wasn't. She put her phone back down.

Judd finally knocked at exactly the time on which they'd agreed, and when Taylor opened the door, he rushed in as if he were late.

"Everything okay?" Taylor asked.

In response, Judd wrapped his arms around her waist and brought his mouth to hers, kissing her with so much intensity she felt weak in the knees — something she'd always considered a figure of speech, rather than reality.

"Everything's fine, now that I'm here."

Taylor found his behavior a bit puzzling. The borderline lateness, and the urgency, were unlike him. Before she had a chance to ask him about it, though, he looked over her shoulder at the spread on the table. "Is that champagne?"

Taylor set aside her uneasy feeling, chalking it up to nerves about giving Judd the gift ... and the potential for him to see her in her lingerie. "It is. I also got you a little something, to thank you."

He took her hand and led her over to the table. "The expression on your face today, when you flipped through two pages of signups for our first event, was thanks enough," he said. "But this bourbon is a really great addition."

"Oh, good. I didn't know what to buy."

He picked up the bottle and ran his thumb over the label. "This was a good choice."

"Good. Still, here's no way I could ever get you a gift that measures up to you helping me with this club."

Judd set down the bottle and took her hands in his. "It's just a small measure of how much I believe in you. From our first conversation, I knew you were special. You're going to do great things, and if I can play even a small part in helping you get there, it's my absolute honor."

Taylor felt tears spring to her eyes. "I appreciate it more than you know. We'd better drink that champagne before you make me all emotional."

Judd removed the cork and Taylor poured the champagne.

"To an opening day that shattered expectations," Judd said, lifting his glass.

Taylor added, "To the best rodeo club co-leader a girl could ask for."

They tapped their glasses together and drank. The champagne bubbled on Taylor's tongue; the sensation extra pleasant in that sweet moment. Glass still in hand, she leaned forward and brushed her lips over Judd's. It started as just a whisper of a kiss, but the quiet humming sound he made signified it would become more. Judd set down his own glass, and then took Taylor's and set it down, too ... which she found an almost unbearable turn-on.

Now free to do as they pleased, Judd's hands wandered from Taylor's waist to her back, pulling her against him. Her own hands seemed to move of their own accord, smoothing over his chest and down to his stomach. She couldn't believe how muscular he was, and all she could think about was feeling his skin against hers. "Maybe we should skip dinner," she murmured, surprised and pleased at how sensual she sounded.

His low, quiet laugh in response sent tingles over her skin. "I think we have time for dinner ... and maybe some more of this."

Between words, he used his lips to explore, moving them along the sensitive area underneath her chin, and then on to her neck and collarbone. She got a little thrill when she felt his breath on her chest, thinking about the lacy bra under her shirt. "I mean, we could cancel our reservations and eat at home," she whispered.

"You're right," he said, his mouth still against her skin. "Hold on."

His left arm remained around her waist, and he used his right hand to pull his phone out of his back pocket. He tapped the screen a few times, and Taylor heard the phone ringing. When a woman answered, Judd smiled at Taylor, giving her butterflies. His eyes on hers, he said, "I need to cancel my reservation for this evening. O'Connor, party of two."

Those words caused a fresh round of butterflies. *O'Connor, party of two.* Judd disconnected and set his phone on the table. "Now. Where were we?"

Judd's hands were under her shirt, against her skin. They made their way up to her breasts, and both Judd and Taylor exhaled as he caressed them.

"This feels lacy," he said.

She smiled against his mouth. "Good detective skills."

His thumbs brushed over her nipples, and she gasped.

"Can I see?"

The nerves from earlier suddenly gone, Taylor said, "I thought you'd never ask."

He unbuttoned the bottom button on her shirt, and then the second one. "Does that mean you put it on just for me?"

"I did."

He unfastened the next two before putting his hands inside her shirt again. "I just want to feel this one more time."

Taylor surprised herself by giggling. She couldn't remember the last time she'd had this much fun making out with someone. Finally, he finished with the buttons. His hands were on her breasts again. "Gorgeous."

"I bought it just for tonight."

Judd made a low, guttural sound. "I was talking about you, not the bra. But it *is* very nice."

He pressed his hips against hers.

She could feel his arousal. "My turn."

His chiseled muscles looked even better than they felt, if that were possible. His skin was smooth, with a patch of dark hair on his chest, and a trail beneath his bellybutton. His bicep, chest, six pack — his entire upper body — was absolutely edible. "Talk about gorgeous."

"You don't know how long I've been waiting for this."

A thrill rushed down Taylor's center. "Oh, I think I have a pretty good idea."

"Take off your shoes." Something about the command drove Taylor crazy, and she managed to comply while letting her lips taste his and her fingers feel the ridges of his six-pack. He pulled her pants over her hips, and with his help, she managed to step out of them somewhat gracefully. She went to work unbuckling his belt and unbuttoning and unzipping his jeans.

"Now yours." He stepped back and pulled off his own jeans. She could see a bulge in his boxer shorts. "When do we take those off?"

He laughed, a low, satisfied sound that both delighted her and turned her on.

"Should we take this to the bedroom?"

"We should."

"Lead the way," he said. "I want to look at you."

Taylor had never felt this powerful with a man before. She took her time walking toward the bedroom, swaying her hips more than she normally would. When she reached the door, she gestured for Judd to go in ahead of her. But he had other plans. He backed her up to the door. With a hand on either side of her head, he leaned in and kissed her, the length of his body pressed against hers. Once she relaxed into the kissing, he started to touch her again. His fingertips trailed over her shoulders, her collarbone, her breasts. They came to rest at the top edge of her panties. "I'm so horny, I'm tempted to tear these right off," he said. "But I don't want to ruin them. I plan on seeing you in them again."

He cupped her butt, then grabbed one of her legs and wrapped it around his waist. She could really feel him then. The pressure was building. He devoured her mouth, feasting on it like he was a starving man. Just when she was thinking she couldn't stand not to have him inside her for another moment, he said, "I want you so badly."

He took a step back, and surprised her by pulling down his underwear and stepping out of them. She couldn't help but stare, and found herself saying, "Wow," before she even realized it.

"I had the same thought."

She started to reach back to unhook her bra, but he reached out and touched her arm.

"Wait. I'd just like to look at you."

While she leaned against the door, he took his time looking her over. If that moment had transpired with anyone else, any other time, Taylor would have found it nerve-racking. Intimidating. Terrifying. But just then, with Judd, she felt confident. Beautiful. And totally aroused. Without another word, he took her hand and led her toward the bed. "*Now* we can take it off."

As he reached behind her to unhook the clasp, he brushed his lips over the swell of one breast. He took her nipple between his teeth, gently. Again, he surprised her — he draped her bra over the back of the chair next to her vanity. He hooked his thumbs into the waistband of her panties, and as he pulled them down, he ran his palms down the outside of her legs. Standing up, he brushed his hand over her center. Her body literally ached for him. She couldn't go another moment without taking him inside her.

"I've always thought you're so beautiful," he said. "I just never had the guts to say it. But now, seeing you here, like this, it would be a crime not to. You are beautiful, Taylor Cole, inside and out."

Her heart might actually be melting. They were kissing, their hands were on each other's bodies, and God, did he feel good.

"I want to make love to you," he whispered.

Taylor decided then there wasn't room for anyone else in her life — ever again.

"I want to make love to you, too."

While they were still face to face, eye to eye, he entered her. They moved together, and within seconds, they both shattered with release.

———

*J*UDD

Afterward, as they lay together, still gazing into one another's eyes, Judd felt totally wrecked. The whole experience – showing up at Taylor's house, wanting her more than he ever wanted anyone in his whole life, realizing she bought pretty and un-sensible underwear just for him, and then making mind-blowing love — had wrecked him.

And it had given him an appetite.

"You know what I think?" he said. Taylor shook her head, licked her lips, swallowed. "I just worked up an appetite, and we should order in."

Her laughter surprised him, and made him feel like his heart belonged in one of those ethereal paintings where shafts of light shoot from a person's chest. "I think you're right. What are you in the mood for?"

He knew it was cheesy, even as he said it, but he couldn't help himself. "I'm pretty sure I'm in the mood for a second helping of the Taylor Cole special. But for now, should we order from Rita's?"

Smiling, she said, "Sounds good. I'm famished."

Needing to clear his head, Judd offered to pick up the food. He hadn't experienced a reaction this strong to a woman ... well, ever. Often, after sex (he was introspective enough to realize he was thinking of intercourse with other women as sex, whereas he thought of it as making love with Taylor), he felt ready for solitude. At the moment, despite feeling completely satisfied by the mind-blowing lovemaking, Judd wanted more Taylor. More of her laughs, more of her kissing, more of her heavy-lidded pleasure when he entered her. And that scared him.

Alone time was the absolute last thing he *wanted*, but he knew he *needed* it.

"I will let you go get the food, only because I am currently a puddle. A very satisfied, exhausted puddle. I don't think I could walk if I tried. And, if I walk into Rita's looking like this, she's gonna know."

Judd put a hand on Taylor's hip, ran it up to her rib cage, and caressed her breasts again. "I think you look beautiful." He kissed her. "You have until I get back — and we eat — to recover."

Laughter followed him all the way out the front door. At Rita's, he didn't even have to wait for the food. The bell jingled overhead as he walked in, and she placed the bags on the counter before he made it across the room.

"Dinner for two?" Rita raised an eyebrow at him, and Judd kicked himself for the involuntary blush he felt creeping up his neck.

"Yep."

Eyes twinkling, Rita wagged a finger at him. "Don't you play coy with me, Judd O'Connor. I know this isn't for you and your sister. She's already been in tonight, grabbing an order for one."

Rita, ever a romantic, took a moment to publicly mourn Katy's singledom, making the sign of the cross before her shoulders slumped and her eyes went downcast. But she recovered quickly, returning to interrogation mode.

"It's Taylor Cole, isn't it?" In the space of time that transpired before he could answer, she pointed at him. "That's it! I *knew* it! I knew it the moment I saw the two of you bumping into each other in this very doorway."

She raised her arms and turned her face toward the ceiling, thanking the heavens. "Finally! *Finally* we've got some romance around here."

From his spot at the end of the counter, Sal grunted. Rita dropped her arms and looked at Judd again, smiling broadly. "I hope you'll mention Rita's Diner at your wedding." She gestured at their surroundings. "The place where the story began. The place where the magic happened. Which one do you like better?"

Judd handed her his credit card and leaned a hip on the counter, crossing his arms. "First option. Judging by the way tonight is going, the magic happens back at her place."

Rita threw back her head and laughed, the kind of loud, unencumbered laugh it was impossible not to join in. She handed the card back to Judd, wiping her eyes. He left a fifty percent tip and winked at Rita as he slid the receipt across the counter.

Judd had spent the drive to Rita's in complete shock, unable to form any coherent thoughts. On the way back to Taylor's, he tried to dial in on what he was feeling. Yes, he liked her. *Really* liked her. Didn't his continued commitment to the rodeo club prove that? And he wanted her. His reaction to the whole lacy-bra-and-panties scenario proved that. But just how much did he want her? How much did he like her?

Was it possible he felt the way he did only because he wasn't working his *real* job — patrol? Was he simply looking for excitement? And what would happen when he went back on the road?

The women he had dated before were incompatible with police life. They were often needy and demanding, using their purported feelings for him as excuses for starting fights about working late or getting called in. Judd sighed. Could Taylor be different? She certainly *seemed* different. His mind flashed on an image of her, laying in bed. His heart sped up.

By then, he had made his way back to her house, and didn't feel like he had gotten anything figured out. If it were possible, he felt even more uncertain. But then he parked, and saw her standing in her open doorway, the light from the house silhouetting her body. She wore loose pants — Katy would call them lounge pants — and a snug tank top, and she was waiting. For him. All the questions fell away. The answer — Taylor — remained.

When he reached her, she lifted her face to kiss him, and he found himself melting into the contact. His stomach growled, and she ended the kiss. "We'd better eat."

She took one of the bags from him and he said, "The secret's out."

They walked in together, and as they started arranging their food on the table, he thought how nice the routine was ... how nice it would be to do every night.

"What secret?"

Judd gave Taylor a recap of his trip to Rita's. "So, she's giving herself — or the diner — credit for getting us together. She wants us to talk about it at the wedding."

Judd had enough composure not to slap his hand over his mouth. What was he thinking, mentioning a wedding, even if it was Rita's idea? Fortunately, Taylor just smiled. "That's a small town for you. Gossip and weddings. Let me get some plates."

"So," Taylor said, her gaze boring into his once they sat down, "I think we need to talk business."

Judd had been about to take a bite of his sandwich, but he put it down.

"Rodeo club," she said.

He felt himself relax.

"Geez, I could see you get real tense right there," Taylor said, amusement shining in her eyes. "Did you think I wanted to talk about the wedding?"

Again, her response caught him off guard. "I don't even know," he said. "But you're right, hearing you say you wanted to talk about business definitely had me nervous for a second."

He picked up his sandwich again and took a giant bite.

"Almost lost your appetite, didn't you?" she teased.

Judd pointed at his full mouth. "Mouth full. Can't answer." She sure looked like she was enjoying herself.

"Anyway. Thanks to our amazing assembly today, if everyone who signed up pays an entry fee, we'll have enough cash to enter a rodeo competition in a couple of weeks. I think, if we do have events every month, we'd have enough to enter the bigger competitions in the next couple of months."

"So what are you thinking?"

"I don't know. Do you think we can do it?"

"Are you kidding? Of course we can! News about our events is only going to spread. We are only going to do better. And, as long as we can keep our rodeo club members out of trouble, then we should be home free. We could even win. What's the prize?"

"Wait. Back it up. What do you mean, 'keep the rodeo club members out of trouble'? Do you know something I don't?"

Judd shrugged, suddenly uncomfortable. He wasn't ready to tell Taylor he'd seen Raven and Zion in an obvious drug deal, or that Ernie had asked him to investigate. "Nah. Just speaking in general terms."

The food was gone, and typically in such a situation, Judd would find an excuse to head home. He realized he felt so comfortable in Taylor's presence, he wanted to stay. The conversation flowed from topic to topic, rodeo club to horseback riding to working at the school. At one point stood up to collect the packaging from dinner, and Judd joined her, carrying their plates to the sink, while Taylor threw away the trash. Meanwhile, they continued talking, and when she asked if he wanted to go into the living room, "Sure," was the most natural response.

"I'm still feeling celebratory. I'm going to open a bottle of wine. Want a glass?"

"Actually, I'll pour myself some of that fancy bourbon you got me."

Judd knew having a drink was committing to at least another hour with Taylor, and instead of wondering exactly when he could leave, he found himself thinking about how far he could stretch the evening. They settled on the couch, then Taylor smiled at him across the space.

Judd thought, *This is everything.*

He woke before Taylor the next morning, and lay there without moving, taking in every centimeter of the work of art he was falling for. He could lay there forever with her. That is, if he didn't have to go to the bathroom. Resisting was almost impossible when he returned from the bathroom and found that she had turned toward his empty spot. He lay next to her, taking care not to disturb what looked like a very peaceful rest. He brought himself closer. Her eyes fluttered open, and he watched, intoxicated, as they focused on his. She lifted the covers and looked down at where their hips met, a husky early-morning half-laugh escaping. "Well, good morning to you, too."

Judd's hand found her breasts, her skin warm against his palm. At the contact, she moaned a sound so sensual, it was all Judd could do not to flip her over and take her then and there.

"Good morning," he said. "I would apologize for waking you, but ..."

He didn't bother finishing the sentence. Instead, he took her nipple between his teeth and teased it until she moved against him.

"I don't mind," she murmured. "It's nice, actually."

She gasped when he entered her, and they moved together as if they'd always been that way — in sync. She cried out and released, and that sent him swiftly over the edge, as well. Arms around each other, they rode the waves of the aftershocks.

"I take it you're a morning person?" she said.

"You could say that." His stomach growled, insistent. "So is my stomach. You hungry?"

"I like to have waffles on Saturdays." At that, Taylor pulled the covers over most of her face so just her eyes were showing.

Smiling, Judd pulled down the top of the covers to expose her mouth and kissed her. "Then I like waffles on Saturday mornings, too."

They went into the kitchen to make breakfast, Taylor in a light, satin robe, and Judd in his boxer shorts and undershirt. Just as they had made love that morning, they moved around the kitchen as if they'd been doing it for a lifetime. She whipped up a batter while he sliced strawberries and put on a pan for bacon and sausage. They talked. About the weather, the school, baking club. Finally, when they'd eaten the waffles, the fruit, and the meat, washed the dishes, and tidied the kitchen, Judd said, "I wish I could stay here all day. Not only because I'd kill for another twenty-four hours with you, but also because I know what's coming from my sister. And I really should man up and go home, get it over with."

"You think she's going to give you a hard time?"

Judd moved around the counter to take Taylor in his arms again. "Oh, I know she's going to give me a hard time. I can't remember the last time I spent the night at anyone's house. Besides my friend Nicky's." When Taylor's eyes narrowed, Judd laughed. "Nicky as in Nicholas. He's a dude. And it's a long story."

"I'm flattered."

He kissed her nose. "You should be."

Judd made it all the way home before realizing he hadn't even thought about his police scanner for the past eighteen hours. When he was with Taylor, he didn't think of anything else. Even as he felt his body sinking into that idea, his mind grateful for the reprieve, he wondered if this thing between them — whatever it was — was going to prove too much of a distraction. Still, as Katy met him at the barn and gave him the ribbing he'd anticipated, he found that he hadn't felt this happy, or relaxed, in as long as he could remember. And that was a welcome change.

Chapter Nineteen

TAYLOR

"The first thing I want to say to you guys is, *wow*," Taylor told the rodeo club members at their next meeting. "I am so impressed with the confidence and poise you demonstrated Friday. If I hadn't seen it with my own eyes, I wouldn't believe we got so many signups for our first event. Fifty-two, to be exact."

"Are you getting emotional, Ms. Cole?" Raven grinned at her from across the room.

The kid might still be in his cool-guy stance, arms crossed, one hip propped against the checkout counter as if he could jet out of the room at any moment, but he wasn't fooling her.

"I might be, and for good reason. You didn't tell me you're such a great salesman."

Raven made a dismissive gesture. "I didn't think I *had* to tell you. It's the word on the street."

Taylor didn't miss the look Judd sent her then, but she didn't let her gaze stray from Raven. "Well, now I'm going to be depending on you every time we have a sale."

"Fine by me." He slid onto the stool then, and put his elbows on the counter.

"And the rest of you," Taylor said. "You guys were on fire. Those signups got fast and furious, and you kept your wits about you. I wasn't sure these events would be popular enough to raise enough money for competition fees, but thanks to you, we are going to have more than enough. How does everyone feel about that?" The girls and Henry cheered. There may have been some squealing. Raven and Zion looked at each other, smug smiles on their faces.

"I take it you're excited about competing?"

A chorus of affirmative answers followed, and in the chaos, Taylor looked over at Judd again. Her body actually warmed at the way he was looking at her, with a mixture of affection and pride.

"Sounds like a yes to me," he said.

"Good," she said.

"We'll dedicate today's meeting to planning our first fundraiser. Then, for our next meeting, we'll meet at the Mint Creek Ranch for practice and a mock competition ... because we have only a few weeks until our first real competition."

"A few weeks?" Henry squeaked.

The girls squealed, and the boys started acting out the various events. Raven held up one hand, pantomiming riding a bull. Zion lassoed an imaginary steer, and Henry jumped off an imaginary horse, tying a calf's feet and finishing the motion with a flourish. The girls had finished their squealing and cheered for the boys' accomplishments.

Judd shot Taylor another look, an eyebrow raised. Taylor's mind flashed to a future where she and Judd looked at each other across the room, over the heads of a whole gaggle of children. Their children. In that moment, she knew with certainty that he would be a great dad. She imagined little girls with his eyes, little boys with his nose.

Then she panicked. That future seemed wonderful. Picture-perfect. But it wasn't possible, she reminded herself. She thought back to how she felt the past Friday, when the assembly had been such a success. It was as fulfilling as having a family, wasn't it? Being an entrepreneur was all she'd ever dreamed of, and she couldn't give her all to a business *and* to a family. Judd was now looking at her carefully, most likely wondering what was going through her mind. She offered him a reassuring smile. He smiled back, and she felt a pang of grief, knowing they would never share that future, with the cozy living room, the couch pillows in disarray, the kids playing on the floor. They may never live it, but it wouldn't hurt to fantasize.

———

The day of the first fundraising rodeo event dawned bright and hot. Taylor awoke to a text from Judd: *Today is day! Fingers crossed.*

She responded, *So glad you are in this with me.*

Check-in started at seven-thirty at the Mint Creek Ranch arena. Taylor's heart leapt when she saw Judd pulling into the arena's parking area ahead of her at five after seven. She parked next to him and her heart leapt again when he held out a cup of coffee. She started to take it from him but he shook his head and said, "Payment first."

She felt so much like smiling that kissing him was a little tricky, but as soon as their lips met, kissing him felt like the only thing to do.

"Now you can have it." He released the cup, and she took a sip.

"That really hits the spot. I've been up since five, thinking about all the last-minute pointers I want to give the kids."

Judd grimaced. "I assume you probably drank a full pot of coffee already. Maybe I should have brought you espresso."

"At this point, I would say my body is eighty percent coffee as it is. One more cup isn't going to affect the balance."

"We'll see about that." He leaned in for another kiss, and Taylor found it fortifying.

At seven-fifteen, trucks pulling horse trailers started pulling up. Tessa and Cody Davis, the ranch's owners, sat side-by-side on the top rail of the fence, elbows on their knees. As truck after truck pulled in, Cody whistled.

"I'd say you're looking at a pretty good turnout, Taylor. I'm impressed."

"I am, too," she said.

The rodeo club kids showed up around the same time, their arrival sprinkled among those of the participants. Each one of them approached Taylor and Judd with the same surprised, excited expression, eyes wide.

"I can't believe this!" Olivia said, and Zion said, "This is fire, man. I know people signed up, but man, I wasn't expecting them all to *show* up."

By eight fifteen, all the competitors had checked in. Forty-eight individuals, many of whom signed up for two or three events.

"Seeing dollar signs?" Judd asked Taylor at one point.

"Yes, and it's making me downright giddy."

"You should be." He pressed a kiss to her temple. "I am, too."

So this is what a partnership could feel like. Sure, Judd volunteered to help her with the rodeo club, but he's genuinely excited because of how much it means to me.

At eight-thirty sharp — right on time — a student sang the national anthem. Then, Judd's friend Nicky, who'd volunteered to emcee, said into the microphone, "Let the games begin."

Taylor felt goosebumps prickle her skin. This was *her* event. It was the first major step she'd taken in making her business a reality — and it was off to an incredible start.

———

*J*UDD

By the end of the day, Judd was so tired he felt bleary-eyed. The event had gone off without a hitch and brought in more than a thousand dollars.

"There are definitely a few things we can do differently next time," Taylor said as they raked the arena after everyone was gone. "I got some really great feedback, but I'm almost in disbelief at how well that went."

"We'll just keep learning every time," Judd said. "I would definitely call the day a success, though."

Not to mention how much fun Judd had watching Taylor throughout the day. In her element, she went from task to task, moving with confidence and ease, friendly and assertive, and so damn sexy. All of that would have ignited Judd's fire, but all of it while Taylor wore jeans that fit her like a glove? He was head over heels.

Finished raking the arena, they hauled the drag to the shed next to the barn. Taylor went to leave the shed, but Judd caught her by the wrist. "Hold on. There's something I want to tell you. She made an adorable, surprised, "Oh!" sound, but her body was soft and pliable against his when he pulled her in.

"I thought you had something to tell me."

Judd kissed her, then grabbed her by the waist and lifted her onto a saddle stand. "This is part of it." He kissed her again, then brought his lips to her neck. "The other part of it is that I couldn't keep my eyes off you today." His lips made their way to her collarbone, and he used one hand to unclasp her bra. She moaned, a quiet sound he captured with his mouth, while his hand wandered up to cup her breast. "I loved watching you work."

"Well, thank you, Officer O'Connor," she said, her voice even huskier as he lifted her shirt and found her nipple with his mouth.

"You are very welcome."

Breathless, Taylor said, "Should we maybe finish this up somewhere a little more private?"

"No," Judd said, pulling her off the saddle stand and unbuttoning her jeans. "You in these jeans all day has made it impossible for me to think about anything other than getting them off you."

He pulled them down, all the way to her ankles, and set her back on the saddle stand. As turned on as he already was, finding her wet and slippery didn't surprise him at all. "Seems like you're ready to finish up right here, too," he told her. He unbuckled his belt and felt himself spring free when he pulled down his own pants.

"Heck yeah, I'm ready," she told him through half closed eyes. "I was just going for propriety."

"Forget propriety," he told her. Then he buried himself in her and brought his lips to hers with more intensity than he ever had. She moaned again, the sound trapped between them. He almost came then and there. Less than a second later, she was undone, her nails digging into his back as she clung to him. The slick, sweaty skin-on-skin contact was almost unbearable. He let go, and poured himself into her, her name on his lips.

Chapter Twenty

*T*AYLOR

The kids could rodeo.

In all the excitement following the first fundraising event, the Davises had offered to open up the arena every day after school for the rodeo club to practice, and to let the club use their horses and tack.

Taylor spent Monday taking care of the paperwork — scheduling transportation to the ranch, printing out liability waivers, and creating schedules the kids could take home. To her disbelief, all five club members turned in their paperwork Tuesday morning, which meant they could start practicing that afternoon.

"This place is gorgeous," Taylor said to Judd when they got there, a few minutes ahead of the bus. "I didn't take the time to look around last weekend, but look at these rolling hills and the granite boulders and the old trees. I think I'm in love."

"It *is* gorgeous," Judd agreed. "And it's perfect for our practices."

The bus pulled into the ranch, then, and Zion came down the bus steps, fanning himself. "It is *hot* up in here."

"Look over there," Taylor said, pointing to the puffy monsoon clouds forming in the east. "We might get some rain. Let's get started, in case the storm does roll in. Cody and Tessa should be here in a minute, but they said we can start putting on bridles."

"Let's go," Judd said. He gestured for the kids to go into the barn first, and when they'd all walked past, he swatted Taylor on the ass, making her yelp.

Cody walked up. "I'm excited to see you guys work today," he said to Taylor. "Should we saddle up?"

From all her talks with the library nerds, Taylor knew Olivia, Scarlett, and Henry had been around horses. They set to work right away, following Cody's directions. What she didn't know was that Zion possessed an unexpected ease with the animals and their gear. He talked to the horses like they were old friends, and handled the tack like he'd been doing it all his life.

"You have horses, Z?" Judd asked as Zion mounted one of Cody's horses.

"Nah," Zion said. "But my grandma used to, before she passed. She lived up in Flagstaff and we'd go up there on school breaks. We rode every day when we could."

Raven was a whole different story. He hung back, sticking to the edges of the barn, watching the horses carefully, as if they might trample him at any moment.

"These things look way bigger in real life than they do on YouTube," he said.

"But you just hung out with them over the weekend," Taylor said. "Didn't they seem this big then?"

Raven's eyes darted around the barn. "Nah, man. You didn't see me anywhere near these things on Saturday. I worked the snack bar, remember? I avoided the arena — and these monsters."

Taylor looked at Judd, who wore a surprised expression that matched the way she was feeling. The rest of the club members had apparently overheard the conversation and they gathered around Raven.

"I mean," Olivia said, "when you joined rodeo club, weren't you thinking horses would be involved?"

Raven's eyes were on Judd's when he said, "Obviously."

Judd spoke up then. "We're going to have to get you on a horse, dude."

"Do I have to?" the kid said, true fear making his voice tight.

"Not today," Taylor rushed to say. "But we do need all five of you to compete. Why don't you spend some time getting to know one of these horses today, and we'll go from there. Cody said Cinnamon is a calm, steady horse. Maybe Scarlett can walk you through a few basics while we finish saddling up."

A few minutes later, the group moved out to the arena, everyone on horseback except Raven, whose only assignment for the day was to get comfortable existing in the same space as the horses.

Taylor was expecting the kids to have some skills. But as they practiced, she found that when they'd talked to her in the library, they'd been humble.

Scarlett, for example, had not revealed that she was a crazy-fast barrel racer, that she could become one with a horse and ride it around those barrels lightning fast, her long braid flying behind her. Henry, usually quiet and unassuming, became a wizard when he had a lasso in his hand. He could rope a steer from any angle. And Olivia was a veritable horse whisperer. From where Taylor stood at one side of the arena, the girl looked more natural on horseback than she did on foot. Zion hadn't yet learned to rope, but he caught on fast as Cody showed him the fundamentals.

At one point, Taylor looked away from the center of the arena to see Judd, feet on the ground and the reins of a horse in his hands, standing next to Raven. The kid had relaxed considerably, and was even laughing at something Judd said to him. Taylor watched as Judd gradually moved the horse closer, shortening the reins until its head was right next to his shoulder.

Raven, who'd been chatting away, animated and smiling, seemed to notice the horse's proximity quite suddenly, and he jumped back, a hand over his heart. Taylor laughed out loud, and Raven glared at her from across the arena.

"Hey, man," he said, redirecting his glare to Judd. "Don't do me like that. You scared the crap out of me."

Taylor could hear the barely restrained laughter in Judd's voice.

"Sorry. I wanted you to see how harmless she is. She was so calm and quiet, you didn't even notice how close she'd gotten. But you could have reached out and touched her."

Raven shook his head, hand still on his chest. "I could have, dude. But I didn't want to. You almost gave me a heart attack."

"Want to pet her? You can rub her neck."

"Nah, man. Maybe next time, all right? She'll probably sense my nerves and kick the shit out of me."

Judd shook his head. "She may sense your nerves, but she won't kick you."

"Are you sure?"

"I'm, like, ninety-nine percent sure."

"Forget it, man," Raven said, taking another step back. "I'm not risking that one percent."

Judd shrugged. "Next time, then."

Raven nodded. "Fine. Next time."

The two of them stood there, both looking at the horse, who looked calm and perfectly still as if she realized the importance of the moment. After a couple of beats, Raven reached out and put a hand on her neck. Judd didn't react at all. He, too, stood perfectly still as Raven's hand moved down toward the horse's shoulder and back up toward her cheek.

Then, almost as if he was in a trance and hadn't realized he was petting the giant creature, Raven pulled his hand back.

"Wow," he said in an almost-whisper. "She's so soft."

Judd nodded. "She is. And she didn't kick the shit out of you."

"I'm going to get away from her before she does."

Again, Raven backed up, stopping only when he was outside of kicking range.

Judd gave him a single nod. "Well done. You were afraid, but you did it. Maybe next time, you get on?"

"I wasn't afraid," Raven said.

Judd shot Taylor a look, one eyebrow raised.

Raven said, "I was terrified. Absolutely petrified. But thanks. That was actually pretty cool."

Watching this interaction, Taylor felt herself falling even harder for Judd. He'd managed to keep the whole situation light while also helping Raven conquer his fear.

As their first practice session came to a close, Taylor had everyone circle up at one end of the arena. "You guys did great today," she said. "I do feel a little like some of you were holding back when you told me you know how to ride." The kids chuckled. "You guys are geniuses out there. We'll do more of the same tomorrow, and maybe we can get Raven on horseback?"

Raven looked at the ground, but the other kids whooped and cheered as if he'd already done it.

"No guarantees, guys," Raven said, and Judd said, "But we'll get him up there, right?"

"Come on," Taylor said. "Let's go put the gear away and brush these horses."

Cody, who'd stuck around for the whole practice, gave the kids instructions and then stood with Taylor to watch.

"Looks like you've got some potential on this team," he said. "I'm looking forward to seeing what they do."

Taylor nodded. "I'm excited, too. Thank you so much for letting us use your space and horses. We're going to owe you, big-time."

"Anything for the sport," Cody said. "I owe everything to the sport — even my marriage."

Taylor smiled. Cody and Tessa had met when she worked as a reporter for the local paper, the *Daily Dispatch*, and covered his bull-riding comeback tour. "Well, we appreciate it," she said.

"We'll get the last kid on horseback next time," Cody said.

"Speaking of Raven," Taylor said, "I haven't seen him since we came inside. I'd better go check and make sure his worst fear didn't come true. He could be laying in the arena, shit successfully kicked out of him."

Cody's laughter followed Taylor out of the barn. She heard Raven's and Judd's voices before she saw them. It sounded like they were just around the corner of the barn. Not wanting to interrupt their conversation, Taylor stopped walking and stood just outside the barn door.

"You can't make me do this," Raven said, urgency making his voice high-pitched and his words come fast.

"You're right," Judd said. "I can't. But listen. I know you've been up to something at the school, okay? Principal Vasquez knows it, too. He asked me to look into it."

Taylor's breath stopped. *Up to something?*

"I ain't scared of Principal Vasquez."

"I'm not saying you should be," Judd said. "What I'm saying is, you've got to stop. You're going to get caught — if not by me, then by someone else. You're putting yourself on the wrong path. This club will keep you out of trouble."

"I can keep myself out of trouble. I don't like horses, man."

"I know. I get it. But I think, with time, you can learn to like them. And I know you can make different, better choices with your life. I want to interact with you in rodeo club, not in juvie."

"Z said that if I don't come to rodeo club, you're going to arrest me."

Judd laughed. "That's not exactly what I said. Just keep showing up, okay?"

Taylor started seeing black spots around the edges of her vision, and realized she'd held her breath throughout that entire exchange. She backed up into the barn, simultaneously exhaling.

What was Judd talking about? What was Raven up to? And what had Judd said to Zion that resulted in him telling Raven Judd would arrest him if he didn't come to rodeo club? And, most important of all, why hadn't Judd mentioned any of this to Taylor?

Taylor had so many questions ... and only one person had the answers.

JUDD

The school bus drove away, the five rodeo club members safely inside after a successful practice. Once it was out of sight, Judd put an arm around Taylor's shoulders and squeezed. "I would say that practice went really well," he said.

"I would agree," she said. She kissed his cheek, and he felt himself leaning into the contact. "I have to say, I was very impressed with how you got Raven to pet that horse."

Judd smiled. "Thank you. We'll have him roping steers in no time."

"I'm confident in your skills, but I'm just happy with baby steps right now."

Judd didn't want the moment to end. He would be perfectly content to remain in that position, Taylor's body pressed against his as they looked down the Mint Creek Ranch's tree-lined driveway, forever.

But then she said, "I overheard you and Raven talking."

His confidence, which rose like a helium-inflated balloon when Raven finally put his hand on the horse's neck, burst, deflated, heading toward the ground. How much had she overheard?

"I didn't mean to eavesdrop," she rushed to add, her body still relaxed against his. "We were cleaning up and I realized I hadn't seen Raven. I wanted to make sure he was okay. I walked out of the barn and I could hear you guys talking. Anyway, where would Zion have gotten the impression that if they didn't come to club, you'd arrest them?"

Judd froze. He should tell her. He'd broken rules—he'd caught Zion and Raven in a drug deal before Ernie even came to him ... instead of threatening them and forcing them to join rodeo club, he should have started investigating, then.

While she waited for him to answer, the cicadas struck up their deafening song, the screeching sound making conversation nearly impossible. The leaves on the trees fluttered in the breeze. Judd took so long to answer that Taylor looked up at him and gave his waist a little squeeze.

A rabbit came out of the weeds at the edge of the driveway up ahead. It froze when it realized it was out in the open, then scampered across to the safety of the weeds on the other side.

He'd done the wrong thing for all the right reasons, Judd thought. To fill the rodeo club roster. To make Taylor happy. To help her turn her business dream into reality. To keep the two kids busy, so they'd be less likely to get into trouble.

But. As the school resource officer, he should have stayed above board.

As suddenly as they started, the cicadas went silent.

"Geez, my ears are ringing," Taylor said.

"Mine, too," Judd said. He could change the subject, talk about cicadas or the weather. He also knew Taylor was waiting for an answer.

"I'm sorry if it seemed shady," Judd said. "I never mentioned this to you because I didn't want to break Zion's trust. I don't know him *well*, but I've known him for a couple of years. He's part of a group of kids I play soccer with at the park when things are quiet on a shift. You should see him use his left foot. It's incredible." Taylor raised an eyebrow at him, and he said, "Sorry. Getting off track. The day of our first rodeo club meeting, when only the three library nerds showed up, I caught Zion and Raven in the breezeway, looking suspiciously like they were in the middle of a drug deal."

Now both of Taylor's eyebrows shot up and her mouth dropped open. "And you didn't tell me?"

Judd shook his head. "Like I said, I didn't want to break Zion's trust. Instead, I told them they both had to join the rodeo club. At the time, I had no idea Zion could ride. It just seemed having him join could be a solution in a couple of ways. One, we'd have enough members to make our club official. Two, it would give him something to be involved in. Keep his grades up. Which I thought would help keep him out of trouble."

"Okay," Taylor said, drawing out the word. "I just wish you'd told me. Not that I would've done anything differently, but it would've been nice to know you invited two delinquents to join the club."

"Every child delinquent is just a kid who needs more direction. I felt like we could give that to them."

"As much as I want to be mad at you for not telling me, I understand. But, as a cop, you couldn't really tell them you'd arrest them if they didn't come, could you?"

The little rabbit he'd seen before dashed out of the weeds again. Tentative, it hopped to the middle of the driveway and stopped.

Some of the anger that had boiled so close to the surface — before Judd became the school resource officer — started simmering. Not because Taylor was calling him out, but because she was right. And he was mad — at himself. "No. And that's not exactly what I said. I told them I would let that interaction slide if they came to club. But, Principal Vasquez called me into his office the other day. Asked me to investigate Raven. Supposedly there's some sort of drug ring at the school. And he's the ringleader."

Eyes downcast, Taylor sighed. "I never would have believed that when I first met him. But now that I've seen him in action, I can understand how he would attract sort of a following."

Good. She could see the nuances. She knew how rarely situations were strictly black-and-white.

"The investigative side of me is going crazy right now," Judd told her. "It's like a wild animal, trapped in a cage, rattling the bars. But the rodeo club advisor part of me is saying, 'Wait, if you track down Raven as the leader of this ring, he won't be able to participate in rodeo club.'"

The beat of silence something.

"So what are you going to do?"

Judd knew his answer was important. "Well, I'm just going to have to go deeper. Like I said, a kid doing bad stuff usually just needs someone to help him turn things around. I just hope I can find the adults Raven is dealing with, so I don't have to take him down."

———

Taylor

Whatever was going on with Judd, Raven, and Zion, Taylor knew she had to keep her eye on the prize. Driving home after practice Tuesday, she told herself that even though she had so much wrapped up in the rodeo club, she had to run it like a business — without emotion.

As soon as she got home, she sat down and wrote a list of goals and deadlines. They had to either get Raven up to speed on at least one rodeo event, or they had to find another club member. The club had to participate in at least two rodeo competitions before the finals, which were in a few weeks. She needed to create a new business proposal, and soon, mail it to a new batch of lenders. It wouldn't hurt to increase the number of competitors at their fundraising events ... she wrote that down as a goal but wasn't sure how ambitious to get. Finally, Taylor wanted a new car. And since this was her list of goals, she wrote, *Buy a new, sexy car.*

List made, Taylor pulled a sparkling water out of the fridge and opened it as she sat down at her laptop. She brought up the high school rodeo competition schedule. The next one was in two weekends, which gave her kids seven more practices to prepare. She didn't spend too much time thinking about it; she registered. Since she was already on the computer, she started a new document to track the club's progress. Eventually, it would become her business plan, and she would show it to potential lenders as proof that her business could be profitable.

When Taylor's stomach growled, she looked at the clock and was surprised to see it was after eight p.m. Feeling good about her progress, she shut her laptop and went into the kitchen to heat up some leftovers. Just as she put her plate in the microwave, Judd texted: *Hey, beautiful. I'm going to start working that investigation tomorrow, so I probably won't be too social during the day. See you at practice?*

She responded, *No problem. You're a distraction, anyway. ;) A fun distraction, but still. See you at practice.*

The microwave beeped, and Taylor got out her plate and carried it to the table.

Judd sent back a laughing emoji and added, *Think we can get Raven on horseback?*

Taylor responded with a .gif of a grown man pretending to ride a child's small rubber horse, and Judd texted, *I hope we do better than that.*

Although she loved these evening conversations over text, Taylor found herself wishing Judd was there, at her house, sitting across from her at the table. She imagined showing him the rodeo competition schedule and the document that would become her business plan. They could even shop for cars together.

When she texted him, *Goodnight,* and he responded, *Sleep well,* she felt such a yearning she almost drove over to his house.

And that, she reminded herself, was why business and family couldn't mix.

Chapter Twenty-One

TAYLOR

Wednesday afternoon, the practice arena at the Mint Creek Ranch buzzed with anticipation. All the kids could talk about was getting Raven on horseback. Taylor didn't want to push him beyond his comfort zone, but she could feel the excitement, herself, when she imagined how triumphant he'd be when he got in the saddle. While most of the kids hummed with enthusiasm, Raven displayed an excess of nervous energy. He rubbed his hands together, bounced on the balls of his feet, and walked in circles around an invisible spot.

Judd had told Taylor he needed to drive separately after school and hadn't shown up yet. Taylor glanced toward the driveway several times each minute. She had to force herself to focus on the kids. Another reason, she reminded herself, romance and business didn't mix.

"You can do this, man," Zion said, giving Raven a friendly punch on the arm. "I believe in you."

Cody brought out Cinnamon, and watching her plod along next to him, Taylor felt hopeful. She did look gentle, and slow. Raven backed away when Cody brought the horse into the arena. Taylor could tell Cody was trying not to smile when he said, "Hold up, girl," and then, to Raven, "We won't come any closer, yet. Why don't you come stand here with us? Just talk to her. Get to know her. Come on, I'll introduce you."

It was the first time Taylor had seen Raven drop his cool-guy act. His walk was no longer a saunter. His mannerisms were subdued. He did approach the duo, but made sure to stand so Cody was between him and the horse. Cody didn't say anything about that, just nodded. "Good. Raven, this is Cinnamon. Cinnamon, meet Raven."

The horse bobbed her head, earning a half-smile from Raven.

"She says, 'Nice to meet you,'" Cody said.

"Nice to meet you, too," Raven choked out.

Cody turned to Taylor. "Why don't you guys go ahead and start practicing? I'll stand here with these two."

"You heard him," Taylor said to the other kids. "Let's go ahead and get started." The kids obeyed. They headed into the barn to saddle the other horses, and Taylor went to work setting up the barrels so the girls could practice. As she finished setting up the first one, she saw Judd rolling the second one into the center of the arena.

"Oh, hey," she said. "I didn't even hear you pull up."

"I'm here. Sorry I'm late. I had a stop to make after school."

"Why don't you go change out of your uniform? I can finish this up."

Judd looked down, as if he'd forgotten what he was wearing. "Good idea."

He positioned the second barrel before jogging back to his patrol car. By the time he came back to the arena, dressed in jeans and a plain white T-shirt that had Taylor's mouth watering, the rest of the kids were there too, on horseback.

They split into groups, Judd working on lasso technique with the boys while Taylor ran barrel racing with the girls.

Although Taylor had promised herself she would become a ruthless business owner, she couldn't help but feel her emotions rising. She gave the girls instructions — sit up straight, keep the reins close to your waist — and watched them improve. She saw Judd laughing with Zion and Henry, at one point lassoing Henry around the shoulders, pinning his arms to his sides. She saw Cody nonchalantly hand Raven Cinnamon's reins, and step away to offer Zion a tip. Her heart swelled. The whole scene was her dream in action.

She was blinking back tears when she heard, "Psst." A couple of seconds passed before she identified the source of the sound: Raven, who was obviously trying to stand as still as possible, while motioning urgently for her to come over to him.

"Ms. Cole," he said in a loud whisper. "Ms. Cole, will you please come over here?"

Taylor had a feeling she knew what he was going to say, and she was right. "What can I help you with?"

"Dude just left me standing here with this horse. Can you take it?" He looked toward his hand, which had a death grip on the reins, but remained still, afraid to move.

"Has she done anything to make you uncomfortable?"

Raven swallowed, his Adam's apple bobbing up and down like a cartoon character's.

"Well, I mean, she didn't do nothin', but —"

"She didn't do anything except exist, right?"

Raven nodded, his eyes wide. "Exactly. She's just so... big."

"How about if I stand here with you?"

"And hold the string thingy?"

"They're called reins. And no, you're doing just fine holding them. Do you want to go over some of the terminology we talked about at one of the earlier meetings? Like the names of the saddle parts and the rodeo events?"

"What happens if I let go of the reins?"

"Honestly? Probably nothing. She'll just stand there. Why don't you try talking to her?"

He shifted his weight from one foot to the other. "What would I even say?"

Taylor shrugged. "Whatever you want. When I was a kid, I had a horse. I didn't get to keep her at my house, but whenever I went to the barn to exercise her, ride her, brush her out, any of that stuff, I talked to her. And you know what I learned?"

Raven closed his eyes then, and shook his head. "No. What did you learn?"

"I learned that horses are really great listeners. And even though they don't speak to you, sometimes they can still give you comfort."

Raven's eyes flicked open. "I want to believe that."

"Tell you what. Why don't you and Cinnamon take a walk? And you talk to her?"

"No way," Raven said. His hand slid up on the reins, closer to Cinnamon's chin. "What if she, like, starts to run or something?"

Taylor put her hand on Cinnamon's cheek. "She's one of the calmest horses I've seen. She'll match your pace. If it would make you more comfortable, you could just do a circle around the arena, inside the fence. And then work your way up to a slightly longer walk." Raven looked doubtful, so Taylor said, "Just take a couple of steps, right here. See what happens."

She stepped aside and Raven took a step forward. "She's not moving."

"She has a long neck. She probably can't even feel you pulling on her reins, yet. Take another step."

Raven did, and sure enough, when the reins were taut, Cinnamon's giant shoulders shifted and she stepped forward. Raven's eyes lit up even while he grimaced.

"Keep going," Taylor said, her voice quiet.

"I'm doing it." The horse took another couple of steps.

"You are. Want me to walk with you, or do you want to walk by yourself, so you can talk to her?"

"I'm good," Raven said, a bit more confidence in his tone. "I think."

Taylor moved out of Raven's path, and kept an eye on the duo as she walked back over to where Judd was standing.

"Good job," Judd said to her. "That's big progress right there."

"It is. Between all of us, we're going to get him on horseback one day."

Thursday afternoon, Raven went into Cinnamon's stall and put on her saddle, then stood by while Cody put on her bit and bridle.

Without much hesitation, he took her reins and started walking her around the the edge of the arena.

None of the other kids, or the adults for that matter, made a big deal of the progress — out loud — but Taylor saw everyone watching Raven, exchanging looks. And, when practice was over, Henry and Zion quietly congratulated him.

On Friday, Cody offered Raven a lesson on mounting, and Raven watched, rapt, as Cody demonstrated putting a foot in the stirrup, grabbing the saddle horn and pulling himself up onto Cinnamon's back.

"Want to try?" Cody said from his perch, and Raven shook his head so fast Taylor wondered if he could feel his brain knocking against his skull.

"All right, man, but we're going to get you up here eventually," Cody said.

Zion spoke up from the back of a different horse a few feet away. "You know, man, we've got a week until our first competition. We need you to do at least one event if we're gonna have a chance of getting points."

"I'll do it," Raven said. "I promise. I just have to work up to it."

———

*J*UDD

Judd was determined to get Raven up on Cinnamon's back by the end of practice Monday. The three of them stood in the arena at the Mint Creek Ranch, the sun a boiling temperature that baked the dirt. A fly buzzed in, and Cinnamon swatted at it with her tail.

"What can I do?" Judd asked Raven. He wiped his forehead with his sleeve. "I'll do anything. I'll buy you ice cream. New shoes." He gestured at Raven's feet. "What do you like? Air Jordans? Cowboy boots? Oh, yeah. I'll buy you cowboy boots. That'll make you feel like a pro."

Raven smirked, but didn't move any closer to the horse. Judd could see the sweat on Raven's upper lip. He wondered if the kid wished for a breeze as much as he did.

Taylor's voice floated over to them from the barn. She'd bought extra bottled water and cooling cloths for the kids to wear around their necks.

"Stay hydrated. Everyone drink a bottle of water right now. I'll keep a bucket of ice water in the barn, and you guys can come wet your cloths whenever they get dry."

Judd lost focus completely. All he could think about was Taylor, wet. Maybe he was having heat-induced hallucinations. He pictured her in a bathing suit, stepping out of a pool, cool water on her skin. In his vision, she looked over her shoulder at him, smiling. Inviting.

"Did you hear me, bro?" Raven's voice brought Judd back to reality, where he was so sweaty (and now, horny), he needed to jump in a cold shower before he even thought about touching Taylor's body.

"No, sorry, man. I got distracted by this heat."

"I said, I don't know if there's anything you can buy that will get me on the back of the horse. I just have to, you know, decide to do it."

Judd lifted one shoulder. "Good point. Pretty enlightened for such a young man."

"I'm scared out of my mind. Like, worried I might die." He paused. "I mean, I know that's really unlikely. But the fear is real."

Sweat trickled down Judd's back. Maybe he'd ask Taylor for a cooling cloth.

"I've been that scared. More than once," Judd told Raven. Just a few weeks before, when Judd first took the school resource officer position, he would have balked at sharing intense stories with high school students. But hadn't he said high school students doing crime often needed guidance? This was a chance to offer it. "Actually, right before I came to the high school, I had a really scary call." He told Raven about the accident, when he'd shown up to find a car that could explode any second. "I could see the gas leaking out of the tank. I knew, if there was even one spark, one ignition source, the whole car would blow, exploding me along with it. The driver was unconscious. I had to pull her out. Just as I was standing at the driver's side door, trying to figure out how I was going to get her out, my friend Nicky showed up. He came over to help me."

"Did that driver cause the accident?" Raven wanted to know.

"No. Some other guy. Texting and driving. But even if she *had* caused the crash, I would have done the same thing."

The cicadas started up. Judd thought the sweltering heat had made them too sleepy to sing, but maybe they were complaining.

"You would've saved her, even though she caused the accident?" Raven's eyebrows drew together in doubt.

"For sure," Judd said. "It's not my job to decide who gets which punishments. It's my job to keep people safe."

"Huh."

"And if my friend Nicky had gotten there first, I would have run up to help him, too."

"So, you were both afraid you were going to get blown up."

Judd chuckled. "Yep. Basically." He wondered whether Raven had any friends with whom he could swap near-death stories.

"So what did you tell yourself, to get yourself to go up there and pull that lady out of the car?"

"I told myself I had to. I told myself I didn't have a choice. I told myself, 'This is what you signed up for, dude.'"

"I didn't exactly sign up for rodeo club," Raven said, his tone pouty.

"Fair point. But you're in it, now, aren't you? It's not a matter of life or death, but this club is a team. And this team is counting on you. Not just Ms. Cole and me, but the other kids, too."

Raven nodded, then turned his attention to the horse. "I hear you. Just give me a few minutes to make that decision, okay?"

"Okay. You got it. I'm going to go get one of those cold cloths Ms. Cole brought. And a bottle of water. Want me to get you one of each, too?"

"Sure. Thanks."

After Raven chugged the bottle of water and put the cooling cloth on his neck, Judd watched him circle the arena for entire practice. With just fifteen minutes remaining before the bus would come to take the kids home, Judd approached him again.

"Time's almost up, man. The bus will be here soon. Is today the day?"

Raven halted. Cinnamon halted, too.

"I don't know, bro. I want to. And I also don't want to."

Judd felt the first surges of adrenaline. His hands shook. He heard a roaring in his years. His hands felt just the tiniest bit shaky. Raven getting on the horse didn't matter in the grand scheme of things, but Judd wanted it — not just for the club, but for Raven. Still, he knew he couldn't let Raven see it was important to him. He didn't need that kind of pressure. So he simply said, "It's no skin off my teeth if today's not the day. It would be cool if you could get in some practice before this weekend. But if not — hey, it's fine. Either way, we'd better wrap this up. Like I said, the bus will be here soon."

Raven looked around. Judd wondered if he was looking for an audience or a way out.

"That Cody guy," he finally said.

"You mean Cody Davis, the owner of Mint Creek Ranch?"

"Yeah. Him. He said all I gotta do is hold onto the saddle horn, here." He pointed at the saddle horn. "And then I just put my left foot in the stirrup, here." He pointed at that. "And then, I just hoist myself up, right? Just swing myself right up there."

"Very good," Judd said. "You've got it. Easy as pie. If you don't want to do it now, maybe you can spend some time this evening visualizing. Just imagining yourself doing it."

"No, man."

Judd opened his mouth, but before he could speak, Raven said, "I'm going to do it now. I just made the decision. Will you just —" he held the reins out toward Judd. "Hold these?"

Judd nodded, took the reins, hoping Raven didn't feel that his own palms were sweaty.

Raven took a few steps back, away from Cinnamon.

"Planning to get a running start?" Judd asked.

That earned him a laugh. Raven circled his arms, windmill style, and then swung them across the front of his body. "No. Just getting the wiggles out." He jumped a few times in place. "Cody, Mr. Davis, the owner of this place, told me I gotta be calm when I finally do it. He said if I'm nervous I can spook her."

Judd nodded, considering. He wondered if that idea had spooked Raven. But, there he was, about to mount.

Raven took a few steps toward Cinnamon. He paused and looked at Judd, as if seeking reassurance that he was on the right track. Judd gave what he hoped was a reassuring nod. Raven took another step forward. Paused. Inhaled so deeply, Judd could see his torso expand. Exhaled. Put both hands on the saddle horn. "Like this?"

"Yep. Like that."

"And then my foot goes here, right?"

"Right," Judd said. He was sure he appeared relaxed on the outside, but on the inside, he was thinking, *Please, please let this happen.*

Raven withdrew his foot and hands from the saddle and took a giant step back. Judd exhaled, but did his best to keep a neutral expression. He didn't want Raven to see his disappointment. But before he could offer any words of encouragement, Raven was back in position, hands on the saddle horn, foot in the stirrup. He pulled himself up, slowing down a little just before his left leg straightened and his right leg swung over Cinnamon's back. There was a moment of silence, and then Judd could feel the rush of energy at his back. The rodeo team, plus Taylor, had come up behind him, and now stood in a semi circle, an audience to Raven's moment in the spotlight.

"I wish we could applaud," Olivia said, her voice a near squeal.

"Me, too," Judd said.

Taylor said, "Should we do a silent cheer?"

The kids clapped silently. Zion did a crazy movement with his arms. Henry did some kind of dance. And Raven sat on Cinnamon's back, grinning from ear to ear. Cinnamon shifted her weight, and Raven grabbed the saddle horn, emitting a sound Judd would describe as a cross between a whisper and a whisper-yell.

"You're fine, dude," Zion told him. "She just took a step, that's all."

"The movement seems a lot bigger from up here," Raven said.

His knuckles were literally white. Judd approached the horse and lifted the reins for Raven. "Here. Hold onto these. You'll be able to tell her where to go. Want to ride her into the barn?"

Panic skirted across Raven's face, and Judd had to suppress his laughter.

"No, man. I'm good for today, I think. Mr. Cody taught me how to get up, but he didn't teach me how to get down. Tell me I'm not stuck up here."

———

The next day at school, Judd found Raven during lunch. As usual, the kid leaned against a wall in Nowhere, under the stairs behind the science building. Judd detected a faint whiff of sulfur, and wondered what kind of experiment the chemistry teacher was doing that day. Whatever it was, Judd hoped he gave the kids gas masks.

Raven lifted a chin, offering a much different persona from the day before. A few other kids shared the space. One girl, dressed in all fluorescent colors, with about a hundred safety pins fastened to one side of her jacket lapel, moped with her chin in her hands as she sat on the concrete foundation for one of the building's support pillars. Another – this one androgynous — sat on the ground, back against the building, a book propped on his or her knees.

"What's up, Raven?" For fraction of a second, Judd wondered how the group of kids would respond if he made rounds, giving everyone enthusiastic high fives. He decided against it. He didn't want to embarrass Raven. He still needed to get information from him.

"What's up?" The kid made it obvious he didn't want to talk. He remained absolutely still, arms crossed, shoulders hunched.

"Can we talk?"

"That's what we're doing, isn't it?" Raven said. Judd wasn't exactly sure what to make of that, but then he saw amusement in Raven's eyes, a hint of a smile on his mouth.

"Fair point. Can we walk and talk?" Judd let his gaze roam over the other kids, hoping to convey the message that he wanted to talk privately.

"Do we have to?" Again, Raven's actions belied his words. He was already in motion toward the sidewalk behind Judd. The other kids didn't seem to notice Judd and Raven left together but Judd was certain they were watching.

As they made their way toward the quad, Judd said, "How's your day going?"

"I know you didn't just ask me how my day is going."

The kid was good, Judd thought. The phrase, "Can't bullshit a bullshitter," came to mind. "I did. But you've got me. I'm not here to talk about how your day is going."

Raven smirked at him. "I know. This is either about your lady, the rodeo club, or some police business up in here."

"Why did you include police business as a possible discussion topic?"

"Isn't it, though? I can tell you're a smart guy. By now, you know there might be a reason to deal with me. But, you also don't want me to get in trouble and get kicked out of rodeo club because you have the hots for Ms. Cole. The sexy librarian."

"You guys can't keep calling her that."

Smiling, Raven went on, "You need me to make the rodeo club work. I'm the fifth guy, right? Whatever I'm wrapped up in could mess up the rodeo club. And that would make Ms. Cole real, real sad. And you don't want that."

While he talked, he gestured with his hands as if he were giving a presentation. If he wasn't so spot-on — and scaring Judd with the admission he might be wrapped up in something — Judd would have laughed.

He couldn't believe the kid's insight.

While all these thoughts ran through Judd's head, Raven laughed out loud.

"Okay, man," Judd said. "Say you're right, not just for the aforementioned reasons, but also because I like you. If you're wrapped up in something, as you say, I don't want this to become your life. So let's say there's someone else — an adult — who's bringing this game to the high school."

"First, bro, you asking me to snitch?"

"What if I am?"

Raven shook his head. "Second, you calling it a game? Because I can assure you, it's not a game. It's dead serious."

They'd come to the quad, and they stopped at the area's edge, out of earshot of the students gathered there.

"I hear you," Judd said. "I'm gathering, from what you're not saying, that there is someone else. Someone higher up on the food chain."

Looking him in the eyes, Raven said, "There might be."

Judd let that idea hang in the air between them for a few seconds before asking, "Any idea how I could find out who he is, which circles he travels?"

Raven broke eye contact, looked out over the quad. "Probably."

Judd had to admire the kid. He was clever. If he were dealing with an adult, Judd would probably be clenching his jaw at the moment. But all he saw was a clever kid who'd end up taking the blame and being punished for the actions of someone older and more powerful. He also saw that he'd made all the progress he was going to make on the topic for the moment.

Raven confirmed that when he said, "All right. Is that it?"

Judd smiled at him, hoping to keep the moment light. "You're not being super forthcoming with your information. I'll hit you up again later."

Judd could practically see Raven thinking, his wheels turning. Instead of sharing his thoughts, though, he shrugged one shoulder and said, "All right, man. Whatever you say."

Judd hooked a thumb toward the library. "I'm going to go have lunch now."

"With the sexy librarian?"

At that, Judd did clench his teeth. "You've got to stop saying that."

Raven laughed out loud as he turned and walked away. A thought occurred to Judd. He turned around and said to Raven's back, "Hey, kid, you got anything to eat for lunch?"

Raven turned back around and dismissed Judd's question with a wave of his hand. "Nah, man. Never do, though."

Judd felt a pang of sadness as he watched Raven walk away.

A few hours later, when Judd saw him at rodeo club, they both acted as if their lunch walkabout hadn't happened.

Raven spent only half the practice walking Cinnamon around the arena before he mounted. Once again, he opted to remain in one spot while he was in the saddle, politely declining offers from his teammates to take the reins and lead the horse on a walk.

As the bus trundled up the driveway a few minutes before the end of practice, Raven said to Judd, "I gotta tell you something, O'Connor."

Judd thought his last name sounded funny coming out of Raven's mouth. "Oh yeah? What's that?"

Judd thought — hoped — Raven was going to drop a name, give him some hints about where to start searching for whoever was supplying him with drugs. He was surprised when the kid said, "I've been practicing at home."

"Riding?"

Raven shook his head. "Lassoing. I set up a little dummy, like they have here. I know it's not the real thing, but it's better than nothing."

"That's awesome. I'm sure Ms. Cole will be happy to hear it."

"I also visualized. Like you suggested. I visualized dismounting. Want to see me try?"

Judd felt a jolt of excitement at that. The kid had listened to him, taken his advice. Maybe they *were* making a connection. "Yeah? Let's see how that worked for you."

Raven gave a single nod, then dismounted as easily as if he'd been doing it his whole life. With much more confidence than he'd exhibited before, he took Cinnamon's reins and started leading her toward the barn. Judd walked next to him, applauding. "Well done, Raven," he said. "Well done."

"Thanks, coach. I'm going to watch some lassoing videos tonight, and do some more visualizing."

———

TAYLOR

Taylor and Judd stood together at the edge of the practice arena, watching the bus drive away. Giddiness felt like champagne inside her body, all fizzy, bubbles rising.

"I can't believe the progress these kids are making," she said to Judd, leaning against him. "Did I overhear Raven saying he made a dummy to practice roping?"

"You did," Judd said. "He also said he took my advice about visualizing, and he dismounted like a pro."

"I saw that," Taylor said. She looked up at him, admiring his strong jawline and the five o'clock shadow adorning it. Imagining those whiskers on her inner thighs, she shivered. "I couldn't have done this without you. Whatever happens, I hope you know that."

Judd turned toward her, wrapping his arms around her waist. "You could show me your appreciation by having dinner with me, since we didn't get to have lunch together today."

She brought her lips to his and kissed him, long and deep. The low near-growl of pleasure he emitted made her think she'd like to do more than dinner. "Again, I am so sorry about that," she said. "Like I said, duty called. The English teachers needed to talk with me about a book order. But yes, I would love to have dinner with you, to show my remorse for missing lunch, and my appreciation for your help with rodeo club. As a start."

He chuckled, and again, the sound sent a bolt of heat to her center. "Let's go, then."

"Wait," Taylor said. "An idea just occurred to me. What do you think about cooking dinner, instead of going out?"

"I think that is a fantastic idea," he said, kissing her on the tip of her nose.

The sweet, casual gesture meant even more to Taylor than the intense lovemaking they'd shared the week before.

"I make a mean Philly cheesesteak sandwich," Judd told her.

"Mmm," she said.

Eyes twinkling, he held up a finger. "But. There's nothing dainty about eating it. You have to be ready to get messy."

"I think I can handle that," Taylor said. "As long as we have some napkins."

"I'm pretty sure that was the best housewarming gift I received when I moved into my own house. Katy got me what has proven so far to be an endless supply of napkins. I admit, I was always a messy eater."

They stopped at the store for ingredients, and a while later, they were back at Judd's house, in his kitchen, cooking together. The smell of the grill heating up came in through the open window, and Taylor's mouth watered as she cut up the bell peppers. Judd, slicing mushrooms at the kitchen island, said, "Grill's ready."

Before heading outside, he held up the dish in which he'd marinated the steak. "Smell that," he said.

She did. "My mouth is watering."

He made a show of looking at her mouth, and then raking his gaze over her body. "Mine, too."

He kissed her, and headed outside through the kitchen door. She loved watching the way he moved, confident and graceful, strong and at ease in the world.

Being there, with Judd, smelling marinades, chopping vegetables — she felt so content. But thinking of her dad, and his belief that a person couldn't run a business *and* have a family — that made her worry. She decided she was enjoying Judd too much to let the worry ruin the time they had.

He came back inside and set the bowl in the sink. "Okay, meat's on. I think we have a little time before we need to start cooking the veggies."

They stood facing each other. "I know how we can pass the time," Taylor said. She put her hand on the back of his neck and pulled him in for a kiss. "This is going to be delicious. I can't wait."

He offered her a cocky smile. "You're gonna love it."

"I already do."

As Judd promised, the sandwiches were messy, and Taylor was grateful for the stack of napkins he set between them.

"Any news on the investigation Ernie wanted you to do?" Taylor asked, just as Judd took a bite of his sandwich.

His eyes smiled as he pointed at his mouth.

"Sorry," she said. "I'll wait."

Taylor could have sworn he chewed for longer than necessary before finally answering. "Nothing new. I did talk to Raven today at lunch, but he's a closed book. He doesn't want to snitch."

"I get that," Taylor said. "I don't think anyone wants to be a snitch, but it's even harder for kids. Just do me a favor. If you end up having to arrest him, don't do it during rodeo season."

Although she was joking — she didn't really think Judd would have to arrest Raven — his countenance didn't reflect any of her humor.

"No promises," he said. Then he took another big bite of sandwich.

"Wait," she said. "I was just kidding. You're not going to have to arrest him, are you?"

"I hope not," Judd said. "But if he keeps calling you 'the sexy librarian,' I might have to arrest him for being a pervert."

This made Taylor laugh, and Judd changed the subject back to the rodeo club and their upcoming competition. Still, as she drove home that night, she couldn't help but feeling like he was keeping something from her. She wondered what it was, and hoped it wouldn't affect rodeo club.

Chapter Twenty-Two

Taylor's phone rang within the first minute after her alarm went off Saturday morning. She smiled when she saw Judd's name on the screen. "Good morning."

"Happy competition day!"

"Thank you." Taylor flopped back down in the bed and stretched, feeling as rested and satisfied as a cat. If Judd were beside her, she'd be purring. "This is a nice start to the day."

"Come to the door. I have something even better."

Still smiling, Taylor did as he said. The Taylor of a month ago never would have dared to go to the door in her pajamas, but wasn't she a new, more confident Taylor now? Judd stood on the other side, looking bright-eyed and bushy-tailed and so damn hot in his jeans and v-neck shirt, Taylor almost wished it wasn't competition day. In one hand, he carried a drink caddy containing two paper cups. Before she could say anything, he grabbed the hem of her shirt. "Is that my shirt?"

She might be the new, confident version of herself, but Taylor blushed and broke eye contact. She looked down at the space between them. "Maybe. You might have left it here, and I might have forgotten to give it back to you."

Judd tipped her chin up so they were eye to eye again. "You look ravishing in it. In Who Wore it Best, you win."

That comment soothed Taylor's embarrassment. "Thank you. And, thank you for the coffee."

She reached for it, and he made a little show of holding out of her reach. "Payment first."

She leaned in to kiss him, inhaling his cologne. "Smells good," she said.

"I know. Rita is trying a new supplier. Some Colombian grower."

"I wasn't talking about the coffee."

"Oh. In that case, thank you."

They kissed again, and Judd permitted Taylor to remove one of the coffee cups from the carrier. Taylor stepped back, holding the door open wider to let him into the house. "Come on in. Obviously, I've got to get ready for the day."

"You look pretty good to me."

"I love that you're saying that, but can you imagine me walking into a rodeo competition like this?"

An hour later, they arrived at the Prescott City Arena, where the rodeo competition would take place. Competitors, coaches, parents, and audience members gathered inside the main entrance, in the concourse.

Two women sat behind the check-in table, clipboards and name tags in front of them. A sign on the table read, *Please check in only when your entire team is present.*

Taylor and Judd moved off to one side to wait for the kids.

"Code red, two 'clock," Judd murmured in Taylor's ear. "That group looks semi-professional."

Taylor followed his gaze to a group of six kids wearing matching plaid shirts, boots, and expensive cowboy hats.

"They do look serious. Let's hope their strength is in uniforms, not rodeoing."

"Roger that. Three o'clock."

"Taylor looked to the right, and saw another group gathered, wearing matching T-shirts: *This is Not Our First Rodeo.*

"We should've done something like that," Taylor said, hoping the lack of a uniform wasn't disheartening to their team members.

"Next time," Judd said.

"If we make it through."

"Oh, we will."

Taylor closed her eyes briefly, visualizing, letting Judd's confidence transfer to her by osmosis. They would make it through. The kids were skilled horse people, and they had demonstrated superior teamwork, which she hoped would give them confidence, and the ability to work through a high-pressure situation. Taylor took a deep breath, nodded. "You're right."

Zion materialized at Taylor's side, his dark eyes round.

"Good morning," Judd said, and Taylor pictured her confidence transferring over to Zion, like fairy dust or magic glitter. She wondered what Zion would think of that image.

"Morning," Zion said.

"Nervous?" Judd asked him.

Zion shrugged. "I guess so." He rubbed his hands together as if to warm them, even though the sun was already baking the ground, making the air a toasty eighty-nine degrees.

The other four kids came in a few minutes later. Taylor's nerves, which had curled up and gone to sleep, sprang back to life when she said, "We're all here. Let's go check in."

They did, and before they walked away, one of the women at the table said, "Remember, coaches! You're not allowed to help your students today. You'll be members of the audience only."

For Taylor, that would be the most difficult aspect of the rodeo competition. She and Judd would be able to watch, but not to offer advice or an extra set of hands.

For the first few minutes after she cut them loose, the rodeo club members stood awkwardly in the space between the arena and the stables, avoiding eye contact, shoulders tense, eyes cast downward.

"They look like they're strangers again," Judd said.

"Exactly what I was thinking."

"I have an idea." Judd got out his phone and fired off a text. A second later, Zion took his phone out of his pocket, looked at the screen for a few seconds, and put his phone away. He looked like he was trying not to smile. He elbowed Raven, gently, said a few words. Raven shrugged and held out a hand. Zion demonstrated a complicated handshake, slapping Raven's hand, wiggling his fingers, and turning around before holding both hands up for a double high-five. Raven shook his head, his cheeks turning pink, a reluctant smile tugging at the corners of his mouth. Zion must've told him to do it again, because they went through the motions a second time. Zion gave Raven a friendly punch on the shoulder, then said a couple of words to him. Scarlett, Olivia, and Henry watched them, looking amused and curious. Zion started to show the handshake to Olivia and Henry, and Raven demonstrated for Scarlett. Within a minute, all five of them looked relaxed and happy, like the team they'd been during the assembly and the first fundraising rodeo.

"How did you get him to do that?" Taylor asked.

Judd shrugged and gave her a smug smile. "I guess I'm amazing," he said.

Taylor had only a moment to bask in the relief of the team's turnaround, because the competition moderator rang her cowbell, drawing everyone's attention. The arena fell silent. The woman welcomed everyone, and then asked them to stand for the national anthem.

Throughout the morning, the big screen at the end of the arena had shown videos of rodeo athletes and important messages. After the national anthem, the screen lit up with information about the first event: barrel racing.

Because Prescott High's team was new, Olivia and Scarlett were seeded lower, and therefore, would take their turns early in the lineup. Olivia was third and Scarlett, fifth. Taylor didn't mind — it meant she wouldn't have to spend too much time nervous, waiting for them to ride.

Taylor looked down to see Olivia sitting on her horse, Jupiter, in the holding pen just outside the alleyway where the riders would start. Her posture was stiff, and she sat high in the saddle. Taylor willed her to look over, and by some miracle, she did. Taylor pantomimed taking a deep breath, and Olivia laughed before actually taking a deep breath. Taylor then tensed up her shoulders and relaxed them, and Olivia nodded, taking another deep breath and relaxing her posture. Taylor gave her a thumbs up, which she returned before lining up for her turn. The first and second riders put up decent times, but Taylor figured Olivia could ride even faster. When it was their turn, Olivia and Jupiter flew past the timer, and went around the first barrel like the horse's heels were on fire. Taylor and Judd were on their feet, cheering, as Olivia came back through the timer at the end of her run.

Breathless, Taylor turned to Judd and grabbed his shoulders. "That was amazing! She was so fast!"

Taylor wondered briefly whether her expression matched Judd's crazed one — wide eyes, even wider smile. She didn't have too long to think about it, though, because Scarlett was up next.

Olivia stopped next to her, and pantomimed taking a deep breath and relaxing tense shoulders, just as Taylor had done for her. Scarlett nodded, and Taylor saw her consciously relax, just as Olivia had. She, too, was fast around the barrels. Her horse's hooves sent the dirt flying. She was back through the timer so quickly, Taylor couldn't believe her run was over.

"I'm so nervous!" Taylor said to Judd. "My hands are actually shaking." She held out her hands to show him, and he took them in his and kissed her knuckles.

"First time is always the worst, in terms of nerves. They're doing great so far."

Next up, Zion and Henry would compete in team roping. From her spot in the bleachers, Taylor could see the two of them outside the arena, having an animated discussion. Zion's eyebrows drew together, like he was upset, but before Taylor could lean over and ask Judd if he knew what was going on, both boys laughed. Taylor watched them mount their horses and ride over to the waiting area. Just like the girls, Henry and Zion were early in the lineup. Taylor's heart started racing before it was even their turn. Judd put a hand on her thigh and squeezed, making her jump.

"Think they're ready?" he said.

"I do," Taylor said. "They've been doing great in practice. Very smooth. I just hope their nerves don't get the best of them."

They didn't. Henry and Zion executed the team rope flawlessly, and in just nine seconds. They wouldn't know how they placed until the other teams took their turns, but Taylor figured they would at least be competitive.

"You can breathe now," Judd said to her, giving her thigh another squeeze.

"Oh! Right."

"Time for our wild card," Judd said, inclining his head toward the holding pen, where the calf ropers lined up. Raven wasn't there, yet, and Taylor's stomach lurched when she saw the two of them just outside the holding pen, her reins in his fist and his jaw clenching over and over.

"I don't know who's more nervous, Raven or me."

"Or Cinnamon," Judd said. "Look at her."

Sure enough, her tail swished and she pawed the dirt. Her ears twitched, turning in opposite directions.

"Oof," Taylor said. "I hope he can get her calmed down."

"Me, too," Judd said. "All we need is for him to finish. If he puts up a score, we'll have enough team points to move on to the next round."

The other rodeo club members materialized then, and after they spent a few minutes talking with Raven and Cinnamon (Henry stroked the horse's neck and talked to her while the others talked to Raven), both boy and horse appeared calmer.

The kids stood back while Raven mounted. He squared his shoulders and lifted his chin, and Taylor wondered if he was trying to give himself more confidence. He rode into the holding pen to wait his turn.

———

A few hours later, as Taylor and Judd walked into his house, she noticed how normal the routine felt.

"I still can't believe Raven pulled that off," Judd said, locking the door and setting his keys on the entry table.

"I know," Taylor said, setting down her purse. "It was amazing. And surprising."

"You could have knocked me down with a feather." Judd turned to face her, and wrapped his arms around her waist. "Congratulations, Coach Cole. We're moving on to the next round."

He kissed her, and all coherent thoughts slipped away.

When he ended the kiss and said, "I think this calls for another celebration," Taylor felt a zing of electricity that started in her chest and ended right between her legs. The last time they'd celebrated, their activities left her with a delicious boneless feeling and the strange but satisfying sense that she would never invite another man into her bed. "Well?"

Taylor realized some time had passed since Judd's comment, and she hadn't answered. "I was just thinking about our last celebration," she admitted, and he gave her a devilish grin, his eyes glinting with promises.

"Yes, we definitely have something to celebrate," she said.

"Should we grab a bottle of wine and an order from Rita's?"

The idea sent a pleasant shiver of anticipation over Taylor's skin.

Once they'd parked at the grocery store, Judd came around to open the passenger door. He took Taylor's hand and kissed her knuckles, a sweet gesture that at once made her think, *Aww,* and ignited a fire in her core. How could she so adore and desire a man, simultaneously?

Inside, a sense of urgency compelling them to get back home to celebrate, they went straight to the wine aisle, where they quickly agreed on a bottle of red. On the way home, they stopped by Rita's Diner to pick up dinner.

Back at Judd's house, Taylor opened the bag from Rita's to find a small takeout box sitting on top of the boxes containing their meals. It contained a perfect slice of chocolate cake with a plastic heart wedged into the icing on top.

"Look at this," Taylor said, holding up the open box.

"Ah, Rita," Judd said. "Always stoking the flames of romance."

They ate in near silence, taking every opportunity to touch one another as they did. Judd rested his hand on Taylor's thigh, and she leaned against him. He fed her a bite of his fettuccine Alfredo and kissed the excess off the side of her mouth.

By the end of the meal, Taylor felt a warmth between her legs, the start of a lovely pressure building.

"Should we eat the cake now, or later?" she asked as they cleared their dishes.

"I'll take dessert first," he said, flashing another grin and leaning against the kitchen counter. "Go ahead and unwrap it."

Although his request surprised — and intimidated — her, at first, the way he looked at her, his eyes dark with desire, intensified the heat in her core and made her feel sexy and a little more confident.

Butterflies in her stomach, her throat tight with nerves, she began unbuttoning the plaid shirt she'd worn to the rodeo competition. Before she unfastened the last two buttons, he pulled her toward him and kissed her. He started with her mouth, and moved his lips to her neck and collarbone and breasts. Then he released her and said, "Carry on, then."

She did, finishing with the shirt and moving on to her boots and jeans. Once she'd stripped down to her underwear, he picked her up, tossed her over his shoulder, and carried her to the bedroom.

Afterwards, they lay in silence for a few minutes. Taylor could see Judd's heart beating. His skin was slick beneath her palm. He ran his fingertips up and down her spine as the two of them caught their breath.

Taylor wondered what would happen when rodeo season ended. Yes, they would continue to see each other at school. But without this built-in excuse to spend all their spare time together, would they? The past few weeks she'd come to think of them as two celestial bodies, caught in each other's orbit. But at that moment, they were in the same universe.

If — no, *when*, she corrected herself — they both left the school, him to go back on patrol and her to start her new business, then what?

"What are you thinking?" he said, his fingertips continuing their gentle stroking.

"Oh, nothing," she said.

"Didn't look like nothing." He shifted so they were facing each other, and put a hand on her hip.

"You got me," she said, removing his hand from her hip and intertwining their fingers. She kissed his before continuing. "I was thinking, I'm really enjoying this. You. Us. I've never had so much fun going to the grocery store, cooking, or making out. Like, more fun than I've ever had in a relationship."

"It sounds like there might be a 'but' in there."

"No, there's no 'but.' Can I be honest with you?"

"Please do," he said.

She huffed out a breath, forged ahead. "It's just that I'm scared, I guess. I feel myself falling for you."

"That's not that scary, is it? I'm a pretty good guy."

She smiled at that. "No, it's not scary because of *you*. It's just — it seems like we met at the perfect time in our lives, right? We met when each of us was at sort of an impasse, professionally."

"But we're good together."

"We *are* good together. Right now. But we're both waiting for other things to unfold. You can't wait to get back to your real job, and I can't wait to start my dream business. I want those things, for each of us."

"I do, too," he said.

"But then what? Will we both be married to our jobs after that?"

"I understand, maybe more than you realize. I love my job. So much so that sometimes it feels like I can't have a great relationship. Or a family. And since we're being honest, I'll tell you that I've been thinking about that a lot over the past few weeks. Especially over the past several days. You make me want that. A relationship and a family. Being here like this, with you — it's perfect. But there's a part of me that wonders what will happen when I go back to patrol. Can we maintain this? I believe we can."

———

The morning of the second rodeo competition, Taylor was standing in the arena concourse when Judd came in carrying a white paper bag. He motioned for Taylor and the kids to follow him, and didn't speak as they rushed around the corner of the building.

"Are we hiding?" she whispered.

"Yes," he said. "Shh."

This made the kids giggle, and Taylor felt her lips twitching.

Judd motioned for them to gather in a shady corner, and Taylor gestured to the bag. "What's this?"

The five kids looked at Judd and the bag and then at each other. A comical silent conversation took place between them. Some of them raised their eyebrows in question: *Do you know what's in the bag?* and others shook their heads. *Nope.*

Judd smiled as he looked around the group. "Not so fast. First, I want to tell you guys how proud I've been of you, not just because of your performance at the first competition, but also because of how hard you've been working at the practices and fundraising events."

Both girls were smiling, pleased with Judd's complements. The boys were high-fiving, cocky. And Taylor was swooning on the inside.

"At the first competition, Ms. Cole and I noticed some of the teams had matching shirts and outfits."

Taylor couldn't believe it. Had Judd really bought them something matchy?

"We did," Taylor said. "And we thought they looked so well put together."

"Nah, man," Zion said. "You did not get us matching plaid shirts."

"Now, now," Judd said. "I wouldn't do anything to tarnish your reputation as one of the coolest guys at Prescott High School." He gave Zion a light, friendly punch on the arm. "But. I thought it would be cool, you know, good for team building, if you guys had something that matched."

"Well, let's see it, man," Zion said. "Don't hold out on us."

Judd held up his hands, the bag dangling from one thumb. "Okay, okay."

He hung the bag on his wrist and pulled out a folded blue t-shirt. He unfolded it slowly, playing up the drama and tension.

"Should we do a drumroll?" Taylor asked. She patted her hands on her thighs, and Scarlett and Olivia joined in. With one final flourish, Judd opened up the shirt to reveal the front: *Howdy* was printed in white lettering, with the outline of a horse beneath it. Judd turned the shirt around to show them the back, where the words *Prescott High School Rodeo Team* were printed.

Zion snatched the shirt from Judd's hands. "All right, bro, that's pretty dope. We'll be proud to wear this shirt."

"Did I do good?" Judd asked. Although the kids all clambered to answer, Judd was looking at Taylor.

The fact that he sought her approval made her feel all warm and fuzzy inside. "You did," she told him. She wanted to add, *I'll show you just how good, later.*

"So good!" Olivia said. "I hope you got one for you and Ms. Cole!"

"Oh, you bet I did."

———

*J*UDD

Judd could literally feel the gratitude and camaraderie emanating from Taylor and the kids when they came out of the bathrooms wearing their new shirts. It hit him in little waves, and he imagined those waves would sparkle and glint in the sunlight if he could see them.

"They look good," he said to Taylor, and as the kids walked away to get ready for their events, she said, "And it's not bad for camaraderie, either. You are pretty much the hero of the day."

Naturally, that led to a kiss — one Judd knew would have lasted a lot longer had they not been in public.

The two of them found a spot in the front of the stands. Taylor's nerves were on full display — adorably so, Judd thought — as the starting bell rang and a high school student sang the national anthem. Taylor kept biting her bottom lip, and although Judd knew it was an anxious habit, his body took it as an invitation. As the competition got underway, Judd forced his eyes off Taylor and did his best to watch the competitors.

Because of how well they'd done at the last event, Olivia and Scarlett had moved up in the rankings and would go a little later in the lineup. When Judd remarked on that, Taylor groaned. "I know, it is a good thing, but it also means we have to wait longer to see how they do."

As it turned out, Taylor had nothing to be nervous about. The girls both did spectacularly, improving their times and coming in among the top half of the group. Zion and Henry also beat their time from the first competition. They hopped off their horses and whooped and hollered when they were done, but Judd found Taylor's reaction even more entertaining. When she saw their time come up on the screen, she stood up, put two fingers in her mouth, and whistled, long and loud. Then she turned to him, bouncing on the balls of her feet, and squealed.

"If you'd told me in high school that I would consider a woman's squealing just about the cutest thing I've seen, I never would have believed you," Judd told Taylor.

She laughed, collapsing into the seat next to him, an arm draped over his shoulders.

"I wish we hadn't picked seats in the front half of the audience," he told her.

Taylor's head snapped to the right so she could look at him. "Why? Do you think they'd have a better chance if we sat in the back?"

He grinned at her. "No. I think *I'd* have a better chance. Of distracting you." He wished he could tuck her hair behind her ear and whisper all the things he'd like to do to her in the back row. Giving his leg a playful slap, she sat up straight again. "We need to send them winning vibes."

"I'd like to send *you* some vibes." At that, she looked at him, surprised. Then she started to giggle. It shouldn't, but the sound of her laughter turned him on even more.

When Raven's turn came around, Taylor sat straight up, hands on her knees, elbows locked.

"He'll be fine," Judd said, putting a hand on her back.

She leaned into his touch. "I know. I know he will. I'm just nervous, that's all."

"From the looks of it, so is Raven."

At that moment, Raven was dismounting Cinnamon with great speed and jogging toward the bathroom.

Some of the tension left Taylor's body. "He'll be fine."

And he was. As Taylor and Judd watched, he executed a near-perfect rope. His time was a little slower than the others in his group, and a little too slow to make the top five, but his technique was near flawless.

The competition was over, and everyone in the building waited for the tabulated team scores to show up on the screen.

"Breathe," Judd reminded Taylor.

He wished he could remind the kids to breathe, as well. The five of them stood in the holding pen, statues among their relaxed, laughing compatriots. Finally, the screen lit up with the scores. Prescott High School's team was nowhere near the top. But, more importantly, they'd earned enough points to advance to the next competition — the last one before the finals.

Before Judd had a chance to react, Taylor threw herself at him, her arms around his neck, her laughter in his ear. "We did it!"

Judd had what for him was an unfamiliar reaction. Sharing all this joy and excitement with Taylor? There was absolutely nothing else like it.

Chapter Twenty-Three

JUDD

Judd was on a mission. He had to figure out who was supplying Raven with his drugs. The Monday after the second rodeo competition, Judd walked the hallways of Prescott High School, deep in thought as he considered how to convince Raven to tell him. The day was so hot, Judd could feel the soles of his boots sticking to the sidewalk. He nodded to a group of girls passing by. They giggled in response.

He knew he couldn't pressure Raven too hard. He needed the kid comfortable for rodeo club. But, if he could somehow get just a little information, bring it to Raven for confirmation or denial, that might work. The lunch bell rang, and kids poured out of classroom doors. On scorching days like this one, they were either subdued and sleepy, robotic and zombielike, or they were bouncing off the walls, spraying each other with water bottles. Judd noticed right away that that particular day would be the latter. He saw one get kid gearing up to spray another one with squeezable water bottle and narrowly managed to avoid getting wet, himself.

"My bad," the kid hollered as he jogged toward the quad, arm still extended, hand clutching his weapon. Judd lifted a hand as if to say, *Don't worry about it*. He could stand to get sprayed with water, as hot as it was.

The hallway felt so chaotic, Judd didn't even notice Taylor approaching. She fell into step beside him and he thought, *Way to be aware of your surroundings, O'Connor*.

"You okay?" Taylor asked, her eyebrows furrowed.

He flashed her a smile. "Yeah. Just a little overwhelmed with all this ..." He held up his hands, gesturing at the craziness.

"I get it. Look over there." One student had taken off his shirt, which he held, bunched up in front of him. Another student was pouring water on it.

"Looks like a good way to cool off," Taylor said as the kid put on the wet shirt.

Judd nodded. "It does. I'll tell you what, there's almost no good way to cool off in this uniform."

"I'm sure there's a small faction of kids who would be more than happy to pour water over your head."

"Very funny," Judd said. He elbowed her, and she elbowed him back. Even in the chaos, Judd took a moment to appreciate the ease between them, the fun. He'd never had that with anyone else.

"What are you doing after practice?" she asked.

An idea hit Judd then, like he'd caught a punch to the nose. After practice, he could follow Raven home. If he trailed the bus, he would end up at Raven's house eventually. And then he could do a little surveillance. But he couldn't tell Taylor. Not yet. She might think he was crazy. But if he could just get to Raven's suppliers, he could shut down the high school drug ring without affecting Raven — or the rodeo club.

"Judd?"

"Sorry!" He rushed to say. He pointed at another student trying the wet t-shirt cool off. This time, it was a girl.

Taylor shook her head. "Kids these days."

"You aren't kidding. Anyway, I told Katy I would come straight home after practice to help with the horses. She has some event going on at her gym."

"Okay," Taylor said. "Sounds good. There's something I wanted to work on at home, anyway."

"Oh yeah? What's that?"

"It's a surprise," she told him, her coy expression making him unexpectedly aroused.

He smiled down at her. "That's fair. I can't wait to find out what it is."

They parted ways, and Judd quashed the guilt he felt about lying to Taylor. Once again, he told himself, he was doing the wrong thing for the right reason.

———

Thanks to Judd's years on patrol, he knew exactly where the activity bus would go after rodeo club. As soon as it drove away, belching diesel fumes behind it, Judd gave Taylor what he hoped was a kiss to remember (it must have worked, because she said, "You know, I could change my plans if you didn't have to feed the horses"), and then zipped home to switch out his patrol car for his personal truck and his uniform for street clothes. Sergeant Barnes would probably strangle Judd if he found out he was using his personal vehicle to do surveillance. But he would never know.

Judd caught up with the bus while it was still in town, dropping off Olivia and Henry in one of the older residential neighborhoods. He waited a couple of blocks back for the bus driver to close the doors, fold up the bus's stop sign, and continue driving. Zion's was the next stop. He lived in the neighborhood near the park where the kids played soccer. Raven lived off the next stop, in a row of gold-rush-era houses once occupied by mining families.

Again, Judd hung back a few blocks. Raven hopped off the bus, but before he started walking, he glanced to his right and left, then turned one slow revolution. *Checking out his surroundings,* Judd thought, *making sure no one's lurking around.* He probably saw Judd's truck, but wouldn't recognize it. He parked at the top of a long, gently sloping hill. From that vantage point, he could see Raven go into any of the houses.

Time to wait. Judd unbuckled his seatbelt and moved his seat back so he could stretch his legs. He'd bet his right arm that he would sit here for a while. Surveillance was ninety-five percent watching and waiting, and only a measly five percent action. But that five percent? It really got a guy's heart pumping — and it was what Judd lived for.

A movement on the sidewalk caught Judd's eye. A humongous orange cat sauntered along, its tail straight up and hooked at the end. As it walked by the house next door to Raven, a petite black-and-white cat — Judd thought people would call it a tuxedo — bounded down the front porch steps. It fell into step beside the orange cat, and Judd chuckled. They must be members of some cat gang, ruling Prospector Street.

Judd's stomach growled. Normally, he'd have packed snacks to pass the time, fill his stomach, and keep him awake. But he'd been in a rush after practice. A small dog on another front porch yapped as the two cats went by. It levitated with each bark. The cats looked over at it, and apparently unbothered, continued walking.

After another hour, Judd finally saw some action. The front door on the house next to Raven's opened, and a little old man walked out. He carried a tray, and on it sat a pitcher and two glasses. Judd could practically hear the man's bones creaking as he made his way across the porch and ever so slowly set the tray on a table next to the rocking chair. His journey back to the front door seemed just as painstaking. He went inside, leaving the door open, and reappeared a minute later, pushing an old lady in a wheelchair. The two of them wore matching light blue cardigans.

Judd could've sworn it took the man twelve minutes to wheel the woman over to the table and turn the chair around to face the street. Another eight for him to pour lemonade into two glasses and hand one of them to the woman. He finally sat down in the rocking chair and lifted his glass toward the woman in an apparent toast. She lifted hers and inclined her head, and they smiled at each other for just a moment before sipping their lemonade. Tears actually prickled in Judd's eyes.

"That is just about the most lovely thing I've ever seen," he said into the silence of his truck.

The tears surprised him, but his train of thought didn't. An image of Taylor came to his mind. He wanted to sit on a porch with Taylor Cole, wearing matching cardigans and drinking lemonade.

Before he had time to explore that idea or desire any further, Raven's front door opened, and Raven stepped out. Judd's inner cop, which had been snoozing as he watched the scene before him, perked up. He could feel the first sparks of adrenaline, tiny bubbles bursting under his skin. Again, Raven checked his surroundings. Finding the coast clear, he walked down his front steps, then looked right and left again. Shoulders tense, he made his way up the sidewalk. The old man called out to him, and he and the woman both smiled and waved at Raven, who smiled and waved back. Judd wondered if the couple had known Raven since he was a little kid. Raven kept walking. Maybe Judd should follow him. No, he thought, if he got out, Raven would undoubtedly see him, as often as he looked around.

The kid was about two seconds from being out of Judd's line of sight, so he put the truck in drive and inched forward. When Raven kept walking, Judd inched forward again. He hoped none of the neighbors noticed him. They would definitely call the cops, and then word would get back to Sergeant Barnes that Judd had gone rogue. He chuckled at that. Raven walked past three more houses before finally walking up the front steps of the fourth house. Judd typed the address of the house into his phone. Later, he'd look up who owned the place. Raven knocked on the door. He stood there for what seemed like a long time. Knocked again. The door opened a crack. Raven said something, and the door opened just wide enough for him to squeeze through.

"Great," Judd said.

For no particular reason, the hair stood up on the back of Judd's neck. Doom weighed on him, as if the air above him had become heavy. Nothing had even happened to make him feel this way. For all Judd knew, Raven was going for a friendly visit to the neighbor's. He could be asking to borrow a cup of sugar or a couple of eggs.

Judd's gut told him otherwise, but he couldn't very well march over to the house, knock on the door, and expect entry. So he waited. And waited. The two cats came back down the sidewalk, still sauntering. They weren't bothered about whatever Raven was up to. Side by side, they climbed the steps of the old couple's house. The orange cat jumped onto the woman's lap and curled into a tight ball. The black and white cat sat under the table, a sentry, ears perked. The sun, which boiled high in the sky, finally seemed to be making a descent. Its light sparkled golden through the leaves on the trees. Judd stomach growled again, reminding him it was dinner time.

As if someone had picked him up and thrown him, Raven came flying out of his neighbor's front door. He landed in a run and galloped down the steps. The whole thing seemed so much like a cartoon, Judd almost laughed. But then he saw Raven's face. The kid was scared.

Judd wanted to run up to him, put his hands on his shoulders, and ask him if he was okay. But, he wasn't supposed to be here. If Judd were on official police business, that would be one thing, but he wasn't. He was on *unofficial* police business, which basically equated to unprofessional police business. So all he could do was watch Raven hurry, head down, shoulders slumped, steps small and close together, as he walked back to his own house.

Judd double checked the neighbor's address where he had typed it into his phone. He copied it and pasted it into a text to Nicky, along with, *Check these guys out. They're definitely dealing. Seems like they've got a pretty big operation going on.*

Nicky wrote back right away, giving Judd a thumbs-up emoji followed by, *Aren't you supposed to be focusing on school, bro?*

Judd sent back a devilish smiley face. Then he put the truck in gear and drove away.

———

TAYLOR

Taylor might be crazy, but she was committed. She sat at her dining room table Wednesday evening, emboldened by a glass of wine (and the mostly full bottle next to it). Armed with a pen and paper, and the only personalized rejection letter she'd received, she finally took the plunge.

She had debated with herself for days, but seeing the kids do so well at the competitions, and the success of their own fundraising events, Taylor felt like she had new information. For about the millionth time, she read through the letter from Kristi Mendez, Senior Loan Officer at Prescott Bank.

Dear Ms. Cole,

I received your application for a business loan. I'm sorry to say that at this time, Prescott Bank cannot offer you a loan. That being said, I, personally, am intrigued by your business idea. Sugar Pine Barn sounds like a viable business that could enhance the lives of people in this area. I could sense your enthusiasm and dedication. The one thing missing for me right now is proof of concept. As a lender, I'd like to see something of a track record. The numbers look good on paper, but I need to see that you can maintain the enrollment numbers you outline in your business plan. And that comes from experience. I encourage you not to give up. I'm confident that, when you find the right lender — and you will — you will get the approval letter I'm sure you are hoping for.

Kristi Mendez

Senior Loan Officer, Prescott Bank

Taylor had originally considered the letter a statement, unarguable. But the more she thought about it, the more it felt like it could be the beginning of a conversation. Kristi Mendez liked Taylor's idea. She thought it showed promise, so wouldn't she be interested in the real-life progress Taylor had made? Taylor was betting on it. Because Kristi had written her note by hand, Taylor did the same.

Dear Ms. Mendez,

Thank you so much for taking the time to consider my business proposal and to write me a personal letter. I wanted you to know that since I applied for a loan through Prescott Bank, I have taken some steps to prove that my business plan is viable. I started a rodeo club at the high school where I work, and we have put on several profitable fundraising events. The rodeo club members have participated in two out of three major competitions, and scored well enough that we advanced onto the third major competition, which is coming up next week.

My business model includes fundraising events similar to those this club has been putting on. I always believed they would be profitable, but now I have proof. Such events would be the bread and butter of my business.

The club members' success at competitions proves that my teaching works — which will make parents feel like they're getting a return on their investment. I plan to work primarily with kids, but you and I both know my true ideal clients are their parents.

I'd like to invite you to come out to the third competition, to see the kids in action, and meet me in person. I would really love to show you what I'm all about, and what my business will be about.

Taylor listed the date and time of the competition, and the address of the arena. She signed off, and then, before she could chicken out, she put the letter in an envelope, addressed it, and went out and dropped it in the mailbox.

There. If Kristi had been interested before, coming out to see the rodeo in person was sure to inspire her towards a "yes" on Taylor's loan.

———

Wednesday afternoon as she was driving to rodeo practice, Taylor's phone rang. She didn't recognize the number, but it was local, so she picked up.

"Taylor Cole?"

"That's me." Taylor braked for a red light and took another look at the caller's phone number.

"This is Cassandra Brown. I'm a senior loan officer at Prescott Bank."

Taylor's grip tightened on the steering wheel. Her stomach churned. "Oh, hi. Hello. How can I help you?"

"I received the letter you sent to Kristi Mendez. She's no longer with this bank."

Taylor's body drooped. The churning in her stomach morphed from nervous to disappointed. "Okay. Well, thanks for letting me know."

"It's no problem," Cassandra said. "But I wanted to let you know that Kristi is still in town. She's just moved on to a different bank. If you feel like you have more proof of concept to share with her, then I urge you to get in touch with her."

The light turned green. Taylor took that as a positive sign from the universe. She pressed the gas pedal as a tiny flicker of hope ignited in her heart. "Oh, thank you! Do you know where she works now, by any chance?"

Taylor could hear the other woman sigh. "I'm ninety percent certain I could get in trouble for telling you. Sending business to another bank, you know? But I could sense your passion in that letter. Just keep this between us, okay?"

Taylor nodded, realized Cassandra couldn't see her, swallowed, and said, "I will. I really appreciate it." Taylor turned on to Williamson Valley Road, grateful to be out of the in-town traffic.

"She's over at the Arizona Credit Union. The one downtown, off Alarcon Street."

"Thank you so much."

"You're welcome. And good luck. I'm rooting for you. If things don't turn out with Kristi, give me a call."

They disconnected, and Taylor felt her throat tightening it at the woman's kindness. She also felt a flicker of alarm. The third and final competition — which would determine whether the team would make it to finals — was in just a few days. There was no time to waste. She called Judd, who picked up right away.

"Everything okay?"

"Yes," she breathed. "That is, if you can take practice for me until I get there. I have an errand to run."

"Sure," he said, and she exhaled. "I can cover practice, but if you want, we can run your errand together afterward."

"That's really sweet of you. But remember the other night, when I said I was working on a surprise?"

"I do," Judd said. "I'm still waiting for you to let me in on it."

"Well, the errand is related to that. So it wouldn't be a surprise if we did it together. It shouldn't take long. I'll see you in thirty minutes, okay?"

"Okay, boss. I'm intrigued."

"I like when you call me boss," she said.

"I'll keep that in mind."

"Please do. And Judd?"

"Yeah?"

"Thank you. It means a lot. Not just for covering practice, but for supporting me. I really appreciate it."

"Any time."

Taylor flipped a U-turn and headed back toward downtown. Heat waves rose from the pavement in the bank's parking lot. Inside, the bank was cool and quiet. A young man, dressed in an immaculate vest and bowtie, stood behind the customer service desk.

"How can I help you today?" He beamed at her.

"Is Kristi Mendez available?"

His smile didn't falter. "Do you have an appointment?"

"No, but I —"

"We really recommend that you make an appointment. You can do that online or through the app. Or, I can make one right here." He put a hand on his computer's mouse, clicked a few times, and looked at her expectantly, his smile still frozen in place. Taylor could practically see his molars.

The unexpected obstacle made Taylor feel like she was wading through wet cement.

"Okay." She nodded, in slow motion. "Okay. Yeah. I'll just do it later. On the app."

"Sorry about that."

Limbs heavy, Taylor turned around and walked toward the door. She couldn't say what fueled her change of heart, but she found herself turning around and marching right back up to the customer service desk. The banker tilted his head. "Was there something else?"

"Yes." Taylor squared her shoulders. "I was wondering if you might be able to just check and see whether Ms. Mendez would be willing to see me. It won't take long."

Although he continued to smile, Taylor could tell he was gritting his teeth. His eyes had lost some of their friendliness, but she didn't care.

He cleared his throat. "Who can I tell her is here to see her?"

"It's Taylor Cole. With Sugar Pine Barn."

Oh, Taylor thought as the man walked away. *It felt good to say that.*

Taylor waited by the customer service desk, unsure of what do with herself. She switched her purse from her left shoulder to her right, and straightened her shirt. She used her fingers comb her hair. Put an elbow on the counter. Tapped her fingernails. How long was this guy going to be gone? And did his long absence mean Kristi didn't want to see her? Or that she did? After what felt like about eight days, the man came back down the hallway.

Taylor couldn't tell whether he bore good or bad news. Then, behind him, she saw someone else. A woman, with expensive-looking high heels and a perfectly tailored skirt suit.

Chapter Twenty-Four

JUDD

Friday night, Taylor planned to have dinner with her friends, which gave Judd the perfect opportunity to do more surveillance. He drove back over to Raven's neighborhood, but this time, he loaded up on snacks. Katy came walking down the path as he loaded the cooler into his truck.

"What're you doing?"

Judd felt himself freeze, just for a second. But it was long enough that his sister noticed.

"You don't want to tell me, do you? Is it something romantic?"

Judd seized on that. "Yes. It's something romantic. But I'd like to keep some semblance of privacy."

He shut the passenger door, and would have walked around to the driver's side, except that Katy had blocked the route, leaning against the front of the truck. She had her arms crossed and a mischievous smile on her face. "Doing a little picnic?"

"Yep."

Katy pushed off the truck and put her hands on her hips. "Is everything okay? You're acting weird."

Judd hated lying to her. He hated making her worry. But he

didn't have a choice. If he told her what he was about to do, she wouldn't like it. She might even go so far as to tell their parents. Childish? Maybe. But also, protective.

Judd plastered on a smile and gave her shoulder a squeeze. "Everything's fine. Promise. I've just got some stuff on my mind."

Katy's posture had relaxed, but her eyes and eyebrows still showed concern. "Work stuff? I never thought I'd hear you say that about the school resource officer position. Which, was going to be, and I quote, 'the most boring, ridiculous assignment ever, with absolutely no action.'"

Katy smiled, and despite Judd feeling like he was in a hurry, he found himself smiling, too. "Exactly. Anyway. Tomorrow is the third rodeo competition. You should come."

As Judd had expected, the change of subject was enough to make Katy forget — at least temporarily — she was interrogating him.

"When and where? I have a thing at the gym tomorrow, but I'll head over after."

Judd gave her the details, and satisfied, she headed off to the barn. He felt a little guilty, but as was becoming common, he reminded himself he was doing the wrong thing for the right reason. He told himself that if Katy knew what Judd was really up to, and why, she would understand.

———

*T*AYLOR

Taylor had looked forward to Friday evening since Jessie and Rose had walked into the library Monday morning, arm in arm, in stride and obviously on a mission.

"We're here for a reason," Rose said.

"We haven't seen you in ages," Jessie said.

Well, we see each other every day," Rose said.

"But," Jessie said, "we feel like we haven't *seen* you, seen you. Like, actually talked to you."

"So." Rose put both hands on the checkout counter. "We hereby demand dinner plans."

It was true. Taylor was so wrapped up in the rodeo club and Judd (she shivered at the memory of being in his bed over the weekend), she hadn't talked with her friends as much as she usually did. "I would love to have dinner. When are you both free?"

"We're free Friday," Jessie said.

"Well that's perfect, because I am, too."

So, Friday evening, the three of them plus Celeste sat in the corner booth at Rita's.

Rita came over to the table, cracking her gum. "What'll it be, ladies?"

"The usual, all around?" Jessie asked Taylor and Rose.

"The usual," Celeste said, giving Rita an authoritative nod.

"I guess it's the usual," Rose said.

Rita snapped her notepad closed and pointed at Taylor with her pen. "It's nice to see you here with the girls. Not that I don't love seeing you with Judd. But girl time is important."

Rita walked away, apparently oblivious to what she left behind. Rose and Jessie's heads swiveled toward Taylor. They wore matching expressions of surprise. As perceptive as she was, Celeste picked up on the shift in mood. "What? Why are you guys looking at Auntie Tay like that?"

"Oh, no reason," Rose said, making an X in the tic-tac-toe printed on Celeste's kids menu. "It's just that, apparently, Auntie Tay has been going on dates. Without telling us."

Celeste brought her hands together in front of her chest, her mouth in an O, her little body tensing with excitement. "A few dates? And you kept them a secret? I thought we told each other everything!"

"It's not that kept it a secret, per se," Taylor said. "It's just that I haven't talked to your mom and Auntie Jessie because I've been so busy."

"Which is why we're here tonight." Celeste gave another nod. Apparently that settled things.

Rita brought their waters and a little peppermint candy for

Celeste, just like she did every time they ate there. Then she winked at Celeste, as if the peppermint was a secret.

Jessie unwrapped Celeste's straw for her and put it in her water before turning to Taylor. "So. Dish. What's been going on with you?"

Taylor filled them in on everything that had happened over the past two weeks. They listened, rapt.

"So you had a sleepover with Judd, Auntie Tay?"

Rose shot a look at Taylor across the table, and Taylor changed the subject. "What about you guys? What's been going on with you?"

Rose tilted her head toward Celeste and said, "We are loving our new, spendy apartment."

Taylor winced. "*Too* spendy?"

Rose shrugged. "Ramen and thrift store spendy, yeah."

"I do love ramen," Celeste said.

"Oh, we know you do, you little ramen monster," Jessie said, poking a finger into Celeste's ribs, making her giggle.

"Do you need help?" Taylor asked. "There must be some way we could help. Groceries, childcare ..."

"I really appreciate it." Rose sighed. "I think things will ease up a little now that we're in the swing of the school year. I was thinking I might be able to get some kind of work-from-home job. Maybe save a little before next school year."

"Let us know," Taylor said.

"I will. Thank you."

"Anytime," Jessie said. "You know that."

Rose nodded and Taylor saw that her eyes looked a little misty. She gave Rose's hand a squeeze, then turned her attention to Jessie. "What about you, Jess? How are things going?"

Jessie cleared her throat, and Taylor risked a quick glance at Rose. Throat clearing was out of character for Jessie. Typically, she launched right into whatever she had to say.

"I'm okay," Jessie said. "But Alvin isn't doing very well. It seems like he's aging right before my eyes. Today I went over and found the stove on — no flame — just leaking propane into the house."

"Oh, honey," Taylor said. "I'm so sorry. I know how much you love him. He's like a second dad to you."

Jessie's eyes filled with tears then, and Taylor felt her own throat go tight. "You're right. And it's so hard that Shane hasn't been around. That's like a double whammy. At least if we were in this together ..." She wiped her eyes with her napkin.

"I wish it didn't have to be this way," Rose said. "I'm so sorry."

Rita swooped in with her tray then, giving everyone time to collect themselves. Even Celeste was somber as she ate her macaroni and cheese.

"So, tell us about your rodeo club," Jessie said, obviously ready to change the subject. "Next steps, competition, all that stuff."

"The kids totally kicked butt in their first two competitions," Taylor said. "I was surprised. I always knew my library nerds knew horses and rodeo, but I am shocked at how well Zion and Raven did their first couple of events. The team is actually in fourth place in our division. We earn points every time one of our kids places in an event, and when the team places at the competition. After the next competition, if we have enough points, we go to the finals."

Taylor could feel the excitement rising in her body, just thinking about the possibility of making it to the finals.

Celeste must've picked up on the energy because she asked, eyebrows raised, "Is there a prize?"

"There is," Taylor said. "The winning school gets a whole bunch of rodeo gear."

Celeste gasped and put a hand over her mouth.

"I know," Taylor said.

"That would be pretty amazing," Jessie said.

Rose nodded. "It would be. And then Celeste and I, if we're ever in need of a slumber party, could camp out at the arena, and use rodeo gear to build a fort."

She dissolved into a high pitched, tittering laugh that alarmed Taylor more than it amused her. She and Jessie exchanged a look, which Rose noticed. She patted the back of Taylor's hand, and then the back of Jessie's. "Don't worry. I'm fine. Really."

Taylor sensed she should dig in further — something about

Rose's deer-in-the-headlights expression set off alarms in Taylor's mind. But before she could ask any questions, she heard a voice from behind her.

"Fancy meeting you here!"

Taylor turned around in her seat to see Katy approaching. She was smiling, but confusion clouded her eyes. Taylor stood up to give her a hug.

"Ladies, this is Katy, Judd's sister," Taylor told her friends. "Katy, meet Jessie, Rose, and Rose's daughter, Celeste."

"Pleasure to meet you," Katy said.

Celeste held up her fork, a piece of elbow macaroni on the tines. "Auntie Tay spends a *lot* of time with your brother." Her tone was accusatory, and Rose shushed her.

Katy didn't seem offended. "They do spend a lot of time together," she said. "But they both seem to enjoy it, so it's a good thing, right?"

Celeste pursed her lips. "As long as Auntie Tay still comes to our girls' nights, I *guess* it's a good thing."

"I'm sure she will," Katy said. "Look how much fun you're all having. Anyway, it was nice meeting you guys. I'm picking up an order, so I'll get out of your hair."

"She seems nice," Celeste said after Katy went out the door, making the bell jingle.

"She is," Taylor said, doing her best to keep her voice bright despite wondering why Katy had looked so confused after seeing Taylor at Rita's. "She's really nice."

———

*J*UDD

As Judd made the trip over to Raven's neighborhood, he thought about the research he'd done so far. The people who owned the property a few doors down from Raven were Becki and Levi and Crouch. He parked across the street from their house.

Based on their front-porch aesthetic (which he'd call white trash chic), along with the way they'd opened the door just slightly to let Raven in before throwing him out, Judd wasn't surprised to find them both in the criminal records system.

He also wasn't surprised that in their booking photos, they both had sores on their faces and missing teeth, and that vacant, dead-eyed expression common among heavy drug users.

The streetlights turned on as dark settled in.

Becki and Levi were born just a couple of years apart, and Judd figured they were married (although, in his line of work he'd seen some weird living situations). The wife, who Judd imagined in her younger days had introduced herself as "Becki with an i," had a longer and more dramatic criminal history.

Cracking open his cooler, Judd pulled out a can of seltzer water and a package of trail mix. He unbuckled his seatbelt and stretched his legs before cracking open the can.

Just like the good old days.

Time to watch and wait. The neighborhood was quiet.

———

Judd's phone rang in the middle of the night, blasting him right out of a deep sleep. Heart racing, he looked at the screen.

"Nicky. Everything all right, man?" He could hear the adrenaline-filled edge to Nicky's voice when he answered. "I'm all good, bro. I hate to do this to you, but I need your help with something."

Judd inhaled deeply, filling his lungs to capacity. He'd once read that deep breathing could snap the body out of the fight or flight response, which he'd experienced when he thought Nicky must be in trouble or injured.

"You there, Judd?"

Another deep breath. Then, "Yeah. I'm here. Whatcha got?"

"We got a kid here. Zion. Says he knows you. Won't talk to anybody else. To be honest, seems like a good kid. But we caught him right in the middle of this thing."

"The middle of what thing?"

Judd heard Nicky's deep breathing, and he could picture his

friend tilting his head back, gritting his teeth before speaking. It was what he always did when he was stressed. "It's a drug deal. A sting the guys are doing. That house you sent me the address for? Those guys are involved, but they weren't around. Anyway, this kid, he's part of something really big. Like, even though he's just a kid, he could go down for some serious shit."

Judd rubbed a hand over his face. "Where are you?"

"Over behind that convenience store off Sheldon and Pleasant Street. But I'm thinking I'm going to haul him in. I want to make an impression. You know, scare him straight, if we can."

Judd nodded, his stomach clenching when he thought of how scared Zion must be. Still, Nicky's idea seemed reasonable. "I'll meet you there."

Less than five minutes later, Judd was dressed and out the door. He was glad Taylor had decided to spend the night at her own house.

At the station, Judd found Zion and Nicky in one of the interview rooms, the kid pale and terrified under the fluorescent lights. Nicky had him cuffed, and Judd wondered if that might be taking things farther than necessary. But then he remembered the way Zion looked that day in the breezeway, doing some kind of deal with Raven: he looked like a criminal. They had to stop him from going down that road, if they could. Judd did the first thing he thought of: he pulled a chair up right next to Zion and sat down, put his elbows on the table like this was a casual conversation.

"What's up, man? Tell me how you got here."

The muscles flexed in Zion's jaw and at his temple. He lifted his chin in Nicky's direction. "He brought me here." Judd smiled, and he knew it was the exact smile he'd seen on his parents' faces numerous times growing up. The one that said, *I know there is more to the story, and you are about to tell me exactly what that is.*

"Why?"

"Do I have to say it in front of him?"

Exasperated, Nicky threw up his hands as he stood up. He left the room without another word.

"Spill."

"I didn't know it was going to be like this."

"You didn't know what was going to be like this?"

Zion balled his hands into fists, one on top of the other, and rested his forehead there. His voice was slightly muffled, but audible. "I didn't know it was going to be this big thing. I told Raven I needed money. And he told me I could earn it. I said okay. And I did what he asked."

"What did you need the money for?"

Zion sat up, then his expression showed nothing but despair. "Do I have to say?"

Judd shrugged, then leaned back in his chair and crossed his arms. "No, you don't. But I can't help you if I don't know what's going on."

"You would help me?"

"Zion, why did you ask Nicky to call me if you didn't think I was going to help you?"

The kid shrugged. "I trust you, I guess."

"What do you need the money for? How much are we talking?"

"I don't know, man. I needed like —" His voice broke. He swallowed. Started again. "I needed like six hundred. But that's just for this month. Next month I'm going to need another six hundred. And the month after that, too. You get the picture."

"What for?"

Zion finally made eye contact, then, defiant, daring Judd to judge him. "For medicine. For my dad."

"Why were you afraid to tell me that?"

"Because, man. Look. You probably don't get it. I see how you're dressed right now. What did those cowboy boots set you back? Like five hundred? You've got hundred-dollar jeans. What's six hundred to you? Plus, your dad is probably a decent, hard-working guy. But my dad? He's a bad dude. In fact, I'm sure if I told you exactly who he is, you'd know the name. But he's still my dad. My pops. And he's sick. He needs medication. Expensive medication. I'm the only one who will help him. When I saw a chance to make some money, I took it."

Judd stepped out of the interview room a while later. His whole body drooped. He had to help Zion. The only way to do that was to take down the guy in charge. Before he had a chance to consider his options, he heard a voice behind him.

"O'Connor."

Judd exhaled, the air hissing between his teeth. Sergeant Barnes had uncanny timing and some kind of Spidey sense. Judd trudged toward his office.

"Have a seat," Barnes said, his deep voice a near bellow.

Out of uniform, Judd felt almost naked, exposed. Barnes didn't seem to care about his discomfort, though. He hurried him in with a *come on* gesture.

Judd sat, perched on the edge of the chair, his elbows on the armrests, his body canted forward.

Barnes inclined his head. "Going to stay a while?"

Judd shook his head. Barnes laughed, and Judd met his amusement with a glare.

"All right, I get it. Down to business. O'Connor, what the hell are you doing here?"

That had Judd sitting up a little straighter. He assumed Nicky had gotten the okay before calling him.

"I assumed the guys got the okay before calling me."

Judd wouldn't single out Nicky, wouldn't throw him under the bus, but his friend should've known better than to call him without getting permission from their supervisor.

Barnes steepled his fingers and rested his chin on them. "I would have assumed the same. But, obviously, they did not. So would you care to tell me what you're doing here?"

Judd opted for honesty. "There's a kid at the high school. The guys picked him up tonight and he asked to talk to me. So they called me. Asked me to come over, see what I could get out of him. Sounds like he's just a tiny cog in a much bigger machine."

"And?"

"And?"

"Did you get anything out of him?" Barnes wanted to know.

"Oh. Yes."

Barnes raised an eyebrow. *Tell me more.*

He'd have to give Barnes something. "Like I said, he is a smaller cog in a much bigger machine. I think we'd do better to go after the big levers, not this kid."

"I believe I asked for information, not advice."

Judd bit the inside of his cheek to keep from groaning. "Right. He gave me some names, but they're street names." *And I'll investigate them on my own time,* Judd thought.

"Look, O'Connor. I get it. You came in to help out the guys." He paused, rubbed his five o'clock shadow with a meaty hand. "You know, I've heard that among the ladies, you're considered quite a catch. And you do have a very fine face. But I don't want to see it around here again. You with me?"

"Copy that. Loud and clear."

Barnes didn't say anything about seeing Judd around town. Still, with what he was planning, he would have to keep a low profile.

Chapter Twenty-Five

TAYLOR

This was it, Taylor thought as soon as she woke up Saturday morning: the third round of rodeo competition. She opened her blinds to look at the overcast sky. Taylor was grateful for the cloud cover, but she also hoped the event didn't get rained out. Kristi Mendez had promised to be there, and Taylor wanted her to see *everything*. Thoughts about a potential business loan occupied almost every cubic centimeter of Taylor's brain.

Still, she wasn't so distracted that she didn't notice the absence of a good morning text from Judd. That was unusual. He typically texted first. But, Katy had been pretty busy lately. Taylor admired the way he jumped right in and took care of the horses without complaint.

She grabbed her phone off the nightstand and texted him: *Good morning. Ready for the big day?*

An hour later, after she'd showered, dressed, and eaten, she picked up her phone in preparation to leave and saw that he hadn't responded. She texted again: *You're not still sleeping, are you? Do I need to come over and wake you up?* She added the smiling devil emoji, hoping he read her text as mischievous and not needy. She got in the car, a strange sense of unease accompanying her. Since they'd exchanged phone numbers, Judd had never not responded to a text. A tiny prickle of worry set in at the back of her mind.

Despite not having heard from him, Taylor expected Judd to show up at the arena at the same time she did, as usual. But he wasn't there when she pulled in. She figured it wouldn't do any good to wait for him, so she got out and went to meet the kids.

Olivia and Scarlett greeted her, grinning as they approached.

"Nice shirts," Taylor said to them, forcing excitement into her voice, even though a feeling of dread knotted her stomach.

"Where's O'Connor?" Henry asked, coming up to join them.

"I don't know," Taylor admitted. "I haven't heard from him this morning."

The girls exchanged a look, and Taylor rushed to add, "His sister has been really busy, so he's been taking care of their horses on his own."

The girls exchanged another look.

"You guys!" Taylor said. "Stop looking at each other like that! I'm sure it's going to be fine."

Henry pointed toward the concourse entrance. "There's Raven."

"Oh," Scarlett said. "He doesn't look like himself today."

He didn't, Taylor thought. She'd seen him around campus doing the cool guy thing, but whenever he was with the club, he was all smiles. Not that morning. Hands in his pockets, gaze on the ground in front of him, he looked like a whole different kid.

They greeted Raven with (maybe a little too much) enthusiasm. All they received in return was a gloomy, "Hey, guys. What's up?"

He didn't even make eye contact with them.

"Everything okay?" Taylor asked. Finally, he lifted his chin and looked into her eyes. "Everything's fine."

Not one word of it was believable. His eyes squinted a little, and his mouth looked pinched, like he'd eaten something sour. Taylor wished Judd were here. He was so good with Raven. He would know what to do. She wasn't sure whether to push for more information. Anyway, it was unlikely he would open up in front of the other kids. So she stretched her smile wide and said, "Okay! Let's go check in."

She headed for the check-in desk, but stopped when Olivia said, in a timid voice, "Um, Ms. Cole? We can't check in until Zion gets here."

Zion! Where was he? For him, too, absence was out of character. Now Taylor was worried about Judd *and* Zion.

"Right! What was I thinking? Why don't you guys go get some water, stay hydrated?"

They did, and she took the opportunity to text Judd again. *Are you okay? It's not like you to not respond, and not show up early to an event. Are you just lazing in bed? Haha. But seriously. Are you okay? And have you heard from Zion? He's not here, either.*

She stared at her screen.. They had ten more minutes before they had to check in. Panic was a butterfly, flapping its wings in Taylor's throat. Her mind spun. Was there any possible way their team could compete, even if Zion didn't show up? She could ask, but not until the last minute. She didn't want the others to know she was worried. She saw them coming back toward her. Raven still looked miserable. His eyes were shuttered, his mouth drawn into a frown. Taylor took a fortifying gulp of air. "It's supposed to be another scorcher. Make sure you drink throughout the day."

"Okay, Mom," Henry said.

The tension had built up inside of Taylor's body, so intense she wanted to scream. She sent the kids off to saddle up the horses, even though they would typically do that after checking in. Despite her best efforts, she was sure that they could sense her angst, and they didn't question her. When she was sure they were out of earshot, she approached the check-in table.

"Good morning," the woman at the table said to her. "Here for check in?"

Taylor nodded. Her jaw worked involuntarily.

"You're going to need your whole team —"

Still nodding like a maniac, Taylor held up a hand. "I know." She took another gulp of oxygen. "But what do we do if one of our team members isn't here? I'm really worried about him. I haven't heard from him. Is there any way to compete with only four team members?"

The woman pursed her lips, like she had to think about it, like the situation had never occurred before.

"I mean, hasn't someone ever gotten sick the morning of the competition? Someone has a fever, they're throwing up, they can't get out of bed? I mean, surely you wouldn't require an entire team to forfeit." Her worry for Judd and Zion was driving her to aggravation.

The woman nodded. "Well, you make a good point. Typically, we require all five competitors to be here."

Taylor ground her molars together. "I know."

"Let me make a call."

Taylor paced in front of the table while the woman made the call. She explained the situation to whoever was on the other end of the line, but after that, her side of the conversation didn't provide much information. It was a lot of, "Okay." "I see." "That's right."

It was all Taylor could do to stop herself from pulling out her own hair. Finally, the woman ended the call and put down her phone.

"I just hung up with the director," she said to Taylor. "I guess the rodeo gods are smiling on you today. You can compete with four. You'll still have to put someone in every event, so one of your kids will have to compete more than once."

Taylor nodded, fast. She could practically hear her brain rattling around inside her skull. She managed to choke out a quick, "Thank you," before scurrying off.

———

"Hi, Taylor!"

Kristi Mendez materialized next to Taylor.

"Kristi!" Taylor did her best to appear composed. Mentally, she straightened her shirt and smoothed out her hair. Physically, she gave her best impression of confidence, offering Kristi a bright smile she hoped did nothing to reveal that she was in full panic mode.

"Thank you so much for coming. I'm so excited for you to see the kids compete. Come on, I'll introduce you."

Without waiting for Kristi to respond, she headed toward the stables. As she'd hoped, Kristi fell into step beside her.

"We have a few minutes before we have to get started. I like to be in the stands before they sing the national anthem."

Taylor kept up her pace, a near jog, as they made their way around the side of the arena. Other coaches and kids called out in greeting, waving and tipping their hats. Taylor responded to each one by name, glad the exchanges took up air space so Kristi couldn't ask any questions. Taylor was afraid that if she had to answer, she would give away her team's tenuous position. She wanted — no, *needed* — Kristi to think she had it all together.

The barn was abuzz with contestants getting their horses ready, putting on saddles and bridles, tying ribbons on manes and tails.

"Guys, this is Kristi!" Taylor said, infusing her voice with joy. "She's here to cheer you on today. Kristi, this is Scarlett, Olivia, Henry, and Raven."

Kristi shook hands with each of the kids. "I'm so excited to be here. What events are each of you doing?"

Olivia took the initiative, listing off their events while counting on her fingers. She got to the fifth event, which should have been Zion's, and started to explain that Zion wasn't there.

Taylor cut her off. "We'd better get going." She looked at her watch. "They'll be starting any minute. She turned on her heel and headed for the stands, keeping a breakneck pace as she and Kristi found seats. Their timing was perfect. The announcer asked everyone to stand, and a student started singing.

It was the first moment since realizing Judd wasn't coming that Taylor was able to stop and think. *Judd wasn't coming.*

How could he possibly miss this?

Taylor went from worrying about Judd to angry he hadn't at least called or texted. One thought repeated itself: *This is why romance and business can't mix.* As the coach of the rodeo team — which very well could determine whether she got a big break with her business — Taylor should be solely focused on the rodeo competition. But Judd's absence was throwing her for a loop.

"Taylor?" Taylor looked over at Kristi, and realized Kristi, and everyone else in the audience, had taken their seats. Taylor emitted a high-pitched laugh and put a hand over her heart. "Silly me. Just daydreaming, that's all."

Still, when she sat down, Kristi looked at her and said, "Are you okay?" Taylor almost burst into tears, but managed to avoid it by letting out another crazed laugh. "I'm *fine*. Sorry, I just have a lot on my mind."

Taylor talked her way through the entire event, explaining the events, techniques, and scoring. Just like she had at the other competitions, Taylor waited, hands clasped between her knees, for the tabulated scores to show up on the scoreboard. When they did, she gasped. Her team's scores were not exceptional. In fact, this was the lowest they've scored yet. But it was just the to get them into the finals — barely.

"You said you needed a sixty-five, and it looks like you got it," Kristi said.

Finally, Taylor let down her guard, just a little. "I know! Can you believe it?"

"I can. Since I received your letter, I've been fairly certain your business is a sure thing. I'd love to come to the finals and watch again. That is, if you don't mind."

Again, Taylor thought of Judd. He'd be so excited to hear that Kristi wanted to come to the finals. At least, before that day, she thought he would. But maybe their relationship didn't mean as much to him as she believed. She'd just have to forge on alone— wasn't that what she'd always counted on, anyway?

"I don't mind!" she said to Kristi. "We would love to have you there."

JUDD

Judd couldn't believe what was happening. And it was all his fault. He paced the police department hallway, waiting for word from the County Attorney's office. Crazy for the adrenaline of getting back to work, like a dog with a bone, Judd had hyper focused on Raven — and completely forgotten about Zion.

"Stupid." Judd ran his fingers through his hair, again. Just because he had a connection with Zion, from all those games at the soccer field, he'd taken Ernie Vasquez's information at face value — and put on blinders.

Someone was brewing coffee. Judd's mouth watered, but he wouldn't pour himself a cup. The last thing he needed was to become even more jittery.

Wasn't one of the first rules of investigations that things are rarely as they seem? Who even knew how Ernie had heard Raven was the ringmaster of the drug trade at Prescott High School? Judd should have looked at alternatives. Specifically, Zion, who he'd seen with Raven at the very beginning of the school year.

"Idiot."

"I hope you're not talking about me, O'Connor," Sergeant Barnes said, coming around the corner.

Judd jumped. "Sergeant. No. I'm talking about myself."

Barnes shrugged, nodded. "I've said the same to myself a time or two. We might have more in common than you think, O'Connor."

He didn't leave room for discussion. Before Judd could respond, Barnes had gone back into his office and shut the door. Judd continued wearing a path in the tiles. His phone dinged. Another text from Taylor. *Is everything okay?*

"Everything is not okay," he said. How could he respond? How could he admit that because of him, Zion wouldn't be at that day's competition? Because of him, Zion might not even make it to the finals.

His lust for a real investigation wasn't the only thing that kept him from doing his best police work. His lust for Taylor had also distracted him. Which was exactly why he couldn't be a good cop and have a life partner. He'd known all along, and yet, he'd been so crazy for Taylor, for her companionship, for her laugh, for her body, that he let himself slip. He put his phone back in his pocket.

"You okay, man?" Judd jumped once more, this time in response to Nicky's voice.

"You sneaked up on me."

"Sorry, man. Usually you're a lot more aware of your surroundings than that."

Judd sighed. "Don't I know it."

"I just made some coffee," Nicky said, holding up his mug. "Want me to get you a cup? Or do you think you're jumpy enough?"

See? Nicky knows you as well as you know yourself. You don't need a woman when you have a brotherhood.

"Jumpy enough. Thank you. Any word from the CA's office?"

Nicky shook his head and sipped his coffee. "Not yet. Nothing official, anyway. I'm waiting on a call back. I tried everything I could think of, but they're pretty determined to turn this into a lesson, if they can. Make Zion's first offense his only offense. And make an example out of him, so other kids think twice before getting involved in something like this."

Judd hissed through his teeth. He understood. Typically, he would feel the same way. A short-term consequence that made an impact could stop a kid from getting into a lifetime of crime. But this short-term consequence would impact Zion and the rest of the kids in the rodeo club. And, of course, Taylor. How could he have been so stupid?

"You couldn't have known, O'Connor,"

"I *should* have known. If I wasn't so focused on the wrong kid, the first suspect. If I had paid more attention to Zion. Dug a little deeper. I might have prevented this."

"Beating yourself up isn't going to do any good. I'll keep you posted." Nicky started to walk away, but then stopped and turned around. "Hey, don't you have a rodeo competition today?"

A heavy weight dropped into Judd's stomach. "Yeah." He rubbed his forehead. "Like, right now."

"Shouldn't you be there?"

"Yes. I should. But I can't show my face. It's my fault we're missing a member." He gestured to the interview room where Zion still sat in a metal folding chair. "And I can't leave Zion now. He's counting on me to help get him out of this mess."

"I hear you," Nicky said. "But don't you think Taylor and the other kids could use your support?"

Judd shook his head. "They don't need me."

"I wouldn't be so sure. I can keep an eye on Zion if you want to —"

Judd held up a hand. "I appreciate it, but I'll stay."

Nicky blew out a breath. "I don't know if you're making the right call, bro. But, whatever you say, I guess. Anyway. I gotta get back in there. Like I said, I'll let you know as soon as I hear anything."

———

*T*AYLOR

Normally, Taylor felt quite like celebrating after a rodeo club event. But when the third competition ended and all the kids were gone, she sat alone in her car and cried. On autopilot, she opened her texting app and tapped on her conversation with Judd. The last ten or so text bubbles were from her:

Is everything okay?

Do you remember there's a competition today?

Are you still sleeping?

It's about to start.

Are you okay?

Not a single response had come through.

She dialed his number. It rang once and went to voicemail. She hung up, dried her tears, and drove home. Instead of putting a bottle of wine to use for celebration, she would use it to drown her sorrows.

She didn't bother turning on the lights, and as the sky darkened she sat in silence, drinking wine and refilling her glass until she real-ized the bottle was almost empty.

Her phone rang, startling her after it hadn't made a single sound all day. Instead of Judd's name on the screen, though, it was another local number. What if it was someone calling from the hospital, because Judd had been injured in a car crash? What if it was Judd, calling from someone else's phone, because he'd lost his in a terrible accident?

Awareness sparked in Taylor's wine-addled brain. While musing over the possible identity of the caller, Taylor had let the phone ring for so long, the call would surely go to voicemail. Fumbling her phone off the table, she tapped the screen to answer.

"Taylor?"

She recognized the voice right away. "Katy."

Katy didn't waste time with small talk. "Have you talked to Judd?"

"No. Have you?"

"No."

Taylor could hear the tension in Katy's voice. Why would Katy be upset? Judd hadn't missed Katy's rodeo club event.

"Have you been drinking?"

Taylor groaned. "A little."

Taylor heard Katy exhale, the sound so much like one Judd would make, Taylor couldn't help but chuckle.

"I'm coming over."

Katy ended the call and knocked on the door fifteen minutes later. As slow as Taylor was to get up from her post at the kitchen table, Katy opened the door and let herself in.

"Well," she said when she saw Taylor. "You look a mess."

"Thanks," Taylor mumbled, stepping back and pulling open the door. "How'd you know where I lived?"

"Judd told me." Katy came inside. "But more importantly, the other night, when I saw you at Rita's with your friends…"

"What about it?"

Katy put her hands on Taylor's shoulders and gently shifted her farther into the entryway. Taylor's hand slid off the doorknob and Katy closed the door.

"I hate to ask you this," Katy said, "but did you, by any chance, have plans with Judd that night?"

Taylor shook her head and gestured for Katy to follow her over to the kitchen table. "Want some wine? I think there's about a glass left."

Katy followed her. "No." She picked up the bottle, walked to the sink, and dumped out the rest of the wine. "So, you didn't have plans with Judd on Friday night?"

Taylor shook her head again, and could feel her brain moving inside her skull. "Nope. I planned dinner with my friends. We *did* have plans today, however." She could feel and hear her voice rising in intensity. "He was supposed to be at the rodeo competition. Didn't show."

"He didn't show?" Katy's eyebrows shot up.

"Right. He didn't show. And neither did Zion. Which left the team high and dry. Didn't even call. Or text. So, in short, he totally proved my point."

"What point is that?"

"That being in love is just a distraction from my business. All day, I couldn't stop pining after your sexy, delicious brother."

"Wait. Did you say being in love?"

Taylor waved her off, the movements slow and dumb. "Ah, so what if I did? It was over before it started. My dad always told me you can't have a family and run a business. I thought he was wrong. Shit, I thought I was *proving* him wrong. With Judd. But he was right. Ergo, things are over between me and your delicious brother. Love or no."

"Hmm," Katy said. "That aside, Judd lied to me. Which is very out of character. Judd wouldn't lie to me, and he wouldn't miss the rodeo competition ... unless something happened."

Taylor's thoughts felt as if they were moving through the heavy weight of water. "What do you mean, unless something happened? Look, Katy, maybe he's not the guy we thought he was, okay? I mean, it is inarguable that he is sexy. But maybe he is not the stand-up, honest, dependable guy we thought we knew."

Katy shook her head. "No, he is. I mean, he can be stupid. There must be something else to this."

Taylor sank heavily into a chair. She lifted her wine glass, and tipped it back. "Empty." She set the glass back down. "That's what I told myself all day today. He wouldn't do this. Something must be going on. But it's late now. And we still haven't heard from him." She picked up her phone as proof.

"I think we need to track him down."

"Track him down? Where could he be?"

Katy sighed, the long-suffering sigh of a sister. "I think I might have an idea."

"I'll drive," Taylor said, wobbling to her feet.

"*I'll* drive. You, my friend, are in no condition."

Taylor's inability to form an argument seemed sufficient proof that she was, in fact, in no condition. A few minutes later, Katy pulled into the back parking lot of the Prescott Police Department.

"I thought so," she said, pointing to the corner of the lot.

"His truck," Taylor said.

Her expression grim, Katy said, "Yes. His truck."

Taylor didn't know what, exactly, the new evidence meant, but she did know Katy thought it was bad. She said, "This isn't good, is it?"

Katy pretended to hit her head on the steering wheel at least four times. "I had a feeling this wasn't going to go well. This school resource officer deal. I mean, once he met you, and got involved in the rodeo club, I thought it might be okay. But, he just couldn't stay away."

Taylor's stomach started churning, and she wasn't sure whether it was from nerves or too much wine. "Are we going in?"

Katy sat up straight and looked across the cab at Taylor. "I don't know. He's not answering our calls or texts. I feel like going in is our only choice."

"Do you have gum, by any chance? To settle my stomach."

Katy reached into the backseat to grab her purse. As she looked through it, she said, "To settle your stomach. Right."

That made Taylor giggle. Ingesting that much wine was never a good idea. Ingesting that much wine and then showing up at her boyfriend's place of work, hurt and angry? An even worse idea.

Katy handed her the gum. "Let's go."

Taylor headed for the police station's front door, but Katy called for her to follow her around the side of the building. Taylor's mouth dropped open when, without hesitation, Katy went up to the side door and pounded on it.

"You can just do that? At the police station?"

Katy shook her head. "Not every day, or anything. And not if I was here to track down an ex-boyfriend or something. But in this town? If it's my brother? You bet your ass I can."

The door swung open and a man, heavy lidded and flat-mouthed with exasperation, stuck his head out to make sure it was just Katy. He startled a little when he saw Taylor, and Katy said, "Barnes. Meet Taylor. Taylor. Meet Barnes."

"Ah, the infamous Sergeant Barnes," Taylor said. Then she slapped a hand over her mouth. "I didn't realize I said that out loud."

Katy shook her head and rolled her eyes. Barnes stood back and held open the door. As the women walked through, he said, "I hate to make assumptions, but it looks like Ms. Taylor here could use something to eat. I'll get her something. You must be here for your brother."

Katy nodded.

"O'Connor, your sister's here," Barnes hollered as he walked back down the hall, leaving Taylor and Katy standing just inside the door.

Under any other circumstances, Taylor would have found Judd's groan in response comical. She heard his footsteps coming around the corner, and felt like two distinctly separate personas woke up inside her brain.

First, the one who loved Judd saw the lines between his eyebrows, the bags under his eyes, and his weary posture. That part of her felt a stab of longing, and wanted to run to him and hug him and ask if everything was all right.

The second, indignant, hurt persona, saw nothing but the man

— albeit the very sexy man — who'd betrayed her. By all appearances, he was alive and well and able to communicate ... but he hadn't shown up, or bothered to call or text or even send a carrier pigeon.

She'd never been a violent person, but that second part of Taylor wanted to walk right up to Judd and give him a good, hard punch in the shoulder.

Fortunately, the warring inside Taylor's mind prevented her from acting. She stood there, silent. Katy, on the other hand, did not seem to have the same problem. She stalked right up to Judd and poked him in the chest, like they were a pair of cartoon characters. "You didn't show up at the rodeo competition, but you're here at the police station. You'd better explain yourself right this very minute."

Judd's jaw worked as he looked down at his sister. He swallowed. He looked over Katy's shoulder at Taylor and said, "I'm sorry."

Taylor remained frozen, still unable to speak. A hand appeared, holding a granola bar in front of her face. She took it, opened the package, and took a bite. She *was* hungry, she realized.

"That's all you have to say?" Katy said.

Taylor took another bite of the granola bar and then crossed her arms and widened her stance while glaring at Judd, who had the decency to look chagrined.

Finally, Taylor found her voice. Heartbeat thundering in her ears, she said, "Then why don't you tell me what the hell happened?"

Judd looked at her for a long moment, eyes pleading. "I know *what* happened. I'm just not clear yet on what's *going* to happen. And I feel like I should have that information before I try to explain myself."

Indignation rose up from the soles of Taylor's feet, through her knees and hips and shoulders. It finally exploded out of her mouth. "You know what, Judd O'Connor? Frankly, I don't care what your explanation is, even if you have a perfectly good one, which I hope you do, because I hope I wasn't wrong about the kind of man you are. But no matter how good it is, even if it's perfect, I'm sorry to say that we can't be together. I can't do this. Ever again. My business is so, *so* important to me and if they hadn't let us compete without our second coach and fifth member today, it would've ruined *everything* I've worked so hard for. And not only that, but you not being there distracted me. It threw me off. Which is exactly why romance and business can't mix."

"Ms. Cole?"

Taylor recognized Zion's voice right away, and she felt her eyes growing wide. She swiveled one hundred and eighty degrees to see Zion standing in a doorway down the hall. "Zion!" She whirled back to face Judd. "You," she spat, pointing at him. "You're the reason my fifth competitor wasn't there today."

"Ms. Cole, let me —" Taylor held up her hand to silence Zion.

"I appreciate you trying to get Mr. O'Connor out of hot water, Zion," she said, "but he's in pretty deep."

"What is *he* doing here?" She said to Judd, her voice dripping with barely constrained anger. She could see his Adam's apple bob and hear the sound as it moved up and down. "It's a long story. I —"

"No! Don't even try to explain!" Rage, burning hot, flowed through her veins. "There is nothing you could possibly say to me to make this right! You should have been there today! And even if you had a perfectly reasonable explanation for missing it, you should have called or texted me. To leave me wondering where you were, all day, that was pretty much the worst thing you could have done."

Judd didn't answer. His jaw muscles clenched, and she could see the tension in his shoulders, but he didn't speak.

Still seething, Taylor dropped her arms to her side. "Look, Judd. I should have known, based on how much you missed your *real* job, how you *couldn't wait* to get back to it. And you know what? I can take the rejection. You missing the competition today, it hurt. It hurt me. But I'm an adult. And now, whatever you've done, which, frankly, I don't even want to know, you've got Zion wrapped up in it. He's a child. A *child*, Judd. I was wrong about you. Don't bother calling me, now. Don't bother coming back to rodeo club, or to the finals. Which, by the way, we made the finals. Even without you. And even without Zion."

"We made it?" Excitement edged into Zion's voice.

"We made it," Taylor told him. "And I certainly hope that whatever is going on here, you can get it figured out in time to be there for finals. We need you."

With that, Taylor stalked out, marching all the way to the parking lot before she realized Katy, her ride home, was still inside.

Chapter Twenty-Six

In the silence Taylor left behind, Judd expected to hear crickets. After a few beats, Katy said, "Well. I guess she told you."

Judd grunted. He couldn't formulate another response. "How could she possibly be this angry? She has no idea what I've been through today." He cringed at the pained, nasal, whiny tone of his own voice.

Katy put her hands on her hips and narrowed her eyes at him. "Probably because you didn't *tell* her. I know you've never had a partner you could trust enough to share this stuff with. But from where I'm standing, you and Taylor had something special. And you're a doofus if you can't see that."

Judd felt the blood rush to his face. "Did you just call me a doofus?"

"Yes! Because you're acting like one. I'm certain you have a perfectly good explanation for why you didn't show up at the rodeo competition today. But there is absolutely no reason why you couldn't have called Taylor. Or hell, even texted her. You left her hanging, Judd. She trusted you, and you left her hanging."

Judd pressed the heels of his hands to his eyes. "I'm such an idiot," he muttered.

Judd realized then that anyone in an office along the hallway could hear every word they said. Even though the damage was already done, he motioned for Katy to follow him, and walked down the hall, the sound his cowboy boots made against the floor echoing against the bare walls.

He led his sister to the break room and sat down at the table. When Katy sat down across from him and finally got a good look at him, her features softened. She reached across the table and laid her hand on top of his. "So, tell me what happened today."

Finally. Judd could spill his guts, and Katy wouldn't judge him. Or, maybe she would, but no matter what, she was his sister, which meant she still had to love him. He told her everything. He started with the day he'd come across Raven and Zion doing a drug deal, and how he'd *encouraged* them to join the rodeo club (he put air quotes on the word). He gave her a bullet-point list of the events leading up to that day, including Ernie Vasquez asking him to follow up on Raven's possible involvement in the school's drug ring, his surveillance of Raven's neighborhood, and how he'd overlooked Zion's possible involvement, as distracted as he was by Taylor. Saying her name felt like taking a knife to his abdomen.

"In hindsight, it's so obvious," he said. "Zion was the main player all along. But, I felt like we were friends in a way, and I let that cloud my judgment." He lifted a hand. "See? More proof that relationships and police work don't mix."

Katy clucked her tongue at him.

"Are you clucking your tongue at me?"

She rolled her eyes.

"You're actually rolling her eyes at me."

Katy, who'd sat back in her chair while he was talking, leaned forward again. She reached across the table and took both of Judd's hands in hers. She looked into his eyes for a long moment and then said, "Judd. I love you. *And* you're an idiot."

"I know. You're right."

She tilted her head at him.

"You always are."

She smiled.

"I wanted to get everything resolved before I told her anything," Judd said. "I wanted to be able to say, 'I made a mistake, but I fixed it.' But nothing's going right. The county attorney wants to make an example out of Zion, and I can't quite figure out how to prevent that."

His sister twisted her lips to one side — her thinking expression. "I know you're going to say you were doing the wrong thing for the right reason. And maybe you were. I just wish you had trusted Taylor more. She would have understood, I know it."

"Again. Hindsight," Judd said.

Judd heard Nicky coming, the creak of his leather gun belt announcing his presence before he filled the doorframe.

"The county attorney won't budge," he told Judd. "Your boy is going to juvie. I'm sorry, man."

Again, Judd was at a loss for words. He'd been expecting that. "Can I talk to him?"

"Sure. Come on back. Just don't let Barnes see you."

"I'll be right there. Can you give us another minute?"

Nicky nodded. "Sure thing. Katy, hit me up when you're done. I'll walk you out."

"Thanks, man," Judd said.

After Nicky left, Judd stood up fast, his chair making an awful scraping sound. He started pacing. "Shit," he said. "Shit, shit, shit."

"How are we going to fix this?" Katy asked.

Judd stilled. "I have no idea. I want to make things right with Taylor. I want to help Zion. He's a good kid. He just made some bad choices. To make things right with Taylor, I *have* to help Zion. I have one week to get him out of juvie, so he can go to finals."

"How are we doing to do *that?*"

Judd stopped pacing and stood facing his sister. "The only way to do it is to find whatever adult has been selling to him."

"And, let me guess. Barnes told you to stick to your new position. So, you're going to have to do it on your own. Go rogue."

"Yeah," Judd said, drawing out the word, anticipating her reaction.

"Well, maybe I can help."

Nicky's voice rang through the hall. "O'Connor, you're running out of time."

Judd sighed. Katy stood up, wrapped her arms around his waist, and gave him a squeeze. "Everything will work out," she told him. "Just wait and see."

Inside the interrogation room, Zion sat in a metal folding chair, as still as a statue. His eyes were so big, Judd could see the whites all the way around his irises. He bounced one of his heels. He licked his lips. "Judging by the look on your face, I guess I'm going to juvie."

Judd shut the door behind him and sat down in the chair next to Zion's. "I'm so sorry, man. I did everything I could. I'm going to bust my ass to get you out as soon as possible. But you've gotta give me some names, man. I've got to be able to give the county attorney something besides an idea. Something concrete. They need to be able to arrest someone — to feel like they're putting a stop to this drug ring at the school."

Zion shook his head. "I hear you. But, even if you get me out, how am I going to get that money for my dad? I've got to do it, you know? If I don't get the money, he doesn't get the medicine."

"I understand." Judd did understand. Desperation drove people to crime. He'd seen it too many times to count.

"What if I helped you?"

Again, Zion shook his head. "I appreciate it. But, dude. Let's be real. I know cops don't make much money."

"I'm not talking about a handout. Although I wish I could. I'm talking about a job. What if I help you find a job?"

"I could get a job? Like, a real job? I thought you had to be older."

"I know a few places that hire at fifteen. Nothing glamorous, you know. Washing dishes, bussing tables, maybe making popcorn at the movie theater. But it's legitimate money."

Zion pursed his lips. "You would do that? After all of this?" He gestured at the space around them.

Judd smiled. "Like I told you before, the way you play soccer, I know you have brains, talent, and determination. I would love to see you use those — legally. So, yes. I would help you. And, it will be a whole lot easier to help you if you help me. I need you to give me something."

———

*T*AYLOR

Taylor permitted herself that one evening to wallow in her misery. After a few minutes, Katy came out of the police station and drove Taylor home. When she dropped her off, she said, "I know my brother seems like a big lunkhead right now. But I hope you can forgive him. The two of you are really great together."

Even in her drunk and miserable state, Taylor noticed Katy's use of the present tense. *You two are really great together.*

She managed not to cry until she watched Katy drive away and shut and locked her front door. Then she burst into tears, massive, ugly sobs, racking her body. She checked her wine cabinet for another bottle, but — nothing.

"It's probably for the best," she mumbled. "Even in my state, I can tell I'm slurring."

After filling a glass with water, Taylor decided to put herself bed. She took off her boots and jeans and slid between the cool sheets. Considering the amount of wine she ingested, she should be able to sleep. But, every time she closed her eyes, she got the spins, which made her cry even harder.

She didn't understand. How could Judd have been so thoughtless, so inconsiderate? How could she have been so stupid? He was upfront with her all along. He loved his job and wanted nothing other than to get back to it. Obviously, their relationship was just a distraction to pass the time.

The ceiling had finally stopped spinning, so Taylor turned onto her side and closed her eyes.

Like she'd told herself a million times, she didn't have room for romance. After her one night of wallowing, she would refocus the next day. She had a team to get ready for the final rodeo competition. She couldn't afford to be thinking about Judd. No matter how mouthwatering he happened to be. That thought made her cry all over again.

The next morning dawned bright and cheerful. The sunshine, in all its joyful glory, felt like an assault to Taylor's eyes and her fragile emotional state. She threw her arm over her eyes as soon as she woke up.

"My head is pounding," she said, wishing Judd were there to get her some aspirin. At that thought, she flung off her covers and sat up. A sharp, stabbing sensation took hold at her temples and she groaned.

"You are a strong, independent businesswoman," she told herself. "You can get your own aspirin."

After downing the aspirin, she showered, making the water as hot as she could stand. A good shampoo, a slice of toast, and half a cup of coffee made her feel somewhat human.

Taylor's phone rang, the sound so shrill, her ears practically bled. She looked at the screen. "Why would Katy be calling?" She answered with as energetic of a, "Good morning," as she could.

"Good morning, sunshine. What's on your agenda for the day?"

"Coming up with some way to salvage the rodeo finals. We don't have an alternate, and I don't know if I'll be able to find a fifth member at this late stage, or if that's even allowed. I'm pretty sure I need another coach. At this point, I would take a warm body. Are you game?"

Before Katy could answer, Taylor had a realization. "Never mind. You heard everything I said to Judd yesterday. He and I are over. I wouldn't expect you to be a warm body for me."

Katy's easygoing laugh came through the earpiece. "I would love to be a warm body for you, since my brother is a certifiable doofus."

Taylor's own laughter sounded foreign to her ears after all the crying she'd done the night before. "Okay. I'd better check and make sure you don't have to be a staff member, but I appreciate your willingness."

"Anytime."

"Wait. You're the one who called me. What did you want to talk about?"

"We just talked about it," Katy said. "I was calling to see if there was any way I could help you. Judd told me how much this club means to you, especially in relation to your business. Ergo, it's important to him. Ergo, it's important to me."

A fresh round of tears threatened to fall. Taylor cleared her throat. "Well, thank you. I appreciate it more than you know."

"You're welcome. Also, I'm at your front door. I called to tell you that I'm taking you out for breakfast. We're going to brainstorm about how to salvage this incomparably terrible situation. Will you let me in?"

Taylor opened the door and Katy stepped back, gasping. "My gosh, you look like death. Please tell me you didn't imbibe any more after I dropped you off."

Taylor shook her head, felt a smile tugging at the corners of her mouth. "I did not. But I had more than enough to result in the beautiful image you see before you."

"It is a sight, that's for sure. I mean, you smell good. But it looks like you got about a minute of sleep and need about a gallon of Gatorade. I think some food will do you good."

Once they were seated in a booth at Rita's, Katy slid a notepad across the table. "Step one. Make sure I can stand in as your second coach."

Taylor nodded. Katy was like a live wire, delivering current. Taylor was happy to go along for the ride. Rita approached the table, smiling. Her forehead wrinkled when she saw Taylor's face up close. "Excuse me for saying so, honey, but you don't look so good."

Katy tried to hide a smile.

"Don't I know it," Taylor said.

Rita pointed her pen at Taylor, then at Katy, and then at Taylor again. "The two of you here, together, you looking like you do," she said. "Tell me there's no trouble in paradise."

"But then we'd be lying, Rita," Katy said. "Don't you worry, though. We're here to get things back on track."

"It's that doofus brother of yours, isn't it?"

Katy's laugh bordered on maniacal. "It is. But I'm determined to fix it."

Chapter Twenty-Seven

TAYLOR

Buying a new car wasn't on the list Taylor and Katy made over breakfast at Rita's. But after Katy dropped her off late Sunday morning, Taylor decided she was ready to take action on parts of her life unrelated to her business. The more she could be the person she wanted to be, the more the pieces would fall into place.

She drove to the car dealership on the other side of town and parked her nondescript car for what she hoped was the last time. She did feel a pang of sadness because the car had been good to her. When she got out and shut the driver's door, she gave the car's roof a little peck. "Thank you for being so reliable."

Inside, she approached the front desk, sure to stand up straight and square her shoulders.

"How can I help you?" The salesman, a twenty-something with close-cropped hair and trendy, thick-rimmed glasses, stood up when he spoke.

"I'm here to buy a truck."

She didn't miss the flash of surprise in the salesman's eyes.

"Okay," he said. "A truck. Did you have something specific in mind?"

She did. "I do. I looked online before I came here. I have it narrowed down to two. I'd like to test drive both of them."

"Okay," the man said, drawing out the word as he started to come out from behind the desk. His disbelieving tone rubbed Taylor the wrong way. "Which two are they?"

Taylor told him, and he stilled. "That's a lot of truck," he said. "Are you sure you don't want to go with something smaller?"

Taylor wished Judd were with her. The salesman wouldn't question Judd if he asked to test drive those trucks. She took a deep breath and figured maybe the universe was testing her, giving her a chance to prove she was serious about being the new, confident version of herself. "I'm sure. I'm opening a barn. A rodeo training business. I'll have horses to feed, bales of hay to transport, and work to do around the barn. I need a lot of truck."

"Okay," he said again. "Let me get the keys."

Taylor felt her jaw tightening even though he was on his way to retrieve the keys. While he was gone, she ran through the details of the trucks she liked. They were almost identical. Although they were two different makes, they both had the same size engine, got roughly the same gas mileage, and featured leather upholstery. One was a cherry red, and the other was an electric blue. Both colors definitely made a statement, and Taylor couldn't wait to pull up to her non-spot in the Prescott High School parking lot in one of them. Not that she would be doing that for much longer, but still.

A few minutes later, Taylor heard footsteps on the polished showroom floor. She looked up, expecting to see the man she'd been talking to, but instead, a woman in a tailored suit and some serious high heels approached, smiling.

"You must be Taylor," she said, extending her hand. "I'm Marisol. I'll be joining you on your test drives. I hear you need a lot of truck."

Marisol smirked, and Taylor laughed, suddenly feeling much more at ease. "I do."

Marisol held up a key in each hand. "Red or blue?"

Taylor thought for a minute.

"Blue."

Marisol pocketed one key and handed Taylor the other. "Let's do it."

As soon as she buckled her seatbelt, Taylor thought she would like driving this truck. When she pulled out onto the highway, she *knew* she would love it. "I love this."

Marisol smiled at her across the cab. "I know. Is it the smell of leather? Or the power? Or how quiet it is in here?"

Taylor laughed. "You're reading my mind. It's all of those things. It's the way I feel in this driver's seat. Confident. In charge. Calm."

"Can I show you something?"

"Please do."

Marisol pushed a few buttons on the touchscreen and the music came on. "This stereo system is top-notch. The red truck? Doesn't have it. It's okay. But nothing like this." She turned up the music, and in the beat of the drums coming through the speakers, the twang of the guitar strings, and the lilt of the country singer's voice, Taylor heard her answer.

"I'll take it."

"You'll take it?" Marisol's voice was practically a squeal.

"Yes. I love it. I don't even have to drive the red one."

And just like that, Taylor bought her first really nice vehicle. And it definitely wouldn't blend into the parking lot.

———

*J*UDD

Katy had Monday off work, so Judd called in sick. He briefly considered whether Taylor might think he was avoiding her or leaving his school resource officer position, but then he decided it didn't matter. All that mattered was getting Zion out of juvie so he could compete in the finals that weekend ... and so — maybe — Taylor would forgive him.

He and Katy climbed into his truck first thing in the morning, and drove back over to Raven's neighborhood.

On the way, Judd explained why they were headed there. "So, when I did that surveillance before, I looked up who owns the house Raven went to. It turns out, it's this couple, Becki and Levi Crouch. Both of them have a record a mile long. When I talked to Zion yesterday, he was pretty reluctant to give me any names. Until I mentioned these guys and his eyes lit up. And you know it: they have street names. B-mom and L-Dog."

Katy guffawed.

"I know. I wish people could put the same creativity into the street names that they do into breaking the law."

"So what's our plan?" Katy wanted to know. "We're not, like, going to go in there and talk to them, are we?"

"We don't have to. But I'm thinking, if I go in there, put a little squeeze on them, maybe they'll give me some information."

They had stopped at a red light, and Judd looked over in time to see Katy shuddering. "Bad idea," she said. "These guys are criminals. Do you really think it's wise to go knock on their door? Especially when you're not in uniform?"

The light turned green. Judd pressed on the accelerator. "I don't think it's the best idea, but it's only one I have. Unless you have a better one."

"Unfortunately, I don't."

The two cars registered to Becki and Levi Crouch sat in the driveway at their house.

"Looks like our fearless criminals aren't working today," Judd said to Katy. "Maybe we'll get some action."

"Should we sit and wait for a while? I mean, maybe they'll come out."

"I guess that's reasonable," he said. "We have all day."

Judd could practically hear a second hand clicking on a clock, even though no actual clock existed in the truck. The neighborhood was still. The only activity Judd saw came from the two cats, who sauntered from one end of the neighborhood to the other and back again. He'd never admit as much out loud, but he found himself thinking about what was happening at the high school. It was only second period, so the kids were still subdued.

"Is this what surveillance is always like?" Katy asked after about an hour.

"Most of the time, yeah. Want a snack?"

"Nah," Katy said. "But maybe we should go around back, spy on these guys."

Judd looked at his sister. "That's what I was thinking."

Katy swatted his arm again. "Judd! I was joking! We can't do that! I'm sure it's illegal. Trespassing."

"Totally illegal. But I'm going to do it."

Impervious to Katy's objections, Judd got out of the truck and jogged across the street. He slipped down the first alleyway he saw, and followed it to the back of the house about three doors down from his target. Those backyards faced the backyards of the homes on the next street over, with a small drainage culvert running between them. Which meant Judd could follow the culvert and hop the fence right into Becki and Levi's backyard. Crouching low, Judd made his way to the target house and peeked over the fence to check for dogs. He didn't see any, but he'd been surprised before.

Judd knew from experience that cement block fences were the hardest to climb. He looked around for something to stand on — a big rock, a discarded crate, or an old piece of furniture — but nothing. At least he was wearing street clothes. Jumping the fence would be easier without the weight of his vest and boots. With that thought fresh in his mind, he put his hands on top of the fence and hoisted himself up. As he swung his right leg over, his knee scraped hard against the cement. It hurt enough that Judd figured it'd leave a good scrape.

He landed facing the house — and a sliding glass door, behind which stood a greasy-haired man in a ratty white tank top and jeans so loose, the waistband of his underwear stuck out above them. The man's eyes widened when he saw Judd.

Judd panicked. He should have come in uniform, on the clock. If the man, who Judd assumed was Levi Crouch, called the police, Judd would be in hot water. As in, fired.

Men like Levi Crouch don't call the police.

Levi's eyebrows drew closer together and the corners of his mouth drew downward. He strode just a couple of steps into the room behind him, and when he strode back, he held a baseball bat in his hand.

Better than a gun.

That's when Judd realized: Levi thought he was some guy off the street. Some guy with a bone to pick related to Levi's drug sales, probably. He had no idea Judd was a cop. So Judd had better not act like one. He looked down at his legs and realized he'd torn his jeans. And his skin. Inspiration hit. He grinned at Levi, as if the guy were his long-lost best friend. Adding an exaggerated wave, he walked toward the sliding glass door.

"Levi, man, what's up?" He spoke in a near shout.

The arm holding the baseball bat relaxed — a little. Levi's expression morphed from menacing to confused.

"Hey, can I come in? I totally scraped my knee, man. Do you have a Band-Aid?"

Still holding the bat, Levi reached for the door lock. It snicked open, and Levi cracked open the door. "Do I know you?"

Again, Judd smiled. "Yeah. We met through Zion, remember?"

Levi frowned again. Maybe he was smarter than Judd gave him credit for. "Huh. Why'd you jump the fence, man? That's some creepy stuff."

Judd shrugged. "Didn't want anyone to see me coming to your place, bro."

"Right. Yeah, I got Band-Aids." He pulled open the door and let Judd inside.

Wasting no time, Judd scanned the living area, which was pretty much as he'd expected. Paper bags and wrappers from fast food food restaurants sat crumpled on the coffee table alongside discarded paper cups. A couple of empty, half-open pizza boxes sat on the kitchen counter. Frozen food boxes pushed out of an already-stuffed trash can. Despite the evidence of a plethora of pre-packaged, pre-prepared food, the kitchen sink overflowed with dishes.

Dirt caked the edges of the threadbare couch cushions. Wedged between the couch and the coffee table sat a pile of clothes, about as high as two bales of hay stacked on top of each other. Judd felt pretty certain those clothes were giving off steam.

He was so busy scanning for visuals, Judd didn't notice the smell at first. It hit him all at once: mold, rotting food, and feces.

Most likely, one of the cats lived in the house — or at least, spent enough time there to relieve itself indoors. Judd was *this* close to gagging, but quickly swallowed down the reflex and turned to Levi, who stood bent over next to the couch. Judd made a show of checking out his knee. After seeing the place, he wasn't sure he wanted a Band-Aid or anything else from inside touching his skin.

A cough from the corner of the couch startled him. He looked over and startled again. It was Becki Crouch. He recognized her from her booking photo, but she'd aged about a decade since that last photo was taken a year before. Her face was sunken in, her chin jutted out, and angry red sores stood out on her skin. Her eyes held almost no life.

"Hey, Becks!" he said.

"Hey."

"I scraped my knee, so Levi's getting me a Band-Aid."

"All right," she slurred. "Cool. Want to smoke after?"

She gestured to an alcove next to the kitchen. Judd's observations hadn't made it that far, but when he saw the table there, he almost gasped out loud. Stacks and stacks of packaged drugs covered the tabletop. If Judd had to guess, he'd say the haul was worth at least twenty thousand dollars.

More importantly, it was way more than enough for two people. Which meant Levi and Becki were dealing.

The stash on their kitchen table was enough to arrest them for possession of drugs for sale, which was awesome — it'd get them off the streets and away from the high school kids they were targeting.

But, it wasn't enough to tie the Crouches to Zion, which Judd had to do if he was going to get Zion out of juvie so he could compete in the finals.

"You hoo," Levi was saying to Judd.

Judd blinked, hard, and then shook his head to knock himself out of the momentary trance.

Levi handed him the Band-Aid, which he took and opened.

"Thanks, dude. Sorry, man. I was zoning out for a minute," Judd said.

"Zoning out on how much meth we have?" Becky said, her voice sounding every bit like a stereotypical, slow-talking addict.

"Yeah, for real," Judd said. "Thanks for the offer, Becks, but I can't smoke today. My sister's waiting in the car. I just stopped by to, uh ..." His mind blanked. Had he ever said why he stopped by? He didn't think so. "I just stopped by to say hey. I was in the neighborhood."

"Oh," Levi said. "Heh heh."

Judd decided to make a beeline for the front door, and leave that way. Before he quite got there, though, Becki came back to life, her eyes focusing on Judd's face. "Invite your sister to join us."

Judd couldn't believe how difficult it was to control his reaction. He almost cringed, thinking about inviting Katy to smoke meth with a couple of tweakers, but schooled his features into a relaxed smile. "Aw, man. I wish I could, but she's got to work. She just got this new gig, you know? She has to be on time so she doesn't get fired. Again. I've gotta run. Thanks for the Band-Aid."

———

"Nicky, my man."

"Judd. Bro. I'm under strict instructions to not talk to you. At all."

"Not even about women?" Judd sat at his shiny, clean kitchen counter and admired his empty sink. It'd been a while since he'd been in a tweaker's house, and seeing his own neat and tidy environment made him feel like he could breathe.

An exasperated sigh preceded Nicky's answer. "Barnes will kill me."

"Okay," Judd said. "Then don't talk. Just listen."

Another sigh. "Okay. Whatever you say. But if the line goes dead, just know that Barnes came in and I had to hang up."

"Wait. Aren't you off today?"

"Should be. Shift bids, you know."

A strange sensation hit Judd, then. Shift bids had happened and he hadn't even thought about it. Typically, he was one of the first to submit the online form to bid on his new shift. He always went for the most action-packed shifts: weekend graveyards. He went to the fridge and pulled out a cold beer.

Nicky's voice broke through his thoughts. "Don't tell me you forgot, O'Connor. You're always the first one to bid. You wanted to talk about women because Taylor's got your knickers in a twist."

For a split second, Judd forgot that he and Taylor weren't speaking. That she was pissed at him. More than pissed, actually. And he smiled when he thought of her. Actually *smiled*.

Then he remembered. Cracked open his beer. Took a long drink.

"Nah, man. I was just joking about women. I don't want to talk about women. I want to talk about what I saw today."

"She's still not talking to you, is she?" Nicky said.

"Wait. I just said I don't want to talk about women."

"Right. But I feel like you do."

Judd took another long pull from his bottle. "I know I don't have to say this out loud, but I'm going to, just in case: everything I'm about to tell you stays between us."

"I'm scared, O'Connor. Whenever you start talking like this, it makes me want to crawl in bed, get in the fetal position, and pull the covers over my head."

"I went to the suppliers' house today."

Silence.

"Nicky? Are you there? Did Barnes come in?"

"I'm here, O'Connor."

"Did you hear what I said?"

"I'm going to say I didn't."

"They have the goods, Nicky. So. Much. Meth. You've got to get in there." Judd could hear the desperation in his own voice. "And we've got to squeeze them, get them to admit they've been using Zion and Raven to run the school drug ring."

"I mean. What can I do, man? You know I can't just bust in there. I need some legit info."

"This is legit info." Judd knew it wasn't. He took another swig of beer, the bubbles dancing on his tongue.

"I mean, info I can use," Nicky said. "You know that. I can't just assemble a team and be like, 'Oh, hey, O'Connor entered their house illegally and saw meth and now we should just go arrest these folks.'"

Judd laughed, the sound bitter. "So get the info."

Judd could picture Nicky as if he were standing there in the kitchen. He was rubbing his chin, nodding, pursing his lips. He was considering.

"Tell you what," Nicky said, after an eternity. "I'll get a stakeout going. But that's it. A stakeout. We get other calls, we've got to take them. I can't guarantee you we're going to spend a bunch of time on this."

Judd's heart leapt. If Nicky were, in fact, standing in the kitchen, Judd would take his face in his hands and kiss him right on the mouth. He said as much and Nicky laughed, gruff and begrudging. "I guess you really don't want to talk about women."

Chapter Twenty-Eight

*T*AYLOR

Although she swore to herself that she'd do her absolute best not to think about Judd for the entire week leading up to the rodeo finals, Taylor found he just kept popping up.

The thrill of driving into the Prescott High School parking lot Monday morning in her electric blue, full-sized pickup truck was tampered only by the thought that she wished Judd were there to greet her, coffees in hand, like he'd been so many times.

She hadn't told Rose and Jessie about her truck purchase — she'd wanted to surprise them — so their bounding across the parking lot, hair flying behind them, lifted her spirits significantly.

"You got new wheels!" Rose shouted as Taylor climbed down from the driver's seat. "I'm so happy for you!" Before Taylor could answer, Rose crushed her into a bear hug that did even more to alleviate her Judd-related sadness.

"It's going to be perfect for work around the barn," Jessie said, opening her arms for her turn at a hug.

"I know," Taylor said. She could feel the wide, goofy grin spreading from one side of her face to the other. "I am so happy I did this. I feel like a whole new person driving this thing."

"It's a beast," Rose said appreciatively.

"If I didn't know better, I'd think Rosie wanted to date this beast," Jessie said, winking.

Rose elbowed her, still smiling.

Taylor also hadn't told her friends about the fiasco with Judd, and decided that the timing wasn't right. That particular start to her day made it possible for Taylor to stay mostly upbeat. She didn't see Judd at all, but she kept thinking she saw him in all the places they'd spent time together.

She imagined him walking into the library that day when she ran smack into him because she had her face in a book. She pictured them hanging rodeo club posters together in the cafeteria. She envisioned them having lunch together at the table outside the library. She wondered when all of these memories would stop causing a painful clench in her stomach, a speeding up of her heart.

The best she could do, she decided, was to change her focus each time she thought of him. Every time his perfectly chiseled, handsome face made its way into her consciousness, she thought about rodeo club. Or her business. Or her new truck.

Taylor wasn't the only one who noticed Judd's absence. Monday afternoon at rodeo practice, Olivia said, "Where's Mr. O'Connor? I didn't see him at school today."

Taylor should have expected the kids to ask. They knew there was more between Taylor and Judd than a professional relationship. But Olivia's question caught her off guard.

"He's sick."

She did know that much — Judd had called in sick.

"Do you think he'll be back tomorrow?" Olivia asked. "I wanted to ask him something about my turn around the barrel."

An idea struck Taylor, and she imagined a lightbulb illuminating over her head. "I'm not sure. But I can call his sister, if you like. She was a champion barrel racer, you know."

Olivia's eyes lit up. "Katy O'Connor?! I've heard of her. She's famous! That would be great."

Taylor hadn't known that. She filed the information away. "No problem. Let's do it after warm-ups. That way everyone can get started."

Olivia nodded and went to join the others in the barn.

Tuesday, Judd returned to school. Taylor saw him from a distance a few times, but devoted most of her energy that day to making sure their paths didn't cross. She busied herself with bigger projects, like changing out the featured books section, labeling and putting security devices on a shipment of books she'd received, and redecorating the bulletin board behind the checkout desk. Even so, her mind wandered to Judd, over and over. A few times a stray tear plopped onto the surface in front of her, reminding her that no matter how hard she tried, she couldn't busy herself out of the heartbreak.

By Wednesday, apparently, the evidence had mounted enough to make people suspicious. Rose texted to set up a girls' lunch that day, and when Taylor met her and Jessie at a table outside the library, her friends pounced.

"What's the scoop?" Jessie said.

Taylor noticed neither of her friends had opened their lunches. They both sat, hands folded, looking at her expectantly.

She played dumb. "What do you mean?"

"Well," Rose said." First, you go and buy a new truck."

Jessie added, "Without even telling us!"

"I wanted to surprise you?" Taylor tried.

"And then," Jessie said, "Judd calls in sick."

"He never calls in sick," Rose said. "Healthy as a horse."

Taylor's laugh probably came on a little too quickly. "We've only been in school for a month or so," Taylor said. "I don't think, based on that short timeframe, we can say he *never* calls in sick."

"And," Rose said, holding up her hand, pointer finger extended. "You're evading."

Rose settled her hand back on the table, and she and Jessie stared at Taylor, waiting. Quite without warning, Taylor burst into tears. She put her head down, but out of the corner of her eye, she could see her friends looking at each other. Jessie put a hand on her forearm. "What's going on?"

Taylor told them everything. How she'd fallen for Judd, thought he was special, felt like he cared about her.

"I can admit this to you guys, because you're my best friends. I actually thought Judd and I proved that I could start my dream business and have a family. I thought we were a great team."

The admission brought on a fresh round of tears. Jessie and Rose came around to Taylor's side of the picnic table and put their arms around her. After a few minutes, Taylor gathered herself and sat up, sniffling. "But. I was wrong."

She told them how she'd found Kristi, the loan officer from the bank, and invited her to Saturday's rodeo competition. When she told them Kristi actually showed up, her friends gasped.

"But that's *great*. Everything is not lost," Jessie said.

Taylor held up a hand to stop Rose and Jessie from getting too excited.

"Except," she said, "Judd disappeared, and he took one of our members with him."

"What you mean?" Jessie said.

Taylor explained while Rose continued to rub her back, and Jessie held her hand.

"So now, we're short one club member. We can't compete without five at the finals. Most teams have an alternate or two. But as you know, we only have the five. And one of them is locked up in juvie."

"You can't, like, grab another student from the school?" Rose asked.

Taylor shook her head. "No. Each member must have competed in at least two of the three events leading up to the finals."

"And the finals are this weekend," Jessie said. "Which means there's no time to find another kid and have him or her compete twice."

Taylor put her finger on her nose. "Exactly."

The three of them ate in silence after that, which Taylor figured was a sign Rose and Jessie found the situation as hopeless as she did.

By Thursday night, Taylor had nearly given up hope of competing in the rodeo finals. Zion still hadn't come to school, and the rules required him to attend school on Friday to compete on Saturday. She planned to show up at the competition, anyway. If Zion did make it, she could tell the competition officials that he'd been sick the day before. Deathly ill. Explosive diarrhea.

Or, she could just position theirs as the story of a fledgling club whose members could simply benefit from the experience. Even if they couldn't actually earn points, at least the kids who were present could compete. She'd gone over the argument in her mind dozens of times.

Friday morning, armed against her despondence with renewed determination to see her club members through the finals, Taylor put on a brave face as she walked past Ernie at the school entrance.

At first, she thought she was hallucinating. Out of the throng of kids, Zion emerged, grinning. He walked toward her, both arms up, like he was presenting himself on a stage. She half expected the hallucination Zion to bow. He even spoke to her. "Ms. Cole! I'm back! Which means..." He did a drumroll on his thighs. "I can compete tomorrow. Isn't that awesome?"

Taylor blinked. "Zion?" She rushed up and hugged him. "It's really you. I thought I was hallucinating."

He laughed. Up close, she could see dark smudges under his eyes. Poor kid. The past several days must have been hell for him. "It's really me. Mr. O'Connor got me out."

Hearing that, Taylor's heart perked up, beating a little faster. "Mr. O'Connor? How did he do that?"

"I don't know, man. I mean, Ms. Cole. He wouldn't say. He just told me I'd better not miss school, and I'd better not miss the finals. And I'd better not put a zero on the scoreboard."

Taylor felt herself grinning just as big as Zion. "He didn't say that last part," she said.

"No!" Zion said. "I just had to say it. For dramatic effect."

"This is great news! Thank you so much for coming to school. I'm sure you're exhausted."

Zion's expression turned serious. "Yeah. Juvie is no joke. But all I could think about in there was getting back to rodeo club. I didn't want to be the reason we didn't get to go to finals. Oh, and I also thought about my mom. How mad she's going to be. But that was second to worrying about rodeo club."

"Are you okay?"

"Yeah, I'm fine. I wouldn't want to go back. But I'm fine."

Taylor put one hand on each of his shoulders and squeezed. "I'm so glad you're okay. And I'm so glad you're back."

"Me too. Although, I'm kind of surprised Mr. O'Connor didn't tell you, himself. When you saw me, it looked like you'd seen a ghost."

"We're not exactly on speaking terms."

"Aww," Zion said, sounding so much like a little kid, Taylor couldn't help but laugh. "Why not? Is it because I was in juvie? That's not even his fault, Ms. Cole."

"It's a long story. Get to class. I don't want you to be tardy!" With that, she headed to the library.

Taylor decided that no matter their differences, she owed Judd her gratitude. So, during the slightly longer passing period between second and third hours, she went to find him. His office door was closed, but the blinds were open and she could see him sitting at his desk, looking at some papers, eyebrows furrowed. She could see tension in the way he held his shoulders.

Maybe because Zion was back, or maybe because some time had passed, the part of her that had been so angry at Judd had simmered down significantly. The part of her that cared for him, though, wanted to go in and massage his shoulders, ask what he was stressed about, offer to help if she could. But they weren't in that place anymore.

Sighing, she knocked on the window, two light, friendly raps. He looked up, and for a split second when he realized who it was, his face lit up. Which made Taylor's throat tight with emotion. No one else had ever looked at her quite the same way. And she wasn't sure if anyone would, ever again. Time stopped, and the two of them remained still, looking at each other. Judd snapped out of it first, his body giving a little jolt before he motioned for her to come in.

The hinges creaked when she opened the door, and she winced. "Somebody really ought to oil those hinges."

Judd cleared his throat. "I know. It sounds like a horror movie in here."

Unsure of what to do with herself, Taylor took her time closing the door behind her. She turned around to face him, her body stiff with the new awkwardness.

"You can sit," he said. He held out a hand, palm up.

She sat, caught off guard when she sank further into the cushion than she expected. She let out a little yelp, and Judd's eyes twinkled at her across the space. "I've heard that chair is a little softer than it looks."

"Well, that's the truth."

Again, time suspended as the two of them sat there. God, she missed him. Why did he have to go and act like such a big lunkhead, as Katy would say? Although she could look at him for eternity, Taylor figured she'd better get down to business. Before she spoke, though, Judd said, "It's nice to see you again. I've missed you."

Because it hurt too much to admit she felt the same way, Taylor said, "I came to thank you. For getting Zion out. He told me you took care of it, but he didn't know the details. Not that I need to know the details. Police business and all that. All I need to know is that he's at school today and he can compete tomorrow. I know you got him out for his own sake, but I know you worked hard to do that in time for him to compete. For him and for me. And I wanted you to know I appreciate it."

Taylor wished she could read Judd's mind. She could see a parade of thoughts and emotions marching across his features, but she couldn't quite make sense of them. After a few seconds, he finally said, "You're welcome."

That's it? Taylor expected some sort of expansion. She could tell he was thinking more than he was saying. At that stage in the game, she decided not to press. She wouldn't be surprised if he had bent the rules to get Zion out of juvie. She was better off not knowing. She returned his quick nod and stood up. "Well, I guess that's it."

"Thanks for coming by," he said.

She cursed herself for wanting to reach out and touch him. Pull him to standing and kiss him hard on the mouth. Why did he have to be so handsome?

"You're welcome." She walked to the door and he said, "Good luck tomorrow."

She smiled, and didn't even care that he could probably see the sadness there. "Thank you."

At lunch, Taylor walked through the quad and saw her rodeo club members in a group, talking and smiling and laughing together. Obviously, they were as excited to have Zion back as she was. At practice that afternoon, the mood was determined. The kids practiced hard, giving each other pointers and pep talks. Still, as they wrapped things up and went to get on the bus, they were all smiles again. For the first time all week, Taylor felt hopeful, and confident about their prospects the next day.

———

Saturday morning, when Taylor's team walked toward her, all of them in step and wearing their matching shirts and hats (when had they gotten hats?!), she felt a rush of pride. Next to her, Katy laughed, and clapped with delight. "I can't believe you took this team from being such a motley crew to being this organized rodeo powerhouse."

Taylor shook her head. "I can't, either. I mean, we all put in the work, but just look at them."

"Good morning!" Scarlett said, hugging Taylor and shaking Katy's hand. "I think we're ready, coach."

"Where did you get those hats?" Taylor asked. "They make you *look* ready, even more than the shirts."

The kids exchanged uncomfortable looks. That's when Taylor realized: Judd must have bought the hats.

"Aren't they dope?" Raven said. "Mr. O'Connor bought them for us. He said any decent rodeo club needs more than just shirts."

Taylor tried not to let that news affect her. She was still mad at Judd. And she planned to stay that way. But it *was* a sweet gesture. "You guys look great. Not just decent, but great."

An hour later, the competition kicked off with the barrel racing. The girls were about halfway through the lineup. After the first few barrel racers made their runs, Katy grabbed Taylor's hand. "I didn't expect to be this nervous!"

"I'm nervous, too," Taylor said. "Less so than I was the first time, because I know they know what they're doing. But, this is the finals."

"I don't know how you stand it!" Katy said.

"Keep coming. It gets a little easier every time."

Katy turned around in her seat. "And wow, there are tons of people here. I wonder if it makes the kids more nervous."

Taylor shrugged. "I'm sure it does. But it's all part of the deal, right?"

A flash of bright pink caught Taylor's eye. Kristi Mendez was coming up the steps into the stands. She waved at Taylor, and as Taylor waved back, she said to Katy, "*Now* I'm nervous."

Without moving her lips, Katy said, "Is that the bank lady?"

Taylor laughed. "Yeah. Kristi."

"Is this seat taken?" Kristi asked.

"I saved it for you," Taylor said.

Kristi sat down and rubbed her hands together. "Two more riders until your girls are up. I'm so glad I didn't miss them. I had a little paperwork I had to finish before I headed over."

"Working on a Saturday!" Katy said. "That's dedication."

"That's right," Kristi said.

The first competitors' times were displayed up on the score-board, and Taylor felt confident that Scarlett and Olivia could hold their own. They had mounted their horses and ridden into the holding area, where they sat side by side, focused, watching. Taylor willed them to look up at her, and after a minute, Olivia did. Taylor pantomimed taking a deep breath, relaxing her shoulders. Olivia smiled and nodded, and then followed Taylor's lead. Scarlett did the same, and they both gave Taylor a thumbs up.

"They look ready," Kristi said. "Are you guys nervous?"

"We are," Katy and Taylor said.

Olivia was up first. She rode up to the starting spot, poised and confident. Taylor saw her take one more deep breath, and then she was flying. Body canted forward, long braid behind her, she looked like a pro. Taylor held her breath for the entire run, letting it out in a *whoosh* when Olivia came back through the eye, putting up a time better than any other that season.

"Was that good?" Kristi wanted to know.

Taylor nodded, licked her lips. "That was good. Her best yet. Scarlett's up." Scarlett, too, appeared calm and in control. Her run was even faster than Olivia's, and when she finished, she jumped off her horse and hugged her teammate tight.

"I feel like a proud mama," Taylor said. "They did so good."

While the three women watched the girls lead their horses back to the barn, Taylor said, "Raven and Henry are next. They haven't roped together, yet. It's Raven's first time during a competition. But with Zion out all week, we had to shift Raven over."

The two of them looked ready though, eyes focused on the calf in the chute until the chute opened. Taylor held her breath. Raven's movements looked smooth and in control, and their time fell well within the average.

Finally, it was Zion's turn. Taylor hoped the time off hadn't made him too rusty. She wished she could go down and give him a pep talk before he competed, but it was against the rules. Unlike the other kids, Zion's nerves were on full display as he waited his turn. His shoulders were practically touching his earlobes, and the fingers of his free hand jumped on his leg. One heel bounced in the stirrup. In a weird twist of fate, the kids who rode before Zion were on fire. Their rhythm was perfect, the lassos swung beautifully, and their steers went down effortlessly.

"Wow! These kids are good!" Kristi said, her excitement palpable.

"They *are* good," Taylor said, biting her bottom lip. "Almost *too* good. I hope that doesn't make Zion more nervous than he already is."

"He'll be fine," Katy said. "He's experienced. He might be a little rusty, but he'd have to fall off his horse to knock you guys out of contention for the top five."

Taylor considered. Katy was right. And it was unlikely Zion would actually fall off his horse. Maybe this would turn out fine. It was Zion's turn. His posture had completely transformed. He was sitting on his horse with his eyes closed. His chest rose and fell with deep breaths. He pressed his lips together, opened his eyes, and nodded. When the steer came out of the chute, Zion eyes narrowed. Good. He was no longer nervous. He was determined, and he rode like it. His turn was over before Taylor could even formulate an opinion about how he was doing.

As he walked back to his horse, he gave her a thumbs up, accompanied by a cocky grin. Then he lifted his arm and his gaze a little higher, obviously giving the same thumbs up and cocky grin to someone behind her in the stands. She turned around to see who it was. "Judd." She was on her feet and a rush of emotions hit her. Surprise, tenderness, love.

Katy stood up, too, and turned around. "Surprise?"

Taylor looked at her and realized she'd known all along that Judd was behind them.

"Judd couldn't miss it. I'm sorry I didn't tell you, but he really wanted to be here. He —"

Taylor threw her arms around Katy. "It's okay. No apology necessary. I'm glad he's here. He's been here all season and he deserves to see it through."

She motioned for him to come down. He reached Katy first, and she threw her arms around him in celebration.

"Thanks for being here," he said to her. "I really appreciate it."

Katy released him. "Anytime. In fact, I was thinking I might want to help coach next year."

Taylor turned to Kristi. "We usually wait about ten or fifteen minutes for the officials to calculate the scores."

"This is so suspenseful!" Kristi said.

"It is," Taylor agreed. "As you can see, everyone is breathing a little easier, now that the competition is over." She gestured at the other spectators, many of whom were standing, talking, and laughing together.

Taylor and Judd both started to speak at the same time. "I—" Taylor said, and Judd said, "Well—"

They both halted, smiled. Then they both said, "You first."

"Awkward," Katy said, her voice singsongy.

Taylor rushed to say, "I was going to go check on the kids. See how they're holding up."

Judd put his hands in his pockets. "I was going to do the same."

"Why don't you both go?" Katy supplied, her tone ultra helpful.

Judd gave her a dark look, and Taylor said, "Oh, it's all right. You can go first. I've been with them all week. Why don't you just bring them back up with you?"

He looked like he wanted to say something else, and Taylor wondered if he wanted to suggest that they go together. But she didn't want to. It would look and feel too much like they were *together*, together. She sat down, and he left without another word.

Katy flopped down next to Taylor. "I don't know why the two of you are making this so awkward," she muttered.

"Geez," Taylor said. "I guess I'm getting a taste of what Judd goes through."

Kristi giggled.

In mock outrage, Katy put a hand on her chest. "Excuse me? What *Judd* goes through? What about what I go through?"

Taylor just shook her head. Having Katy as a sister-in-law would be pretty amazing.

Fortunately, Kristi took that opportunity to change the subject. "How high are you expecting to score?"

"I wasn't even expecting to get to finals this season," Taylor said. "But now that we're here, I would be thrilled if we placed in the top five."

Kristi smiled. "From what I've seen, that might just be possible."

———

JUDD

Down at the barn, Judd found the kids taking the saddles off the horses.

They greeted him in chorus. "Mr. O'Connor!"

"You guys looked great out there," he said. "Really great. No matter how you place, I'm proud of you for all the progress you've made this season."

"Thanks!" Olivia said.

"We saw you sitting next to Ms. Cole," Scarlett said.

Zion added, "We did. She told me you two weren't exactly on speaking terms. We noticed you sat way up high in the stands, as far away from her as you could get."

Judd smirked. Why did these kids have to be so perceptive? "How do you know I wasn't just avoiding my sister?"

Henry shook his head. "We know a romantic breakdown when we see one. What happened?"

Judd looked at Zion, whose gaze remained steady when they made eye contact.

"I made the mistake of putting work before romance. Let me tell you, it's a real buzzkill." That answer seemed to satisfy the kids.

"Maybe we can help you," Raven said. "Have you heard how good I am with the ladies?"

The others shook their heads and rolled their eyes.

"I take it this is a popular topic for conversation?" Judd said.

Olivia elbowed Raven. "Just because Raven won't stop talking about what a ladies man he is. But, you should let us help you. Apparently, you're not so great in the romance department."

Hearing that from a teenager stung a little, but Judd knew it was the truth.

"Okay," he said. "You guys can help. But nothing crazy."

"You have to do everything we say," Olivia said.

Judd cringed, but agreed. "What first?"

"We're going to get pizza," Scarlett said. "After they announce the results."

TAYLOR

A low murmur rising in the audience drew Taylor's attention to the scoreboard. She hushed the kids, who'd come up from the barn, and they all looked up.

Taylor started at the bottom, with twelfth place. As she scanned up the list, she felt her excitement rising. And there they were. She saw their team name just as the announcer said, "And in fourth place, at their first finals competition ever, is the Prescott High School Rodeo Club!"

The next full minute was a cacophony of squeals and shouts and laughter. There were hugs and high fives and more than one I-told-you-so. Somewhere else in the stands, Taylor heard another round of cheers go up. Her body literally buzzed with excitement, not just for her team, but for the other teams who were cheering, too.

She felt someone squeezing her arm, and looked over to see Kristi smiling at her. "Can I talk to you, over here, for just a moment?"

"Sure," Taylor said. She let Kristi lead her away from the ruckus.

"Remember when I said I had to finish up some paperwork before I came over this morning?"

Taylor nodded. "On a Saturday. That's dedication."

"Right. I'm dedicated because I believe in my newest client."

She pulled an envelope out of her purse, opened it, and removed a few sheets of paper. Unfolding them, she handed them to Taylor. "On behalf of Arizona Credit Union, I'd like to offer you a business loan for Sugar Pine Barn."

Taylor couldn't even read the words on the first page, as much as they shimmered.

"Taylor?"

Taylor closed her mouth and looked up at Kristi. "I'm speechless. Thank you so much!"

The paper still clutched in her hand, she hugged Kristi, who hugged her back. "You're welcome." They broke apart, and Kristi handed her a tissue. "You may not know this, but I watched you at the last competition. I saw how you stood up for yourself, how you got the officials to let your team compete, even though you were missing a member. I came to a couple of your fundraising events, too. I didn't tell you, because I wanted to see you in your environment. I love the way you interact with your clients. I love the way you think of all the details. I love your authenticity. And I like *you*. To be honest, although your business looks like a bit of a risk, only because of your lack of experience, it's a risk I'm willing to take. I'm quite confident that you will make a successful entrepreneur."

Openly sobbing by that time, Taylor hugged Kristi once more. Kristi laughed. "I have to tell you, I've never received such a nice thank you."

"I don't know if a business loan has ever meant as much to anyone else," Taylor told her.

By that time, the kids, Judd, and Katy had stopped celebrating the fourth-place finish and were watching Taylor talk with Kristi. Taylor released Kristi from her embrace and held up the papers. "We've got a loan! Sugar Pine Barn is happening!"

Taylor had thought she was happy when Kristi handed her the loan papers. Nothing compared to the feeling when her team members, co-coach, and alternate co-coach rushed over to hug her.

She'd always thought she couldn't run a business with a family. But at that point, she knew she couldn't run a business without one.

Chapter Twenty-Nine

*J*UDD

An hour later, the nine of them — the five kids plus Judd, Taylor, Katy, and Taylor's new banker friend Kristi — walked into the pizza place. The kids did all the talking, carrying the conversation, filling the space with stories and pieces of gossip from the day.

At one point after everyone had eaten, the kids disappeared from the table. Judd assumed they went to the arcade, an assumption Olivia and Scarlett confirmed a minute later, when they came back and asked Katy and Kristi if they could help with the basketball and claw games.

For the first time in days, Judd found himself alone with Taylor. Nerves hit him like a Mac truck. Almost instantly, he could feel his palms slick with sweat, a stone-like weight in the pit of his stomach.

"Hi," she said, looking at him from under her lashes.

Good. She was nervous, too.

"Hi," he said back.

"They did good today."

"They did."

Was this all they were going to talk about? The server approached the table, a pitcher of beer in her hand. Setting it down on the table, she said, "Here. This is courtesy of your rodeo team members. Only, they want you to know that they didn't buy it. Seeing as they're underage and all."

Taylor giggled, the sound a perfect expression of how Judd was feeling inside all of a sudden: giddy.

"Thank you," he said to the server.

She set down two frosty glasses and said, "Cheers," before walking away.

Judd picked up the pitcher and started pouring. "I figure I should be up front and tell you, the kids planned to help me get back on speaking terms with you."

"It's funny they thought beer would aid the process," Taylor said, raising an eyebrow.

She might be joking, but after a healthy drink of the cold, foamy, bubbly beer, Judd had to admit, he felt more at ease.

"I forgot a toast." He lifted his glass and Taylor tapped hers against it.

"To a great first season," he said, "and to the beginning of your successful business venture."

"Cheers," she said.

They sat without speaking for a few seconds, until Taylor leaned to one side to look at whatever was behind Judd. "I think they're spying on us," she said.

"Good thing we're speaking," he said.

"Good thing," she echoed.

"Taylor," Judd started, but then he stopped because her name caught in his throat. He swallowed. "I need to say that I am sorry. So very sorry for what I put you through. The whole thing started out because, instead of just focusing on the drug ring at the school, like Ernie asked me to, I went bigger. I was so hungry for real police work, I took things too far."

She wiped her hands on her thighs and waited for him to go on.

He took another sip of beer. "Then, when I messed up, and I knew Zion was going to juvie, all I could think about was finding a solution, so I could come to you having already fixed the problem. But I couldn't do it fast enough. I was so afraid you would be upset. I was so afraid of disappointing you. We've both been worried this thing between us wouldn't work out, that we both loved our careers too much. And I thought that what happened with Zion was proof that was true. Especially when I couldn't call you with a solution."

Taylor took a deep breath. Her face was a mask. She wrapped her hands around her beer glass. Judd set down his beer and gently took Taylor's from her, setting it aside as well. Then he took both of her hands in his, and looked into her eyes. She blinked at him, offered a tiny smile.

"I am so, so sorry that I misjudged the situation. I love you."

At that, her mouth formed a little O.

"I do. I love you. And I should have trusted you — and our love — enough to tell you what was going on. Maybe we could have worked together to find a solution. And if we couldn't, at least we could have commiserated ... at least we would have gone through it *together*. But because of my actions, we both ended up going through it alone."

"We did," she said. "And it was awful. I missed you so much during that time."

He nodded, squeezed her hands. "I want nothing more than to be with you. I want to spend every day with you. I want to be there by your side when you open your barn. I want to help with lessons. I want to come home and tell you about my day. If I could, I would give you all the stars. You mean everything to me."

Taylor blinked. "Judd, I — I forgive you. When we weren't speaking, I felt like part of my body was missing. I wanted to do rodeo club for the kids, but it just wasn't the same without you. I kept seeing you everywhere I went. School, the arena, my house. Because you'd already become such a huge part of my life. I was envisioning us being together. Forever. I don't want to be mad at you. And I understand why you did what you did. And you can trust me. Because I will always, always want what makes you happy."

"Awwww."

Judd turned his head to see all of the rodeo club members sitting at the booth across the aisle, cartoon hearts coming out of their eyes.

———

*T*AYLOR

"Come home with me?" Judd said to Taylor after all the kids' parents came to get them, and Katy and Kristi said good-bye.

"I would love to," Taylor said.

They dropped her truck off at her house. Taylor got into Judd's truck, and he turned up the radio.

"Aw, you're listening to country. I take it today wasn't a heavy metal kind of day?"

Judd reached across the center console and took her hand, intertwining his fingers with hers. "Even though we weren't exactly on speaking terms this morning, or maybe because we weren't, it was a love song kind of day. Possibly a sad love song kind of day."

"This sounds like a happy love song," Taylor said. She turned the volume up one click and settled back against her seat. "I'm glad we're on speaking terms again."

"You're going to be really glad, once we get to my place."

She looked over at him, one eyebrow raised. "Is that so?"

"Yes." He wiggled his eyebrows. "I'm going to show you exactly how much I missed you." Heat blossomed in her center, and pooled between her legs. She couldn't believe, that, even for a few days, she thought she could live without him. She squeezed his hand. "I can't wait."

And she couldn't. For the duration of the drive, her body continued to heat up, to vibrate with need.

As soon as Judd parked in front of the house, they both jumped out, and rushed to the front door. Taylor got there first, and instead of unlocking it, Judd backed her up against the door and claimed her mouth with his. The kiss held hunger, desire. And, Taylor noticed, tenderness.

Judd took half a step back and tucked Taylor's hair behind her ear. He leaned his forehead on hers. "I love you, you know," he told her.

She gave him a gentle peck. "And I love you. Now, take me inside and show me just how much you missed me."

Chapter Thirty

One year later

Taylor

Taylor turned her electric blue pickup truck off the main road and onto the driveway of *her* business, Sugar Pine Barn. She squealed when she saw the banner strung across the gateway sign. *Grand Opening! Welcome to Sugar Pine Barn.*

"Oh my gosh! I love the banner! It even has our logo!"

She looked across the cab at Judd, who grinned at her. "I knew you would. It was a team effort. A gift from me, Katy, Jessie, Rose, and Celeste."

"I feel so emotional," Taylor said, her voice thick with all the big feelings. "I can't believe it's finally happening."

Roxy, the ugly, now-giant shelter dog they'd adopted after their wedding, picked up on Taylor's feelings and expressed her own excitement by licking Taylor's face.

"I *can* believe it," Judd said. "And look. You have a whole fan club who believes it, too."

They'd come around the bend, and Taylor gasped. She saw the group assembled there. Not only Katy, Jessie, Rose, and Celeste, but also the kids from rodeo club, a handful of students from the high school, and some colleagues. They held balloons and signs, and when they saw Taylor's truck, they jumped and waved and cheered.

"I can't believe this," Taylor said, her eyes smarting with tears for at least the twelfth time that day. "This is just so wonderful."

Behind her friends stood her barn, newly constructed and bold against the bright sky. Taylor had been on site for every step of the construction process, from laying the foundation to putting on the roof. But seeing it on grand opening day, behind the people she loved most, took her excitement to the next level.

"The open house starts soon," Judd said to her. "Should we get out, celebrate a little before we have to tone it down for the public?"

"Yes, absolutely," Taylor said. "But I don't think I can tone it down. We have a lot to celebrate."

The End

Preview: The Whole Sky

Book Two in the Love Under the Arizona Sky Series

The Whole Sky, Chapter One

Rose Coffey was becoming a master at making the best of a situation ... and she was exhausted. Even a master sometimes breaks, especially at two-thirty in the morning. For the fifth night in a row, the sounds of Rose's inconsiderate college-student neighbors woke her.

Each night, it started the same way. Tires crunching on the gravel parking lot as these kids — young adults, really, and shouldn't they start acting like it? — came home. Headlights sweeping across her blackout curtains, coming through the cracks despite her best efforts to close them as snugly as possible. Car doors slamming shut. Voices. Sometimes talking, sometimes singing, almost always laughing.

There was typically one considerate kid in the bunch, shushing the others. More often than not, someone bumped into the wall of Rose's apartment as the group made their way to the metal staircase, which was completely unforgiving when it came to noise.

Directly above her bedroom, at their front door, her apartment mates fumbled with the keys, stumbled into their apartment, and slammed the door. If Rose's daughter, Celeste, didn't wake up as a result of any of that, she began to stir as the college students settled in upstairs. Sometimes they thumped around the whole place, a herd of elephants overhead. Sometimes they turned on music. On this particular Wednesday night, they started what sounded like a racquetball game.

"What is that, Mommy?" Celeste asked, her voice croaky with sleep.

"Oh, I don't know. It sounds like they have an enchanted ball up there, and they're playing catch."

"An enchanted ball?"

"Yeah." Rose infused her voice with cheer and calm. "It's like magic."

Celeste sighed and rolled onto her back, away from Rose. Moonlight came through a crack in the curtains, illuminating Celeste's wide-open eyes. "I mean, that sounds like a lot of fun. It's just, it's the middle of the night."

From the mouths of babes. "I know, it does make it hard to sleep." Rose had discovered recently that one of the most difficult things about being a mother was the constant need to make everything seem like it was okay. To not fall into pieces, even though she wanted to. In that moment, Rose wanted to fall apart. She'd worked *so hard* to save for the security deposit on that apartment, because it was supposed to be new and quiet and safe. And she kept them on such a tight budget to be able to afford the rent payments. She felt like she couldn't win. All she wanted to do was give her daughter a good home, a home where she could have the essentials. And one of those essentials was a good night's sleep.

"Mama, are you crying?"

Rose felt a tear escape the corner of her eye. She hadn't even realized. "No, sweetie. My eyes are just watering because I'm tired."

"I'm sorry." Celeste rolled towards Rose and laid a hand on her cheek. "I'm tired too. Let's go back to sleep."

Rose remained wide awake, but Celeste drifted off for a little while, until a huge *thud* shook the walls. It was so loud and so thunderous, Rose had to remind herself earthquakes don't happen in Arizona.

Celeste startled awake, her eyes wide. "What was that?"

Shaking her head, Rose said, "I don't know. But it was really loud." Rose decided then and there that they couldn't live like that any longer. "How would you like an adventure?" she asked Celeste.

"You know I love adventures," Celeste said. "But it's the middle of the night. Maybe we should adventure tomorrow. Shouldn't we be sleeping?"

"We *should* be." Hearing the exasperation in her voice, Rose took a deep breath to calm herself. "But, since we're not sleeping anyway, what do you say we go on an adventure?"

She turned the bedside lamp on low.

Even the dim light made Celeste squint as her eyes adjusted. "Okay," she said, her eyebrows knitting together in doubt. "I think someone might be on the crazy train."

"Oh, honey, I've been on the crazy train for a while. Now, I'm going to give you your very own ticket."

Celeste giggled at that.

As Rose got their things together, she thought about where they could go. She knew she could call either of her best friends, Taylor Cole or Jessie Monroe. They had told her innumerable times she could call or come stay, whenever she wanted (or needed) to. But she didn't want to burden them. And she knew from experience that being woken out of a sound sleep in the middle of the night felt like a burden.

She folded the outfit she'd chosen for Celeste and put it in the suitcase, and then did the same with clothes for herself.

She could call her parents, but she couldn't stand the thought of them thinking she wasn't making it, wasn't doing a good job raising her child.

Toothbrushes, toothpaste, and a roll of toilet paper, just in case, went into the suitcase.

You could call Jared, a mean voice piped up from the back of her mind. She slammed shut the suitcase and zipped it, her movements hard and jerky. *No.* She would never call Jared. When she'd finally gathered up the courage to leave him, he'd tried to convince her she wouldn't survive without him. It almost worked. She had almost stayed with him the last time because of how incompetent he'd made her feel.

She wouldn't call anyone, she decided. She would rely on herself.

So, car loaded and Celeste buckled into her booster seat, Rose headed for the only place she felt totally capable: Prescott High School.

Rose was great at two things: being a mom and being a teacher. During her five years as a high school English teacher, she'd gained more confidence more quickly than any other time in her life. The building felt like a home away from home — and, for one night, it was going to be.

"What are we doing at your work?" Celeste wanted to know.

"Having an adventure!" Rose used her key to unlock the main building's side door.

She let Celeste in ahead of her, then locked the door behind them. She'd already decided the teachers lounge would make a perfect camping spot. It had two couches, a microwave, a fridge, and a sink. She flicked on the florescent light, which gave off its typical humming sound.

"It feels creepy in here," Celeste said.

Rose happened to agree. "I think it feels cozy. Look. We can each sleep on a couch. And there's a microwave. And the bathroom is *en suite*."

"What is en suite?"

"It's a fancy way of saying it's connected."

"En suite." Celeste imitated Rose's French.

Noticing the dark smudges under her daughter's eyes, Rose felt another pang of guilt. "Here, let's get your sleeping bag set up."

They unrolled Celeste's mermaid sleeping bag and she wiggled into it. "Good thing I'm still wearing my pajamas."

"Good thing," Rose said. She brushed Celeste's hair away from her face and kissed her on the forehead. "Go ahead and go to sleep. I'm going to be on the other couch."

"Are you going to turn off the light?"

"Yep. Right now." Rose flipped the switch, shook out the blanket she'd brought for herself, and lay down on the couch. Within seconds, she heard Celeste's breathing become deep and even. A clock ticked from its spot on the wall, next to the door. The sound, which normally would drive Rose batty, lulled her into a deep sleep. Her alarm went off at five-thirty the next morning. Zero hour started at six-thirty, and generally, the teachers showed up at six-fifteen. Rose folded her blanket and got dressed, then microwaved the breakfast sandwiches she'd packed.

Naturally, Celeste had a hard time waking up. Rose really couldn't blame her, and did her absolute best not to rush her through the morning routine of dressing, eating, and brushing her teeth — but the closer it got to zero hour, the more stressed Rose felt. She left Celeste in the teachers lounge while she made a trip to the car to load the sleeping bag, blanket, pillows, and suitcase. By the time she returned, Celeste had eaten only a few bites of her breakfast sandwich, and hadn't put on her shoes. The clock next to the door read twelve minutes after six, and Rose knew the zero hour teachers could show up any minute. She knelt in front of Celeste and slipped her shoes onto her feet, then stood and hoisted her onto her hip.

"Mommy!" Celeste said. "You're so silly! Why are you carrying me like a baby?"

"I just don't want you to be late for school."

Fortunately, Celeste couldn't yet tell time and wouldn't realize they had an hour to kill. They made it all the way through the building without seeing anyone, but when Celeste pushed on the door that led outside, she pushed it right into someone coming in. That person pulled the door open and stepped back. Rose was about to offer a hurried thanks, and then she saw his shoes, and lost all coherent thought.

"Johnny Mac." She recognized his shoes only because she'd memorized every detail about him. The brown loafers were one of twelve high-dollar pairs of shoes he wore to school. Delirious from exhaustion, Rose allowed her gaze to travel from Mac's shoes to his thighs, his package, his trim waist, and his chiseled chest, finally coming to rest on his gorgeous, gorgeous face. She could get lost in those deep green eyes. Her own face flamed when she snapped out of it and realized what had just happened.

"Morning, Ms. Coffey. To what do I owe the pleasure, this early in the morning?"

Face still hot with shame, Rose spluttered, "I — my daughter — we —"

"We had a campout here." Celeste's voice was so loud and clear, there was no way to pretend she'd said anything else.

Mac raised his eyebrows, and Rose let out what she hoped was a believable laugh. "Oh, honey! You tell such wonderful stories!" She turned her attention back to Mac and said, "We had a campout in the living room last night. And when it was time to leave for school, we realized we left Celeste's water bottle in my classroom yesterday. She needs it for school."

Mac smiled at Celeste, warm and genuine. Rose's heart melted. "You know, you're lucky to have such a nice mama, that she would come early to school just to get your water bottle. Have a great day, both of you. I've got to go in and teach."

With that, he was gone, leaving behind a leathery scent that made Rose weak in the knees. She made a beeline for her car.

"You're so silly, Mommy! Why did you tell that guy we didn't have a campout?"

Rose didn't know what to say. She buckled Celeste into her booster seat. "I don't know." She got in the driver's seat and started the car. "Here, I'll put on your favorite station."

Rose turned on Celeste's kids' station and turned up the volume, hoping that would keep Celeste from asking any more questions. As they drove away from the high school, Rose's heart rate finally slowed down.

Although Mac was the absolute last person she wanted knowing she was in such a desperate situation, she also felt a thrill at their interaction. She'd lusted after him for years since he returned to Prescott from San Francisco, but never had the guts to actually converse with him. The fact that they'd exchanged more than a few words would stay with her the rest of the day.

About the Author

Hilary Dartt loves great adventures, whether she's writing, reading, or living them. The author of twelve novels, Hilary lives in Arizona's high desert with her husband, their three children, and her Weimaraner, Leia. She loves camping, exploring in the Jeep, and dance parties with her kids. Learn more and sign up for her newsletter at www.hilarydartt.com.

www.ingramcontent.com/pod-product-compliance
Lightning Source LLC
Chambersburg PA
CBHW061647190726
48289CB00006B/1775